Elaine was a beautiful, struggling widow of World War II. Hug... ...med by a bold de... ...that would set a sn...

"ABSORBING!"—*Philadelphia Inquirer*

"ROMANCE ON A TEXAN SCALE."
—*Publishers Weekly*

"RICHLY IMAGINED . . . DANSVILLE has enough mesmerizing prose and sheer narrative thrust to keep a reader turning pages long after midnight."
—*Dallas Times Herald*

"Football, dance halls and thick, hazy summer nights when bodies cling to each other to blot out small-town blues—these are the atmospheric ingredients of Robin McCorquodale's brooding first novel . . . If you enjoy smoldering romances and have a soft spot for cowboys, try DANSVILLE."
—*Glamour*

"WONDERFUL FROM BEGINNING TO END . . . DANSVILLE beautifully chronicles Elaine and Hugh's long, turbulent affair . . . a high-level romance . . . a dynamite ending!"
—*Waldenbooks Review*

More . . .

DANSVILLE

ROBIN McCORQUODALE

BERKLEY BOOKS, NEW YORK

A portion of this work originally appeared in *Redbook*.

This Berkley book contains the complete
text of the original hardcover edition.
It has been completely reset in a typeface
designed for easy reading and was printed
from new film.

DANSVILLE

A Berkley Book/published by arrangement with
Harper & Row

PRINTING HISTORY
Harper & Row edition/January 1986
Berkley edition/November 1987

ISBN: 0-425-10410-9

A BERKLEY BOOK ® TM 757,375
Berkley Books are published by The Berkley Publishing Group,
200 Madison Avenue, New York, NY 10016.
The name "BERKLEY" and the "B" logo
are trademarks belonging to Berkley Publishing Corporation.

For my husband, Malcolm

Prologue

ELAINE MUELLER HAD been every bit a tomboy when, in the spring of 1936, she met Foley Menutis. She had matured late, and so the ongoing battle for physical equality with her three brothers had been prolonged, and had given her a false confidence that her eligibility for the contest might remain forever fixed. But at fourteen, her thin, hard-fleshed, shaftlike body began to change, and by the start of her fifteenth year, she had been transformed. Her waist drew in, her chest filled out, her hips took on the kind of flesh that usually attracts even the most obtuse male observer. Her thighs broadened and her legs filled out at the calves. Even her eyes changed, deepening to the color of the sea at the two extremities of the day. Only her mouth remained the same: The lips stayed full and red, as if nature had swept over them without swooping down, since they were already perfect for her purposes.

Despite the alterations that overcame her, her toughness and strength stayed with her, and if her muscle and flesh were now arranged in a dazzling shell, her character was a thistle in the heart of a rose. She had endurance and a tolerance for pain. She was a fine athlete, and even after her sudden transformation, the gym teacher continued to tell her so. For three years, she had been the best runner at school; at basketball she dominated, not because she was tall—she was of only medium height—but because she was the fastest, the most aggressive, and her shots were deadly accurate. She was captain of the team; she had a purple and gold letter jacket with three stripes, which she wore to the limits of the season. Like all people of her type, she had a healthy

1

loathing of suffering and physical weakness. If she was hurt, she would cry out in rage. Only humiliation could bring on her tears, and these she hid so cleverly that those who knew her might well say, "Elaine Mueller never cries."

On the afternoon that she met Foley, she was a senior in high school and he was in his last year at the state university. He was twenty-one years old, a big, strongly built man who looked like a cross between a Swede and an American Indian, blond and fair, with chiseled, angular features and a very square jaw. As is most often true of really attractive men, feature by feature, Foley was ugly. His mouth was too wide, his chin too square, his cheek-bones a bit high, his nose irregular (it had been broken and set, and broken again), but the parts came together in a not unpleasant whole. The effect was enhanced by a kindly disposition, which he owed one-half to training and one-half to his nature. In clear weather his light eyes almost faded away in a kind of apologetic diffidence; on a cloudy day, or if he was indoors, they were actively aggressive and startlingly blue. Above all, he moved his huge frame (he was six four and weighed over two hundred pounds) with the grace of a mild but successful exotic animal, so that, in spite of his haphazardly molded features, he was a male who was thought of as highly desirable by a number of young (and not-so-young) women whom he let entertain him occasionally, but whom he rarely wooed.

Like many men who have yet to find their mate, who have tried a few times and been disappointed, he was on a kind of somnambulant search, from which he was occasionally awakened by a creature who displayed even a single characteristic of his unconsciously perceived ideal, but who could not sustain his interest or heat his blood sufficiently to spur him to attempt to capture her. "Foley, you'll never marry," his mother would say to tease him, recognizing that, in terms of energy, power, and an affinity with nature, there was too big a gap between him and the women he knew.

His mother had rarely criticized him, or any of her other children, but instead had given them continual attention and judicious praise. She ignored what they could not or would not do, and bragged about their achievements. His mother's nurturing had fostered in Foley a sense of worth and self-confidence that neither sorrow, nor time, nor adversity could erode, much less erase. The hardships of his childhood, after the death of his father, had left him unmarked, not because he was insensitive but because he was stable. He knew where his place was, his feet were planted firmly on the ground, and it seemed to him that, in spite of a damning poverty, he could do anything.

His father, who had owned a service station with a small general store attached to it, had died in an influenza epidemic when Foley was eleven, and his mother (she was only fourteen years older than he was, twenty-five at the time of his father's death) had had to sell it and, eventually, to take a job as a waitress in a truck stop. The money that Foley made working, all of it, went straight to his mother for household expenses. There was no other way, she said; and he knew it. He never argued with her, nor complained much. Her face was drawn enough with grief, her body strained enough with fatigue; it would be too cruel to add to her burden a quarrelsome and dissatisfied son.

He had a four-year football scholarship at the university, every dollar of it earned, paid for in the beatings he took, the punishment to which he had to subject his hard and resistant but still vulnerable body. Yet he hid his pain and injury: When his face was swollen and bruised, he stayed in his room; when his muscles hurt, he walked at a fast stride and kept his expression steady and quiet. As tough as it was, his body sometimes held itself back, resenting the abuse, as if it complained at a depth below consciousness. *But so what*, he had thought. *I can't change it*. Foley had to get through college.

It was late March, a week into spring, when Foley accepted an invitation from Elaine's brother Albert to spend the weekend on his parent's farm near Seguin. Foley offered to drive them; the trip was pleasant—one of those afternoons where the flow of bright green pastures is interrupted generously by islands of asters and wild indigo. In the side yard of the farmhouse, azaleas with purple blooms leaned into the garden. At their feet, daffodils rose out of the damp greenness of leaves. The marigolds were bright yellow; and around the old pump, pansies, open-faced in velvet, sprung out of a blanket of ivy. An amaryllis bloomed; four red trumpets, heavy on a hollow stalk, were tied with a string to a sturdy switch.

As Foley's Packard took the turn off the road and came down the tree-lined drive, Elaine was setting the table for dinner. She heard it, the motor's powerful acceleration at the curve; she went immediately to the window and looked through the lacy knots of the curtain. The car was huge, and it looked new. The shade of the oaks fell waving and dappled on the curves of its hood and fenders; its windshield, reflecting the great branches, was shot through with spangled bursts of movement in the recurrences of light, so that it seemed to whirl the gold and silver extravagances of late afternoon in a fiery, metallic kaleidoscope. Just before it stopped, a wheel bumped, and the heavy car was jarred. Elaine frowned. That hole should have been fixed; it was unlike her father to have left that undone.

A blond arm rested on the car door, and the driver, saying something to the person beside him, looked toward the house. Elaine pushed aside the curtains and leaned on her hip against the glossy black wood of the window frame; she was holding a fistful of silver. Behind her the polished dining table mirrored the room: the glassware and the heavy glass compote, which captured the needles of light permitted by the long, thin windows; the twin candlesticks; the dark walls; and the portrait of her grandmother, a symbol of tradition, grace, and peace—not wealth, but comfort, and the kind of family pride and honor that are the fruit of at least two generations of labor, augmented and strengthened by orderly and careful minds in a countryside which for nearly a century has known neither anarchy nor war.

Foley shut down the trunk of his car and followed Albert through the gate of the white picket fence and up the walk, taking care to close the latch. He wore dark slacks, and the sleeves of his white shirt were rolled to the elbows. He had no watch, no ornament of any kind. As he stepped forward she saw that the tumbling thickness of his hair echoed the scrolls and whorls and arabesques in the decoration of the trim on the porch. When he reached down to touch the leaf of a geranium, he seemed wary of brushing the petals of the red flowers or disturbing in any way their brittle stems. He moved as if fearing that he might break whatever he touched, not out of clumsiness, which he could control, but because of an intractable strength, which he could not always trust to stay settled down and keep still. Likely he had been warned, and warned again; he was careful.

Elaine called to her mother through the long, high-ceilinged dining room to the kitchen, "They're here, Mama—Albert with that boy Foley!"

As Elaine watched him, her mouth, slightly open and showing the tips of her teeth, lifted into a smile, which was caught in the high reflection of the broad windowpane that she had washed that morning before the school bus came. She had never met Foley, but she had anticipated his visit since Albert had talked of him the previous summer, and she had begun to think of knowing him and finding out his secrets.

She went into the front hallway, and when he offered her his hand (and she had to shift the silver from one hand to the other to accept it), she began breathing fast, and the beat of her heart changed. The silver glittered in the slant of the late afternoon sun. There was great purpose in its presence—Elaine had polished it herself, and it was wedded to her meeting with this man, a symbol of his quality. One of the knives slipped from her grasp, and when she stooped with Foley to retrieve it, her arm brushed his, and her red hair glanced across his cheek like a silk sash. Again she saw herself in a reflection: In the mirror, encased in the somber, ornate wood of the frame, was her blushing face, her mouth peculiarly aggravated in stress—and the blond head was there, too, in profile, bending toward her, solicitous and friendly.

"How was the trip down?" she asked him.

"It was fine."

She tried to smile, to seem to meet him casually, to think of him as just anyone; but her voice dipped, and for conversation, rather than saying what she had rehearsed, she had to fall back on convention. "It was a good day to be on the road. The wild flowers have started. The buttercups are . . ."

He smiled, then let his smile grow as he watched this younger sister of his friend. "It was a good day," he said.

She continued to look up at him. There seemed nothing more she could say; she was uncomfortable in her silence but was unable to leave the room. While she watched him, he made observations about farming and the weather.

"And the bluebonnets?" she asked him. "Did you see . . ."

"Just a few."

He was welcomed by Elaine's mother and then followed her upstairs to the spare room, carrying his overnight case in one of his huge hands. Just before the landing, he looked back at Elaine and caught her staring at him. He smiled again, much more strongly. Immediately she looked away. He was all that Albert had said he was, and she understood why he was famous. She wouldn't have to be told again. He emanated a perfection that she meant to emulate; she could see in the way that he moved up the steps the courage in his shoulders and spine; she observed the resoluteness in his legs. She imagined that every muscle had been trained, controlled, disciplined, and even punished in order to keep it at his command. She both understood and envied the determination that must have required.

When Elaine went back into the dining room, her heart was

pounding; if she was going to breathe, she would almost have to make a conscious effort to do so. She arranged the table perfectly, even better than she had intended, because she was angry at herself for having let him make her nervous. She must be calm if she wanted him to take her seriously and help her. As she worked, she could hear footsteps above her in the room where he was unpacking. *I'll ask him at dinner,* she thought. She had never known a real athlete; there was not a boy in her school who would play football in college next fall. She listened again for the tread of his feet. *He'll know everything,* she said to herself. *All of it.*

The sun was bright in the upper panels of the windows, and dinner was nearly ready, so there would be plenty of time afterward for a game. She heard the murmur and flutter of a bird. On a gray flagstone beside the birdbath, a squirrel was sitting on its hind legs. Its mouth was moving fast, and its paws, holding a few of the sunflower seeds that Elaine had scattered earlier for the birds, were pulled up tightly to its chin. She shouted through the window to scare it. It ran toward the tree, hesitated, and then glanced back at her, its round eyes shining, its tail lashing in irritation.

The light flared, then lifted on the panes of the window; at a surge of the rough March wind, the brightness was replaced by shadow. The wind blew under a hanging basket of fern; the fronds leapt suddenly, and the basket jerked and twirled. A pigeon on the telephone wire struggled for its balance, then lifted its wings. In search of a quieter place, it disappeared in the bluster of a yellow elm.

"Elaine!" her mother called from the kitchen, where the steaks were already frying and the biscuits were in the oven. She would also be preparing a bowl of cream gravy, speckled with pepper and seasoned with thyme. On the back porch, where the greening feet of the new vines had already crept halfway across the latticework, a table held a gelatin salad in the shape of a star, and Elaine had even been able to talk her father into buying ice cream in town. She put the heavy serving pieces and the fat silver salt and pepper shakers beside her father's place and answered the call from the kitchen. As she moved away from the window, she seemed to flow through the room with the precision of a beam of light, not disturbing anything but merely existing as an example of what nature at her best can do, if everything works right.

At the dinner table, after the dishes had been laid and the family assembled, not a half-hour after she had met Foley, and only a short time after her fear of him had been mitigated by the passion of her interest, she was leaning across the table and questioning him: "Yes, but if it was a T formation, and I had to pass, wouldn't I . . . ?" "Well, what would you do if . . . ?" "In that case, wouldn't you do better to use a single wing back?"

Foley had never met a girl who took such an interest in football, and amused by her seriousness, her strange desire to play a sport in which it was impossible for her to excel, one of the sports that might have been designed, at the outset, by men who wished to exclude women, he answered her questions readily. She seemed to regard him as a teacher; she watched him, her face close to his, sometimes biting at her lip, sometimes serious and nodding.

She even brought him a pencil and paper (he was trying to eat), pushed aside his sweating glass of iced tea, and hung over him while he made diagrams of the plays. Her breast touching his shoulder caused him to shiver and to draw a very deep breath to contain it. She listened to his explanations, thinking about what he said, paying him as much careful attention as if he were reciting poetry or reading from the Scriptures, and that the things he was revealing, both those unknown to her and those expected, moved her deeply. She seemed to be seeing in his features something that told her more about the mystery of the game than his conversation revealed. Nodding her head gravely, she appeared to be memorizing arcane information; and he observed that she was hard, competitive, and difficult—beautiful in her wild earnestness to learn. Actually she already knew a lot; her brothers had taught her a good deal about movement and strategy.

In the car coming down, Albert had warned Foley: "Don't pay any attention to Elaine."

"Why?" he had asked. "She ugly?"

Albert had laughed. "Oh, no; she's good-looking enough." He had watched the fleeing army of young corn with sharp green spikes through the car window. "She's mean."

Foley had put his hand out the window to adjust the mirror. "How old?"

"Fifteen . . . no, sixteen. I think she had a birthday."

"That's too bad," Foley said.

"Why?"

"She's too young." He was surprised that Albert had not guessed.

Toward the end of the dinner, after she had absorbed the best of what she thought he knew, she challenged him to a game. It was almost seven.

"It's pretty dark," he remarked softly, no longer smiling, not teasing either. He had never played football with a girl and he wasn't going to start now—a man couldn't do that. "I don't think so. You'd just get hurt."

"Why would I get hurt?"

"It's not a game that girls play."

She glanced at her brothers, and when she spoke again the tone of her voice showed shock at his refusal. "But I play it all the time."

"That's not smart." He gave a shake of his head and a signal with his hand that the subject was closed, and when her eyes flared angrily, he looked away from her and served himself from the big glass dish of ice cream.

She glared at him, her fists half-clenched, one of them on her hip, jabbing Albert. "It's just as smart as majoring in football," she said.

He looked up quickly and set down the dish of ice cream harder than he had intended.

"As smart as having a coach arrange with the professors about grades," she went on. "Or taking easy courses because you can't pass any others."

Albert pushed his glasses back on his nose and shouted: "Shut up, Ely!" Elaine knew that her brother admired his friend and was proud of himself for having secured his friendship. On introducing him in the hallway, Albert had said: "Foley plays center on the football team" in the same way that he might have said: "This is a brave soldier, a respected leader, and he fights courageously and intelligently. He does well. You should respect him."

Foley, holding his spoon suspended halfway between his bowl and his mouth, waved his other hand toward his friend in a gesture of such tolerance that Albert raised an eyebrow. "It's all right," Foley said. "Let it alone." He lowered his eyes, but his hand shook slightly, and his face was drained of color.

Foley knew that Elaine's outburst deserved a reproof, but he couldn't answer her hostility: The good manners that his mother had so carefully taught him when she had realized that he was going to be big, rough, and imposing put him at a disadvantage. He was a guest in Elaine's parents' house, eating their food and sleeping under their roof. He had to keep still.

Implicit in her invitation was the fact that he had now become her adversary. No longer her mentor and friend, he was like one of her brothers, the enemy, and she had lost her respect for him. Why? It was as if the long, warm, seductive look he had given her when he had laid his hand gently, in increasing friendship, on her back, caressing her really, in answer to her body touching his (he had read that as an invitation, and it was one he was ready to accept with all the energy of his nature) had offended her and made her change her mind about him. She seemed to resent him for appreciating and responding to the girl who attracted him rather than the one whose challenge was absurd. It was as though the sweeter options of womanhood had never occurred to her.

She is daring me, he thought. *That's it.* He assumed that, like many girls who were brought up as the unique female in a family of boy children, she had been taught to be tough, and her tyranny was not only tolerated, but expected. The boys could not hit her; part of their masculine training was to tolerate her female anger. And Foley was perceptive enough to see that she had every reason to be angry. As bright and vigorous as she was, still she was relegated to second best, schemed against by nature to follow rather than to lead, to mind the material fortress rather than to provision or protect it, to appease human beings rather than to confront them, to praise others rather than to be praised, and probably to love more than she was loved. She seemed furious and impossible in her frustration, hemmed in and deeply resentful, as though she had seen the light of opportunity in her childhood and lost it. She was a superb athlete (Albert had told him as much) but she was still a girl, and she couldn't compete. Half her rivals would outdistance her . . . simply because they were male.

Foley talked to the others then; he ignored Elaine. But even as he asked for another glass of iced tea—which he sugared but didn't drink—he was thinking about her. He saw that he would be unable to get to her with clever insights or remarks on human nature or public events. She was too physical; at least with him she would be. But he felt that in spite of her hostility (maybe the hostility was a manifestation of it), she was attracted to him. The cautious handshake at the door, her darting examination of his face, her quick disappearance after he had smiled at her from the landing—all this he could not have misread. Yet now it was as though a war had been declared, one that he would win, but not before he had been flayed in a number of skirmishes. Well, so be it. He would not shrink from this first encounter: He would meet her on the turf and see what she was up to; he would enter the contest, and, if necessary, he would rough her up a little, if just to touch her again.

"All right," he said, speaking to her across the table. He gave no explanation as to why he had changed his mind. "What position do you play?"

"Quarterback," she whispered, reaching down quickly to recover the napkin she had dropped. "Or anything."

"Are you going to change out of that dress?"

"Yes."

"What?"

"I said yes."

While the others were finishing their coffee—she had refused hers—Elaine changed into slacks and a thick sweater, then went outside to inspect the playing field, to make sure that it was still as perfectly groomed as when she had left it that afternoon. She bent down, picked up a rock, and threw it into the trees. From the center of the field, she looked in both directions, a serious inspection; then she smiled and pushed the sides of her thick hair behind her ears. She ran a little way, limbering up; she reached down, touching her toes with opposite hands, and then she stood with her arms folded in front of her, watching the others come out, Foley leading, her brothers just behind. She announced that she would play quarterback to Foley's center and ordered Albert to play end. Her two smaller brothers, Larry and Jack, and the hired hand's two young sons she would use as flankers, wing backs, or receivers, according to her whim and the requirements of the plays.

When she had set up the first play that Foley had diagrammed for her, she crouched against Foley for the hike, concentrating so intently on her movements that she was unaware that her closeness to him, her body touching his where it did, might be disturbing, might ultimately ruin the game. Her attention was focused on giving the signals correctly, remembering the blocking assignments, trying as hard as she could to get everything right and not embarrass herself.

She amazed Foley by throwing a series of incredibly long and accurate passes to Albert and Larry and Jack, one of which must have gone fifteen yards, maybe twenty, and after which she bragged insufferably, grinned, tormented her brothers, and even tortured the hired hand's meek and silent children, who had been so delighted when she had asked them to play. She criticized each successive play like a coach who is exacting, but at least marginally perverse. She made everyone miserable.

But two plays later, Foley snapped the ball to the halfback, feinted back behind the line of scrimmage, and tackled the quarterback, who in no sense had possession of the ball when she was downed and, worse, was still ostensibly a member of his own team. Both of them were breathing hard and wet with perspiration when he crushed her to the ground, pinning her down, while her body thrashed under his, not hurt badly, but shamed in front of her brothers, a thing that, to Elaine, was much more serious. He had humiliated her before all the others. He had made her cry. She bared her teeth like a dog and called him a filthy name, one that she had never uttered to anyone other than her brothers, though it summed up her feelings about all men, and her rage at their strength. She ran from the field, tripped, and was up again before the bewildered center could catch her.

"Come back here, Elaine," Albert yelled. "He didn't mean..." Albert was worried about his mother's reaction. He and Larry and Jack had been warned never to harm Elaine; no matter how obnoxious she got, they were not to hurt her. There was no excuse for that. "When this happens, there's always hell to pay," he told Foley. "But don't feel bad. She started it. My mother saw how she was at the table."

When her daughter came into the kitchen, her face warmed to burning, her teeth clamped tightly together, her hair ruined, Mrs. Mueller was distressed; when she went toward the sink, panting from exertion and rage, trying to hide her face with her arm, that distress increased. But on questioning Elaine, Mrs. Mueller immediately understood the kind of masculine attention that that tackle represented. It was blatant, and had she not known that in a certain sense Elaine had provoked it, she might have felt obliged to reprimand their visitor. As it was she spoke quickly and emphatically to Elaine, for she disliked what she had seen. Elaine was going to punish Foley for being attracted to her, and he was unlikely to stand for it. He was different from the docile, accepting boys that had attempted to pass Elaine's trials and had failed. If this man wanted Elaine, he would get her; it was her duty as the girl's mother to make sure that this happened only within the limits of custom and Elaine's consent. "You don't realize what you're doing, Elaine. You can't..." She tried to read her daughter's face, but there was no emotion in it. It retained the hot, flushed redness produced by fury and the demanding physical struggle of the game but revealed no more: She was hiding the rest. "Go call Arlet and see if you can spend the night, Elaine. Your father can drive you over in the truck." Arlet Simons was Elaine's best friend; she lived in town. Ordinarily Mrs. Mueller would have required Albert to drive his sister, but Foley might want to accompany them, and for the time being, that was out of the question.

Elaine shook her head at her mother's suggestion, and then she leaned over the sink and threw water on her face and dried it on a dish towel. Mrs. Mueller was silent, but Elaine knew what she was thinking. "I play fine," she said. "Albert brought him home to show me that I don't!"

"Albert brought him home because he admires him, Elaine. It has nothing to do with you."

Elaine's mouth trembled, and her tears interfered with her sight. Her mother's protection weakened her, held her back, suffocated her. She wouldn't even let her ride her horse off the property anymore; if she wanted to go anywhere at all, she had to wait for her daddy to drive her. She twisted the towel violently and then threw it on a chair. "I don't believe that. Albert hates me. . . . I play with Larry and Jack, and I play all right. I pass better than Jack. Even Albert says I do. When that person, Foley, isn't here, I do fine." She turned her back to her mother to show that she was no longer interested in the conversation and began putting away the dishes.

"He's not even trying, honey. When he plays with you, he's not playing football, he's playing something else."

"I don't—"

"He plays for the university, Elaine. He's paid to play football. They give him his tuition, his room, and all he wants to eat just to play that game."

"Then they don't know what he's like. I don't care how good he is. If he cheated like that in a real game, he'd be sitting on the bench."

Mrs. Mueller had been drying the coffee cups; she put the last one down. "I doubt he sits much on the bench."

"But you don't know, Mama."

"I do know." She took Elaine by the arm and moved her into the dining room. In the dusk, in the gray and violet light that had moved over the vegetable garden and the pasture, the silver and black Packard coupe gleamed like a jewel in a box with an iridescent lining. "College students don't have cars like that, Elaine. Do you know how he got it?"

Elaine hid her face in the thickest folds of the lace curtains. The polished window glass made her remember how eagerly she had awaited the football player, and again the tears came.

"Some rich businessman gave it to him. Do you know why,

Elaine? So he'd play for the university and refuse an offer some-where else. He plays that well."

That was true. Mrs. Mueller had heard from Albert how one night in March, during Foley's last year in high school, a man with a car dealership in Dalhart had left the Packard in front of Foley's house. When the sky was still lavender and blue from the dawn, and the clouds were still soft and lacked description, two little neighborhood boys had knocked on Foley's window to tell him. The keys and title were in the mailbox along with a cheerful anonymous note saying that the car was his whether or not he played for the university, and that the insurance was paid up for the next four years.

Elaine shrugged and went back into the kitchen. "Who cares how he got his car? Other boys have nice cars. J. Henry Fisher..."

Her mother followed her. "Claude Fisher is rich; J. Henry never earned it."

"Foley didn't earn it either—just playing football."

Her mother began drawing the cold water in which the nap-kins would soak. It beat like a hammer on the bottom of the pan. "That's earning it, honey."

Elaine looked out the window, where the game continued without her. It was nearly dark. In the east, the sky was washed out and fragile; in the west, there was still a hard band of gold melting over the steep roof of the barn and into the tops of the great trees that stood behind it, separating the corral and the plowed and newly planted fields. She saw Foley squat down a moment and look toward the house. "It's no fun unless you play somebody good," she said weakly. When she turned to look at her mother, her lashes were so wet they looked like the petals of a flower; her eyes searched for something to rest on; she fidgeted with her hands. She was remembering the passes she had made and one particularly spectacular play. He had admired those things; there had been admiration for her in his calm face and in the quiet of his body as he had watched her; she had been proud before him. But her time was over for engaging him in play, and she knew that.

Mrs. Mueller put down the dish she had wiped more than dry. "Why are you so angry, darling?" She took the girl in her arms. "I never understand you." Elaine's muscles hardened to resist, and she pushed away a little; but then she went soft on her mother and let herself cry.

* * *

That night, Foley, afraid of Elaine because he had upset her—
he had no idea how much she had told her mother—found her
sitting on the stone bench beside the birdbath. She was wearing
her purple basketball jacket, her red hair almost long enough to
cover the three gold stripes on her shoulder. He spoke to her
casually, something about the stars, the Seven Sisters and Orion's
belt; something about the unusual visibility and brilliance of
Taurus the Bull. When he sat down by her, he felt her stiffen and
move over slightly, yet he was in no way disappointed, for he no
longer cared. Despite the extremely affirmative reaction of his
body to hers as she had struggled under him in the grass, he had
decided to remain only a friend to her. She was too young, and as
Albert had warned him, she was mean; she had a temper that he
did not care for. He could never be attracted to her: Her apparent
obliviousness of her own sensuality had to be insincere. Still, he
was a guest in her family's house, and he had to fix this. "I hope I
didn't hurt you out there," he said suddenly, interrupting his dis-
course on the constellations.

"I don't get hurt," she answered. She looked away, not only
from him, but from the sky he was so intent on describing.

He tried again being impersonal, speaking to her about the
presidential election and his support of Franklin Roosevelt, but
again felt his resolution destroyed by her, and once more he
found that he was approaching her through the intelligence of the
flesh. Something was happening to him. It was as if once he had
taken the notion of making love to her, once it had occurred to
him that he would like to do this, he had been unable to stop the
forward motion of the desire. He tried to halt that motion by
abandoning his efforts to talk to her; he joined her in her silence
and in her preference for looking toward the vague, dissolved
landscape rather than at the eager and clearer sky; and yet, he
realized, he was breathing with an agitation that she apparently
shared. And yet, and yet . . . he seemed to have recovered himself, to be thinking of something else, miles away from this, at a
safe, safe distance, when suddenly he brought her around to face
him, lifting her to her feet, his head dipping down, his square,
angular chin pushing her head backward, until he was kissing her
on the mouth, pressing so hard that she had to open not only her
lips but her teeth. She had to give up to the explorations of his
tongue, which, since she had scarcely been kissed before, hardly
been kissed at all (she would almost never permit it), startled her.
He was crushing her; she panted for breath. She remembered a

kiss as the flat touching together of lips, softly, shyly. Not this.
This had to be a mistake. Maybe he did not know what he was
doing. When he released her—she had been pushing against him
violently—she thrust herself away from him, rubbing her wet
mouth and chin with the back of her hand, and zipping together
the panels of her jacket. In disbelief at what he had done to her,
and in shock at what she had felt, she turned away from him,
stumbled on the first step of the porch, took the others rapidly,
now surely, and went upstairs, silently seeking her place of retreat.

She undressed quickly and lay on her side in bed without
sleeping. Again and again, thoughts of the kiss and the tackle
swooped through the maze of her brain's excitation like frenzied
swifts after a violent change in weather. She was helpless to stop
them; helpless to do anything. The flow of acid through her loins,
astonishing for the way that it weakened her and brought on a
peculiar and indefinable pain, made her throw angry glances out
the window through the innocent, obstinately mute branches of
the red oak and the golden rain tree to where their limbs parted to
let in the stars he had talked about. During the rest of his visit,
she decided, she would stay in her room.

On Sunday, Foley made Albert wait until the end of the day to
leave. He had wanted to see Elaine at least once before going, for
no other reason than to be in her presence. He had paced anxiously, feeling foolish, in the entrance hallway as the purple twilight entered the glass panels of the front door and moused
around his feet while Mrs. Mueller, at his request, had gone
upstairs, her shoes rubbing each ascending tread with a quick,
scrapping sandpaper hiss, to Elaine's room, to ask Elaine to come
down so that he could tell her good-by. And maybe he could get
her out on the porch alone, even briefly; not really to apologize,
but to tell her what he was thinking.

With one hand on his hip, the other on the pate of the newel
post, he waited at the bottom of the stairs. He was in love with
Elaine, and since he could not declare it to her, he declared it
over and over to himself. He had thought so when he first met
her, holding a handful of silver—and certainly he had known it
the first time he had seen her reach back to execute a forward
pass and deliver it like a discus thrower at Olympia. *I love her,* he
had said to himself as he was packing, *but it's sure begun badly.*
At last, Mrs. Mueller came down the stairs. Her hand moved
along the rough pine strips of the bannister, which, last winter,
when there was so little to do outside, the hired man had painted

for her in what the hardware store called Dresden blue. She stood before him, in front of the hall table, her cheek licked blue and yellow in the stuttering leaps from the flame of the kerosene lamp, and she told him: "I'm sorry, I apologize for her. She isn't able to come down right now. Elaine is sometimes . . ."

Foley blushed at what she had had to tell him, a deep red insinuating itself brutally across the planes of his cheeks. It was half anger, half bewilderment. He shook his hostess's hand and thanked her for her hospitality, but since he had been obliged to hold his jaw a fraction too tightly, his face quivered. And though he had cleared his throat to prevent it, his voice cracked from the shame, which was so unfamiliar to him that he had no idea how to control it.

As he started the engine of the Packard, as he drove it slowly away from the lighted farmhouse, as he took one last look at Elaine's window on the second floor and thought he saw the yellow shade pulled aside, he knew that the agitation inside him would continue until she was his. He wanted, he thought, to tell her all about himself, all the stories about his family, to slowly unreel before her his whole life, even to imagining its end; and then he would want to listen to her recounting her own, until he knew everything about her and could learn why she was so competitive and harsh, and why, right now, she disliked him. Mainly he wanted to make love to her. He wanted badly to possess that particular arrangement of flesh and bone and warmth and temper. She might be thrashing or acquiescent, furious or calm—it no longer mattered. He wanted that body beneath his at least one more time; he would make that happen, only this time he would finish it properly, to the satisfaction of them both.

Driving the sixty miles down the narrow black highway, he remained silent, keeping his eyes on the road, his jaw set, his expression grim. He was a different man from the one who had come down this road in the opposite direction two days before. As the headlights fanned out over the farms and settlements, briefly illuminating fragments of the landscape, he was unable to remember what that calm, casual, undistracted college senior of two days ago had been like. He kept his thoughts from Albert, answering his friend's questions obliquely; he avoided the subject of Elaine until the last crossing of the Colorado River, when he said, "I would consider it a favor if you would ask me home again next weekend, Albert."

Since he got along poorly with his father, Albert avoided his home as much as possible. But he was proud of his friendship with Foley, glad that this renowned person favored him and was now giving even his family attention. "Good," he said and did not question his friend's motives until Foley let him off in front of his boardinghouse.

"It's Elaine," he answered, looking up without raising his head.

"You think she likes you?" That afternoon she had pulled him into her room and berated him. "And don't bring him back here," she had added. He was sure she had meant it. He looked at Foley with sympathy and asked, "You think she wants to see you again?"

Foley pushed his foot down on the accelerator and let the engine race. "She will."

Foley had been meeting adversity head-on for so long that he rarely expected anything to be easy. When his father had died, he had recognized at once that a burden had fallen on him, that the days of a childhood which had been fiercely protected by an earnest and capable man were over. He guessed he was ready, and in any case, his mother had already begun talking to him as if now the two of them had a partnership. He had thought about his three younger brothers, one of them still in diapers, the other two not yet old enough to be left alone at home, and realized that he would not only have to go to school but also have to play surrogate parent when his mother was at work, and to go out to a job when she was at home.

He was forced to convince the grocer of his abilities, claiming that, though he was only eleven, there was nothing too heavy for him to carry; that he already knew how to sweep, dust, and polish windows; that he could stock even the highest of the shelves—couldn't he climb a ladder?—and that since he knew everything there was to know about horses, he could even drive the delivery wagon during the hour that he had off from lunch.

The small salary at the grocer's had satisfied him until he had grown old enough to build roads and do maintenance work for the highway department, where he could make real money, and where he could learn about life by working beside every kind of man there was—men who were young and strong and who planned to move on when something better came along; men who were old and tired before their time; men who were crude; men who were too sick to work but had to eat; men who had a certain refinement but who had gotten trapped in a peculiar mode of itinerant life that obliged them to snatch work anywhere they could find it. Some of them shirked, but most of them, Foley included, worked hard. He had never let a foreman see him slacking, and not because he necessarily felt a loyalty to the people who ran what was a harsh and sometimes heartless enterprise, but because nothing must happen to make him lose that job, or any job he ever had, since he would then have to look at his mother's face while he told her that the only person she believed she could depend on had let her down, just as his father had failed her by losing his health and his life.

His work left him little time to cultivate or be aware of his own emotions, but he was still attractive to women, partly because of his physical excellence, partly because he had grown up so early and had been forced into responsibilities that are usually those of older men. At fourteen, he had gone steady with a girl at school, to whom he gave his heavy wool letter jacket; at sixteen, he had had a brief affair with the woman who owned, managed, and staffed the only beauty shop in town. At the end of his sophomore year at the university, he had had an understanding with a tall black-haired girl who possessed both dignity and refinement, qualities that especially pleased Foley since he had seen so little of them when he was young. She was sophisticated and worldly; she came from Dallas. They might have married that next year; they had spoken vaguely of a wedding at Christmas; but after the summer separation, the relationship ended. The girl who left him in June—she and her mother had traveled to Europe that summer, stayed in hotels he knew nothing about, eaten food he had never heard of, toured cities he would never see—came back to him different and changed. He no longer felt the same about her; he didn't know exactly why; and when on a walk by the lake he told her, she was dazed, then angry, and finally, she cried, embarrassing and shaming him. The crying made him want to erase what he had said, but erasing it would leave his feelings unchanged. He must not try to make it easy; it was kinder to leave it as it was.

The guilt he felt, the error in choice that he had made, caused him to be wary of women, and for nearly two years, his times with them were imperfect and brief; but now, with two months left of college, and the image of Elaine in his mind, he did something different, and not simply because he was seeking to relieve his pain but because, since she had come into his life—rather he had come into hers—he was a different man.

On the Monday after he had met her, after his classes were over, and after he had gone to the bank to draw out sufficient money, he stood before the display window of a jewelry store on

the main street of the capital city. His blond hair blazed like a
helmet; sunlight swept across his square shoulders and solid
back. He was bending forward slightly to look long and intently
at the glittering diamond rings, lighted artificially and couched in
dark, loose waves of velvet. He examined them scrupulously, and
then, finally, finding one that was both pretty and affordable, he
went inside and bought it.

Appraising the man and appreciating at once what some girl
was getting, the saleswoman smiled and said in the sensuous
voice of a knowing matron, "Your fiancée must be very happy."

Foley pushed the stack of bills across the glass counter toward
her waiting hand. "Not yet," he answered.

She counted the money and placed it in a wooden drawer
under the counter, then gave him his change and a handwritten
bill of sale. "Do you want me to wrap it?" she asked.

The box that contained the ring was covered in soft black
suede. He could imagine Elaine's opening it; he could almost see
the flash of her green eyes. "No, ma'am, it's fine like it is."

Outside the shop he held the box in the palm of his hand, and
when he opened it, and the top locked back precisely on its
hinge, he could see the diamond's facets blazing against the royal
blue velvet, while the tiny baguettes flanking it twinkled in the
sharpness of the sunshine. She would like it. He stood rapt in the
pleasure of having in his grasp this symbol of his future com-
pleteness, and it was only when he noticed two women glancing
at him that he smiled at them broadly, snapped the lid shut, and
moved swiftly toward his car.

Every night that week, Elaine's sulky interludes during meals
kept the family on edge; in the afternoons, she took moody strolls
through the house, dragging the dusty heels of her school shoes
across the flowered carpets, startling her mother by refusing to
leave them at the kitchen door as was the custom. She found no
good in anything, and when, late on Thursday, Mrs. Mueller
found her in her bedroom crying, Elaine refused to talk about it,
even when her mother held her in her lap, stroked her hair, kissed
her, and tried to coax her.

When the Packard came again, Elaine was riding horseback.
She turned her horse quickly toward the back pasture, for she
needed time to think, to ask herself why Albert had come home
two weekends in a row, and why Foley Menutis had accompanied
him. The answers she came up with, the implications of this
second visit so close on the heels of the first, caused her to

wander farther from the house than her mother liked, to take her horse through a muddy slough she had never meant to cross, and at the corral, to let him step on one of his reins and break it—a thing that would cost her a wearying lecture from her father.

That afternoon Elaine did her best to evade Foley, but he continually asked her parents and brothers where she was and waited where he thought she might come. He planned every movement and every step he took was with one thing in mind—being in the presence of Elaine. When he did finally manage to ambush her, she hardly spoke to him, and though he stared at her constantly with his blue-gray eyes all during supper, she kept her green ones averted, never giving him the satisfaction of catching them. That she was trying to avoid him and that he was seeking her out was clear to everyone, though no one could quite find the nerve to suggest that, in order to save his pride, he either be covert in his pursuit or abandon it—until Albert, frankly embarrassed by his friend's abasement, drank a beer, took courage, and while the two of them were playing cards in the quiet of the living room after supper, mentioned it. Foley cursed softly, threw down his hand, left the room, and went upstairs. He could not understand why she would not come around. When he had given her the box of candy he had bought, a three-layered Whitman's Sampler, she had taken it, and had thanked him, not without warmth. He had thought she would stay with him then and talk to him, that the candy had broken the spell; but soon after unwrapping the box and offering it around, she had put it on a table, available to them all, and gone to her room, leaving him in the company of her parents in awkward silence.

He pulled up the window shade in the guest room, and looked out at the part of the yard that they had used as the playing field, now palely lit by the moon. Did he regret the tackle? No, he told himself. That had been the only right thing he had done—and the kiss, too, because it was honest. He felt that she must be rejecting him for something else. Silently he pressed his fist against the sill and touched his aching forehead to the glass. What did she want from him? He got into bed, wishing to drift off quickly into a deep sleep, but lay for many hours held awake by his failure.

The next morning he woke late to the sound of voices in the garden—Mr. Mueller giving a command, the boys protesting, another command, then the movement of tools into the area that was fenced in with waist-high white pickets to keep out the chickens and dogs. He dressed quickly, politely refused Mrs.

Mueller's offer to prepare his breakfast, and went outside to help with the work.

Elaine was sitting on the porch in a wicker rocking chair. When he stopped to speak to her, she answered his question quickly, motioned him toward her brothers, and glanced away.

It was a deeply shadowed morning, yet there was still enough new vegetation to set everything glowing in yellow and lime-green shade. The landscape whispered with sound, the blades of the lawnmower clattering in interrupted bursts of action while the wires of the rakes clicked in more or less constant exchanges. Elaine sat rocking, her head resting on the woven twigs of the ample chair back, her lazy, half-open eyes occasionally widening when the boys laughed at one of their own jokes, which she was usually unable to hear. She sighed then, stopping her rocking, and fanned herself with a palm leaf; the ten o'clock warmth was almost uncomfortable. She looked across the lawn and remembered what her mother had said in the kitchen at breakfast: "Why don't you be nice to Foley, darling? You know he's here to see you."

She had turned away from her mother to lash the butcher knife over the whetstone, though it had its edge, and she had answered, "I *am* nice."

"No, you're not. You don't talk to him . . . or to your brother."

"I never talk to Albert. When do Albert and I ever talk? You told me to leave Foley alone. That's all I'm doing, Mama." She had continued the redundant activity of honing the knife, and if her mother tried to say anything, she couldn't hear it.

It was not long before Foley left the rake he had been using, propped it against a tree, and came to the porch. He sat on his heels beside her chair, took the palm leaf out of her hand, and fanned her himself, making a steady and agreeable breeze. She reached to take the fan back, but then, judging from his expression that he would not release it, she let her hand drop. On the road, a truck was passing fast in a cloud of red dust; it interested her; she sat forward a little. Foley was perfectly still, as though he was trying not to intrude on her thoughts. She could see that there was pain in the deliberation of his campaign to draw her to him; it was painful to watch. She noticed that the work in the yard behind Foley had ceased, and the workers had turned their heads to the porch.

"You want to organize a game this afternoon before dinner?" he asked. He looked at her steadily, his blue eyes hard on her.

She turned to him, amazed. Nothing he could have said would

have been worse. How could he be so insensitive? Her mouth opened slightly, and she blinked.

"We could play football after it gets cool," he went on.

She sat up straight and, with her feet flat on the floor, stopped the motion of the rocker. "Why?" she cried. "So you can take advantage of me again? Cheat?" She pushed the fan aside so that she could glare at him with nothing in her way. "So you can roll on me when the play hasn't even started?"

Foley cleared his throat and settled himself better on his heels. "I only meant to tease you," he said.

"To tease me?" She shivered with rage. "Did you think you were playing with a baby?"

"You asked for it," he said quietly.

"How?" she shouted, her startled eyes filling with tears.

"You were obnoxious."

"Then why do you bother with me? What are you doing up here on this porch?"

Tears had started down her cheeks, and when he reached out to dry them, she pulled away.

"You would never have done that to a real team member," she cried. "How dare you do that to me . . . just because I'm a girl!"

Her righteous eyes searched his face, hoping he would find something, anything at all, to say to her, to assure her that he regarded her as an equal, as a competitor whose challenge interested him. When he was silent, she turned her head away from him and stood up so abruptly that the back of the chair hit jarringly against the wall of the house, rattling the windowpanes behind it. He had to catch it to stop the hammering of its rockers against the floor boards. Slamming the door, she fled inside.

He waited a moment, outcast and brooding; then he tried to slink back to the rake (impossible for a man of his size), knowing what the boys in the yard had seen, knowing that he dared not look at them, because if one of them glanced at him wrong, showed any pity, he would be unable to control his temper. They understood that and resumed their work quietly, keeping their eyes to their tasks and their thoughts to themselves. It hurt them all, the whole male cast, to see the giant so helpless. Their sister's conduct, while consistent with their knowledge of her, was still an enigma to them. Why Foley was unable to have her groveling at his feet they did not know. They were just as puzzled as to why he would even want Elaine. She had a wicked tongue, and she was too rough for a girl. Yet Foley was rough himself sometimes: On the playing field, he could be terrible. And he was not

without his competitive side; if he saw an advantage, he took it.
Elaine acted that way, too.

When Mrs. Mueller came outside with a pitcher of lemonade
and glasses and left it on the stone table, the boys sat down to rest
on the lawn, Foley leaning against a tree, watching the house,
describing distractedly a project at school. All of them knew that
he was just passing the time; that what he wanted was what he
watched for; that what he was missing was what, because of the
walls, he could not see; that what he was thinking about was what
he could not say. Yet they went on talking with him, every one of
them playing out a somewhat specious part while a set of tight
white clouds held itself tensely above the barn, the drop in the
wind quieted the trees to silence, and all activity within the house
apparently stopped.

For the rest of the morning, Elaine managed to evade Foley,
but when the family gathered for lunch, he used every kind of
seductive masculine mannerism, trick, and convention that he
could think of to draw her to him. In the kitchen, while Elaine
and her mother prepared the food, he leaned back in an oak chair
with his knee against the table edge, so far back that he risked
falling over. Each time Elaine carried something from the kitchen
to the dining room, he would reach ahead of her to open every
door that she approached—though once she turned abruptly,
veering away from the door he held. He undid a jar that she could
not open (she gave him a filthy look for that). She knew that the
favors he was doing, that he volunteered to do so willingly, were
in no way done because Foley wanted to please her father; they
were done because he wanted to please her. If he thought she was
watching, there was no task he would not undertake.

It was only after lunch that she imagined he had retreated and
she could relax her guard. He was nowhere around; she thought
that he had given up. She read in her room, she worked awhile at
training her new dog, she went to her vegetable garden and
pulled the new weeds from between the seedlings. As she went to
check on the litter of kittens in the loft of the barn, she passed the
washhouse window and halted when she saw Foley through its
wavy pane. He had taken apart the broken wringer of the washing
machine and was now beginning to put it back together. He was
quiet and still and quick. There was a sensuality in the silhouette
of his secret concentration, and she began to feel a disconcerting
isolation from him. A desire to be the object of that formidable
concentration swept over her like a flare, and she took a quick,

strong breath, as if she had been hurt. His shoulders and arms were heavily muscled, but this never caused him to slump. He had large hands with heavy clumps of blond hair above the knuckles, and though they moved thickly, his fingers were agile and fast. Looking at them frightened her, took her strength, made her ache. He still had not seen her. She watched him—the insistence of his flanks, the gracious curves of his torso, the great arms and chest, the hair on him, flaxen hair that seemed to be all over him, would have been on his face had he not shaved it so closely twice a day. He took a bath and shaved before dinner. He came to the dinner table in clean clothes. She had never known a man to do that. He smelled of soap, and his skin fairly gleamed with health and well-being. He advertised his faultless constitution in every move he made. His teeth were strong and white, and he showed them often in his smiles. He seemed to participate more fully in life than other men she had seen: He had an affinity with the natural environment, and he exemplified manliness; he had energy, and he sought occupation. She felt that only a deep, innate, humane respect, a charity of sorts, held him back, kept him from using his power in a dangerous way.

Yet the potential of his outrageous maleness upset her; it made her angry; it made her hate him for possessing it and parading it, however inadvertently, before her. She could hardly look; she could hardly bear to see what she admired in him. He was like her father's bull, with his powerful, changing eyes, and was as blond as that beast. Yes, that was it, the bull; the unexpected aggression of the animal's manner, violent without warning, everything about its nature in contrast to a heifer's meekness. The cows were brought to that bull! It was awful, and she hated her father for letting things like that happen.

When she was still in grade school, she had often heard boys talking, giggling over their bizarre daydreams, their artless obscenities, their lewd humor, ringing alarmingly of truth. Even then she was aware that implicit in the business was the abjection of the female, and the triumph of the male. Once, two of the older boys with yellow fuzz and pimples on their cheeks cornered her in a silent, after-school hallway which was heavy with the smell of chalk, pubescent children, and stale lunches. "We know how to kill a girl," one of them whispered, grabbing her arm with his damp hand and invading her face with the odor of garlic from cheap lunch meat. Pale with loathing, she broke through them. She wanted to tell her teacher and then her mother, but of course she could not, since to do so would be to admit to knowing what they meant, to being tainted—would be to join in the corruption that these things implied.

After a period of sober musing, an interlude of worry and realization, she had in a state of need and with a hunger to know, gone as a scientist to observe the mating of animals from the square window of the barn loft. The hatch was wide open, and so she had to lie at an angle in order not to be seen. She had watched between two wired bales of acrid-smelling alfalfa hay, as wide-eyed and suspicious as a doe in a thicket before a clearing; she lay flat on her stomach in the dust and derangement of the feed; she remained there in the invisible, ammoniacal mist, witnessing the coupling of cattle until at last, with lost innocence, she rolled onto her back, unable to continue looking. She closed her eyes and listened to the harsh, effortful sounds, but she dared not look again.

From that day forward, her childhood was erased. She spent many days in shock from it and felt guilty for having gone there at all. She was puzzled and uncomprehending, shocked and changed. It was sinful to have looked; she should never have done it; she should not have been present. If she had been Catholic, she would have been able to confess this sin behind a screen, and she would have hoped the priest would absolve her. But how could she tell her minister, a confessor whom she would have to meet with face to face? She lived with her knowledge instead.

As the weeks passed, she controlled her anxiety with study and activity, but then suddenly, one afternoon when school was over—she could never explain it to herself—she went to the drugstore and bought one of the romance magazines that the druggist kept behind the nicer things. She bought first one, and then several more. She hid them under her mattress and, when she was done, tore them up, or crept like a criminal to the incinerator and watched them redden, curl, turn black, and fly upward in the filthy smoke.

She thought of the humiliation of giving herself up to someone. Would any woman do that of her own free will? No. Maybe fathers, in rites and rituals (there had been a story like that in a magazine!), betrayed their daughters, permitted their disgrace, abetted it. She began to look at her own father with new understanding and, for a month or two, feared him. She hated to ride alone in the car with him and, at the table, kept her eyes from meeting his. She was cross and, though she never told her why, kept close to her mother and sought her protection. Only the passage of time caused her to see her father again in the old way, as her guardian and provider, though the days of thoughtless caresses while sitting on his lap, or pressing his hand against her cheek, or embracing him and hanging on his neck after he had come home from a night or two away were over.

She had believed that she had recovered, that she had pushed the trouble out of her mind; and then, unexpectedly, her favorite cousin became engaged. She grieved; she tried to understand it; she asked herself why this sound and sensible girl would submit willingly, go to her fate so stupidly? While the older girls rejoiced and prepared presents, she sulked, was often rude. The marriage ceremony irritated her; at the reception she was so sullen and withdrawn that her mother questioned her about it. She would not answer; she complained of a headache and asked to be taken home. Two months later, when her cousin announced that she was pregnant, Elaine was stunned. She saw young mothers in church and wondered how they could show their faces when everyone knew what they had done. The sight of the grotesque swelling of pregnancy sickened her; it seemed a ghastly trick of nature; men coming to court a woman were no better than a pack of matted-hair mongrels circling a witless bitch, a scenario she herself had observed from the upstairs window when her dog, Juno, whom she had tried to keep penned, was let out by her brothers to tease her. Yelling invectives at the astonished boys, the inside of her head roaring with anger, she ran from the house to drive away the gasping dogs; and then to fight with her brothers, to pay them back for the outrage to which they had surrendered her dog, until her mother had to pull her off and put her head under the pump; and when the boys laughed at her for her wet face and streaming hair, she laid into them again.

For bloodying Jack's face, she was punished—for a week, there would be no horseback riding and no swimming in the tank by the spring. There seemed to be no one with her point of view. She tried sharing her indignation with her friend, an old black woman who came to clean, and again she was disappointed.

"She's better off," the servant said. It was like a slap in the face to Elaine. "Poor Juno . . . you pen her up. Let nature take its course."

Elaine would teach nature.

Her other confidante was Edna Sandomir, a young, rawboned Polish girl who planned to join a convent in San Antonio. Elaine liked her, often rode her horse the three miles to visit her at her family's farm. They spoke little of God and religion, but incessantly of independence; and both of them wanted to oppose the masculine threat. Though Elaine was not Catholic, she considered following Edna's example of chastity and living in a colony of women, and there was even a secret exchange of letters between Elaine and the Mother Superior of the convent where Edna was going. But her father lost his temper when the prioress telephoned Elaine (in his stolid German insolence, he intercepted the call); and though Elaine refused food for two days, that was the end of it.

But the seasons passed; she grew two, then three years older, and either time healed her, or her intolerant soul sweetened. The mystery, like a tangled skein, unraveled until, at last, when she saw a broad, well-shaped man, the solid, thick, sunburned back of a male neck, the heavy, well-formed chest or arm, the well-made head, the spare loins and square hands; when she noticed the way a man stood or moved or walked, or the way he held his eyes, or how he spoke carefully or spoke little; when she perceived these things (as she did with increasing frequency), she would swallow hard and try to get back to her lesson, or to the sermon at church, or to the conversation at a party. But she was changed, and bit by bit, she accepted this new condition; a germ of consent planted itself in her psyche, and the bud of complicity began to grow. Without objective, her flesh yearned and prepared to join the rest of nature, the assemblage of failed angels; and, at last, she began to ask herself when and where the male would appear, and if she would know him. Yet she continued to be afraid or, if not afraid, baffled. Her surrender to her sensuality had not accounted for the possibility that she would allow herself to be mastered. But she was female, and the nature of that act, implicit in it, was the male confronting the female, subduing her, and winning from her whatever it was that she had, that he wanted. Hadn't she seen this with the animals?

So, that afternoon, watching the man whom the state university paid to play games, this man who seemed to be as cruel as he could be careful, Albert's friend, watching him fix a washing machine, deep in her disturbing reflection, forgetting her need for secrecy and concealment, she moved slightly and stroked with her fingers the ridges of one low windowpane. He fascinated her; she feared him. All the ways in which he was different from her, the aspects of physical power she simply did not have, intrigued, reassured, and disquieted her. He was opposite to her; he always would be. He would never be familiar, though she might search out his mysteries eternally with all the guile and hope of a scien-

tist in a laboratory. That was why she would have to keep returning to this image before her, never learning anything.

Her eyes focused sharply as she took him in; she watched him
nervously, particularly the deep curve in the center of the mouth
that had kissed her, that had promised her in that kiss a delivery
of himself that might engulf her in such heady pleasures that she
would be made dependent. She needed to know about the hair on
his chest, to see if when she placed the palms of her hands flat
there he would be as warm as he had been on the two occasions
their bodies had come together. She had never seen his bare feet
or his knees, and this was a deprivation. She needed to know
more about his tongue, the shape of his ears, the outline of his
mouth, and especially the form of his neck: If she could have
been sure that he would stay still, she would have put her arms
around it, just to see. She wanted to touch him without his
knowledge. If she could have thought of a way to weaken him
temporarily, like Delilah, to shear away his hair, but only for a
while, so that when she was ready, he could rise again in power,
she would have done it. He complemented her; she felt equal to
him. Her hand moved on the pane.

Sensing the motion, he turned toward her. Their eyes came
together for a moment, and a blend of disparate sensations affected her. Through the distorting rippling of the old glass he
smiled at her like a caressed infant, and, making a motion that
was an invitation to come inside, called to her.

Instantly, furious for having revealed herself, she was gone.
Furious also (it had leaped into her consciousness at last) because
he seduced her terrifically, she hid herself, crouched behind a
wall, a fugitive; and when she heard him call to her again, she
forced her eyes shut and hid her face on her knees, frightened
because she had almost answered him. He had become a problem
she would have to solve unless she could avoid him; in letting
him see her, she had been inexcusably careless.

He had left the washhouse quickly, but she had vanished, and
he had missed the direction she had taken. If he had been able to
catch up with her, he knew the timing would have been right, and
he would have had his chance. She had come to him. He called to
her and then, getting no answer after several tries, sighed in grim
disappointment.

He stood in the gravel yard outside the washhouse and drew
his hand slowly across the back of the neck that Elaine had been
so curious to embrace. Before him, the lawn was shaded by swift
clouds. Each successive canopy of shadow lasted only a minute

or two, then was replaced by another. The brief intervals of light
shocked the eyes with their brightness. In the distance, behind the
house, was the pear orchard, where the tops of the trees, already
full-leafed, rippled in the breeze, like spinnakers that have been
neglected and left to run wild by an absent-minded mariner. He
started when he saw a slim woman walking toward the door,
holding her billowing skirt gathered with one hand and a basket
of eggs in the other; but it was not Elaine, it was her mother.

Foley sat on his heels to pet the black-satin dog, who, sym-
pathizing with this man's isolation and despondency (the genius
of good dogs), slowly wagged her cordlike tail. He let her ears
flop in the loose cups of his hands. Panting as heavily as the
engine of an untuned machine, the dog rolled to her side under
the large considerate palm; and he stroked her in long, open
strokes always in the same comfortable direction. Finally he
shook his head, murmured something, an affirmation of his condition, and went back inside to finish his job with the washer
while the dog remained on her back, her rear legs spread to allow
the warming of her freckled belly, her red tongue lolling over a
ridge of pointed teeth, wagging her tail residually.

When the sun began to fall and the shadows lengthened, Foley
put down his work. The wind had calmed, and as he walked
across the yard toward the house, he looked for Elaine as he
always looked for her since he had come to this farm. He took the
porch steps slowly, searched for her behind the long trails of
wisteria—she might be there, she had been once before. The hall
was quiet, the house seemed empty, yet he heard from the kitchen
the faintest movement, maybe a curtain blowing across the sill,
maybe the movement of fabric on a shirt or dress. He went to
see. She was in the kitchen alone, standing before the sink, leaning against it, facing him, and with what he imagined to be a
softness in her eyes, a difference in the way she regarded him.
From over the sink in the window behind her, he noticed that
there was a view of the washhouse.

"Why didn't you come inside and help me?" he asked. He
stood in the doorway and leaned against the frame. One hand was
stretched to the high lintel, grabbing it from in front; the other
was arched low on his hip.

"Where?" Her face was shadowed with worry.

It was an answer he had expected; he had thought she might
lie to him. "When I was fixing the machine," he said. He spoke
softly and with the nasal tone of his home, a town near Pecos.

"I didn't see you." She rarely lied, and the lie was unfortunate because it betrayed her a little.

That was it, he thought. That was what he needed. He crossed the kitchen in three hard strides, but she ducked swiftly under his arm and disappeared. He heard her moving on the stairs, taking them two at a time. A door slammed, and there was silence.

"She's fast," he whispered at his loss. "She's so damned quick."

No one else was in the house. He stood at the bottom of the stairs looking up. He wanted to follow her, to go into her room and pull her to him, as he had done eight days before on the porch. He should have kept her then, not let her loose at all. He should have put her in his car, and left with her; driven fifteen hundred miles to the West Coast, then written her parents a letter of apology. So what if he lost his chance to graduate? The memory of the tackle and the kiss invaded his mind. He frowned; his eyes were suddenly pained by the cool Dresden blue of the stairwell and he wanted to climb the stairs, two at a time, just as she had climbed them. As a bird follows another in flight and imitates its movements—soars, dodges, flashes, glides—he wanted to follow her; and then to catch her and keep her. He smiled at the insistence of his imagination; then, biting down hard on his lip, he bowed his head and moaned pathetically.

Upstairs he heard quick footsteps, then the click of a latch. She had locked her door. he would have given anything to see her face then. Was she scared, self-satisfied, smiling? Did she ridicule him? No; he knew she was not that kind of woman. She was a pure element, armored in a special version of morality that he recognized but could not yet decipher. Whatever she did was primarily a foil for what he did, and the rhythm she created with him intensified his anticipation.

During supper, Albert talked to Foley about the horses, particularly a two-year-old that his father had gotten from a young farmer in exchange for a harness and a pair of sheep. Before it got dark, they would set up the barrels, and Foley could try the horse. Although they invited Elaine, she shook her head, showed no interest, and left the table early; but when they had gone outside, after an interval, she followed, sitting down on the grass away from the group but near enough to see. She looked up occasionally, but when the saddled horse was offered to her, she refused it, implying that the activity did not interest her.

Foley rode Albert's horse fast among the barrels without

brushing a single one. He leaned into them, helping the horse to keep its balance on the turns. Albert held the stop watch.

"Oh, hell, Foley," Albert said. "It's not anything you can brag about. It's easy for you." The Mueller brothers were amazed. It wasn't so much that Foley had not knocked over the barrels—all of them were good at that; it was the speed at which he had taken them, and on a mount he was unaccustomed to. Albert brought his hand down hard enough on the rump of the horse to make it shy.

Slapping the left rein hard against the animal's neck, Foley whirled around toward Elaine so that he could see her expression, hoping for a look of praise. He leaned forward and twisted his hand in the long mane where it parted. The horse, a bay with white socks and small feet, danced on its delicate front hoofs, snapping beneath them the dry hulls and scattered shucks; its eyes full of fire, it foamed at the mouth and jerked its head up and down against the curb bit.

Like the rider in a fine equestrian sculpture at the head of a park, Foley sat straight and still. He ought to have had as a backdrop a curtain of yellow and orange leaves, a lashing, pearlized fountain, and the thick, steel-colored trunks of ancient trees. Instead, the dust on the floor of the corral churned up in little puffs and blasts; the man and the animal panted from the pleasure of their exertion; and Elaine, as if she had seen nothing, got up from the place where she had been sitting, turned her back, and began walking toward the house.

Albert called to her. "Ely!" She kept to her path as if she had not heard him. "To hell with you, Elaine!"

The smile of triumph that Foley had prepared for her froze on his face, and it cost him an effort to alter it. She was killing him. He was exhausting himself. He put his hand on the pommel of the saddle and stared blankly. Albert and the others looked away from him and kept silent.

She would not even come out to watch the races from the corral to the first cattle guard—a competition that ordinarily she would have participated in—and for the rest of the evening, if Foley came near, she pretended not to notice. For Elaine, he was not in the room, he was not in the house, he did not exist. She would talk to someone else, giddy and strained; she would bury her face in a book; she would listen to the radio, raising her hand, motioning anyone away who might try to interrupt her delight in the program. At her mother's suggestion, she fixed popcorn for the boys, but when she offered the buttery and fragrant dish to

Foley, she kept her eyes averted, smiling neither at his thanks nor at his compliments. And when in a little while he went over to the easy chair where she was curled up listening to music and asked her if she might like to go for a walk with him, she reached over wearily to twist the wooden knob of the radio, then left the room, her feet moving rapidly on the stairs.

After church on Sunday, Elaine changed into some comfortable clothes and went to read in the hammock that was strung between two oak trees. When, spurred by hours of neglect, Foley risked humiliation by taking her a glass of lemonade (he brought it to her filled with cracked ice from the ice block that he had driven into town to get), she held her book closer to her eyes than she needed to, answered him in murmurs and grunts, then flipped herself over and turned her back to him, not responding at all. He sat down beside her in an uncomfortable green metal tube chair that he had carried down the slope from the porch. He stared silently at the curve of her back, at the red hair spread out around her head and on her shoulders, feeling pain that to him was more serious than physical injury; impulsively he brushed her arm with a switch of straw he had been twisting nervously in his hand. She shuddered, and lashed at the switch with her hand, as if she were wiping away something nasty.

"Leave me alone, Foley," she said. The whine in her voice gave him hope; the plea seemed languorous, a bit coaxing.

He decided that this was the moment to declare himself. It was not exactly his plan, but then, if she refused him, he would be no worse off than he was; and maybe his heart would stop jerking in his breast, and maybe he could sleep. "I want to talk to you about something," he said.

"What?" She was looking neither at him nor at her opened book. She seemed to be watching for something on the far horizon, straining to catch sight of an anticipated object or caller.

He touched her arm with his hand. She trembled, and he felt it. "I want you to marry me," he said. "In June, after graduation."

As she flipped over on the hammock toward him, her golden legs were almost totally uncovered, and they shone like the breast of a lark. It took all the force of years of disciplining his will not to seize her; but he had come dangerously close.

Her eyes traced his face over and over in a scrupulous search that apparently satisfied her, and she finally said, "You are insane, Foley." Then she flipped herself around again, the book in her hand, the pages turning at appropriate intervals. If his question had raised any turmoil in her, it now seemed to have been dispelled.

He went on: "I'd make a good husband for you. I have a job beginning in the middle of June. The pay is good . . . so, if you like, we could begin a family right away. . . . If you want to, that is. . . . Although I wouldn't mind waiting a year or two if you think you're too young to be a mother."

"I'm going to college."

"I've done that; only one of us needs to."

"No," she said. She turned a page. "No."

"Why don't you think about it?" he asked with devious mildness.

"I'm too young for you."

"I'm twenty-one."

"And I'm sixteen. That's *five* years!" Impatiently she rubbed a page between her thumb and forefinger.

He waited. "My father was six years older than my mother."

"Yeah . . . and look what they got. You're too big and you act wild." She shrugged. "You're probably okay for football."

He pushed the hammock gently. "Just think about it, Elaine," he said.

"I have." Still on her side, she turned away from him even more, and she drew herself up like a snail.

He cleared his throat. "Don't you like me at all?"

"No," she said brutally. "I think you're a cheater and a liar. I think you take advantage of people."

"I never lied to you," he said, wounded.

"You made me think that you thought of us as equals. That was a lie, Foley."

It was true; he did not think of her as an equal. She was a woman; not worse than a man, but different. Of course, she came the closest to being his equal of any woman that he had ever met. He would make up the difference. "Please think about it . . . at least until next weekend," he said.

Her feet stretched out nervously to the end of the hammock. When the breeze played in the hem of her skirt, she pulled it down over her leg. "Goodness, Foley," she said, "are you coming back next weekend?"

"I am."

She groaned, and her eyes moved across the page of her book from left to right, then downward; after a time, she turned the page.

He stayed with her, rejected as he was, rocking the hammock

from time to time, occasionally saying something, to which, now, she would not even reply. When they were called in for lunch, she hurried on before him, as if he had not been walking behind her at all, or carrying the still-full glass of watery lemonade, which she had not drunk, and which he had felt too bad in the pit of his stomach to drink, either. He poured it out on the grass.

There had not been the slightest question of presenting the ring. It remained in Foley's pocket, exactly where he had put it on Friday afternoon.

The third weekend he came without the ring, thinking that, if he left it behind, it might work as a contrary talisman, making him less agitated and less vulnerable. He had already decided to visit her as many weekends as it would take; and if summer came and still he did not have her, he would give up the promise of the job he had in Victoria and look for one in nearby Seguin—even a bad job, that would waste his time, spoil his future. His mother would be sad about that—she was so proud of his achievement —but what choice did he have? Whatever he had to do to be near Elaine he would do. He would continue to court her.

As his car pulled into the drive of the Mueller farm, he saw Elaine leaving in the truck with the hired hand. The two vehicles passed each other; Elaine was looking straight ahead, and as Foley turned around to see, the truck receded rapidly under the speckled shade, past the last two matched trees. He was aston-ished when an hour later she telephoned her mother to say that she was spending the night in town with Arlet, who had been elected Halloween Queen that past fall and had got to keep the glittering scepter.

It was late Saturday afternoon when she came home. He saw her from the window; all day he had been pacing around the house, or trying to read her father's farm magazines, or helping Albert with work. (Albert had given up trying to placate him, to tell him that his sister, Ely, wasn't worth this kind of torture, that she was just a spoiled kid, and just because she could heave a long pass was no reason to...) Now she was coming down the drive, and he felt incredible joy at the flash of her red hair. He came out the back door to greet her, but she turned out of his path and ran lightly, friskily, shaking her head as if enjoying the rush of air through her hair, smiling as if she had a secret memory that did not include him, ran toward the kitchen, calling to her mother with news. Later, in his presence, she kept her eyes riveted to the floor.

Just before supper, when Foley entered the house from the porch and saw her pass before the staircase, he changed directions swiftly, turned into the hallway, and headed her off. He grabbed her arm, pulling her against him with all the force of his disappointment. Her eyes were huge; her fear was genuine. "I love you, Ely," he said brokenly. "Can't you respond to that at all?" He felt her leg against his; she straightened herself as best she could and pulled away slightly. Then she looked up at him, tipping her head back farther than necessary. There was a kind of mockery in that gesture, and she must have sensed it, because she corrected it instantly by lowering her head, relaxing against him as she stood quietly, her cheek pressed against the hard, tense muscle of his arm.

"You want to kill me," she said softly. "Look at you now. You're breaking my arm. Don't you ever do anything nice?" She thought of another college friend of Albert's. He had delicate hands, long tapered fingers, and a physiognomy much like her own. For her, at least for now, he was right. His name was Joel Amerman; he was a classics major, and he could read Latin as if it were English. He knew Latin and Greek poems by heart, and he would recite them in front of anyone. That was courageous, Elaine thought. She had sat on the porch swing, and while he had pushed the swing with his soft, white hands, he had recited four of them, giving, after each line, its translation. She had liked him, and once, when they were walking together on the shell road that led to the old tenant house, she had, at his request, let him kiss her. It had been languid and sweet, like the petals of two primroses brushing together by an accident of weather. He had let her participate. Unsubstantial as it was, she had had an equal part, a kind of sharing in it, that a man like Foley, too undisguisedly sensual, too profoundly self-satisfied, would never permit. As far as Elaine could see, there was only one thing that Joel had in common with Foley: He was never nervous. He was sweet and timid with her; he would never take hold of her like Foley did, or do the things to her that Foley would. He would never kiss her the way Foley had. Foley would be all over her, tearing her apart, shaking her, injuring her, like a fox taking hold of a chicken. "You're not like . . ."

He made her look up at him, his face an inch from hers. "Like who?" he asked miserably. "Are you in love with someone? Is that it?" He shook her. "Is that what's wrong?"

"No," she said. She had moved against him in a kind of swift caress.

"Albert told me you don't have a boy friend."

"I don't need one."

"You need me."

She giggled. "Really? To do what? To break me in half? To cheat me in games? To make your own rules?"

Elaine's eyes passed Foley's, then came back to them, slowly, fixedly—enigmatic and soft for once and free of hostility. They swarmed with some mysterious intelligence, and for the first time since that evening at dinner, when he had been explaining football plays to her she held her gaze to his, even if just for an instant; then she giggled again softly, giving him hope of a recurrence of her playfulness. Speaking quickly, in a hushed voice, she teased him: "I couldn't make you happy, Foley. You'll need more than me to do that. . . . Listen, I know a big Norwegian girl at church, as blond as you are. She's strong, and she could take care of herself with you. If you come to church tomorrow, I'll introduce you. I could . . ."

"Stop it," he whispered furiously. He squeezed her arm so hard she drew in her breath.

"See?" Tears were in her eyes from the pain. She pulled away from him sharply. "Do you see how you are? See how you do, Foley?"

No, she just could not give in to him. There would be no middle road. He would never meet a woman on any ground other than his own, and that she was unprepared for. There would be no waiting for her to catch up, no temporizing, no favors; it would be fast and cruel and terrifying. She was unable to make that sacrifice. She moved away quickly and left him.

In the space she had occupied he now saw his own image in the hall mirror, and it alarmed him: He was different. His face was an assemblage of features new to him, and though he stood there quietly, though he controlled his anguish, his instinct was to bellow. He wanted to run after her, to catch her right there in front of her mother. Until he had her promise to love him and to live with him, he would never let her loose. It would take her father, the hired hand, his timid children, and all three of her brothers to pull him off.

When this crude fantasy had exhausted itself, when he was rational, his imagination moved on, and he thought for a minute or two about what course of action he might take. At last he saw his head nodding slowly in the mirror, and he knew what had been decided. "That's the only thing left," he said; and his reflection looked better.

After supper, while everyone was listening to the radio, a serial she usually liked, Elaine excused herself. This surprised even her mother, who, although by now almost convinced that Elaine was not interested in Foley after all, and that there must be something else wrong with her, understood the capriciousness of some feminine maneuvers and waited, not yet sure enough to be willing to concede that she had misread the signs.

Elaine kissed the foreheads of both her parents, telling them that she had a headache—which she wearily referred to as a migraine. She wished neither Foley nor Albert good night, and as she was going out the door, just getting ready to close it, her mother reminded her of that fact. The young men, playing gin rummy on the sofa, sat staring at her, Foley with a watchfulness and concern that made him seem almost possessed. Elaine turned and waved her hand lazily and left.

Foley raised his chin and jerked his neck as if his collar were too tight, then listened to her ascent, raising his gray-blue eyes to the quivering yellow circle of lamplight on the ceiling, following the sound of her footsteps down the hallway above him. He heard the bath water running. Two games later, both of which he had lost, her bedroom door slammed shut, and soon afterward, there was silence upstairs.

"You used to play better," said Albert.

"I used to do a lot of things better," he replied grimly, shuffling the cards and then dealing ten to himself and eleven to his friend.

The absence of the sound of her agitated Foley more than the indication of her retreat. He brooded. He was angered that she refused him the small pleasure of sitting in the same room with her, however petulant and silent she might be, however distracted by everything and everyone else in the room except him, however cruel, however ungrateful—yes, ungrateful. Why shouldn't she like him? Everyone liked him. Why couldn't she return his affection and like him just a little? Why not, for Christ's sake? He would have been willing to begin anywhere with her, to court her long and carefully, to hold himself back, as patient as a knight. He would have waited for her in ascetic misery, done anything for her, if she had just been nice to him, civil; if she had turned her head in his direction every now and then and given him a nod, even a hint of a smile. But she was insisting that he court her differently. She had proved that in the hall before supper. She was forcing him to deliver himself to her in a way that was unacceptable to him, although he had, he realized, agreed to do

it. He bit into the inside of his mouth so hard that blood ran over
his tongue, salty and slightly metallic. Under his breath, he
cursed. Mrs. Mueller looked up at Foley, caught his eye too
quickly, then looked down again, leaving both of them embarrassed. She shook her head, then continued knitting a kellygreen
sweater for Elaine to take to college in September.

Resigned, sure of what he was going to do now, certain of
what she was calling on him to do when she had rubbed against
him at the same time that she teased him about another woman,
Foley laughed out loud, looked straight across at Albert, and
kicked his foot with the toe of his shoe. "What's the name of the
game, Albert?"

"You gin?"

"Yeah."

They started another game and continued playing until Mr.
and Mrs. Mueller said they were going to bed. Foley glanced up
quickly again at the space in the ceiling where he had last heard
Elaine, and told Albert that he was going to bed, too; that he
thought Albert should as well so that they could get up early in
the morning to see if they could figure out what was wrong with
the gearbox on the tractor.

Without lighting his lamp and without undressing (he had
washed up and combed his hair carefully), Foley sat on the side
of the bed in the small spare room at the front of the house,
weighing the mattress down so much that the part of the bed
opposite rose up like a sea swell. He leaned over, his arms on his
knees. Overall, he was content with his plan. He knew he must
succeed, just as he had known years earlier that he had to be
more than good, that he had to be perfect—one freezing day in
November, too cold to snow, but just right for a vicious cross-
wind to come down from the hills and hammer the football field.
A quarter-hour before the beginning of the game, the water boy,
Bobby Joe Kuehm, excited to breaking, had reported to him that
there were three recruiters from university football teams in the
bleachers, ten rows up on the fifty yard line in the spot, always
deserted until now, that, since Foley had been playing, the coach
had reserved for them. So he learned that they had managed to
find and to visit the high school in the town where he had lived
all his life—a town without trees, nothing much alive other than
desert willow, cactus, and yucca; six thousand people; and the
few pets they could afford to feed (he had never been able to have
even a dog)—just to watch him play football, to see if what they
said about him in the four-county newspaper was true, or simply

an exaggeration of the worth of a youth in their desolate, isolated, and miserable region. He did not yet know, as he sat on a bench in the locker room pulling at the stiff leather laces of his cleated shoes, that because of his dread, he would play better than he had ever played in his life. Well, there had been so much at stake. His performance that day had been the difference between getting a college education and not getting it.

And now, four and a half years later, he had the same terror within him that he'd had that night, a terror he'd vowed never to let return. Yet here he was shaking, and though he'd just drunk a glass of water in the bathroom, his throat was dry. His hands trembled every time he held them out straight to see if maybe they had stopped, and in clearing his throat, he made a sound as disappointing and unresonant as if he had shouted into the hollow of a damp tree. Outside, in the direction of the windmill, he heard an angry metal rasp; Elaine's dog barked; sometimes there was the sound of an animal, muted by distance, air currents, or the movement of trees. He thought he heard a train. On the road a car passed, then died away. He waited, not only because he was afraid but because it was not yet time.

After the house had been silent for a full hour, he unlaced his shoes and pulled them off. He straightened his clothes and again ran the comb through his hair. He was ready to go to her; he crossed the room without hesitation.

When Elaine heard her door open (she had not been asleep), she raised herself swiftly on an elbow and jerked her head toward it. He closed the door softly, passed the chair, and crossed the hook rug without making a sound. Then he hit against something and let out a pitiful, muffled groan. In the darkness, as he was moving toward her (his eyes had not yet adjusted to the dim light of the moon, so he had nothing to guide him to her except his own sense of her), he had crashed his knee into the corner of the oak trousseau chest at the foot of her bed, in which her mother had already stored pillow slips and sheets appliquéd with flowers and fruit, a crocheted tablecloth, crewelwork napkins, a handworked quilt, a rag rug of wool and velvet, and two double blankets from Scotland; all of this waiting in the dark cedar-scented box for a monogram that could only be applied when the new name was known.

Foley had kept himself still, holding on to his knee and squeezing his eyes shut against the jets of pain coming up his thigh to his groin and then going back down to his foot. He was quiet; he would not let himself be defeated by this small accident.

Elaine sat up in bed, clutching the quilt high around her shoulders, stretching her neck to listen, opening her eyes wide to see, the cool air from the window at her back making her cold. It was Foley. Although she couldn't see him well, she knew his movements; from behind the pages of books, from windows, out of the corner of her eye, she had observed them all. She started to shiver, not just because of the draft or because Foley was in her room, but because the moment for the encounter had come, and all at once she understood what was going to have to happen, and realized that she should have figured that out before and decided to protect herself from him, or not to protect herself, so that she would be neither seductress nor victim.

"What are you doing, Foley?" she asked in a hysterical whisper. She wondered why she was talking to him like this. Why hadn't she screamed and brought the house into her room? He had unbuckled his belt, pulled out the tail of his shirt and undone his buttons, and was now peeling off his socks.

"What does it look like?" He had to lift his hurt knee to free himself of the trouser leg.

"Get out of my room. . . ."

He went on undressing and said nothing.

She watched the silent shadow of him approach the bed. "But why?" she asked. "Why, Foley?"

He leaned over the bed and spoke to her in the way that an imposing man, used to being successful in his life, confident of his position and of his righteousness, speaks to a child who is in serious error. "Because it's the only way I can think of to get your attention," he said.

There seemed nothing outside of him, neither darkness nor light; there was no space that he did not fill. To balance his authority with her own, she pulled her feet under her and sat on her heels, lifting her chin in such a way that she would seem dignified and in command. "You don't love me," she whispered urgently.

"I do love you; I told you; you don't listen!" He hesitated. "I'm going to bed with you so that you will."

"No, you're . . . I can't . . ." She was unable to finish a phrase; her fear manifested itself in the suspension of her intelligence. She was telling him no, and telling him why; she was adamant, but she wasn't making sense. "Foley. . ." Then, suddenly, she stopped trying to talk, to plead, or to explain, and what she did then would undermine the force of any argument she might have made. With closed eyes, she reached up, slipped the flat of her

hand under the strap of his undershirt and ran her fingers through
the hair on his chest. She had never seen Foley without a shirt,
but she had noticed that hair, all she could see of it when the top
buttons of his shirt were loose. She had wanted to go through it,
to leave her hand in it, to touch it all she wanted, even to rub her
cheek there, her chin, her nose. It was rather coarser than she had
expected. "Since when have you loved me?" she asked. The
question was redundant. She was stalling for time, not to drive
him away, but to keep her hand where it was.

"Since the game. . . . No, at the table. . . . Oh, god." He trembled because, on her own initiative, she was touching him. It was
the first time she had voluntarily touched him anywhere at all
since she had hunched over him in order to receive the football
fifteen days before.

"Then you want me," she said quickly. She drew her hand
away from him, depriving both of them of an extreme pleasure.
"You don't love me."

"It's not different."

He gave her time to absorb this idea, and when he thought that
she was reconciled to it, asked, "Will you let me stay, Elaine?"

She hugged the cover around her. "I would hate you afterward."

"You hate me now," he pointed out. "You can't stand to be
around me."

She hid her face in her hands, wondering if she would be able
to endure the assault she expected and if she would be spared
punishment for her complicity in not revealing to the house his
presence in her room.

"I think it's the way we are," he said. "Not you and not me,
but the way we mix. Let me settle it, Elaine."

She held on to his arm, her nails going into his skin; and then,
her face embellished with an ingratiating smile, she reeled out a
litany of promises that would give him hope but, at the same
time, make him leave her room: She would talk to him in the
morning, right after breakfast; she would wait for him wherever
he said; she would meet him outside, and they could go to the
orchard and talk; she would go with him for a car ride without
Albert, just the two of them.

"You'll see," she said. She ran her fingernails along the back
of his wrist and hand, in exactly the same way that, years ago,
she would have caressed her father if she had needed money or a
favor. She meant for him to go away, yet at the same time she
knew she was leading him into something. She wondered

whether if you touched a man the way she was touching him—a man who thought of you as he thought of her—there was any going back.

"I'll be nice," she said. "I'll talk to you. You'll see. . . . Foley?"

Her personality seemed to have collapsed under the burden of his purpose, and his silence answered her suggestions negatively. Her body felt hot, yet she trembled with a chill as severe as the one she had had the winter before last when she had developed pneumonia, and on the third day of the fever, the circuit doctor had told her mother that if she didn't start sweating soon, she'd die—saying it right in front of her.

"I'm scared of you, Foley." She had never said this to anyone.

"You're not scared. It's not that. That's not what's the matter with you. In a few minutes you'll be fine." He waved his hand toward the hallway. "Anyway, I'm not going back in that room by myself."

"Not now . . . not yet."

"Of course," he said slowly, "you can go back in there with me if you like, Elaine. That's okay, too. It doesn't have to be here." Actually Foley would have preferred it; it was farther from her parents' room, and he wouldn't have to be so silent and careful. He was smiling.

He waited, but she said nothing; he couldn't see her expression very well, but he felt her shiver. He put his hands on her shoulders, feeling the heat of her skin under the neutral ruffles of her nightgown. It was so magnetic that he almost took advantage of her then. To stop himself, he had to remove his hands from her and hold them together between his bent knees.

"I'll call my father!" she said abruptly. She made her eyes huge, twisted her head sideways, and looked toward the door.

"Go on."

"I guess you'll tell him that I invited you in?" Foley realized that she was testing his courage and that it would be by passing a series of trials of her invention that he would win her. "I won't lie to your daddy, Elaine, but if you're going to call him, you'd better do it pretty quick."

Her voice went up in pitch again, as it had during her recitation of promises. "I didn't think you could be so—"

"Yes, you did, Ely. You found out everything about me on the football field. You understand me perfectly."

He leaned over her, half-dressed, his back hurting from being so long hunched in the same position. He was uncomfortable, but he had further to go. If he even quivered unintentionally, he might lose his advantage; and he was close now. He spoke to her tentatively, easily; he was wary of spoiling what he had so far accomplished. "What are you going to do? Are you going to call him?" He shook her. "You're not answering me."

Her head drooped to the side; she started to speak but her voice trailed off. She pulled the wayward strap of her nightgown back onto her shoulder, giving the impression that her hand was almost too weak to do it.

A wave of remorse flashed over him. He thought of his church; he had a fleeting vision of his mother putting on her flowered hat to go there. He questioned the soundness of his judgment and the humanity of his decision to capture Elaine in this way, but his hesitation was brief, and he cast it aside because of the strength of his conviction.

It never once occurred to him that her dejection might be feigned in order to elicit his pity, nor was it. Correctly he had trusted in her integrity, and in his own sense of what she wanted of him. He knew that if she had shouted for help, she would have destroyed him—undone his audacious act of coming to her, his gamble on the hint that, since she had watched him through the washhouse window (and lied to him about it afterward), she might love him. But he had not believed that she would shout for help; he had thought that in suggesting that she introduce him to the lusty girl from Norway, flattering him by the implicit concession that he was too much man for her, she had thrown down the gauntlet, challenging him to seduce her. Her silence in the living room afterward, her early retirement, and her rudeness he had interpreted as a dare. The choice of weapons and the time of resolution she had left to his ingenuity and discretion. *I've not disappointed her,* he thought.

Yet when he sat down beside her, she pushed him away with the flat of her hands. He terrified her really. She looked away. She was unprepared; it was too soon. *I won't be ready for him for years,* she had said to herself that night as she had lain awake thinking about the way he had just kissed her in front of the porch. Rolling to the other side of the bed, she turned over on her stomach, clutched one of the pillows to her breast, and whimpered something inaudible.

He touched the nape of her neck, ran his fingers into her hair as softly as he could, so as not to scare her. He tried to keep his hand weightless on her so that, at first, she would hardly know it was there; yet she reacted immediately, and her back arched. The places he touched pressed back at him like answers to questions, and he was gratified. Like all people who act out of courage rather than nerve, he had become self-possessed as soon as he had encountered the object of his fear. It was only his imagination, fallible and untrustworthy, that had caused his anxiety.

"No, Foley," she whispered.

He was turning her over toward him and tugging at the pillow she held, gently, not insistently; then he let it go a little and tugged again, carefully, until finally he had the pillow away from her and over the side of the bed, where it dropped on the floor, solid and silent. He put his hands under her arms and lifted her up to him, cautious still, though with taut, unequivocal resolution. She put her face into his neck, swallowed hard, blinked two or three times and then dropped back her head.

He said her name and stroked her cheeks. He looked down at her face and, in a last instant of uncertainty, hesitated. The kiss on the porch had been a disaster; Foley realized that he had miscalculated. He had thought that, because their initial contest had been physical, she would respond only to a brutal attack by which, as vanquisher, he could quickly claim her. That first night, when he had lain on top of his bed, not yet having drawn back the covers, he had looked at the moonlit ceiling of the room to which Albert's mother had assigned him, and pondered his failure. He had been confused. He had seen again and again the specter of that infuriated though still exquisite face, dabbed with moonlight; saw again the back of the hand scrubbing at the mouth that he had kissed so spontaneously and with so much feeling. His kiss, a kiss that would have kept another woman in his arms, would have caused a surrender, a melting of flesh, was, for her, too direct, too frankly aggressive. It had dismayed her, and from that time, they had been estranged. In the hammock, and then again in the hallway, she had accused him of being brutal. So, thinking with his head and denying his flesh—though his instinct fought against this, told him that he was a fool, that he could do much better, that he should bend to his inclination and nature, and enjoy her—he kissed her warily, giving her nothing but the most tentative knowledge of his mouth, the most cautious brush of his mouth against hers, and with no command.

Instantly, unmistakably he felt her recoil. Could he have again misunderstood her terms, misinterpreted the signals? Did he have no intuition at all? How was he to know her? It was senseless to try. He should have let his instinct guide him. Hadn't he gotten as far as her bed? Wasn't he embracing her in it now, without having transformed himself? He was the same man who had lain on top of her outside on the playing field; who had mussed up her hair and rumpled her blouse. Was it possible that, having permitted him access to her, she had dropped the pretense of requiring him to be what he was not, that she preferred him to make love to her as he was?

"Elaine . . . ?"

She spoke to him. "For God's sake, Foley. . ."

She turned away from him then and, with a grace reminiscent of that she had displayed as a quarterback, she flung her legs away from him and across to the other side of the bed, trusting herself to the accommodating darkness. He had no idea what she was going to do, only that she had changed her mind about staying with him, and that, if he failed to do something to stop her, she would escape, just as she had escaped that afternoon in the kitchen. He lunged at her retreating form and missed. In an instant, he was out of bed, fast upon her—a quick and supple and silent move that only a man of his skill could have made to capture as agile an adversary as Elaine. He had her at first only by the wrist but then swung her around toward him in an almost complete revolution that brought her up against him, one hand clutching at his neck and shoulder to keep her balance, the other touching his mouth as if to keep him from talking. He said something to her, spoke against her fingers, something halfway between a curse and a command.

She cried out softly. They struggled together—he to keep her, and she, not to escape, he realized, but to adjust her position against him and to explain something vital.

He bent down toward the snuffled sounds. "What?"

She spoke against his chest and repeated to him what she had said before, what he had not heard. "I don't know . . . I don't know anything! I never . . ."

He smiled at her, and his voice was calm. "I'm amazed, Ely. I thought you knew everything."

"Not that."

"I do."

"What should . . ."

"Nothing."

He put his arm under her knees, lifted her back onto the warm covers, and then he removed her gown and his shirt in two simple, almost sleight-of-hand movements. He kissed her mouth, then started downward along her neck, and soon she lay there unaware that she was panting, dangerously loud, yet unable to do anything about it; that her head was spinning around; and that she had lost her sense of direction and had no points of reference at all. She had chosen, she realized, though the choice was not rational. She squeezed her eyes shut.

When she had first cornered Foley to take from him his power, to neutralize the threat that he represented to her, she made inevitable the act that she had half dreaded, half longed for, and which was now going to take place. From that instant when she had lashed out at him across the dinner table with her searing and outlandish outburst and his face had gone pale, not from anger but from incredulity that the sister of his host would attack him, a person whom she hardly knew, and whose only mistake had been to pat her back and shoulders a little; from that instant on she had known that she was offering him a challenge, and that her estimate of his value to her would depend on whether or not he accepted it. Since the war had begun at the dinner table, and she had reacted so strongly against his interest in her, against the surprise of his infatuation, she had known in her bones what lay ahead, that what was happening to her now was going to happen and that all the rest had just been incidents in the infinitude of variations that might lead up to it.

With the entire front of his body pressed up against hers, the capitulation was complete; she accepted him, gave herself up to him. She made so much noise: at first sharp inhalations from the exasperation at the pain he submitted her to without concern or apology, as if he were getting back at her for her unwillingness to let him into her life until that moment; and then astonished, mournful exclamations in a series of inverted mordents, so dangerously loud that Foley had to make himself still to quiet her. He had to suppress the sounds of his passion; he had to lift himself up, clamp his hand over her mouth, and keep it there until her fast breathing was just in her chest and not moving through her vocal cords, until she was occupied in just holding on to him, pressing herself to him. When he had freed her, when he lay beside her, there was a slow, steady diminution of gasps, and finally his breath became less labored, until at last he was still and so silent that he was like a felled tree, blocking all the passages her life might have taken. She pulled upon him, put her head in the hollow of his shoulder, and closed her eyes. She was someone else; she was another girl, and she was stroking him with a more significant hand. She began telling him, over and over again, things that had never been wrenched from her before, things that did not seem to him either banal or precious because they were thoughts that no woman had ever shared with him before; at least not shared with this passion, which was at one instant puerile and groping, at the next, womanly and exact. He smiled. She went with him; she was swift and strong. When she held on to him, he felt it; when he embraced her, he had what he needed.

"I hurt you?" he asked. His eyes were still closed, and his weakness was still apparent.

"No." This lie was her final effort to preserve her past self-image.

"You sounded like it."

"So did you."

Then she said something that startled him, for he had, in his need to make love to her, forgotten what the act was for. "I hope we get a baby out of this," she said.

He was, to her dismay, silent—maybe just recovering his strength. Had she heard him correctly from the hammock? Did he love her as he had said? She had heard that sometimes men . . . She squeezed his hand urgently. "Don't you?"

He hesitated, then spoke slowly. "That's all right. . . ." He turned his body around to hers, kissed her gently, and waited. "Sure." Then, feeling the sudden tautness in the arms that had slipped around his back, and the swift compression of the lower part of her body against his thigh, he kissed her in another way.

Before dawn, well before the drift of morning hazed across the sill of the window and spread onto the broad, worn pine plankings of the uneven, slightly slanted floor, he prepared to leave her, first going to the bathroom to fill the china pitcher with cold water to wash the blood off her sheets. He rubbed at the smears, which he could see by the low wick of the lamp, the globe of which he had shadowed with his shirt so that the beam was focused on the bed and would not be visible from under the door.

. When he had finished the task, she pulled him back toward her, whining his name; but he pushed her aside, giving her a perfunctory kiss on the neck, avoiding her mouth. She fell back on the covers. The next phase of his plan was already in progress; he was leaving; he would spoil it if he was caught in her room. He dressed and crossed the floor quickly, closing his mind to her murmurs, shackling his desire with his will, as frightened, as certain of the danger, as sure of his weakness (it would only be luck if he got out safely), yet every bit as resolute as Odysseus when he bound himself to the mast of his ship so that he could

resist the sirens' songs. A bird shrieked. He recognized it as a
bluejay; and then the first rooster crowed, trilling on the last note,
the length of which it exaggerated since the morning was going to
be fine. Foley dared not look back at Elaine, dared not risk seeing
her softened green eyes, toned with expectancy, or this new way
she had of looking at him, this slow lazy smile.

Lying in her bed alone, reminded by a slight ache that she
belonged now to the man who had just left her and that she had
told him so, she struggled to remember her past. At first she
could recall only his having entered her room, and then her memory began to extend itself to his weekend visits. She wondered if
her provocation of Foley had not been due to her first impression
of him, when she had seen him walking up to the porch, had
noticed the intrusive, mote-sprinkled shafts of the late afternoon
sun, halting reverently on his blond hair; had scrutinized his
strong face; had admired his massive though not ungraceful form;
yet had not been able to run up to him, hold him around the waist
and say: "This is mine, this one is mine!" and thus have saved
herself the stupefaction and anguish when he came into her room
and saved him having to be so inventive, obstinate, bullish, single-minded, patient, and shrewd.

But then, why not? She moved over, lay on her stomach on
the side of the bed that had been his and, in a strong rippling
motion, pressed herself to the mattress. She had meant to stay
awake and savor in memory what had happened, but her exhausted and sated consciousness began to recede. In a minute
more she was asleep.

It was almost noon when she fixed Foley's breakfast: fried
ham, scrambled eggs, boiled grits, stewed pears, black coffee,
and a glass of buttermilk. She had to substitute for her mother
because they woke late; she had waited to hear Foley in the hall
before going downstairs.

Mrs. Mueller heard their voices from the porch; she walked
silently down the hallway on the soft wool runner and looked
through the door of the kitchen. Her daughter was at the stove;
Foley was behind her, towering above her, touching her and teasing her, and Elaine was putting up with it. In fact, she answered
his teasing with such faint mutterings that it was clear she was
making no defense whatever, and that she encouraged, if not
actually sought out his attention. Slipping away down the hall,
the girl's mother blushed. She had seen Foley lean over Elaine,
and while her arms went around him—a wooden cooking spoon

was still in her hand—he had drawn her up against him until she was on her toes, and he had kissed her in a way that made Mrs. Mueller tremble in recollection. She had never before seen Elaine submit to anything like this: As far as she knew, she had never been kissed. The flood of warmth, the radiance that she had witnessed between them was so apparent, so unmistakable that had she not known better, had she not been certain that this could not be so, she would have concluded that they had been intimate.

After supper, Foley and Albert climbed into Foley's Packard (Mrs. Mueller was certain that Foley had kissed Elaine on the darkening porch in the shadow of the willows) and left for school (during the meal Elaine and Foley had stared at each other exhaustively and gravely, neither saying a word to anyone else, and addressed each other in short, careful bits and pieces, cryptic messages), and Elaine washed the dishes without being asked.

When the car had disappeared at the base of the alley of trees on the dusty road, Mrs. Mueller turned to her daughter, who was drying the last of the china, and said, "You've changed your mind about Foley."

Elaine looked surprised. "I always liked him."

"But you were horrible to him, Elaine." Her voice caressed her daughter's name. They would be very close during this beautiful time for women.

"Not really..." was her mysterious and mysteriously delivered reply. She turned, put her arms around her mother's neck, and then abruptly, either laughing or crying, she ran to her room. Her mother did not see her again until, wishing to tell her good night and hoping to learn more about her happiness, she knocked at her door—and she found her elated about her love and, at last, willing to talk about it.

On Wednesday of that week, Foley spoke with Elaine's father. When the telephone rang, the family was sitting around the table in the kitchen eating dinner. The phone was at eye level on the wall near the back door, so that Mr. Mueller, standing before it, still unused to the instrument, looked like a soldier at parade rest, the back of his left hand flattened against his buttocks, his legs spread apart to make sure of his balance, nervous and trying to make a good impression—not on the speaker (he came from stock in which the masculine members, at least, prided themselves on not being afraid of any man), but on the instrument itself. His reddish hair, touched with gray and combed flat to his head, was parted down the middle with the exacting deliberation of perfectionism, and it was exactly in line with the center of his chin and the knifelike bridge of his slender nose.

The previous fall, at Thanksgiving, Elaine had wanted to go to Austin and see Foley play—Albert had urged them to come—but her father was against it. He never did anything extra like that; no family trips, not even short ones. He would never waste money, not even to watch Albert's friend. "The Depression didn't hurt us much," he would say, "so let's keep ourselves that way." He was a quiet man, and he believed to the point of prejudice that the less you said, the more likely you were to be heard. He distrusted discussion and despised argument. He ran a fine farm, and though his sternness was hard on his wife and children, they never wanted for anything, not even during the lean years when other families suffered poverty and shame.

Mr. Mueller rarely smiled; he was a serious, silent man, who had never had anything much to do with his four children. He fed them and kept them in clothes and loved them distantly because they were his own, but children, unless they needed to be punished or put to work, belonged to the woman, just as the duties of putting in the crops and taking pains with the livestock belonged to him. It was the wisdom of this generation, a reason for their long, comfortable marriages, that their labors never crossed.

Yet Elaine was his daughter, and she was his to give or not to give to the man who might want her. He was sympathetic enough to the plight of women to know that he had to be careful in his judgment, for his daughter's choice was a crucial one. A man who married badly might solace himself in adventure or in a career; but for a woman, the family was everything.

"You haven't known her very long, son," he said.

He frowned and looked toward the window, avoiding the eyes of his wife, who might by a look of tenderness or pleading cause him to make a mistake.

"I don't know whether she's in love with you or not," Mr. Mueller finally said. Unobservant of his children as he was, he had missed the spectacle of Elaine's transformation on Sunday, even though his wife had tried several times to excite his interest, so that, basing his reaction on Elaine's behavior toward Foley up till then, he didn't suppose she even liked Foley, much less loved him. Although he was so isolated in his male experience that he had to feel sympathy before he could feel affection or friendship, he did feel sorry for Foley, and so tacitly wished him well in his quest. He brought his hand around and covered the receiver, turned to Elaine and contracted his lips into a thin smile that softened his features, which were usually so severe and harshly drawn that just looking at him frightened his children.

"Are you in love with Foley, Elaine?" he asked. "He thinks you are."

Elaine looked down at her plate while her mother, her two younger brothers, and the hired hand stared at her, their forks at various distances from their partially eaten food. Only Mrs. Mueller knew what her daughter's answer would be, and certainly what she had seen going on between Elaine and Foley in the kitchen at midmorning on Sunday had made her, in her mother's heart, hope for this request. But the others felt sorry for the man because they were certain that he was going to be hurt. They liked him, admired him, and thought, all of them, that Elaine's imminent rejection of him was going to be a shame. But they knew that she valued her isolation, the singleness of herself, her independence. They could not believe she was going to relinquish her pride for the sake of the voluptuous lassitude of most other young women in love. As far as they knew she had never let a boy kiss her; and even now, she was so uninterested in her father's question that she was carelessly pushing her creamed potatoes around her plate, covering and uncovering the blue flowers and birds that were painted there.

"Well?" asked her father.

"I love him," she said softly.

"What?" he asked, jerking his head forward on his neck and squinting one eye. "I can't hear you, Ely."

She looked up, awkward and shy, but her face broke into a strange smile. "I love him," she said. She cleared her throat and said it again.

The boys teased her until Mr. Mueller hushed them with a heavy, downward motion of his hand. He uncovered the receiver and spoke to Foley. "You're right," he said. "She is in love with you."

There was a pause, and then again the blocking of the receiver with the farmer's rough hand. "He thinks you want to marry him. Is that possible?"

She bit down on her lip, trying desperately to contain the smile in front of her brothers. Then she nodded her head, and the voices started again, only to be quieted once more.

"Does that nod mean you want to get married to him?"

"Yes, Daddy." Her voice, placed so low in her throat, had such warmth that it startled everyone. "I want to marry Foley . . . when school is out."

"What about college?"

"We want to get married."

"It's important to us that you go to college; we've given up things to make that possible." He waited; when there was no reply, he said, "We want you to be a teacher so you can take care of yourself if you need to. We've always talked about it. Elaine, you're not going back on that?"

His voice frightened her, and the immobility of his face made it hard to tell if he was disappointed or angry. "I'm sorry, Daddy. I'm sorry I can't be a teacher." She tried to sigh heavily, to make her voice sad, but it was impossible, so she turned her eyes away from him and looked at her mother. "I guess I'll just have a family," she said.

"You'd made up your mind before this call?" her father continued. "This is not something sudden you didn't know about?"

Her mother smiled at her, reached out her hand, and touched her hot cheek.

"No," said Elaine. "Yes, I had made up my mind." She paused, and the beatific look on her face and the tears in the corners of her eyes reinforced what she said. "I want to live with him all my life. I don't care about anything else."

The receiver was uncovered. Mr. Mueller stood taller, a bit more confident with the phone.

"You're right again, Foley. She will marry you. . . . Yes, certainly . . . if that's what she wants." He lowered his voice and shot a sideways glance at his wife. "But she's young, you know —hardly sixteen. Her mother was twenty. Uh-huh . . . I'm sure that you will treat her well. . . . No, I don't doubt that. . . . Yes, if you have employment and can provide for her." He laughed without opening his mouth. "But she's used to having what she wants, you know. I haven't deprived her any. . . . Yes . . . well, that's right. . . . Yes, I'm giving my consent."

The next weekend, when Foley came to Elaine, he was wearing a hat, the brim of which was slanted over one eye. He had on a gray suit and a bow tie. Even apart from the fact that he was more dressed up than he had been before, he looked different, changed, much older. Stepping ahead of Albert, he came up the walk concerned and serious. From the window of her parents' bedroom over the porch, Elaine had seen the handsome car turn into the drive, seen it come down swiftly under the canopy of leaves, raising the white dust halfway up the trunks of the two rows of oaks. She had seen it promptly because she had been watching for it, waiting for over two hours, angrily shouting downstairs, leaning on the hall railing, her elbows cast out like wings, demanding of her mother to know if she could think of any reason why Foley and Albert had not yet come, blaming the delay on Albert, mentioning every real and unreal flaw in Albert's character in order to make it obvious that it was he who was culpable, and not the man she loved. At last the car turned into the drive.

"He's here, Mama!" She ran out to him, letting the screen door bang behind her, and flung her arms around his thick neck. He lifted her off the ground, swung her over the hedge of dwarf yaupon that bordered the walk up to the house, half-carried her to the bench under the elm tree, and with her sitting on his knees, expectant of favors, the solid blue shadow of the tree falling over her lap, he pushed the diamond engagement ring that he had bought three weeks before onto her finger. He gave her a bottle of perfume, a present wrapped in satiny pink paper and tied with a matching ribbon, which she would decide to leave unopened until supper. "I don't want to see everything at once," she said. She kissed his face in several places, lingering on his mouth. She was so persistent, in fact, in touching him and rubbing against him that at last he put his arms fully around her, bent her down strongly, knowing that it was wrong to kiss her like that in the company of her family, but unable to do otherwise.

From the porch the three brothers observed all this, rocking back on their heels or leaning on the narrow white pillars of the porch, their hands in their pockets, their thumbs hooked into their belts. For the first time, they were estranged from their sister, uncertain of what they should think in witnessing the change in her personality, wondering how it was that she was so diminished. For the time being, they could only be happy for Foley, the big bearlike man who had won her. She kept smiling at him. He kept smiling back, confident, admiring, absurd, while she stroked the edge of his jaw with the hand on which he had placed the ring.

Two months later, three days after Elaine's graduation in early June (Foley and Albert had graduated a week earlier; the Muellers had taken Elaine to Austin, where she had not only attended the ceremony but had met Foley's mother), they were married by a Baptist minister in Elaine's garden, under the latticework arch at the foot of the double row of yellow roses, not two yards from the area where, in late March, they had played the game of football which had been the catalyst for their future.

Albert was best man, and Arlet Simons, the Halloween Queen, the girl whom Albert would marry five months later, was maid of honor. Among the guests, particularly the young, the wedding festivities were heightened by the gaiety and buoyancy of the graduation season. Elaine's mother had wanted them to wait until August, so that the two occasions could remain separate, and they could savor them; but neither would discuss a delay. Even two months was intolerable and, as it turned out, impractical.

After the ceremony, Foley and Elaine stood close together like docile children locked in alertness, showing a quiet and secret pride. They had assimilated all the many suggestions about married life that had been made to them since their engagement, and they were ready to set out accordingly. They talked enthusiastically and planned, or they were glowingly silent. They left that night for Victoria (Foley had a job in a bank) and detoured for a three-day honeymoon at a dude ranch in the Hill Country, where they shunned horseback riding and shooting the rapids in inner tubes in favor of walking beside the river under the brooding cypress trees, or wading on the rocks in the shallow currents, Elaine exaggerating her ineptness on the slippery rocks to call for her husband, and Foley exaggerating his attention, not only because he loved being near her but because she was carrying his child. Three days after the new year, Jimmy Menutis was born, a week before Elaine became seventeen.

Even before the child was born, maybe at the time of its conception, she had already accepted her new role. As a melody in a romantic etude, with the striking of just one decisive chord, slips from the minor to the major mode without any perceptible transition, yet without the least trauma to the form of the piece, she had undergone a transformation. Until Foley's death, she would display, except on rare occasions, a passivity with which she was content; and since she was happy, she never questioned or perhaps even acknowledged his mastery over their lives. Yet it was a fact that she made him more than he was, lent him her strength to graft onto his own. They never fought, he never shamed her or made her cry, and there was hardly an unkind word between them. She rarely argued with any of his ideas; she accepted his tastes and his habits. It was no privation for her. It was her choice. What he liked she accepted, what he defended became right, and she never thought of it again. His continuing love for her and his constant and vigorous expression of it burned out and cleansed her of any latent ambivalence that might have caused her, had she made a less fortunate choice, to question her position. He didn't need, ever, to assert his mastery, and her submitting herself to him did her no harm. There was scarcely a day that went by as long as she lived with him when she was not happy. She would always believe that, and the serenity of that notion became the finest memorial to him. Foley came first; what he said was law; she would accept it for reasons she would neither worry about nor try to understand. In sum, the only bad thing that Foley ever did to her was to cease to exist.

On August 5, Doccey Allen telephoned Elaine from the railway station telegraph office to tell her what had just come in over the wire that summer of 1944, when in the town of Dansville, Texas, with a population of ten thousand, some half-dozen women were made widows; when, on that hot afternoon, the men who delivered telegrams, their khaki shirts soaking wet, the sweat glancing out in ellipses like tides around their collarbones and under their arms, went up the familiar walks and paths to the doors of people they knew, had known all their lives, gone to school with, in tears themselves, so that the families did not even need to open the windowed envelopes and read the messages. After the people who had delivered the news to Elaine had come up from the railway station, they heard the shrieking from beyond the Menutises' porch, through the handsomely ornamented, double-screened doors that Foley had made from a sketch that Elaine had drawn ... until Molly Webb Jones's stout, red-faced farmer husband had to shake Elaine to get her still and then catch her spinning arms, hold on to her (almost exactly as Foley had had to do three years earlier in the corridor of the hospital when they had come back from getting dinner and had been told by an intern, whom they had never seen before, a stranger, that their one-year-old baby girl, Laura, who had seemed to be doing better, had died of polio, had quit breathing, suddenly and inexplicably, and not even in Elaine's arms), and finally thrust her sobbing into the lap of his wife, who was also hysterical, not entirely with empathy, but rather with a presage, because her twenty-year-old son would be wounded four days later. ... And then the long, still stares out the window beyond the place where a gold star hung, into the landscape of roses and elms and picket fences; that star-symbol fading in the heat and brightness of September and October, vanishing like the shattered soul it represented; the knowledge that Foley had died in a field hospital two days after he had been picked up by medics, unconscious and hemorrhaging, in an apple orchard behind the broken gray walls of a French farm, approximately fifteen kilometers inland from Caen in the direction of Lisieux, and that on the second day, he had regained consciousness and called for her and for his family.

And finally, after weeks and months of the shock of waking in the first hour of the sunlight to the steady illumination of the wartime photograph: Foley taken in uniform, with two silver bars on his shoulder, the Christmas before, 1943, when he was only a year away from thirty, the perfect age for a man—old enough to be sensible, but young enough to still have the vigor that makes a well-made man a delectation—his image in the nacreous frame on the dresser, the frame too much like, too near the tones of dawn itself; finally—it must have been well into November— Elaine, the derisive red and gold beauty of morning hanging in the lashes that had parted briefly when she wakened, then closed quickly, forced herself, because that day, Sunday, she had promised her minister to leave her house, if just to attend church, sat on the edge of her bed, her hands stroking, with an unrhythmic downward motion, the cold and still though once vigorous, striv- ing, and responsive body that was not Foley's but her own. Days were shadows; events were without edges; she seemed to be looking through a smoky piece of glass that only other people could see through to identify objects, yet she lacked even the spirit to ask them what they saw.

For three years she kept her mind and her spirit in check in mourning; and her flesh, dazed and indolent in its grief, followed along obediently.

Chapter 1

IT WAS NOT that Hugh Littleton did anything worse than most of the other boys in Dansville; it was just that the exuberance of his renegade behavior exaggerated his sins. What was considered to be a fault not to be disturbed about in others, smiled at and whisked aside with tired clichés and earthy aphorisms, was condemned mercilessly when it involved Hugh. He was rich: Out of gratitude, he should have been good. He was well educated: Out of respect for that advantage, he should have been better. But Hugh never listened with even half an ear to either logic or lectures, so whether he was coming out of the bar in Ganado or the canteen in Cuero or the pool hall in Richmond, he was more trouble than anyone else; and if he had been without the good will of a couple of friends, and the heavy hand and cunning wit of Matt Kirkland, his father's ranch foreman, he would have spent a good part of the last several summers in jail. He thought of himself as a god, a descendant of the Olympians, born with advantages but plagued with problems, a few imposed by fate, but most, he admitted, of his own making. Hugh had just enough good in him to be troubled from time to time by a sense of responsibility for his shortcomings; he would shake his shaggy head, rumble around a bit, and think of reforming, but then go back to the shelter of his immunity, to his bold leaps and terrifying roars.

He was not exactly spoiled, or if he was, it was in compensation for his parents' having neglected him in his early years, having brought him up by giving him whatever he wanted and by letting him do as he pleased because they simply were not

going to take the time to correct him. He had been thrown out
to sink or swim, and in almost every way, he was swimming
nicely. He had a big car that he had not yet wrecked, a herd of
cattle, a half-dozen quarter horses (as nice as any in the state),
two Hanoverians (the only ones in the state), and a practically
unlimited supply of money. By the fourth quarter of his nineteenth year, he had few rivals in terms of his accomplishments
at the university, his wealth, his endurance, his energy, his
irascibility and violent temper, or his appearance.

He was over six feet tall, and his body was already solid, so
that he moved with the grace and assurance of a man who knows
himself, has discovered the direction of the track he means to
take, and avoids apology for his manner or for his actions. His
features were yet big for his face, his eyes were like his father's,
dark and deep. He had black hair, heavy and curly and thick, and
he wore it a little too long.

He had been admitted to Princeton, by the skin of his teeth
maybe, but nevertheless admitted—and he was doing well, or
had been since the second semester. After he had found out that
the professors meant what they said when they told him that he
was required, in preparation for an examination, to learn everything, not just the highlights, he delivered it. The life of a student
during the cold months up north in New Jersey was one thing,
though, and the hot, glary, sun-violent summer in South Texas
was another. At the end of the year, all the restraint of the student's life crumbled, like a dam before the force of a boiling
current, and as always when he arrived in Dansville, he was wild
and ready—bigger, stronger, and smarter than he had been the
year before.

In the summer, he let everything go. He quit shaving very
much, didn't bathe much either, and spent most of his time on
a horse, doing what Matt told him to, and not protesting because the life suited him, and because Matt was mean enough
to keep him in harness, and smart enough to know that he had
to. The fatigue of that work, the aching muscles, the raw skin
and sore back, soothed his blood and made him able to go to
sleep swiftly, to sleep soundly, and rarely to dream.

But one thing was different this year. He was looking for
something that he did not have, that he had never had. Hugh
wanted a girl friend. He already knew he could buy a woman's
company; he knew how and he knew where. He had been
enough of a regular at Lilla Mattox's place over the last three
summers to be comfortable going there, where he felt pam-

pered and at home; since he had the double advantage of being attractive and rich, and the wisdom to be generous (he had been known to leave a girl enough money in addition to the required fee for a month's rent, a weekend in New Orleans, or a coveted outfit she might have seen in a dress shop window in El Campo or Victoria), he was encouraged to return, and he was welcomed when he did.

Lilla was a good merchant and knew how to keep her customers coming back; she also knew how to keep her pleasant place in Allensdale from being torn up by a man who was almost too young to be there, but too rich to turn away. When he caused trouble, something he nearly always did (drunkenness usually being the catalyst for his visits), Lilla gave him to Ruth, the first of seven daughters of a tenant farmer. She was fat and pretty and young, and had already learned how to handle dangerous children, to make them think they were doing what they wanted when really she directed the play, at her convenience, and in line with her understanding of the conventions. Years before, at a time when he had known little about drinking and nothing about women, it was in Ruth's arms that Hugh had lain crying and maudlin, feeling sorry for himself after his second double whiskey and in despair after his third or fourth. He had slept it off (she had stayed with him), gone home when he was sober, and paid her anyway. Such a breakdown had happened only once; the surprise of a woman's solicitous gentleness had prevented its reoccurrence. If Ruth was busy or indisposed, he got Aileen or Janie. They suited him less well, but they kept him relatively quiet and out of trouble, and that was Lilla's main concern.

The bedding down had been fine, and the variety had been intoxicating, but it was not enough: He never thought of these women after he left them. Then somehow during that past year —maybe it was because of his roommate's successful relationship with a girl from a school in New York—he had gotten the idea that to buy love was unfair, and that it showed a lack in him that he had to. That summer, in the five weeks that he had so far spent at the ranch, he had not only stayed away from Lilla's but he hadn't gone a single weekend to Mexico with any of the men at the ranch—Mexico, where, at a bar, one foot on the brass rail, the other planted firmly on the bright mosaic floor, the guitar music and folk ballads drowning out only a small part of their shouts and obscenities (at which they were equally adept in two languages), they would get drunk on

dares to one another to down shot glasses of tequila, followed
by the licking of salt off their fists and the sucking of lemons.
Then, drunk enough, their nerves cleansed and sharpened, their
young minds rebelling furiously against the restrictions of their
upbringing, they egged one another on to argue, to fight, and
to do things with women that Hugh was ashamed to remember
—even though he had paid them well, much more than they
asked, bought them quail and *cabrito* dinners served on ornate
plates of Mexican silver, given them French perfume or a pair
of earrings bought from the hawkers; and when he was sober,
he had apologized in pretty good Spanish for his crimes. But
never once this summer, which was unlike last summer, unlike
the wild, drunken summer of 1946, when he had driven away
from the ranch almost every Friday night after dinner and not
come back until Sunday at two o'clock for the big lunch in the
cookhouse kitchen. When he had arrived home this year, he
was different. His friends in town shrugged their shoulders.
"The girls ask about you," they said. They told him about the
allure and youth of the two new ones, twins from Wichita Falls
who resembled each other so closely that you couldn't . . . But
their stories did not stir him, and eventually they had to go on
alone.

Hugh could have had the pick of the young women locally;
none interested him. The girls he had met at parties at his
home in Houston were pretty and sweet like his mother; the
ones he had met at the schools close enough to Princeton Junction for him to visit were studious, officious, and lazy about
their looks. It occurred to him that he might find the right one
if he changed; maybe he lacked the right manner with women.
He had been told that he was too harsh and rough, and so he
had made a point of watching other men, noticing how they
acted with their dates and mimicking their behavior. But he
was to learn fast that the women they had he would never
want, and that the manners he imitated were too counterfeit to
satisfy his nature.

He was waiting, and he had very romantic notions about
what he would find. He wanted another kind of woman, one
who would never be worried by him, who would adjust to him
no matter what he did, yet who would possess a sensuality free
of the corruption he had so far experienced. He wanted one
who would somehow understand his nature; or, better still,
would act as a foil for it, and make it better or more interesting
than perhaps it was. He had no plan to stop drinking for her,

or fighting, or cursing, or playing rough; but it was one of his expectations that she would know how to make him feel so comfortable and happy—in contrast to the way that his whoring and dissipation had hurt him and left him angry at himself and troubled by his life—that he would stop automatically. Hugh imagined that though he had participated in the act of mating, he had never actually bonded his spirit with that of his partner and therefore had kept his innocence. Now he wanted to obtain the consent of a woman of his choice; he wanted to have the courage to let her make an assessment of the kind of man he was, and choose him on the basis of that assessment. He thought that he would be able to see his manhood reflected in the quality of her love for him, and that when she had understood the essence of his nature, he would understand it, too. He felt redeemed by this notion, and with his discomfort over his past offenses put to rest by the purity of his objective, he felt that he could wait in a state of serenity.

This would be the summer, he had promised himself, that he would find his match; but June had gone by and so had the first week in July, and still he was without her.

Clarence Littleton made a point of never doing business with a woman if he could avoid it, and it might have been for that reason that he sent his son to Elaine Menutis, rather than for the more obvious one of wanting him to have the experience of buying, on his own, a large tract of land. Clarence had a way of looking past women; he was teasing, careless, and sweet with them if he cared to notice them at all. If he could pass the responsibility of dealing with Mrs. Menutis on to Hugh, he would do it gladly.

The Littletons owned fourteen sections in Brazoria and Wharton counties, a savage property that Clarence had received during the Depression of the early thirties as payment for a debt, and which, in a decade, he had developed into the most valuable grazing land in the area. The ranch enhanced the whole region, and certainly it was the pride of those who owned it. There were gas pipelines buried beneath its long open spaces, beautiful pastures, fenced meadows, the finest herd of beef cattle for two hundred miles, and the prettiest registered cattle anyone knew anything about.

The tract for sale, the place next door, belonged to the Greeleys and was undeveloped, though it had crude roads, a few of them spottily topped with shell. By gaining it the Littletons would add twenty percent to their holdings, and since half the new property was covered with hardwood good enough to be harvested, it would generate on its own enough income to finance new fences, improved roads, and the cleaning of the two lakes.

For as long as Hugh could remember, he had dreamed of owning the Greeley two thousand and developing it himself. He had been all over the property, with and without Greeley's permission. As a boy, he had gone into it with a .22 rifle slung over his saddle and a knife in his belt, pretending to be an Indian, a spy, or a scout. He had even dared to hunt a little, to take out a squirrel or a rabbit now and then, not because he could not have killed them on his own land but because it pleased him to do it there. He would not have called what he did poaching: It was simply one lord accommodating another, though he would never have let the red-faced Greeley kids onto his property.

But Hugh now thought of the Greeley land as his father did: In the condition it was in, it was a slum, and it looked unsightly next to their place. They'd have to fix that, and the way to do it right was to buy it and get it up to Littleton standards. He planned, at the least, to clear part of it, improve the forest, and build a hunting camp.

It had been his hope, and that of his father, that the property would not pass through a broker, but because Clarence had quarreled with Abbot Greeley years earlier over the fence lines, Greeley had specified in his will that Elaine Mueller Menutis, Foley's widow (Greeley's nephew, Denton, had been a close friend of Foley's and had, in the early spring of 1942, gone with him to Houston to enlist), would act as agent for all his properties, which also included a few small scattered tracts along the Colorado River. He had made Clarence's acquisition of the land as difficult and costly as possible by handing it over to Elaine.

Until he saw her, Hugh had intended to get the survey map from Mrs. Menutis and then to check out the land with Matt. He had meant to make his visit with her as brief as possible, no more than was necessary to pick up the survey. But one warm July night, after the movie had let out, he saw a light in her office and—he had an appointment with her the next morning—decided to save himself a trip into town. He went up the steps and looked in the window. She had several papers on the surface of the desk before her, at which she was glancing without interest; she held a pencil which she was not using.

That afternoon she had unsuccessfully shown a young couple a property, a half-section a hundred miles from Dansville, ten miles south of Ganado. They were the kind of buyers who would search out the back roads of every county for a bargain, not because they lacked the money or were unable to get a mortgage but because the pleasure of the purchase was in the bargaining itself. They had noticed nothing; they had hardly seen a bird, an animal, a sweep of prairie, a rise; although the man had claimed to have done farming, he had neither bent down to examine the quality of the black soil nor observed that the fields drained well into a bayou with well-planted slopes. At the end of the day, they had failed to comment on the sunset that hung on the top of the sycamore grove, then stayed over the roof of the barn, pausing in full parade-color before retreating behind the old garden of onions, asters, and sunflowers, into the beautifully animated eye of the water tank. The cotton field, filled thickly with sturdy plants a foot high or more, was green and promising. It was a good year. But they wanted the asking price lowered, and finally, a few miles out of Dansville, they had attacked Elaine, as though she were responsible for the figure the seller had set. They had exhausted her, not by wasting her time, but by being the kind of people they were.

It was nine-thirty. In the dark office the circle of light above her shaded her in amber and exaggerated the soft red of her hair and the paleness of her skin. As she looked down, a wave of her hair fell across her lowered face, like a curtain over a scene in a play. Her slender hand held the pencil, and she tried to work. Her eyes were on the paper; her bare arm lay on the green blotter like a swatch of white satin across a lawn. Closer up, the blotter showed blemishes, ink blotches, and scars, the stress of engagement in an activity for which a person has worked to make herself well-suited.

She watched him open the door and step into the room. Standing just inside the entryway, he was practically in obscurity, and since he was dark himself, she saw only the gleaming silver of his belt buckle and his white shirt, which shone dully like a moon in a hazy night sky. Though he was dressed like a country man, she recognized immediately that he was generations away from the land; standing before her without the stoop of expectancy, doubt, or diffidence, he appeared to her to be, like all successful men of cities, immune to the effects of the natural catastrophe and disillusionment that plague people who work the soil. She had yet to understand how the transition from country life to city life was made, what the intermediate stages were. Even before he moved into the light, she could sense that he was very young, hardly twenty, or not much more than that. He removed his hat and dropped it onto the table in front of the sofa. He stood for a moment, silent, and she felt that he was assessing what he found. When at last he came nearer the light, she knew who he was. He did not look like his father, yet he had the same coloring, aspect, and hard manner.

As she straightened herself in her chair, he walked up to the desk, picked up the photograph that stood in the etched leather frame, looked at it, and then returned it to its place. She was thinking: *This has to be Hugh. Only a Littleton would dare to touch something on my desk before even asking my name.*

"You Mrs. Menutis?" he said, smiling down at her. He spoke like his father, though with less of the studied country accent and tone of voice.

"That's right."

"My father called you?"

"Yes." She watched him from her little stronghold of light. "But I thought I wouldn't see you until tomorrow, Mr. Littleton."

The tips of her fingers, the only part of her still in full light, touched the edge of the desk. She wore two rings, both gold, one with a small round diamond. Her nails were neither long nor painted.

"Won't you sit down?"

"No, I'm all right."

She attempted a smile.

He gestured toward the desk, the photograph of Foley. "That your husband?" he asked.

"Yes."

"You run this business together?"

"My husband was killed in the war," she said. She had said that a hundred times. To herself, she had said it a thousand, and still she seemed to lie; she seemed to have misunderstood what had removed Foley from her life.

"In Europe?"

"Yes."

He backed up, and on the edge of the darkness, where the pool of light bled into the shapeless space, he sat in the comfortable wing chair, facing her. He was confused by her obvious discomfort with him. Her husband must have died at least three years earlier; it was inconceivable to him that she could still be grieving, incongruous that this attractive woman was alone hours after the time for work had ceased. "When you finish what you're doing, let me buy you a beer," he said.

"Haven't you ever seen the Greeley property?" She had dodged his invitation.

He rubbed his hand along the arm of the chair. His features were sharp and patrician; and his eyes, in a face too close to adolescence, flashed with a too-open expressiveness. He was finer looking than Clarence, but unlike Clarence, he was careless. He would be impulsive, where Clarence was calculating and advised. "I've seen it," he said, casually. "But that's not what I asked you."

"I can't go out," she said. "I'm sorry." She pulled a paper toward her from a stack on the corner of her desk. "Did you look at the copies of the aerial photographs that I sent your father?"

"Yes." He seemed to make her vaguely uncomfortable by keeping silent for a moment. "Just a beer," he said finally. "It wouldn't take long."

Her hands moved along the edge of the desk. "I can't leave," she said. "I have some work to do."

"Do it tomorrow."

"I'll be with you tomorrow."

He leaned back in the chair, put his ankle over his knee, took out a pipe, and began to fill it. "I'll wait for you," he said. He sat behind the glow of the tobacco. Smoking gave him the dimension of maturity he had needed; so did the ambiguity of his expression and his silence.

He watched her walk across the floor from the desk to the bookcase to replace a book. He had absolutely never seen a woman walk like that, and being a man of spirit and extreme self-assurance (and since he'd attained that spirit and self-assurance on his own, rather than its having developed in the normal way as the result of the concern and attention of his family), he immediately decided that the way she had moved was for his benefit; and when she turned to him smiling cautiously, he believed that this was intended for him, too. He complimented her on both her walk and her expression with a casualness that underlined the insolence of his presumption. He thought she would be pleased, and so he was amazed when, rather than leaving with him at once, she went back to her work and ignored him.

For a quarter hour she attended to her papers. If she glanced up, she saw that he was watching her through carefully accomplished twists of smoke. Elaine had regretted instantly what she had done to elicit his daring flattery. She had known exactly the effect it would have even before she had gone to the bookcase, yet she had done it anyway, against her better judgment, concealing her motives from herself by thinking that he was too young to respond to her, though she certainly couldn't have believed that. She had provoked him, had felt herself making an effort to please the dark young man, and wondered why. He was big like her husband, comfortable in himself, a well-adapted human animal with an undercurrent of confidence and pride that spoke to her character. Some people seemed so alien, so perplexed by existence; some people went through life, it seemed to Elaine, as if they were in a house in which they didn't belong, being polite, deferring to a world of strangers, and never demanding their share. But not Foley, and not this boy who had walked into her office and then sat down with such ease that he might have been in a room which they had shared for years. But she had encouraged him, and she was sorry. It wouldn't happen again.

However hard the conditions she imposed on him, he seemed to want to stay with her. She looked at his dark hands spread carelessly over the red printed dragons on the arms of the chair, much prettier now in its faded, worn condition than it had been when she and Foley had first furnished the office. She knew he was unlikely to leave; she could tell by his slumped position, the comfort of his long, easy body, the big shoulders pressing against the high back of the chair.

"You want something to read?" She pointed to the coffee table before the sofa. "Get a magazine. You can turn on the other lamp." She spoke to him with a soft sweetness that she often used with her son. She was being patient, not so much to please him as to wait him out.

"No," he said, drawing on the pipe. "I'm fine." He showed no reaction to her condescension but, on the contrary, made himself more relaxed, or at least the lazy smoke in its directionless drift made him seem so. When a curl of black hair fell loosely across his forehead, he ignored it.

Hugh, for his part, was struck by the loveliness of her, the way her green eyes had a sleeply laziness that contradicted the character she tried to present. When she spoke, the tilt of her chin might have been an affectation, but he thought otherwise. She had lit a cigarette and handled it as some women handle a small flower. She didn't inhale the smoke, but she was not delicate. The more he watched her, the more he needed to see. He began to ask himself a series of questions, which only the sure, steady observation of her would answer.

Finally it had gone on too long, and Elaine sighed. "Mr. Littleton . . ." She was satisfied in her widowhood; she had cultivated sadness, and she had become used to its regularity and predictability. She was the product of her mourning, stable and firm, like a crystal whose temperature had been radically changed and for which another change would mean ruin. She wanted him out of there, and she planned to ask him to leave now. But instead she decided to leave herself. In a sputter of brief irrationality, she dropped her pencil, snatched up her purse, and pulled so harshly on the tiny metal bell of the lamp string that, before she could extinguish the light, the lamp made a convulsive swing over the desk, like a croupier sweeping his hand to collect the winnings. She stepped into the squares of light coming in the window from the street. When she passed Hugh in the dimness, he was leaning down to pick up the pencil she had caused to roll off the desk, and her leg brushed his knee.

"Are you coming with me?" he asked.

She mumbled something he couldn't decipher but knew to be affirmative. He stood up quickly and reached for his hat, followed behind her, and shut the door.

"Do you lock it?"

"No."

He held her arm, and with the ingrained courtesy of a second-generation gentleman, he helped her down the steps in the direction of his car, which was parked a half-block away on the square. As they walked under the trees in the sprinkled light, she looked at him in amazement, unwilling to admit to herself that she understood him, understood his haste and urgency, unable to think about what she should do, and wondering now if it was really useful to think beyond one beer.

"Do you mind going to Leon's?"

"No, it's all right."

Leon's Drive-in was in an area with neither street lights, curbs, nor sidewalks. It was where the poor lived, and the youth of the middle class went to drink. It had no sign, and the yellow lights under the roof were kept dim. Colored Christmas tree lights ringed the two windows, but they were only lit in December. If you wanted service, you honked the horn of your

car, and a fat woman with black hair and deep, beautiful eyes
came out of the trailer that served as a shelter for the preparation of food. She was familiar with everybody in town; her
name was Lupe, and she was Leon's wife. Apparently she
knew Hugh well, and with her crude, generous warmth, she
joked with him; he laughed and parried with her, immediately
imitating her style.

Elaine kept to her part of their agreement by having a beer
with him but disappointed him by drinking it very fast and then
refusing to let him buy her a second. He asked her questions
about her life; she answered them perfunctorily, obviously not
desiring to discuss it with him. Instead she talked about the
Greeleys, what they offered, the terms and conditions. She
described the boundaries of the property and a stand of unusually fine timber in the south section, then suggested ways of
dealing with the acreage around the lake that in late fall was
subject to flood. When he tried again to find out something
about her, she headed him off by giving him details of the
livestock show and rodeo at the Fourth of July picnic, seeming
to have forgotten that as they were driving across town, he had
told her he had been there. He had given her up much sooner
than he had planned, but consoled himself with the knowledge
that she would meet him the next morning at eight o'clock.

After he dropped her outside her office, where she bid him
a polite good evening, he left his car and watched her pull her
truck away from the curb. His inclination was to follow her
home. He wanted to follow her. Where did she live? He would
find out. He had friends who would know, or he could ask the
sheriff, Lonnie Teague, who was parked in his sheriff's car in
front of the darkened gas station, waiting to pick up someone
like him for speeding or being too loud. He considered this
seriously, but then, remembering that his impulsiveness sometimes cost him, he got in his car and turned in the opposite
direction.

The Littleton ranch was northeast of the river, almost fifteen
miles from Dansville on a road whose bridges crossed a half-
dozen bayous and sloughs. That warm night, a haze grew up
from the ditches and low places in the pastures and concealed
the houses and livestock in a way the darkness could not. The
weight of the trees seemed to have increased, become heavier
than when, in the sunlight, the branches had appeared separate
and the leaves hung in distinct buoyant clusters. Blurred land-

marks took on a different character. A farmhouse outside of
Pledger had lost its solidity to the mist: Only yellow pinpoints
of light, flickering in the upstairs windows, revealed it.

At night few cars traveled this road; except on Saturday, activity stopped at sundown. Hugh passed the small darkened settlement a mile from the entrance of the property, then turned into
the ranch, driving fast enough to raise the dust and disturb the
wild lantana and palmettos. As he got nearer the group of houses
where the ranch help lived, he seemed to have forgotten it was
there, to remember only at the last minute, braking just before the
bunkhouse steps. He sat in the darkness a moment, looking for
what he wanted to find, at last seeing it in the sudden glow of a
cigarette. Before his marriage, it might have been Luther, Matt's
lieutenant, for whom he was looking, but now Luther would be
with Lettie in their cottage, so this had to be Matt. He slammed
the car door noisily, though the lights went out in the windows of
the bunkhouse and in all of the neat identical houses that spread
out from it and from the cookhouse like wings, and walked over
the short-clipped grass, which still smelled sweet from the morning's mowing.

As Matt pulled on his cigarette, he revealed the high points
of his face. His lips were thin, and his mouth lengthened out
toward his cheeks; his nose was slender, and the nostrils were
narrow; from looking into the sun, his eyes were small and
tapered at their corners into three lines like the print of a sparrow's foot. Once he might have been a handsome man, but he
had lost his looks, not because of age, but as the result of a
conflict or an injury that had come early in his life.

Matt had worked for Clarence Littleton since the drought of
1936, when he had lost his property at Marlin. In 1935, when
the government people came to his farm and told him to kill
his livestock, and that they would pay him for it, he refused;
and when he heard that a vigilance committee was coming to
his place to kill the stock for him, he went into town, bought
two boxes of twelve-gauge buckshot, and sat on his porch
waiting, the gun propped on the rail, the barrel pointing at the
road. The vigilantes must have heard about Matt Kirkland's
purchase, though, because they never came. Matt's wife died
shortly after that, and then, when he was forced to pay a penalty for planting a hundred acres of cotton and refusing to plow
under thirty acres of it, the bank foreclosed on his farm. Without an earthly father to bail him out and without sons to share
the pain, he was a lot like Job, except that Matt had never

learned to love a higher spirit—that is, not until he had met Clarence Littleton.

He had been working in Mineola as a roughneck, and glad to get the work, when in the middle of a rainstorm, he found himself in a makeshift shelter, staring into Clarence's commanding black eyes, and sharing his bottle of whiskey. Both of them were down and out, though Clarence was wrestling with tax payments on vast acreages all over East Texas, selling some (only a fraction of what he had) at a loss to pay taxes on the others, and Matt was wrestling for close to his very existence, doing a job he hated and living a life he loathed. The two men spent the three hours the downpour lasted talking about Matt's past losses, Clarence's future plans, and both their dreams— and by the time the storm was over Clarence had offered Matt the task of taming the wildness out of ten thousand acres, building fences, cutting down trees, clearing the land, hiring and managing a crew of men who were talented with animals and strong enough to make ragged, neglected swamps and forests into pasture land. It was all spit and polish with Matt. He did for Clarence what he had done for himself: He gave his lifeblood to the land, not just for profit (or for his now handsome salary), but because his father had done so, and his grandfather before him, and all his people; because they had taken pride in the land and the stock and loved it like a religion, with gods they could touch and work for instead of just think about.

At sixty-two, Matt was arthritic and slowing down, but he was still rough, his arms and shoulders were powerful, and when he got drunk on holidays, people stood away from him and gave him his head. He was exactly Clarence's age, and Clarence would come down each February to celebrate with him: an all-night poker party, four tables, twenty men consuming nearly a case of whiskey, nearly everyone waking up in the morning sick, yet bragging about their consumption of alcohol (some of them waking up bruised and hurt because they had blustered, argued, and fought) while they ate pancakes, slab bacon, and slippery fried eggs, and drank coffee floating with grounds and laced with Clarence's French brandy.

Matt watched Hugh climb the steps up to the porch. "Can you slam that car door any harder, Hugh?"

"I don't know. You want me to go back and try?"

"I thought you said you were going to the pool hall."

"I changed my mind."

"I know that. Martin came in from there and didn't see you. Where the hell'd you go?"

"The movies. You should have thought to send Martin over there. You're slipping, Matt." He brought up a chair beside the foreman, as he must have done a thousand times before as a prelude to a conversation. Half the things he knew that he could use, he had learned from this farmer.

"I've just met a woman," he said. Biting down hard on his lip and keeping his eyes steady, he expressed his feelings about her with an obscenity, not because of an indelicacy toward the woman but because Matt would expect it, since that was how he and Matt always spoke of women whom neither of them knew very well.

Matt looked behind him. "Keep your voice down. People here got to get their beauty sleep. Some of us work for a living, big shot. . . . If she's so goddamned easy, what the hell are you doing home before midnight? You sure got kicked out early."

Hugh was quiet. You couldn't tell Matt anything. It was wrong to have tried. He had no judgment with respect to Matt— he just opened up to him, letting himself get hurt.

"Don't tell me you ain't got that far," Matt said. "You had since six o'clock."

Behind them, a window slammed shut somewhere in the house. Matt kicked at the railing with his boot and then left his leg there, pushing backward in his chair. "Who you courting? You going to tell me, or is this something you mean for me to find out on my own? We got some mystery?"

Hugh's eyes followed the tiny lights of a car far away on the road, until they were lost in the trees. It was a way of keeping his attention away from the conversation. Having unwisely brought up the subject, he now wanted to drop it.

"Okay, I give up," said Matt. "Who's the lady?"

"Mrs. Menutis." Hugh's voice trembled a little. It was the first time he had said that name out of her presence.

"Didn't she tell you her first name yet? She making you talk to her like she was your schoolteacher? You ain't nowhere." Matt laughed and shook his head. "Her name's Elaine, if that helps you any."

Hugh spoke softly, his eyes burning into Matt's profile, with its slightly lifted chin. "Honest to God, Matt, I hope you fry in hell."

"You ain't the first to have that wish."

Hugh listened to the whistle of a train, to the wind in the

oaks, to the sound of an animal in a distant pen. He wanted now to keep his interest in the woman away from Matt, to keep it completely to himself, but he realized that if he was going to get near her, to do better than he had done tonight, he'd have to find out at least one thing. "She in love with anyone?" he asked.

"Nope. I haven't heard of it. . . . But I miss things now and then since I don't go to no sewing clubs." He kicked at something Hugh couldn't see and kept his gaze on the toe of his boot. "She like you?"

Hugh took out his pipe and dug it into a pouch of tobacco. "Why wouldn't she like me? I'm nice, I'm easy to get along with, I can give her any damn thing she wants, and I'll be gone in six weeks."

Matt recognized at once what the boy's bravado meant: His ego was involved. At once he felt sorry for Mrs. Menutis, as he sometimes felt sorry for himself. He had seen this determination countless times before when Hugh wanted something: a horse that still had a good mouth but was spoiled in temperament; a bull he thought was right for the herd, but that Matt knew was wrong in disposition. Sometimes the boy showed good judgment, and when he was right, Clarence let him have his way. But when he was wrong, Matt would have to try to talk him out of it; if he was unsuccessful, then he and Clarence would find some way to make it work. But this situation was unworkable, impossible. A wild kid escorting Foley Menutis's widow around Dansville? Never. He decided at once to tell him so.

"So that's your idea of a girl friend?" he said. "Damn it, Hugh." He dropped his arm and mashed the butt of his cigarette against the raw boards of the porch floor. "Elaine has a son nine or ten. What you looking for, a mother? You're too damned old for her to mother you, and you're too young to be of interest to her in any other way. Forget it."

Hugh cursed him and tried to get up, but Matt put his heavy hand on his arm and restrained him.

"I'll tell you something else: She don't go with men no more. Not since her husband was killed. She was well married, and she intends to stay single. Not you or anybody else is going to break into that. Leave it alone."

When Matt saw that Hugh had started listening, he lit another cigarette and gestured with the hand that held it, making wild stops and starts and an occasional arc. "And hell," he continued.

"If she picks anybody, it ain't going to be a college boy. Plenty of men in town have tried to take Foley's place, and she won't even have dinner with them, much less any of the rest. She don't take nobody home."

"Maybe I can wait around in her yard for her to call me in. Maybe she'll think I'd make a nice pet."

"As a pet you ain't no bargain, and she's not going to give you the time of day after she sells you Greeley's ranch."

Hugh rested his head on the back of his chair and folded his hands over his chest, hoping that he wouldn't have to say anything more to Matt, that Matt would just divine what he wanted to know and tell him. After waiting sufficient time to realize that that wasn't going to happen, he asked him where she lived.

"A house outside of town... property back beyond Caney Creek, I think.... No, I don't know. Spanish Camp Road, maybe. I've never been there. She sold the house she and Foley owned.... God, that must have upset her kid."

"He nice?"

"Not too. He's rough and loud, 'cause he ain't got a daddy to ride herd on him. I think he lives with his grandparents part of the time, so he gets straightened out a bit by his grandfather. They've got a farm someplace."

"Why did she sell the house?"

"Money. Why else would she leave a pretty place a block from her work, with all the memories of her husband in it?"

"I'd give her money."

Matt looked at the edges of Hugh's profile, the definite descent of the brow and nose in one line, silhouetted against the gentler blackness of the night. "I'll bet you would," he said. "And she'd be worth every penny she cost you. But she ain't going to take it in return for what you want, kid. She's one of them women takes care of herself, all her needs. You understand me?"

"She let her husband take care of her."

Matt sat forward and looked toward the corral, as if he were expecting something to come into his vision through the darkness, and then turned around to look at Hugh. "That's right," he said. "You getting married?"

Hugh was silent. Both men stared out at the outlined form of an oak, holding their hands still and steady like spectators at a performance. "A romance your idea or hers?" asked Matt.

"I don't know. How the hell should I know what she's think-

ing?" Hugh slapped at a mosquito on his arm and turned up his
collar to keep the insects off his neck.

He considered what it meant to be a widow. One of his
cousins had lost a husband in the war. "What was her husband
like?" he asked.

"Perfect."

He waited, hoping Matt would alter that assessment a little.
He did not. "Nobody's perfect," he finally protested.

"Except you, maybe. Huh, Hugh?"

"We're not talking about me."

Matt reached a thumb and finger into his shirt pocket. A
square of white paper flicked in the darkness. Matt never
smoked while he was working; away from work, he never did
anything else. "Foley was perfect. He really was. Everything
he did turned out good. Look at that woman! He was good at
what he tried, and he was the best shot with a rifle I ever saw
in my life. He could make five out of five. I saw him do it.
She's a good shot, too; at least at popping tin cans off fence
posts. Gun would kick the hell out of her, but she'd never
show it. They didn't hunt, though. Foley was as much a Baptist as Luther, maybe worse. He was one of them regular
churchgoers who listens to the message. He gave help himself,
or he got other people to help. He got hold of your daddy once
about a farmer with a lot of kids whose place got in the way of
a tornado."

"Dad do anything?" Hugh tried to remember whether his father had mentioned this incident to him. He didn't think so.
"What did he look like?"

"Foley? Great big. But he was built right. He just wasn't
good looking in the face; he had big, coarse features, but he
had a fine smile, and he was generous with it. He always held
himself to his full height—God, Jesus, he was strong. Elaine
hung all over him; she was always with him. Even worked
with him at that office. They did everything together. Maybe
she did that because she knew she wasn't going to have him
long."

"Nobody has anything long."

"You're awful young to know that." Matt paused and made
a noise in his throat like something had hurt him. "It broke the
heart of this town when he died, when them goddamned Krauts
killed him. I was in the drugstore when I heard some lady
behind me telling it in whispers to Dr. Jackson's wife . . . and
she was crying. I remember I opened up one of them wide

picture magazines. Put my face down in it and made myself keep real still. I hoped no one would see it, but I guess they did, and were good enough to keep their mouths shut. Soon as I could, when I got quiet and had found a place to wash my face, I walked up to their house, but there was so many people on the porch, I felt funny, and I went on home. I never did tell her nothing. You have to do those things right away. If you leave them till late, it's like apologizing, and nobody apologizes around the death of a man like that—ain't no sense in that happening. It hurt the town real bad, and it sure as hell changed her. God, she used to be a beauty."

"She's a beauty now."

"Not like she was. You should have seen her when she was happy. One Easter, I remember her coming into church on his arm. She looked small beside him, though she ain't a small woman. Then I saw her looking up at Dr. Mengden in the pulpit, watching him, closing in on every word, with that beautiful face, white like one of them china cups your mama has behind glass in the big house. . . . War ain't nice. You see some little drunk like Bobby Jerabeckus come back and sit on a curbstone irritating everybody, taking punches at his wife, beating up on his kids, never earning no living—and yet, him, the best we had in this town, he lands on a beach in France and catches a bullet from some bastard strafer who probably never even saw him real good. I don't understand it. I don't understand nothing like that."

Matt looked at Hugh, saw the stubbornness in the set of his shoulders, and worried about the boy's intentions. He was sure Elaine would never give him the time of day, but he couldn't take a chance that a miracle wouldn't happen, like her taking him on—which would bring Clarence down here asking him why he never watched out for anything.

"In the morning, we're going to take some steers up to auction in Beaumont," he said. "Why don't you drive the truck for me? Get your mind off that woman you can't get. We can go to Galveston after. You ain't been real drunk in a long time."

Hugh, hardly listening, bent down distractedly, emptying his pipe, tapping it on the edge of the porch, so the cooling ashes fell into the flower bed. He thought about how he had tried to put his arm around Elaine, and how she had drawn away quickly in the corner of his car, as far away from him as she could get, where she had finished off a half bottle of beer so fast that her throat must have stung. "You'll have to excuse me, Matt," he said finally. "I'm buying a ranch tomorrow." He leaned back in his chair and looked out farther into the darkness than he could see. "And I'm courting, too."

Well, that was it. He'd either win her and mess up a whole bunch of people, or lose her and raise sand. In any case, Matt was going to have some broken pieces to pick up. "You going to get Greeley's place and Elaine?"

"That's right."

"Your mama's going to be upset about that last. A farm girl turned real estate agent, and a good bit older, ain't going to fit her plans."

He wasn't aware of his mother's plans; she never mentioned girls to him, or much of anything else, for that matter. He wondered if she even knew where he was. "I'm not tampering with her plans," he said. "I'm just figuring out how to get myself through this summer." He stretched his arms over his head and groaned.

Matt recognized the gesture and knew Hugh was nervous from anticipation, and if Hugh was scared, that was bad. He thought about going to see Elaine, at least phoning her.

The tops of the oak trees struggled in a sharp, sudden wind; Hugh raised his head and drew in a breath. "It's going to rain, Matt."

"No, it ain't. It's not hot enough."

Matt rose to his feet. After he had spent the day on horseback, his sixty years showed. He put his hand on Hugh's shoulder and, remembering Elaine's husband and the friendship he had felt for him, said: "If you get her attention, Hugh—and I know you won't—be careful with her feelings. You hear me? You listening? She's had enough bad luck without getting a man like you, who'll stray off. She's got a business to keep going and a kid to raise." It was useless telling Hugh no about anything. He ignored negative orders, and if Matt rode him too hard, he'd just quit confiding in him. At least if he could keep the lines open, he might minimize the damage. "Be careful of her feelings, that's all."

Matt tossed his cigarette into the yard in a long, high arc and watched while it splashed sparks on the black serpentine root of an oak. The top of the tree blacked out half of the purple sky and one of the recognizable constellations.

Hugh picked up his hat, dusted it, paying attention to the roll of the brim. "Don't you care if she's careful with mine?"

"I always figure you'll make out, Hugh." He turned toward

the bunkhouse door, then reconsidered. "Why don't you go with one of them girls who comes to watch you play tennis at the club? Be so much simpler. The only reason they're there is to look at you. They don't care nothing about tennis."

"Maybe they come to see Tony beat the hell out of me."

"Tony's Mexican. White girls don't watch Mexicans."

"They do if he's a champion." Hugh pulled off his boots, and throwing them onto the dark porch, he laughed. "They can be very forgiving."

"Can't you like one of them little girls who comes to ride horses with you?"

"Little girls get in trouble."

"Widows don't, huh?"

"Something like that."

"A woman's a woman, Hugh."

Again Hugh stretched his arms toward the ceiling of the porch. "I've been waiting all my life for the right one."

"With you, that ain't very long."

"Cheer up, Matt. Maybe I'll be over it in the morning."

"You think so?"

"Why not?" Hugh lurched forward, then stood up quickly and hit Matt on the fleshy part of his arm. Matt struck him back. Hugh lost his balance, fell against the side of a post, and recovered himself, cursing Matt, wiping his mouth on his sleeve, and laughing. He raised his arm toward Matt again but changed his mind and relaxed. He laughed from deep in his throat and put his arm around Matt's shoulders. He had been the taller of the two for better than a year. He said: "A civilized man's no better off than that stallion you bought, Matt. He's got to wait around for someone to be kind enough to open up the door of the corral."

Matt held his finger up in his protegé's face and, then, in slow motion, grazed the boy's chin with his fist. "And she ain't going to do that for you, Hugh." His face twitched as it always did when he thought he had made his point and wanted to stop a discussion that, as far as he was concerned, was finished.

But Hugh ignored the implied warning. "Yeah, she will," he said. "I just have to find a way." He looked down at his foot and worked it against the crude planking of the porch floor.

There was a callousness in the boy's certainty that annoyed Matt, and when Hugh turned his head toward one of the dogs, who was growling at something going on at the foot of the yard, he hit him again, half-pushing him, this time less playfully, and so hard that Hugh fell against the bright blue metal of the glider. Matt's face had gone hot. "You don't lack for confidence, Hugh, but you ain't Foley."

Hugh was breathing easily, so Matt almost expected him to get up, wheel around, and knock him off the porch for his comment. It was too hard; he realized that right after he had spoken. But Hugh kept still. "Bring me a beer, Matt," he said quietly, with not a little maliciousness. "You owe me that for busting my rib."

"Go to hell." Matt was not moving a muscle. Although he saw Hugh's teeth flash in the dark and knew he was smiling, he was still unsure of what Hugh was going to do. *He really wants that woman,* Matt was thinking, *maybe more than he knows. Nothing else in the world would cause him to be so careful with himself just now.*

"I'm the boss, Matt." Hugh's tone of voice was quiet, measured. "You've got to do what I say."

Matt grinned. He was sweating from the roughhousing with Hugh, but he felt better. "When your daddy tells me so."

Taking his time, Matt picked up his hat and got his cigarettes off the railing. "You coming in, kid?"

Hugh lay still, one leg jackknifed across the glider, the other stretched out. He had put his hat back on, but it was low over his eyes. "Yeah, I'm coming," he said. But he stayed on the porch.

Twice Matt headed for his room but changed his mind. He shuffled around the bunkhouse living room, rearranged the magazines without really reading anything, replaced a chair before the table, picked up a jacket that had fallen from its hook. On the desk was a photograph of a boy seven years old on a wide, tired-looking horse. He was frowning in anger and shame because he had been refused the privilege of riding Matt's mare, Dolly, who shied and was mean. On his head was a Stetson, way too big for him, but still not covering the tangled black hair he kept everyone from combing, except his nurse, Cana. The first time Matt had seen him, he had put his hand on the top of that black, matted head and asked him his name. "Hugh Clarence Littleton!" the child had shrieked, and shaking his head violently to rid it of the foreman's hand, he had run screaming into the ditch and then into the pasture, his short legs working hard, his arms tracing circles like windmills, his fists doubling up and hitting at the legs of the dispersing, terrified animals while he hollered: "Red cows! Red cows! Red cows!" That was the first summer that Clarence had dropped him off with Matt, and every year afterward, he would come back on his own like a migrating bird, older, taller, better coordinated, but just as mean and almost as wild. Glancing at the picture, Matt thought of how Hugh looked now, and how Elaine would look beside him, that sublime woman whom Hugh fancied he cared for and whose image, even yet, Matt could not separate from Foley's. His heart went out to her. "Ain't she had enough?" he asked the empty room. "Ain't she?"

Hugh woke before dawn; by a quarter of eight, he was sitting in the chair behind Elaine's desk, his feet on the desk corner, watching the door. When he had entered the office, he had been surprised to find Felix Fuller, the middle-aged schoolteacher who helped Elaine on weekends, already there. Felix had been a prisoner of war for two years in Germany, something he never talked about. He seemed too withdrawn and frail to have ever been a soldier, and in a helmet he must have looked like a caricature of one; but he had four robust children under ten; and he had Lily, a loud, lusty wife who adored him and praised him in front of people, amazing his male friends with the zest of her regard.

At eight-thirty, Hugh broke their silence. "She always late?" he asked.

"Nope. She's never late. . . . You sure she said eight?"

"Positive."

"She usually likes to start out later. She's not a morning person, she says."

Hugh leaned even farther back in the chair, picked up a paper clip, and bent it harshly. His disappointment in the fact that she had apparently not shared his desire that they be together showed in the frown on his face, and in the rigidity of his body. He should have been able to control his displeasure, but he was unable. Hugh could argue with incredible finesse, his mind was a generously provided labyrinth of finely tuned receivers, and he never forgot what he learned from books, but when he was slighted or crossed, he was aggressively defensive, and his emotions would disintegrate like those of a teased child. "That doesn't surprise me," he said, keeping his eyes on the twisted paper clip.

It was nearly nine when she arrived. By then he had drunk three cups of coffee, alternately sitting and pacing; he had exhausted himself talking to Felix about cattle prices, the early cotton crop, and the unpredictability of the weather.

"Mrs. Menutis," he said, as soon as she was in the room, "if there was any way on earth I could purchase this property without going through you, I assure you that I would do so."

"I'm sorry," she said, breathless from hurrying. "A phone call came just as I was leaving my house."

"If it was a business call, it would have been made here."

"Not necessarily."

"And if it was not a business call, you shouldn't have spent time on it."

"Why, Mr. Littleton?"

"Because you had an appointment here with me," he said. "And I have been waiting one goddamned hour!"

She listened to Hugh; while she was pulling on her boots, she apologized again, and then she ignored him. She would take him out—she had to do that—but when they got back, after they had walked the boundaries he insisted on walking, her job would be finished. She was dead certain that he already knew the property, that Matt Kirkland had showed it to him years before. He had no reason to see half of what he had suggested they see last night. All he really needed to do— Clarence had told her as much on the telephone—was check the 1940 survey and make sure that it tallied with the fence and landmark descriptions on the contract. One full day should do it. She would handle the sale, but she would not throw herself into the bargain.

In the time it took to walk from the door of the office to the truck, Hugh regained his composure. She guessed from his behavior that though he had a temper and could be nasty, it never lasted. All you had to do was be nice to him: A smile and a few kind words on the steps of the office had done it. She took care to be compliant when he wanted to guide her to the truck; she thanked him as he helped her in. But when, on the way out of town, she saw a friend and pulled over briefly to speak to her, she felt his impatience. Clearly he resented sharing her attention with anyone else, and he complained about the delay.

She glanced up at him, but since he was staring at her in the same way he had looked at her the night before, she returned her eyes to the road, made comments about the hot summer (much hotter than almost any they had ever had), and then talked about other properties, as if they might interest him. She quoted him the prices of things on the market and those already sold. She advised him on the agricultural potential of his purchase—though he had already told her he would not put the new land into fields—as if she were lecturing to the local chapter of the FFA.

He let her talk, he listened to the broad vowels; he listened for, and after a while stopped expecting, certain final consonants to appear.

"You're not from around here," he said.

"I was brought up on a farm near Seguin."

"You go to school there?"

"Until I married." She took the barrette out of her hair and refastened it harshly.

He offered to drive for her, but she refused him. He shrugged and looked out the window. They were crossing a bridge. The river was high; the different currents jostled one another, carrying the clay-colored water toward the ragged banks. The limbs of the willows traveled free and light, then were suddenly jerked backward like whips. "My driving scare you last night?" he asked.

She didn't reply.

"I hope I didn't bother you by asking you to go with me for a beer?"

She might have hurt him then and alienated him as well but instead calmly said, "You didn't," and pulled the truck sharply onto the side of the road, parking at an abandoned dry well. "We'll walk in from here. I'll take you around the back side later."

They spent the entire day together; he was tireless in walking the fences, in examining the lakes and the marshes. They both played the game according to the rules each of them understood the other had made. His scrutiny was minute and exaggerated, but that evening, as they parted at her office, he insisted that they go out again the following day.

The next morning, he appeared early, and this time she was ready. They cruised over the balance of the property in her truck, along the open firebreaks, and then on the roads; and when the roads ran out in the darkness of the tangled woods, they walked through the dense underbrush, looking for streams, slopes, edges of ponds, a collapsed building, a dilapidated corral, any landmark. Elaine recognized and identified them expertly, and Hugh remained quiet. He let her guide him over and over again into areas where he had already been, into places where his childhood seemed to have begun.

When they had walked as far as the first lake, he came up behind her and turned her head with his hands to show her a white heron. She stood still a moment, hardly looking at it, and patiently waited for him to release her. He had hoped to please her—she had pointed out other birds to him—and he smiled at her close to her face. But she walked quickly away, brushing at her jeans, as if they were dusty, as if she had just done something to get them dirty. It was a gesture he was sorry to see.

Later they spread the map and the aerial photographs on the hot fender of the truck and circled with pencil the area they had just walked, their fingers marking the paper yellow with the sulfur they had used to keep off the insects. They decided to walk in all the way to the second lake on the north corner of the property.

It was ghastly with heat in these places hung with vines and dense with scrub, where breezes never came. At the base of a hackberry tree, Elaine stood still, raised her hand to stop Hugh, and pointed to where, not three feet from where she was standing, a copperhead was coiled quietly, sunning itself on a muddy little island. It moved only slightly at their approach, then flinched all along its length and remained still. In the gray changing shadows made by the leaves, it was as beautiful as a jewel in a dark, suede-lined case. Behind her, Elaine heard the hammer click of a pistol. She swung around and caught Hugh's wrist, hard enough to leave the prints of her fingers. "Why would you shoot it?" she said roughly. "It's not hurting anything! It does good things. You just want to kill something, don't you?" Her voice made it clear that she despised the kind of man he was. The snake slithered into the water, leaving its trail in a thread of silver.

Hugh answered her quickly, and with brutality rather than tact: "What would your husband have done, Mrs. Menutis? Reached down and picked it up?"

Her face went white, and her expression changed from anger to a suppressed terror at this highly successful invasion. "He would never have killed it," she whispered.

He saw that he had crossed into her deepest refuge by superimposing his image onto Foley's, by letting them blur together; and that it was his first step toward her. It was the husband's position and authority that he would have to assume.

He looked down at her hand on his wrist, glanced at her face, and smiled; then, quite surprising her, he covered her hand, twisting his fingers through hers to hold them. Still watching her, meeting her eyes until she had to look away from him, he slid the pistol back in its holster and repeated what he realized must have been a line out of a bad movie, but which, because it was almost a reflection he did not intend for her to hear, was perfect all the same. "You're a pretty woman," he said. "And you act as if no one ever tells you so."

She stayed near him an instant too long, spoke when she should have been silent, and lowered her eyes briefly when she should have kept them fixed and still. "I don't need anyone to tell me," she said abruptly.

"Why not? I'd tell you."

There was a hint of arrogance in his voice, and she caught it. Under the dark protection of the trees, he had been daring, and she knew he was waiting for her to make what he had said acceptable, to approve it, or else, by rebuking him, to erase his advances altogether, to make him dislike her, but she turned and strode back to the road as swiftly as the underbrush permitted.

Although for the rest of the day Elaine made a point of being even more self-reliant and professional than usual, Hugh continued to believe that he saw a vulnerability in her, that for all her seeming toughness, there were moments when she lapsed into a sadness that attracted him profoundly. That she was a beautiful woman had drawn him to her, but that she had a secret life apart from him, intrigued him on another level, one that was not without unexpected power. He understood that it was her allegiance to someone else that caused her sadness, while at the same time giving her an unapproachable serenity that he longed to break into; he would like for her to retain it, he thought, yet to know that he was the cause.

They had a late lunch in a café in West Columbia. She restricted her conversation to professional remarks, and if he asked her a question, she answered him disinterestedly.

"Tell me about your son."

"He's with my parents," she said.

"Your father's taken him over?"

"Yes . . . and sometimes he stays with my brother."

"Don't you miss him?"

"Yes."

"But you think he's better off."

"I know he is. I have to work. He needs a man with him."

At first she had resisted sending Jimmy away from her. The idea of giving up his company was unthinkable. Yet the child's behavior—that he often disobeyed and then was rude when he was corrected, had worried her father and he had spoken of it, arguing with her that for Jimmy's welfare she should let him come to live at the farm. Jimmy needed discipline and planned activities, Mr. Mueller said. As it was he had too much time on his hands and that caused him to get into trouble. Before making her decision Elaine watched how her father dealt with the child. Jimmy might get angry—he was furious when Mr. Mueller punished him for sneaking out of the house before dawn to saddle a spirited horse and ending by letting it escape into a ravine, where it tore its pastern on a twist of barbed wire—but afterward, she saw that Mr. Mueller had established a rapport with the boy. He might punish Jimmy, but he also gave him time: He let him help with the work even when the child's participation slowed things down, he explained with seemingly endless patience the workings of the farm equipment, he answered Jimmy's questions about the animals and the crops. So while it grieved Elaine to be separated from her son, she had agreed, at least during the summer and holidays, to send him to her family.

"Why do you wear a wedding ring?" Hugh asked her.

"Because I was married," she said and immediately turned her head away from him, denying him the expression on her face.

In a way, she could not imagine what he wanted, what he was doing, and she refused to believe the most likely explanation. It was lost to her vocabulary of possible situations, and lost to her imagination. His attempts to make her needful of him challenged her preferred image of herself, that image that she had had before her marriage, and that she had now. Furthermore, they were a way of separating her from her sorrow, and except for a few letters and pictures that was all that remained to her of Foley. If she wouldn't let a mature man break into it, why would she accept a boy? She longed for him to relent in his pursuit, and she thought about telephoning Clarence, but, good Lord, what would she say?

Finally Hugh stopped flattering her and trying to distract her with conversation, and he waited. In spite of Matt's warning, he had expected this to be easier. He thought that he and Elaine were alike: vigorous, smart, independent, and a little mean. Each of them would take advantage of the other if he

could. In opposing him, he guessed, she was testing his
strength, seeing how far he would be willing to go to get her.
It never occurred to him that she might not desire him. Why
wouldn't a widow, a small-town woman, like him? At first, he
considered that he was doing her a favor by courting her, or if
not doing her a favor, then paying her a compliment to which
she could not fail to respond. He believed he understood why
she would dislike the men she might meet in Dansville, and
thought of many reasons why she would prefer him: If he was
unprepared for a long siege, self-assurance was his excuse.
But, like an untested army that has lost its first skirmish, he
was now preparing carefully—thinking ahead, foreseeing the
difficulties, solving all the possible problems beforehand.

At the end of the day, when they returned to the office, he
asked her to have dinner with him, arguing that he wanted to look
over the draft of the contract of sale after the revisions he had
asked for had been made. She tried to refuse; he could have
looked over the papers in less than ten minutes. "I've work to
do," she said.

"You will be working."

"I really can't."

"Is anyone taking you out?" They were standing in front of the
office. The sidewalk was shaded by oaks whose roots broke the
concrete squares at intervals as regular as swells on the sea. "You
have to eat, Mrs. Menutis."

She waved at a passing car. The wind blew her hair across her
face like silk; she pushed it back, and when she looked again at
Hugh, the request was still there, apparent in his silence. "I'll
pick you up at six," he said.

"What time is it now?"

"Quarter of five."

She seemed to be seeing all the store fronts on the street at
once, the metal pillars, the plate glass, the crude signs. She had
no choice.

"You want me to pick you up at home?" he said.

"I'll meet you here."

"I'd be glad to come by for you."

"No, thank you."

A little over an hour later, he arrived, clean-shaven and in
different clothes. She was beautiful in a pale green blouse and
matching linen skirt. She had not dressed for him; she had simply
dressed for dinner. She rarely went out, and so, in spite of her

discomfort at being escorted by a man whom she thought of as a spoiled child, it was an event.

He took her to the nicest place in town, a small, pretty restaurant in the downstairs portion of a wood frame house. The dining room was pleasant and comforting with its checkered tablecloths, pretty floral china, candles in colored-glass cups, and on the mantel of the old brick fireplace, hurricane lamps with bases of blue and white porcelain. On each table, a heavy pewter ash tray in the shape of a fish sat beside the glass sugar bowl. It was obvious to Elaine that, before coming, Hugh must have spoken to Mrs. Rockwell, the owner. They had a table in the back of the room, the only one with fresh flowers.

He again asked her about her life, but she remained distant, told him nothing. He tried to tell her about himself, but she was uninterested. Her eyes took in everything in the room except for him, and when she talked, it was business or country-town gossip, so feminine in content as to be deliberately insulting. When their dinner came, she ate in silence, even though the food was the best she had ever eaten there or at any other place in Dansville. If Hugh was frustrated, it was his own fault. She had come out with him against her better judgment and against her will, and he knew it. She sat at the table wishing that he would regard her differently, that she would emerge suddenly from this disturbing dream and find across from her only a client and friend.

When they were back in the car, Hugh offered her champagne, which, before picking her up, he had gone to a great deal of trouble to obtain and to chill, even providing the right kind of glasses. She refused it, not only disappointing him but embarrassing him slightly by stating that she never drank with clients, an assertion that was both unkind and untrue.

"You drank beer with me," he reminded her.

"I was tired . . . and you surprised me. It was wrong. I never do that."

She had taken a cigarette out of her purse and lighted it before he could do it for her. He frowned. She seemed to be tallying up her victories over him, thinking of everything she could do to keep him in his place, to keep him from crossing the line she had drawn between them. Being nice to her, he realized, was fruitless: a mellow, self-sacrificing gentleman would get nowhere with her. *I know what she wants,* he thought with characteristic bravado. *I'm just not there yet.*

He had already decided to buy the land. He had talked to his
father; everything was in order. He sensed that Elaine knew this.
He was confused himself by his tenacious, obvious, and now
shameless pursuit of a woman he should have ignored, should
have used only as a mediator, but he kept on. The past two
sleepless nights had exhausted him, and the difficult days with
her had injured his pride. He was inexperienced in the ways of
the heart. He was a novice at love-making where the two shares
were equal, and he had been brought up to think that he deserved
what he desired; yet, in this instance, he was willing to work,
think, and wait.

For now, he had to take her back to the office and let her go.
Typically, after such a defeat, he would have gone to get drunk.
In the Mexican drive-in, or in the saloon in Refugio, he might
even have picked a fight: All he had to do was flaunt his eastern
school superiority over the local boys. They really hated that.
Some of them thought that an education made a pantywaist out of
a man, and when they talked of one of their own who had won a
scholarship to Harvard, they pretended to be drinking from a cup
like a woman, holding out a little finger to balance it. When the
world disagreed with Hugh, he could throw body and soul into a
conflict of his own making, and he could come out exhausted,
dissipated, and satisfied. He loved a fight: It was regenerative to
him.

He sure couldn't go to Matt, not with a report of this route.
And Matt would know, even if he didn't confide in him. After
two minutes of quiet observation, he would say: "It's going
bad, huh? You thought it would be easy. Didn't I try to tell
you? Let it go." Also, Matt might laugh, and Hugh would kill
him, or at least he would try to, and then he'd get twenty
minutes of Luther's time, one of those quiet lectures that he
listened to because he liked Luther, and because Luther soothed
people with his presence as much as by what he said.

He started for the ranch. He drove slowly through the
black-shaded, tree-covered streets, smoking a cigarette, hardly
listening to the garbled music of the two crossed stations of the
radio, but too preoccupied to turn off the sound.

He had been on the highway for some time before he began
to feel the full impact of his disappointment, and then he began
to accelerate. He was driving almost too wildly to keep to his
side of the road when he began to reproach and throw blame
on the obtuse, meddlesome gods who were thwarting him. He
was soon at a speed where the center of the road plunged away

like quicksilver, and had he not known the way like the back of his hand, he would not have known when to slow. A car came around a curve, and its headlights fell briefly across his face. Its horn blared at him, and as he held his car just far enough to the side to avoid a collision, its tires scattered the loose rocks on the shoulder and into the ditch. The wind had forced his black hair flat to the sides of his head, his hands were tight on the steering wheel, and he held his lips pressed tightly together. He was enough in love to find her without blame, incapable of being complicitous in making him miserable. Something other than Elaine's will was standing between them. He hated the failure of all things to fall into place quickly, the perversity of fortune, its teasing methods, its dull, mean, easily sidetracked intelligence. He was impulsively greedy for what he had been deprived of; he had never been smothered by kind hands and unlimited affection; he had never had a relationship in which there had been a reciprocity of feeling. Against the wind that was roaring through the inside of the car, he heard himself yell out her name.

Driving into the ranch, he caused a cloud of yellow dust to cut through the darkness and to curl up to the undersides of the oaks that bordered the road. The car stopped so abruptly that the back of it swung around, causing the loosened earth to fly against the fenders of the cattle truck and the side of the water tank.

That night, Hugh did not seek out Matt or Luther or anyone, but went straight to the bunkhouse and slammed the door of his room as hard as he had slammed the door of his expensive car. He pulled off his boots and threw them against the wall and then, without undressing, fell on the top of the bed, cradling his head in his arms in the attitude of an irritated child. If Matt knocked, he would get no answer. Hugh planned to be unresponsive to any and all words spoken from outside that door. He lay fighting drowsiness in order to keep his memory of Elaine alive and his concentration active, to keep the hope he still had free of the treachery of a sleep that would search out his misery and sprawl his failure into one long, depressing dream. Later, he smoked awhile, and then poked around in the top of his closet for the bottle of whiskey that he kept in reserve for moods as bad as this.

One thing was clear to him: Unimpressed by his money or his resolution or his attraction, Mrs. Menutis was holding out. He had hoped to return to the ranch that night different,

changed, successful. God knows, if he had, he would have
looked for Matt. He would have walked up to the bunkhouse,
loud and heavy, jarring the walls if he could, scraping his
boots; he might even have tried to get Matt to fight with him.
He would have had a terrifying happiness he would have been
unable to live with alone. He would have needed to exhaust
himself, to fight until he was breathing hard and dripping wet.
Afterward, he would have gone down on his haunches, hung
his wrists over his knees, and waited. Staring at the ground, he
would have been patient for the return of his breath; and then,
hardly moving from that spot out under the trees, in the blackness lit only by the flare of a match or the tracings of the
lightning bugs, he would have talked to Matt quietly until very
late.

Instead he turned on his back, one hand behind his head,
his black eyes following a gray column of cigarette smoke to
the ceiling. Over and over, he told himself that he would have
Elaine, that never again, after today, would she refuse him. He
said this without believing it but had to keep saying it to keep
his ego aloft, well above these swift, drowning currents of
failure.

He slept very little. As soon as it was light, he got up and
dressed. He took his horse into the pasture alone. He avoided
everyone: He did not go to the long table in the cookhouse for
pancakes and eggs, nor did he pick up Lettie and swing her
around just to hear her shriek like a baby for Luther, nor did he
devil one of the other women by stealing from the piles of sliced
bacon and ham that were draining their salty grease on thick
brown paper before being set out on the table on heavy white
platters.

That afternoon, the fourth day that he had known Elaine, he
stood close to her desk with the beginning of the sunset in the
window behind him, blazing around his head. He had lost his
calm of the evening before. The frustration of his exhausting
suit had made him too impatient to hide his feelings. The idea
of having to separate himself from her again, to have the night
stretch out before him, empty of her company, seemed unbear-
able. He was helpless, and it seemed to him that Elaine knew
it. His hands were in his pockets; he was standing over her,
too close, uncomfortable and strained. The composition was
disturbing. Elaine felt it, and Felix, having glanced up at them

briefly from his position at the second desk, had looked down quickly at his work, and kept his eyes on the page before him.

"I'll see you in the morning," Hugh said coldly, reminding her that she would be in his company for at least a part of the next day to ascertain whether the Greeleys had met his ridiculous demand to clear the lake area of rubbish and an old truck. She had refused his invitations to both dinner and a movie, and she had been firm. She had told him that she was visiting a friend; and he had known she was lying, because he perceived a satisfaction in her refusal which she had not even tried to hide. But he had sulked and let her see it, and he was angry now, not only at her but at himself for being unable to conceal his childish reaction.

She pushed away from the desk without looking at him; walked with him to the door, both of them silent. She was finally ashamed of the way she was treating him, but she did not call him back. After he left, she shut the door and leaned against it, as if she meant to keep him from returning and pushing it open. "Good God, Felix," she said softly. She was not looking at Felix but at the red roses on her desk: a dozen of them, huge and fresh, hardly out of the bud, and with stems a yard long. They must have cost a fortune. "Take the flowers home to Lily," she said. "They burn my eyes."

Felix glanced up from his work. "Looks like you've got yourself a boy friend," he said.

She sighed and dropped into the armchair.

"He ask you for dinner again?"

"How do you know he'd asked me before?"

"You were seen at Rockwell's last night."

"The advantages of living in a little town."

"There are some. . . . You like him?"

She took off her watch and synchronized it with the big clock above her desk. Avoiding his question, she asked, "Do you know that he's buying two thousand acres so he can bring his friends down to hunt?"

"Maybe he needs friends."

She put her arms over the sides of the chair and slipped down into it. "Felix, what in the hell do those people think of us?"

Felix rolled his chair away from the desk and turned to face her. "I don't know. They're rich as Croesus." He spread his hands out and tapped the ends of his fingers together in a regular rhythm. Then he got up slowly and went to the window, where he put his hands in his pockets and curved his head and shoulders toward the glass.

"Do you like them, Felix?"

"I can't afford not to. Their being here improves the economy. In a few days, it's going to make you some money. Foley was nice to them. He was damned nice to them."

"Foley was nice to everyone," she said too quickly, and with bitterness.

Felix was silent. Maybe it had been the wrong time to mention Foley.

But she went on sharply: "And Hugh? What do you think of him?"

Felix turned toward her, a bit surprised at the tone of the question. His fingers moved in his pockets, quietly shaking some coins. "I think he's a hell of a good tennis player and a nice looking boy," he said slowly. "What more?"

"Have you seen him play tennis?"

"I saw him play in the tournament last summer over at the country club. He's almost as good as Tony Cuevas, and he doesn't even want to play for a living. He could."

"Why doesn't he?"

"Littletons don't become athletes."

"What do they become?"

Felix went back to his desk and closed the notebook he had been working on. "They work real hard at staying rich, and they're good at it. I expect Clarence gets to his office every morning at seven-thirty and doubles his income every year. They're not lazy."

"What does Hugh want with me?" she said, looking up at him. He had walked across the hook rug to where she was sitting, taken her hand, and sat down on the arm of the chair.

"You want a compliment? You feeling bad, Elaine?"

"He's too young to be interested in me."

"You're pretty. You make men want to do nice things for you."

"Not for nothing."

"No; but he may not want so much. He may be young enough to be content with just squiring you around . . . be proud to do that."

"I doubt it." She remembered his response when she had stopped him from using the pistol. She could still feel the strength in that hand that had held hers, the big fingers that had slipped between hers and made them ache.

"Be real careful, Elaine. Be as nice to him as you can. Just because he's offended you by thinking he's man enough to take you to the movies doesn't mean he's evil. Maybe he can't help it. Anyway, don't throw away your four percent." He laughed. "Maybe Clarence sent him to you to teach him humility and help him grow up."

"He's grown up. He doesn't need me for lessons."

She crossed the room and riffled through her mail, seeing nothing, cursing as she impaled a piece of thin, yellow paper on a steel spike and wondered how she was going to pay the amount written on it.

Felix took off his glasses and rubbed his eyes like a man who has seen too much and wishes he hadn't. He had come home from the war with gray hair, the result of neither stress nor bad treatment, he said, but diet. Since the war, he had experienced enough to know that most changes are for the worst, and so, though he worried about her some, he rarely tried to influence Elaine. They worked together like two men, each of them living in a secluded, carefully managed, ideal world, thoroughly occupied, a little withdrawn, and vaguely unhappy. "You don't have to like your clients," he said gently.

Then strangely, as if she had not been attending to the conversation with Felix, and with the impulse of a creature, ignorant, trapped, and helpless, she launched into a tirade against the Littletons, not just Hugh but the whole family; and though it might have been true that they had faults, and that fortune had smiled on them unfairly, her criticism was unjust, arbitrary, and ridiculous. "They're too dark," she said from out of the prejudiced depths of her primitive, ancestral, Teutonic biases. "Their hair is black, coal black. I hate that. And so are their eyes. I've never liked dark people." Her outburst was so outlandish that Felix could only regard it as a last-ditch stand before a terrible capitulation. "I should have let you take him out," she finished.

He had his back to her. "No. For that much money, he's entitled to his time with the boss."

She shook a cigarette out of its package and struck a match so violently that she broke it. "Go to hell, Felix."

He shrugged. "Don't look at him, then."

"What will I look at?"

"The wild flowers." He replaced his fountain pen in the pocket of his shirt, a preliminary gesture in a series of ordered, habitual preparations for going home. "Get your wild flower

book and identify the species. Show him how oblivious you are
to male persecutors."

He lit her cigarette for her and watched her become lost in a
kind of revery that was maintained by the smoke and the dusk.
There was feminine mannerism in the way she smoked, her
fingers curving into the air, and her chin tipped up. She turned
her eyes toward the window, where the light was fading and
where a heathery tinge, borrowed from a rainbow, outlined the
glass. The evening star was already hanging in one of the panes
of the rapidly darkening glass.

She changed the subject and reproached herself. "I don't make
anywhere near the money out of this business that Foley did. I
think I hardly make a living at all. What the hell is going to
happen to me?"

"Nothing bad. You do fine." He paused. "You might get married, though. Why not Besley Staub?" Besley owned a farm between Edna and Cuero. When he was in town, he stopped by the
office, and sometimes Elaine had lunch with him. She liked him;
he was quiet and competent. He ran a farm as fine as her father's,
the kind of farm where a woman worked only in the house and
had a maid occasionally; her mother had always had cleaning
help and someone to cook the meals at harvest time and then
again to do the canning, and Elaine was impressed by that kind of
thing.

She brushed the end of the cigarette against the edge of an ash
tray. "No," she said, keeping her eyes lowered and her attention
on the business of smoking.

Felix frowned, and for a moment, he didn't speak. He admired Elaine. She was one of the few women he had ever
known who had a job other than pouring knowledge into the
heads of unreceptive and vicious children, or giving shots and
emptying bedpans for miserable people, or standing behind a
counter handling someone else's nickels and dimes. "Come
have supper with us," he said. "Lily wants to see you anyhow."

Elaine had work to do at home; she should not have gone;
certainly she should have written to her son. But in the back of
her mind was the disturbing thought that if she went home, she
might be called on, or she might even find a visitor waiting
there. By going with Felix, she might frustrate the enemy at
the door of her lair, her place of legitimate privacy. She
crushed out her cigarette, dumped the ashes in the metal waste-
basket, turned off the desk fan, and followed him outside with

the obedience of someone who has been robbed of choice by
the anarchy of chance.

As she stepped onto the porch, she was caught for a wild
instant in an act that amazed her: She found herself looking for
the gray car, and she felt a surge of disappointment when she
saw that the place where it had stood was empty. Her eyes
flicked down both sides of the street, and then she closed them
tightly. Though the heat was still oppressive (the sunset had
been driven by swollen rain clouds into a premature twilight),
she shivered at the recognition that she sought the company of
a boy whom she found to be unbearably insolent and whose
life was so clearly discordant with her own.

Instantly, contrite for her treason, ashamed that she had
looked for the car and for the man, she called silently for the
bright appearance, the resurrection of her dead husband in her
vigilant memory; then she spoke to Felix on the sidewalk, and
because of the tone of her voice, he turned to her alarmed and
dismayed.

"I need you to do something for me," she said. "I don't want
him to . . . I can't . . ."

As the dark, sweet-smelling rain clouds crept up blind and
consoling from the east, and Felix put his arm around her, she
lowered her head on his shoulder until all that he could see of
her were swirls of pale red hair. Having crossed unconsciously
and unwillingly over a line of involvement, she began to cry.
"He'll hurt me. I won't do this. I just can't let that happen."

To Foley's wife, Felix wanted to add, but he said nothing.
Goddamned war.

Near seven the next morning, a violet glow pressed against the
blinds. Through the partially raised window, damp breezes
moved the ruffles on the curtains; and at intervals, increasingly
further apart, raindrops fell from the eaves onto the wooden front
steps while mild winds shaking the branches of a mimosa tree
caused quick, noisy showers.

Elaine lay in bed on her side thinking and waiting, knowing
that something was going to happen, expecting it. She had a
sense of anxiety similar to that which precedes a performance
or the delivery of a speech, a feeling she thought she had left
behind when she graduated from high school. She finally sat
up, slid her feet into her slippers, went to the window, and
raised the blinds. The clouds, clearing after the rain, had left
the area over the pasture the ash blue of high summer; the sky

to the north was scrubbed white; in the east, the color flared.
As the tree limbs appeared clearly in their familiar patterns,
birds broke the silence. She looked over the green pasture, full
with rough-leafed asters and daisies and thick-bladed grasses,
green imitations of fine grains. Yellow-breasted birds flew into
it and disappeared like fish in the troughs between waves; insects, birds, and grasses hovered and melted together, steaming
between the dampness of night and the oncoming warmth. In
the misty breeze, a huge blood-colored rose bruised its petals
on the window screen and gave off a heavy perfume; below,
the earth, heated and moist, reeked with strength and seemed
to boast of a robust health, rediscovered with the appearance of
the sun. To the left of the house, fine shadings of lavender
blended easily into the horizon over a strip of silver that lay on
a cotton field. The crowded plants, hard with thick, green
bolls, stood firm against the risings of the hot wind like a
phalanx of soldiers. The wet, oak-dark road was quiet and
empty. Elaine let the cord go, and the wooden slats clattered
against one another as the corner of the blind swung into the sill.

A telephone call interrupted her bath. She dried slightly and
went to answer it, picking it up after a dozen rings. A fra-
grance stayed on her skin, heightened by the warming air
around her.

"It didn't work," Felix said.

"What did you tell him?" She pressed a towel to her wet hair.

"That I'd take him out, drive him anywhere he wanted to go.
He let me know real good that that was not interesting to him."

"Is he there?"

"No, he's on his way to your place. I think it hurt him. He's
pretty mad, Elaine."

From the hallway, where the telephone stand was, she could
look out the living room window to the road. It was empty. "But
he doesn't know where I live, Felix. I never told him. Did you?"

"He knows where you live, honey, and anyhow, he wasn't
waiting around for anything to get complicated, like my offering
to give him directions."

"Well, there's no sign of him."

"You want me to come over there and look after you?"

"No," she said slowly. A car approached her house but passed
by and continued on the road. "He's all right. He's just not used
to being crossed. I'll listen to him fuss if he wants to. He's just a
kid."

Felix shot back a warning. "He's a hell of a lot more than a kid, Elaine, and if you don't start thinking faster than you're thinking right now, you're going to lose this round."

"No, I won't."

"What are you going to do to prevent it?"

She looked down at her damp body, her free hand moving to the curve of her waist. "Get dressed," she said.

She was ready. From behind the curtain, she had watched for him. His car passed once, slowed, then turned around. Her name was on the mailbox in small black print; there was no address number. When he came up the stone walk and up the three steps, she was waiting on the porch. She was dressed in jeans and a white tailored shirt; her hair was combed through, but not arranged. She wore no make-up whatever. He was immediately aware of her effort to look unattractive, and realized that it was totally ineffectual. His impression of her was already indelibly stamped on his spirit and intelligence; her attempt to understate her beauty gave him hope, for it might be a sign that she understood and was worried by his intent.

As he stepped onto the porch, she turned toward him, her back to a post, in the attitude of a caryatid on a superb building; her chin was raised and her eyes were startlingly alive. "Good morning, Mr. Littleton," she said. She made a great effort to keep her eyes steady and her voice clear. Behind her, the trees flashed from a warm, fresh wind, and the collar of her blouse lifted and brushed her cheek. Though her heart beat fast, she managed to smile. But she could do nothing about the blush that rose to her face.

He smiled back and echoed, "Good morning, Mrs. Menutis." He looked at her giddily, absorbed in his fascination.

"We can take the truck," she said, proceeding directly to business. "I'm afraid, what with the rains, we won't be able to see the area you had talked about. That's why I told Felix to . . ."

"I don't think that's why," he said abruptly. He put his hand on the post behind her so that he had her fenced in and could look down on her. He was not angry now but spoke gently and watched her reaction to what he said with reverent patience. Coming over in the car, he had not only gotten hold of his temper; he had changed the spirit and tone of his campaign. "I think you worry too much about keeping me out of your way. Will you tell me why?"

She did not answer. He took the pause well, but she blushed again strongly.

"When are you going to like me?" he asked and then, breaking into a smile, said, "I brought you something." He took a small, flat velvet box out of his pocket. "Here." He pushed it toward her.

The box opened on a hinge. In it was a chain with a gold heart.

"I can't accept this," she said quickly. She closed the lid and gave it back to him, avoiding his eyes.

"Only candy and flowers, huh?" He shrugged and put the box back in his pocket. "All right."

Her eyes slanted up to his. He was beautiful, and she forgot how young he was.

"Would you like a Coke before we start?" she said. "It's terribly hot." It was five days after Independence Day. The refreshing effect of the morning rain was gone.

He looked toward the screen door, at the cool darkness of the interior of the house. He nodded and followed her inside. He had rarely been in such a small dwelling, and then only in the country. The entire structure would have fit into any one of the reception rooms of his parents' home, yet, at once, he felt at ease in it. It closed over his spirit gently, not in its individual features—they were less than interesting—but in its seclusion, its cool, ungreedy, small-town prosperity, its heavy, generous comfort, and the exclusiveness of its smell of a woman: of bath powder, ripe flowers, and somewhere, a damp silk robe.

He could see into the bedroom, the bed yet unmade, a sprawl of white rumpled sheets and tumbled pillows, a white garment on the rug. Overwhelmed by the leap of his imagination, he looked away quickly.

There was only one central room, half of which, covered by a patterned rug, was the living room; the other half, defined by a dark table and six matching chairs, was the dining room. On the table was a milk-glass compote filled with purple figs, some of which had burst their skins and showed the fuzzy whiteness of their fruit. He followed her through the doorway at the end of the room into the kitchen. She got two bottles from the refrigerator. He took them to an opener on the side of the cabinet, which he had noticed as he entered the room. She faced the window to the garden and arranged a series of little flowerpots with violets in them, picking off a leaf on one, pinching at a few dry flowers on another. She told him about their success, that it had nothing to do with her, but rather the filtered light that reached them there. He watched her as she raised the pale green Coke bottle to drink, as she took each swallow of it, all the while neglecting to look at him, her attention riveted first on her plants and then on a lilac bush she must have seen every day. When she had finished the drink, she dipped her head and touched her mouth with the back of a paper towel she had wrapped around the sweating bottle.

She began to leave the kitchen and, noticing that he had hardly touched his drink, said, "Are you ready? You can bring that with you."

He murmured something she didn't stay to hear. What he had not drunk he poured into the sink, and it hissed into the wire trap of the drain; then, turning to follow her outside, he copied her motion of dropping the bottle in one of the compartments of a wooden case. He had been silent in her house; no words had come to him; he had just existed there, glowing sadly, sad because he had to leave it without taking her in his arms, and glowing because he thought he understood by the blinking, nervous eyes he'd seen looking out the window at the familiar lavender bush, and the light, carefully measured breaths she took high in her chest, that her mood, while still guarded, was changing. He would study this hint of success, savoring its implications.

In the corner of the back yard was a garage, a small building, built years after the house, and though not as well constructed, it was well kept and neat and was partially hidden from the back of the house by tall clumps of pale green fern, yellow day lilies, and jasmine. It held only one vehicle; the bed of the truck just barely fit. He opened the doors for her and pushed them back against the outside walls, where they caught in the grass and stayed fixed. "I'll drive for you," he said, reaching out to take the keys.

"No, please . . . I prefer to drive myself."

He lifted his hands in compliance. "Okay."

He got in, and she backed the truck out the gate and over the culvert. As they drove, they didn't talk at all, and though he was watching her, and she knew it, she never took her attention from the road. Intermittently the clouds covered the sun, blocking the excess of summer light, smoothing the sharp edges of the shadows. The sky was almost covered with huge, stiffly rising thunderheads; and to the west was a row of clouds roofed by a blurry crenelation. An eye of blue in a round mass of white seemed to close without wanting to while strayed

mists reached out to meet larger and more solid formations.
The oak trees, the corn, the meadows themselves seemed to be
sending up steam and wilting in the heat. The livestock, listless
and quiet, seeking the deepest grottoes of shade under the
limbs of the trees, had lain down or were standing motionless,
like toy farm animals in dim, neglected corners of children's
rooms.

The roads of the Greeley tract were still slick from the
heavy rain of the night before, for the sun had not been freed
long enough to dry them. Holding the truck to the road was
almost impossible, and though Elaine had experience in this
kind of driving, she was doing badly. Staying in the center was
no better than keeping to the grassy sides, and both were dangerous. She knew Hugh would be more successful, that he was
observing her discomfort with that in mind. Instantly she resented him for being smarter, more able, and better—not just
better than she, but better than everyone else. The hotter the
day and the more difficult the driving became, the more she
disliked him for supposing that he could win her, that he would
be able to invade her sanctuary. She blamed him most for the
antipathy she felt in his company, and the loss that she felt
when he was gone. She was unwilling to attribute that sense of
loss to attraction, though even a cursory review of her courtship with Foley might have warned her, had she been willing,
in Hugh's presence, to invoke that memory. A tree branch
slapped against the windshield, and then another. She could
hardly see the road before her, as much because of her tears as
because of the undergrowth, and though she wanted to curse,
the hand that had found its way to her shoulder, and which she
pushed away violently, brought her to herself. The trunk of a
sycamore rose before her, and she swerved the truck to avoid it.

She left her thoughts behind in the orchard of ruined pecan
trees or the pasture with the devastated corral when he put his
hand under her hair at the back of her neck and called her by
her name, Elaine; said that name so lovingly and disconcerted
her so much that she began to tremble. It was what he was
saying and what that declaration implied that made her do a
thing so crazy that it was almost as certain to lead to trouble as
driving the truck off a cliff. She didn't know what she had
been thinking when she drove the truck into that swale—when,
all of a sudden, she decided to take the shorter way behind the
lake. As they entered the lowest part of the hollow, the road
almost disappeared, and the vehicle stuck fast. The left rear tire

spun helplessly, deepening the rut, and again the wet, low-hanging branches of the trees fell across the windshield. She could not see. She could not think. Worst of all, he was advising her. He was telling her what to do. "Put it in reverse and let it rock," he said; and then: "I can get out and put some brush underneath the tire. If you would..." She had made a mistake, and he was taking advantage of it.

She was so hot, the weather was so oppressive, the mosquitoes so terrible that she ceased to care if he bought the property or not. The commission that she would gain if he did had become irrelevant before she had even reached this swale. It was as if she had already let herself be held in his arms, already given herself to him, already accepted from him the pleasure that the solidity and strength of his presence promised. Certainly he had caused her to take the wrong turn and come into this impassable trap. Was this the last event in his calculated plan? *What for?* she thought. *What the hell for?*

He spoke gently then, with a patience that she knew wouldn't last because it was so completely out of character. "Let me get us out of here," he said. But she kept working at the truck, knowing that she should stop and let him take over, but unable to. "Come on, Elaine." There was not a trace of condescension in his tone, yet all she could hear in it was his own sense of superiority. "Why do you have to do everything?" he said. "Can't you let anyone help you?"

Not him. She bit her lip white.

When she raised her arm to push him away from her, she cried out feebly, not from fright, but as a defense of her last redoubt of isolation and her understandably pessimistic view of the outcome of love and commitment. She resisted him strongly, but he somehow managed to come closer to her, and she recognized that she was fighting equally the stubborn will of a truck wheel and the stubborn body of a very young male. She had confused the two, since both were joined together in her mind in this one hopeless predicament. She would not have been helpless in either struggle but for the heat and her longing, and loneliness. There had been a war, a great grief, a loss of faith, and a sense of the failure, not just of her ruined life but of the whole universe in which she might have to live for another half-century without the man she had felt predestined to mate with, to live out her happy life with, and to love forever, even in an existence after death, which she believed in because this seemed logical and reasonable, and because her church, her parents, and Foley had made the belief seem a credible one.

Hugh reached over to lift her across his lap so that he could move behind the wheel, and she could say nothing about it. His face blurred across her vision when, as they exchanged places, he took her face in his hands and kissed her. Though she returned his kiss with a willingness of her own (she was so puzzled at her response that she was silent and astounded), afterward she slapped him. She heard her hand, even over the harsh noise of the idling truck engine, make contact with his face, felt her hand sting, but her reaction did not involve any forethought, any judgment as to its necessity.

She had never slapped anyone in her life, but she had struck Hugh full in the face, swinging the flat of her hand as hard as she could within the limits of the space in the truck's cab; and she reached back at once to hit him again. It was her intention to annihilate him; no other punishment she could imagine would have been severe enough to placate her. He caught her by both wrists, somewhat more roughly than he had intended (so that she cursed him yet again for hurting her), and he uttered a perfunctory apology. When he then moved toward her abruptly, instinctively, she ducked and hid her eyes.

"I'm not going to hit you," he said. His black hair, untidy and wet, fell loosely across his forehead, and he had to wipe the perspiration off his face with his sleeve. He was frowning, and his cheek burned, but he was not angry; he had avoided the contamination of a hostility that might weaken his purpose, belie his self-control, and cause her to condemn him for his youth. And because of the way she was now talking to him, because of the accuracy of many of her accusations, he smiled. "Okay," he said. "That's all right, Elaine."

What she said then, and the manner of her saying it, was so irrational that he recognized in the diatribe the commencement of a surrender. He welcomed the implication and reflected, with incredible self-importance, that he would soon be able to sweeten her humiliation by giving her himself. He was coming to the finish line in the lead. His victory was the result of a chance accident on a washed-out road, but he understood now that it could have been the outcome of any accident, any problem he could solve, any argument he could win.

He had come to a conclusion about Elaine that was perfectly accurate, and it was this: Heaven help the man who wanted her, if he could not show her up, do what she was unable to do, at least once. She would relinquish neither her widowhood nor herself without exacting a proof from the thief. She would see him crucified otherwise, and she would never lift a finger to stop it; without a murmur of pity, she would allow him to suffer. She would be capable of remaining morally unscathed by the torture she would devise and implement to punish a man weaker than she, who had the temerity to want her and to let her know it. On the first night, when he had seen her in all her splendor under that lamp in her office, he had been awed and innocent, and she had chastised him immediately with her contemptuous indifference when the only crime on his head was to have admired her, wanted her too quickly, and shown it. She had scorned him pitilessly, and she had outraged his recently matured, especially sensitive masculine pride.

She sat in the corner of the cab, her chin slightly raised, her hands folded in her lap, her back rigid and very straight. He was kind enough not to make an effort to see her expression, and he had the good judgment not to laugh. He was grave, careful, methodical. He would not humiliate her further, for he admired her; and if he was in love, he was also in awe. Her reticence, her masculine thoroughness and seriousness in her work, her country wisdom and courage and adaptability, a chameleonlike way of according her nature with that of whomever she was with—truck driver, restaurant owner, farmer—won his respect and fascinated him. She did not belong by character or behavior to any class or race; she was just herself. He saw her as existing alone, abandoned, defeated, bruised and shaken, but surrounded by fire. He had never met a woman like her, nor had he ever had a woman of her worth as a friend. His observation of women close to him, particularly his mother, had taught him that trusting in their affection, or taking their counsel, was unwise; and his observation of his father in the company of women bore out that conclusion completely.

Hugh, his head out of the window to see the wheel, put the truck in reverse and stomped the gas pedal to the floor. At the instant he felt it lift, he jammed the gear into low and slapped his foot to the floor again. The brutalized motor and gears screamed, the wheel smoked, then fell back, was lifted forward again, the process repeated three times, until the rear end skidded sharply, putting the truck dangerously offbalance, requiring of Hugh an extreme effort to move it away from a declivity and put it on course for the slick, torturous climb. At the top of the ridge, he said: "I saved you the cost of a wrecker, though I guess you'd have made me pay for it." He was smiling, and he was very proud; his cheek was quite red where she had hit him. *She may not like me*, he thought, *but she'll let me make love to her. She'll do that now.*

She crumpled over, crying, her face on her knees. As he again reached to hold her, she fought with him; but because of the way he felt against her, her anger lost its purity, and the struggle of her tired arms, her twisting motions, were ineffectual. He asked her to be still and not to cry. "What the hell difference does it make who got the truck out of the mud? I hope you're not crying about that."

With her, it made all the difference, and he knew it. Because of his success, she was miserable; he must try to talk her out of it. "You wouldn't do what I told you," he said softly. "It would have come loose if you had. Why don't you listen? Don't you ever listen to anyone? I don't think you do." He had heard his father talk to his mother like this; it was effective in calming Clara, and it was, for the time being, all he could call on.

Tears streamed down Elaine's face. Unlike his mother, who would have been soothed by such a speech, Elaine answered in full vendetta. She no longer remembered that she was talking to a client. She was only aware that on two counts she had experienced defeat, and that by hurting him, she would make him pay for it. "I don't need anything from anybody," she said, "and if I listened to anyone, it wouldn't be to you, you son of a bitch!" Her cheek was against his chest; her lips moved against his shirt, which was wet through with perspiration and tears, but her enraged body was already responding to the insistence of his. Her anger, which was becoming more and more isolated in her mind, had, like many vital things abandoned, simply sought vengeance before giving up its strength.

He attempted neither to defend himself nor to answer her back. He had planned his strategy far too carefully to risk an altercation with her now, to trade a verbal victory for the more important one. Her green eyes were searching his urgently, pleading with him to change the direction of what was happening, to let her loose, to take her home, to leave her there, and to vanish. If at that moment he made a mistake, she might be free of him.

While holding her tight against him with one arm, he reached under the steering wheel and turned off the ignition. He shifted his weight to bring her up to him, and as if she

were a partner in a dance, she raised herself. She felt her arms
go around his neck; though he had placed them there, she let
them remain and tightened them in sympathy with the arms
that had closed around her back. She raised her head as he
lowered his, and with the same degree of insistence with which
he gave them, she returned every one of his kisses, pressing
herself to him with all the expressiveness and passion that for
so long she had kept not only from him but from everyone
else. He would release her now and then to look at her with
that same dazed expression that she had seen several times
before—an expression which, on a man she could not have
loved, she would have despised, but which on him looked
appropriate.

Whatever resistance was left in her was revealed in what
she murmured after her ability to think had been robbed of its
precision. She told him that it was too hot and uncomfortable
where they were; the hair around her shoulders and neck was
wet and clinging to her skin. "Hugh"—his first name, and it
was all the more unexpected because he did not even know that
she knew it.

"Where do you want to go?" he asked. He had only half-
listened; his question was more a response to the sound of her
voice than to the words she said.

"To my house," she answered.

He considered her request and tried briefly to move away
from her, but it was beyond him, and it occurred to him, too,
that she would criticize him if he did so, and that she might
even change her mind about letting him make love to her at
all. Telling her that he loved her, he put one hand under her
and slid her down across the seat while with the other he began
the discovery of her body. Staying true to the ritual, knowing
its mystique and understanding its purpose, she tried at intervals to escape him; but each time he held her fast, acknowledging the venial lie of her reluctance. And when she moaned
sharply, her mouth struggling away from his to do so, it was
not in pain (she was perfectly prepared for him), but in relief.
The predicament that had fallen upon her in the summer of
1944 had ceased as abruptly as if a door had been slammed on
it by the urgency of this man's possession.

Hot as it was, with more mosquitoes around them than there
were leaves on the tree branch that scraped inside the cab, the
steam of humidity surrounding them, the heat increased by
their closeness, the sounds they made more communication be-

tween them than anything previously said, they finished what
they had begun three days before; and both of them trembled
from the task. Hugh, soaking wet, hardly able to take breaths
in regular succession, his back wounded with scratches and
swollen with mosquito bites, pulled her up with him into a
sitting position and fanned her with a piece of folded newspaper that he had found on the floor of the truck. He looked after
her well-being, even to the draping of her blouse around her
shoulders, as concerned for her modesty, once his sanity had
been recalled, as shortly before he had been eager for her to
abandon it. Certain that she was his (he had understood her
integrity from their first meeting), he asked, "You want to go
home now?" With her cheek pressed against the hard bones of
his wet shoulder, she began to laugh softly. He continued inno-
cently, "Or we could go to the ranch . . . to the big house. Do
you want to go there?"

Once on the road he drove with one hand, his other arm
stretched out across her flank. Her head lay in his lap, her arm
limp over his knee. Her body might have been without nerves;
nothing could disturb her. Her mind seemed to have stopped
functioning, to be narcotized, everything having given itself up
to the experience, as voluptuous and soaked with heat and
smelling of life as the moist veils of vegetation strewn across
the ditches and hanging in the trees. More than once he
stopped the truck and attempted to lift and embrace her, but
Elaine, reduced to incoherent responses, protested, almost
whining. She insisted on languishing in her satisfaction, and
she paid no attention at all to the man who had provided it.
She was unyielding to any intrusion, and at last, he understood
that she was not ready for him. It was useless now to try to
awaken anything in her; but the knowledge that he had been
responsible for such contentment pleased him. He had learned
something valuable. He left her alone and drove on.

Her hands shook when she tried to unlock her front door; he
took the key from her but hardly did better. She asked him
dully, scarcely thinking, the standard questions for any guest:
Was he hungry? Would he like anything to drink? He spoke
absently, made a few nervous gestures and remarks, then led
her into the bedroom. At first, his haste, his selfishness, and
his lack of refinement frightened her, particularly in a man who
should have been more gently bred; but then, though the realization came as a shock, she sensed that his impetuousness
suited her, and that she was unwilling to modify it.

The blinds were still down and closed. The ceiling fan turned its slanted paddles, moving the air vaguely across the dresser, around the flowered, pleated skirts of the overstuffed lounge chair, and over the disordered tucks in the unmade bed. It was nearly noon, but the room was still dim and cool. Hugh did everything that needed to be done: It was not that he desired her passivity, or that he needed to dominate her; it was just that he didn't require her to do anything. Undressed without thinking about it, in bed without knowing how she got there, and experiencing pleasure no matter what her involvement, she let him do as he liked, because it pleased her absolutely.

Lying on his back with his eyes closed, Hugh expressed an earnest, unnecessary gratitude in phrases in which the key words were mostly omitted. Later, when she questioned him, trying to hide her expression, he forced himself into a certain alertness and made her look at him, and said, as if offended, and with more directness than he had shown even in his passion, "I do love you. Good God, Elaine." She felt guilty for having suggested that it might be otherwise, especially when he tempered his sternness by looking down at the long, white, audaciously interrupted column of her body, whiter than the sheet on which she lay, and complimenting her on the possession of it.

"Are you tired?" he asked.

"No . . . What have I done to be tired? That's not how I feel."

"Do you want to get up?"

"Do you want to? Why would you want to?" She laughed. "Aren't you happy where you are, Hugh? You're not bored?" She had never spoken to him like that before. No one had ever communicated so much love to him, and all this in a series of short phrases, almost whispered, while she looked up at him from her damp pillow.

For the rest of that morning and into the afternoon, two vehicles were parked in front of Elaine's house where there was usually none. The truck had been drawn up behind Hugh's Chrysler so that the bumpers touched and reflected each other in the water-stained chrome. The sun was so insistent that, by noon, even in the dark shade of an oak, the mud on the fenders and sides of the truck had dried into a smooth, taupe-colored crust. A breeze from the prairie came up, and a window slid open to receive it. One mammoth cloud lay halfway across the sky, a big fleecy blanket, dragging its train. A magazine sat uncollected in the open door of the tin mailbox. Birds came to the darkened rim of the birdbath and beat their wings carelessly. As a man passed on horseback, a dog chased along a fence, barking frantically, though the man passed at the same time every day going home to lunch. A child in a neighbor's yard gave a cry in imitation of the distant train whistle—that, too, habitual. In the house, the bed gave a sound which, in that house, it had never made before; and for the first time in his life, Hugh was making love to a woman for whom, afterward, he would not have to leave money on the dresser or the pillow for the privilege.

It startled him how much she enjoyed him and let him know it. He had not thought that would be the case. The lore in the locker rooms or among the boys in the cars that cruised the main streets of the little towns was that a woman had other reasons for giving in to a man: to trick him into marriage, or to get her way. She had a commodity for sale, something that a man needed desperately, but to which she was indifferent. Elaine was nothing like that: Sometimes she initiated their love-making, calling to him softly but directly, or beginning to caress his still and silent body with a firm, expectant hand. With the same serious, extravagant insistence with which he came to her, she gave herself to him. All of the love that she had kept contained for so long, she gave to Hugh without exacting a price.

To go to bed with a man who would not offer her marriage was a thing that would never have occurred to Elaine before she met Hugh; and yet, even after she had admitted her love to him and to herself (in that order), she did not expect him to marry her. He would not; it was unnecessary for him to tell her. On the other hand, she expected him to stay with her, as faithful and loving as a husband. For him to leave her, she thought, would be an insult to nature, since they were perfect together, and he had to know that. The only danger she foresaw was that he had nothing to compare with their relationship, since she was the first woman he had loved. She was aware from the beginning of the possibility of his being drawn to other women simply by virtue of his sensuality, his restlessness, his continual need to prove himself.

Yet, however great a risk Hugh represented, however serious a threat to her peace of mind, he satisfied her completely. He had none of the usual inhibitions that women found in men of his class and race and time. He was like the tough, well-hewn men in his father's family before him, not a throwback but the result of a successful genetic strain that had prevailed. Novice that he might have been at showing love, or acting out passion despite the trappings of civilized behavior, he was by nature affectionate, and in her arms (a sensual woman too long deprived of sensual encounters), being able to express his dramatic though somewhat obsessive temperament freely, he was easily made happy. Though he was defensive and quickly hurt (in this he showed his age most), there was not fit of temper, no sullenness, no sadness that could not be placated almost at once by a display of desire for him that came effortlessly to a woman as much in love with a man as Elaine was after that morning. Though for vastly different reasons, both of them were starved for physical love and comfort; similarly deprived, they were similarly grateful for the abundance of mutual affection. Both of them were by inclination generous, and what they had come to was nothing more than the affirmation of a hardy attraction between two affinitive, corresponding natures.

That first evening, when they were eating supper in her kitchen (steaks that he had gone to the ranch to get for her; his first offering after his success), he repeated a question that he had asked her two days before, though now with the need for a real answer. "Why do you still wear your wedding rings?" He spoke softly, lifting his eyes to hers, and taking his time over his words.

She looked self-conscious and uncomfortable, and she was silent.

"Are you going to keep wearing them now?"

She would have smiled were it not for the seriousness with which he was looking at her. "I love you," she said. "What difference does it make if I wear my rings? They're pretty." She did smile then in an attempt to change his mood. "I'm used to them. It doesn't—"

"I don't like it," he said with swift violence. "I don't understand why you would want to."

Since her marriage, eleven years before, she had never removed her rings; they remained where Foley had placed them, and she had meant to wear them all her life. She thought that Foley would have expected her to. "I wouldn't fight about it," she said.

He leaned across the table, putting both his hands out flat. His shirt almost touched the food on his plate. "Then don't. Go take them off."

"I'd like to wear the diamond," she said, and her voice was deadly quiet. "I could wear it on my other hand if you object to what it means."

She watched him steadily, wondering just how cautious she had to be, wondering how one man could possibly be jealous of these symbols of possession when the other was unable to return to reclaim her. Hugh looked at her menacingly, a gesture that seemed childish to her, and disappointing. *What have I gotten myself into?* she thought. *What in God's name have I done?*

He had put on a fresh shirt at the ranch; it was light blue, and the sleeves were rolled up to his elbows. He had wonderful arms; he was thin and the muscles under the black hair were outlined strongly. She thought about how they felt when he held her.

She got up, slipped her chair back, and moved away from him slowly, with the same elegance in her step that he had observed that first night in her office. She was wearing a thin cotton robe with a fringed sash and satin mules that slapped against the bottoms of her feet. Once in her room, she opened the lower drawer of her dresser and slipped the rings off her finger, letting them fall under a stack of sweaters, next to the gold star, the public acknowledgment of her husband's heroism that had hung so long in her window. Then she pushed aside the blinds and looked out at the orange border of the day, which was sinking behind the pear trees and her neighbor's mimosa. A squirrel, feeding on something in the grass, his tail held tightly to the curve of his back, rushed to the safety of a tree trunk as she lifted the window a little.

With a clearly articulated sigh, she turned to see Foley's picture; his signature and a message were in one corner, written with black ink over the sleeve of his military uniform. The photograph had been taken in England; he had sent it to her at Eastertime, four months before she had received the news of his death. She slowly removed it from its nest of a ruffled lace doily, folded the stand into the back of the frame, ran the doily over it, as if to dust it, and laid it face down in the same drawer in which she had placed the rings. Her lips moved slightly; she thought about the last time she had seen her husband, walking toward the car that waited for him, leaving her stunned and silent, standing in the doorway of a rented bed-room in Oklahoma.

From the kitchen, Hugh had heard her, heard the opening and shutting of a drawer, the raising of a window. When she returned, the rings had been removed, though the white marks from them were visible on her finger. He caught her by the arm, and his dark eyes flickered over her face, searching to find in it any sign of what she felt. But there was nothing, no message for him, and nothing of her thoughts about the man who had given her the rings. For a while, she was unable to look at him, and she answered his attempts at conversation softly and distractedly. She seemed disturbed rather than angry; her mood worried him, and he feared its implications.

Hugh bought the land he wanted, and though, at her sug-gestion, he had made a handshake deal agreeing to pay $48.50 an acre over five years, after talking to Clarence, he went back and offered $45, all cash, and it was accepted; and Elaine received her four percent. He would clear part of the property, sell off a portion of the hardwood to pay for the fencing, have the hunting camp constructed, and build the deer blinds him-self—platforms in the limbs of the great oak trees, just off the clearings.

Chapter 2

HUGH'S CAR MADE its way with difficulty under the ragged hutch of cedars. Limbs scratched at the hood, and small branches scraped at the fenders. As the wheels bounced in and out of the dry ruts, pulling the car through the tunnel toward a clearing, a trumpet vine caught on the windshield, held an instant, then snapped and retreated, its red flowers splattering against a wall of yaupon. At the base of the clearing, behind the forked trunk of a hickory, was an unpainted shack, surrounded by a wire and pine board fence. Hugh drove to the front of it, turning sharply to miss a pump and wash tub, and pulled up before a small, solid gate of cedar strips and plywood. On the porch, a rabbit, so recently skinned that it shone like a fish, hung from a plow hook. In the peculiar light, a mixture of dusk and intense shade, the carcass no longer resembled the animal's body. It was a big rabbit, close to seven pounds skinned and dressed; a pearl of blood gleamed on the raw neck, where it had been shot with a .22.

Behind the man who had come out on the porch, a baby girl toddled in a trailing cotton gown; when she tried to grab the hand that swung empty, she was snatched back by the thin arm of a woman whose face stayed out of sight. There was a swift howl of infant anger, and then silence, except for the cawing of grackles, the call of a mockingbird, and the hollow sound of the man's feet on the warped treads of the porch stairs. The man wore overalls without a shirt and unlaced boots without socks. He looked scarcely older than Hugh, but he was twenty-eight; he had been married a dozen years; and he had

111

served his country for the duration of the war. His skin was the color of wet sand; his frame was delicate for his extreme height; and his hair was cut close to his head. Since his mother had been twelve years old, she had cleaned and washed houses in Dansville. His father owned a good farm near Garwood, but he had never done anything for this son or for the woman who had given him birth.

"What kind, Jake?" Hugh asked him, when he had come up to the car and nervously pushed the package inside.

"Walker's . . . and it's good . . . some of what they hold back."

Hugh had his arm around Elaine; she had stayed close beside him, the side of her body touching him from the shoulder down. He motioned toward the rabbit. "You going to sell me that, too?" He turned to Elaine. "You know how to cook it?" She nodded. She and her mother had prepared rabbit at the farm, letting it marinate for days, then making a rich, sour stew, heavy with herbs. Foley had liked it and so had her brothers.

"No, sir," said Jake nervously. "That's my wife's. I can't shoot enough . . . I got a trap, too."

"You have a baby coming for Christmas, Jake?"

He shook his head. "November."

"You've got four. What the hell? Aren't they enough?"

When Jake smiled, his eyes nearly disappeared between his high cheekbones and the strong ledges of his forehead. "I got five," he said. "I'll be all right so long as they don't start selling whiskey in town. We gotta keep it that way, Mr. Hugh."

"I don't mind, except getting down here tears all hell out of my car."

Elaine had never been to Jake's farm before, but she knew him. Foley had lent him money once, and when Jake was unable to pay it back, he let it go. Elaine had suggested letting him work it off. "He's working an eighteen-hour day now," Foley had told her. "What could he do for me in the other six?" Then Foley had gone to talk to Jake's father, not to get his money back but to convince him to help Jake, or at least to let Jake and his family join him on his farm; but it did no good—the man had been loading a hay wagon, and during most of the interview, Foley had been talking to his back. *Even Foley*, Elaine had thought, *not even Foley could work that*. Whenever she saw Jake in town now, he apologized for his debt. He would take off his straw hat, brace himself against a railing or against the wall of a store, and begin talking fast,

running all his words together, as if he thought by doing that
he could conjure up the money and ease his mind. She had
told him to forget about it; his farm, less than fifty acres, was
on the wrong side of the river, so that while he could sometimes stay even, he could never get ahead.

Jake stooped to see inside the car. "Hello, Miss Elaine," he
said.

Elaine peered forward, stretched out her hand, and shook his.
"Hello, Jake," she said softly.

Hugh handed him three one-dollar bills. Jake pushed them in
his shirt pocket, uncounted, and then turned around and went
inside. The car pulled away from the shack, casting loose earth
and sticks away from its wheels.

"I'll carry the bottle inside the hall," Elaine said. "If I have it,
they—"

"You just open it."

"Don't get us in trouble, Hugh."

He maneuvered the car through the narrow tunnel. "I won't."

She unwrapped the newspaper from the bottle and wadded it
under the seat. She tried the cap, squeezing hard; when she
made a wincing sound, he stopped the car and took it from
her. The blended smell, the harsh sweetness, entered the car
and filled it. He took a deep, noisy swallow and pushed the
bottle at Elaine. She shook her head, and after turning the
liquor up to drink, he handed it back to her. "You going to
want any more?" she asked.

"No," he answered, moving the car off the side of the road.

She capped the bottle, slipped it beside her on the seat, and
put her head on his shoulder. He steered with one hand, hook-
ing his wrist over the centerpiece of the wheel; he kissed her
mouth quickly, yet so effectively that she drew her hand over
his chest and turned to him to bury her head against the side of
his neck.

"You want to go to this dance or not?" he asked her; and his
free hand, as if repeating the question, tightened on the back of
her neck. Acting then on his own preference, he stopped the car,
pulled up the brake, and gathered her to him. He moved across
the seat, turned her around to face him, kissed her, and put his
hands beneath her clothes.

At once, she shifted her weight away from him, and she told
him to leave her alone. She pushed at him, ducked her face into
his neck, and tried to loosen his grip. Then, with her cheek
against his, she smiled at this encroachment on her will, at her

weakness, and at her body's strong reaction to what he was beginning, this ceremony which had such a high rate of success with her that it appalled her reason. "Stop it, Hugh . . . come on . . . please don't . . . please . . ."

She complained strongly, struggled a little; and he let her move away. Her head fell back against the seat; she began straightening her clothes; but she was unhappy with the choice she had made, and underneath her sigh was an unmistakable disappointment. His eyes shifted back and forth over her face; he was still leaning over her; his amused expression suggested that he had only now discovered the wickedness of her nature, and that this had surprised him. "What do you want to do, Elaine . . . huh? What do you want, baby?" After a moment's pause, during which she refused either to look at him directly or to reply, he laughed and rubbed the side of his hand against her cheek. Laughing, he moved back to his place, reached down to release the brake, put the car in gear, and shoved the accelerator down close to the floorboard, the sole of his boot hitting it like a slap. The car leaped away from the cedar and jolted across the ditch, skidding on the clutch of vines that the tires were crushing. It jerked one last time in leaving the shoulder, then eased out onto the road, growing quiet and purring.

The sun had set, and the trees at the horizon were rimmed with gold. A gentle wind articulated the rows of dark-leafed cotton plants, above which hung a purple fringe that seemed to complete a landscape almost too rich in color and composition for nature alone to have invented. There was just enough light to provide a contrast between the rich black soil and the whiteness of the spreading bolls. The car flew smoothly over the shell topping; the county road had recently been graded, and the rain had been insufficient to start new potholes, or to cause the crumbling of the shell into the coarsely flowered ditches.

Hugh put his arm across Elaine's lap and pulled her close to him. "If that dress was any tighter, you couldn't get into it," he said.

She ran her hand along the inside of his leg. "I'd try."

"I'll bet you would." He pinched her; she cried out and pushed away from him; he caught her and kissed her again. "You're beautiful in green, Elaine."

"Redheads always look good in green."

"Not this good."

"Hadn't you better watch the road?"

"I thought you liked my watching you."

She pushed in the lighter, tapped a cigarette on the dashboard, and lit it. As she picked a thread of tobacco off the tip of her tongue with a red fingernail, he took the cigarette from her and kissed her hand. They shared the cigarette, talked through the smoke, their cheeks sometimes touching.

Hugh turned the car left on the main street, and the wheels bumped over the railroad tracks as they passed the train station. Weeds, stunted red oaks, and undernourished shrubbery were the only vegetation on this side of town. Street lights had never been installed here, and most of the shacks and cottages, scattered along streets that were more like paths than roads, lacked electricity; except for the headlights of the cars, the lanterns on the dance hall porch, and the boys twirling flashlights to show the people coming to the dance where to park, the countryside was dark.

The dance hall was a structure with a vaulted ceiling where cotton, waiting to be taken to New Hampshire and Vermont to the textile mills, used to be stored. But cotton remained in the state now—it went to Dallas in trucks that picked up the bales at the gin on the river—so the city council had had the storehouse rehabilitated for social events and revivals.

Hugh pulled his Chrysler beside a pickup truck, slammed his door, and went around the car to get Elaine. It was a warm, humid Saturday in early August, one of those nights in which the air around a country dance hall is thick with cigarette smoke, mosquitoes, and music. Once every two weeks, all summer long, the old building, red now with shiny black trim and reeking of alcohol and perfume, trembled beneath the drums and guitars and the heels of dancers. In the open anterooms, people milled around; on the porch, they paced restlessly, looking for something special to happen.

As Hugh ushered Elaine into the hall, he kept his hand on her arm and his eyes straight ahead, as if he were handling a thoroughbred mare, having to guide her only ever so slightly, since she was not only exquisite but well trained. He hardly spoke to his friends and tried unsuccessfully to contain a smile. It amazed him still that Elaine was available to him, that she had recalled her womanhood in response to his insistent affection. Before he had met her, Hugh had been the kind of young male who had mused with his friends and shaken his head at the predicament of women, knowing that, one day, he was going to be the more fortunate half of a union in which it would be his duty to balance out the ledger by keeping the woman happy and creating the illusion that their positions were equal. Most women were slothful, stupid, and weak, he had thought; the few who were smart were cunning. All of them spent their time waiting for a man, who, because of the Achilles heel of his sexuality, would have to take her on, take from her father's house to his own. But Elaine did not fit this characterization; Hugh, in response, had forgotten the role he was supposed to assume. The acquisition of Elaine had increased his self-esteem. He swaggered; he was likely to be boastful. But anyone misunderstanding his pride, or thinking that he was too inexperienced and too inexpert to defend what was his; anyone who underestimated his temper and volatility put himself at risk. Halfway through a bottle of whiskey, Hugh thought himself invincible.

And why would he react differently? He had had neither the guidance of parents nor the chastisement and occasional humiliation from siblings to check his insolence and shape his behavior. As smart as he was, and as well educated, as much as he had memorized and parroted the classics, as civilizing as his education had been, as perfectly as he understood the teachings of outcasts, geniuses, heroes, martyrs, misfits, and saints, he still had a poor understanding of altruism—at least, in so far as it pertained to him. He had been neglected by his mother, and taught to be selfish by a father who idealized him but who gave his less of his time than he would ever have given to even the most minor financial involvement in a drilling venture or the purchase of securities. Hugh had nonetheless learned a lot by observing Clarence, but it was the devitalized education a student receives from the back of a huge lecture hall, where the view of the teacher is always obstructed by other people, and there is never a chance for questions or discussion. He admired and emulated what he thought to be the true image of his father—the tough, hard, uncompromising, successful, work-driven man— but he did not know him. Hugh had many of the qualities and the foibles of his father, the obsessive energy and occasional cruelty, and all were heightened by the circumstances of his indulgent, aristocratic upbringing. He had the royal demeanor of a prince, with all the outward arrogance and inner confusion of that station, and he would sometimes ravage in order to succeed like one.

His taking of Elaine, his increasing insistence on her subservience, and his failure to underwrite her future emotional protection were in keeping with that arrogance. His demand that she remove her wedding rings had been only the first of many; but he was fortunate to have in Elaine a lover who saw unsentimentally that his despotism, if it could not be successfully challenged, was, on the whole, benign. She had seen this clearly about a month after his success with her in Abbot Greeley's woods, when already he was spending fewer and fewer nights at the ranch, but before it was clear to anyone, except to Hugh himself, that, in fact, he had changed his summer headquarters of the last dozen years, and had moved in with her.

"You can't stay here," she had said. She had been on her front porch watching him unload the ranch pickup. "People will . . . Hugh, I can't possibly live in this town if . . . Jimmy is coming home!"

A cigarette hung in his mouth, the smoke of it bluer than the hot sky which boiled up behind him, pale with clouds that looked as if the ripe cotton bolls in the fields beneath them had floated up and swelled. "I'll take care of what people say," he said. "And I won't bite Jimmy. You know what kind of teeth I have." He showed them. Then he kissed her quickly, absently; and later, as he passed her with an armload of things, he looked at her in such a way as to make it immediately clear that the matter of his staying or leaving was up to him, and that it would go better unmentioned, not, she realized, because he was tyrannical or unreasonable but because he would have been unable to bear the humiliation and disappointment of being turned away—nor could Elaine have borne to see that happen. So she neither helped him nor hindered him but simply observed his work with an uneasy anticipation from her place on the porch; watched this very young man, who, after having taken over her heart, was taking over her home as well.

"You won't live with me in the big house," he said. "So that's okay, Elaine; I'll live here. Want me to make your mortgage payments?"

She laughed. "That's safe. You know my house is paid for."

"How do I know?"

Her eyes slanted upward toward his, and her face lifted softly into the smile that would stay with her for most of the rest of the day. "I told you."

"I forgot."

When he had finished unpacking and had put things in place, he called her inside, and she found him lying on top of her bed on the tufted, pearl-white satin spread, his ankles crossed, his mouth open a little, his eyes gazing through her, his hands behind his head on her silk and lace pillow, his fingers lost in the abundance of his black hair; and when she moved toward him, in the direction of his coaxing voice, he held out his arms to her and began to speak to her with that incredible sweetness that he reserved unashamedly for those times when he wanted her.

Hugh was good to Elaine. In that little white house on the outskirts of Dansville, he was amazingly gentle. But the better he was with her, the more he gave himself up to their relationship, the worse he was with everyone else. Matt had warned him of this, but he had shrugged, dismissed it, and gone on his way. When it came to Elaine, he was deaf to Matt, or to anyone, so that on that hot August night, so early in his life with her, when he could hardly be in her presence for more than a few minutes without giving her signs and indications that he needed to take her to bed, there was not a thing in the world that could have made him either give her up or share her.

They had chosen a table away from the band and two deep from the dance floor. The hall was cool and dark inside; sawdust covered the floor; the peak of the ceiling disappeared under the shadows that the rafters made. In the corner of the room, a big, square dais, decorated with lanterns and twisted streamers of crepe paper, held the musicians. A girl in a tinsel dress, floor-length and decorated around the neckline with fringes, stepped onto the stage and gripped the stem of a microphone. Frightened at first, she looked out at the crowd with a hard, challenging stare, but after she got out the first few phrases, her face flooded with warmth and her voice became huge, jerking at the vowels when the lyrics turned sad, so that they came out like sobs. As she finished each song, the crowd clapped wildly, called out her name, and shouted their approval.

Whatever the dance—polka, waltz, or two-step—couples on the floor moved in the same direction. Some of them swayed close together, locking arms and fingers; others danced wildly, pumping their arms, swinging in twists and half-circles, feeling agile, strong, even talented. It was a vigorous exercise, and they were proud of their body's part in it.

Elaine loved this place, she was enjoying the party, and she wanted Hugh to take her out on the dance floor almost every time. Each song seemed her favorite. "Oh, we have to dance to that," she would say; or, "I love that one. . . . Yes, that's the

one I remember." Her arms went around him, her cheek
pressed against his face; sometimes she turned her mouth to
his, anticipating or requiring his kiss. She gave him all her
attention; she flirted with him; she drank her beer out of the
bottle, holding it by the neck. It was rare for her to drink at
all, but this night, the delight of the festivities, the pleasure of
going out for the first time since her husband's death, made the
occasion an exception. There could be no doubt in the mind of
anyone who had observed them for that first hour that Elaine
was in love with Hugh, that she was sleeping with him, and
that she had allowed him to take Foley's place. From time to
time one of the men, a friend of Hugh's or one of the Littleton
ranch hands, stopped to talk to them, or to sit down for a
moment at Hugh's nod; but the women, timid, fearful, or critical, stayed away.

For Elaine to appear with Hugh in town at a public gathering, particularly a social one, was a mistake. She knew it even
before she raised her foot to the first step of the dance hall
porch, and certainly it came to her plainly when she saw the
amazed glances of people she knew, people with whom she had
conducted business. But her relationship to them was clearly
different now, and she was convinced that had she looked in a
mirror at that moment, she would have seen a different face,
just as they seemed to. *It's because of Hugh*, she thought,
*because he's so young, and they think he's wild, and because
he isn't really a part of this town*—and she wondered if anyone who had known Foley would ever forgive her, or if she
would ever forgive herself.

"Maybe we shouldn't be here," she said to him sadly when the
band had left for a break. "Maybe we'd better go. I—"

"To hell with it."

"I mean it."

"Good God, baby." Pleased to exaggerate their intimacy, he
pulled her closer to him. "We can go where we like. I don't give
a damn what people think."

As they moved through the hall, she avoided whomever she
could, and spoke only to the people who faced her directly, a few
town mavericks whose approval or disapproval meant nothing to
her. She was glad, at last, to be in the safety of the dimness of the
table inside, to be able to hide from everyone who had known her
as Foley's wife; and when Hugh put his arm around her and drew
her, chair and all, close beside him, she was grateful to be able to
hide behind him as well.

But she had been content the first part of that night; after two beers in quick succession, she had forgotten everything except Hugh and the happiness that he gave her. When she went back out onto the dance floor, she moved on her high-heeled sandals with provocative extravagance. In every respect, her allure was enhanced by the man who had brought her, who smiled at her, who kept his arm around her, and who, from time to time, leaned over her and kissed her. The loose, unreserved way in which she danced, her noisy laughter and conversation, did not trouble him. If she was showing off, it was for him; her gaiety was aimed at him, to evoke his response and no one else's, and he knew it. As far as he was concerned, she was having fun and she could do as she pleased. But it was folly for Elaine, who, because she was a stranger to the situation she had made for herself, was acting dangerously outside the framework of her temperament.

Only beer was served in the dance hall, but Hugh had his bottle of whiskey, which, since their arrival, he had been drinking steadily. Elaine wanted to speak to him about it; she thought that she should; but she feared spoiling the moment by intruding upon it. They were having fun; nothing was serious; they could be selfish. The strength of their union insulated them from criticism.

When the band began to play a song to which neither of them cared to dance, Hugh got up to go across the street for cigarettes. She watched him break through the crowd. He was beautiful, she thought: his broad back, his shoulders heavy under the white cloth of his shirt, the wealth of black hair. Near the door he stopped to talk to someone, a man his age; laughing, he shook his head, motioned back toward her, and went on. It was hot in the room now. Elaine held the whiskey glass against her cheek to cool it. She sat there alone, smiling, smoking what was left of their last cigarette, focusing her mind on erotic reminiscences of the past month, letting it wander unhindered through the rich scenery of that territory.

Across the dance floor, a man who had just arrived took off his hat, greeted a few friends, and looked around for people he knew. A group of men invited him to join them; they cleared a space; one of them got him a chair. After sitting down, he motioned for a waitress to bring him a beer, and then he began to listen to the usual exchanges of jokes, observations, and news. He might have sat there all evening, smoking, talking to these men with whom he worked during the week; he might have had

an uneventful but pleasant time had the man on his right not
pointed out to him that the woman whom he had had on his mind
all that summer, and whom he had yet to find a way to attract,
was in the room, and for the moment, alone. He turned his head
in the direction the man's finger was pointing, immediately wondering what had brought her out of her mourning. Attentively he
watched the side of her beautiful face, the bands of light on her
crossed legs, and the occasional movement of her graceful hands.
When someone stepped between him and this vision, he stood up
and broke away from the group, bought two beers, and moved
toward her.

"You with someone?" he asked. He handed her a beer.

"Yes," she answered; and after a pause, she told him who.
The happiness she felt carried over in her tone of voice, and
Gerdine misinterpreted her elation. She seemed glad to see him;
she was different, and he felt encouraged. Instantly his manner
became relaxed and confident, and he forgave her for past injuries.

"Aren't you robbing the cradle?" he asked. He put down his
beer and leaned toward her, his hands on the back of the chair
where Hugh had been sitting.

"He doesn't mind."

"I'm sure he doesn't." His voice was thick and happy, and
when he asked her to dance, she nodded.

Gerdine Bowen had been trying to court Elaine Menutis
ever since a Sunday, three months before, when he had been
eating a plate lunch in the drugstore on the courthouse square
and had seen her crossing the street in a jersey dress. The day
had been windy, and the skirt had clung to her legs, so tightly
that she might as well have just come out of the Colorado
River, soaking wet. That image had startled and amazed him;
and it had filled him with a welcome kind of expectant dread,
which he had experienced only a few other times in his life,
and not at all since his divorce two years back, at the end of
the war, when he had come home, weary, disillusioned, and
changed.

He had asked Darrell Tarpley about her: "She married?" The
druggist's face was deeply lined, and his mustache was badly
cropped. His eyes were watery, like those of a man who drinks
too much, although Darrell didn't touch liquor: Three years before, his youngest son—so young, in fact, that he had had to lie
about his age and enlist in Canada—had been reported missing in
a plane over the Aleutians. "The worst is not knowing," he said

to friends. "My wife runs to that phone every time it rings, and then she whimpers like a hurt dog when it's nothing about Ross. Every time she sees one of his friends from high school, she invites them in to talk about him, but those kids want to go about their business. For the ones that came home, it's over." He moved slowly, and his hand trembled a little when he handled things. After he had run up Gerdine's bill on the register, he said, "She was married."

"Her husband get killed?"

"That's right."

"Pacific?"

"France."

Gerdine took a toothpick out of a glass and held it loosely between his teeth. "Damn shame to have to leave a woman like that."

"Maybe." Watching Gerdine, Darrell moved his fingers slowly through the drawer, picking up change and letting it fall. "Worse shame never to have had her."

Gerdine folded his wallet and pushed it into his back pocket. "She go to church?"

Darrell nodded.

The following week, Gerdine had gone to the big all-brick Baptist church, with its rose garden running along the side, and its six privet bushes sculpted in the shapes of flower baskets with hoops for handles. After Sunday school and the pot luck lunch in the basement recreation room, he had driven Elaine home. As they were going up to her porch, he had tried unsuccessfully to take her hand. Afterward, when he had both telephoned her and stopped in at her office, he had received the same polite, brisk, negative response that she gave to everyone, the same indifferent courtesy: She had to work, she was tired, she had other plans.

Yet now she agreed to dance with him, and saw no harm in doing so; in fact, the invitation pleased her. It would be all right to have Hugh come back in and see her with someone else. Perfectly sober, she would never have considered responding to the attentions of another man or, at least, would certainly have been more circumspect. But she was giddy with what she had drunk, and she had lost any benevolent impulse that might have checked her inclination to irritate the man she loved with the idea of a rival.

As she accepted the hand that Gerdine offered to take her onto the dance floor, Hugh returned, easing his way through the crowd, drawing a cigarette from the package he had just bought, stopping to scratch a match on the underside of a table. As his head lifted, he squinted through the smoke at what he could see of Elaine, now almost entirely hidden by the dancers. He left the cigarette in the corner of his mouth and proceeded to the table, where he slid low in his chair, sprawled his legs to the side, and began to do what he had never in this world expected to be doing that night: watch dancing with another man the woman in whose bed he had spent the better part of the afternoon.

Matt Kirkland and Luther Kelly had been keeping an eye on Hugh all evening, both what he did and what he was drinking, and they could see him now through the spaces between the tables. Matt had nudged Luther when Gerdine had approached Elaine, each of them aware that their vigilance would be required. Matt rolled a cigarette, and a man from behind him lit it; he nodded his gratitude, but didn't turn around. He finished his beer, pointed at the empty bottle, and the waitress quickly replaced it.

Surrendering to the heat, Luther rolled up his sleeves and ordered a Coke, flipping a dime on top of Matt's fifty-cent piece. With his calm, sure eyes—the best shade of blue to reflect that condition—he watched Elaine. Luther had rough features, rough even for the kind of man he was, the work he did, and the life he had known. His muscles were as tight as ropes dragging a wagon uphill; there was no unessential flesh on him, and there was never a word in his mouth that need not be said. He was extraordinarily cautious, as thorough and as conscious of detail as a cavalry officer taking his company through Indian country, and famous for his patience. Already, at thirty-one, he knew that what he needed to do was not so much to attend to the world outside as to watch what was going on within himself. For an instant his expression turned inward to do just that.

Matt had kept his eyes steady on the situation before him. "Well, there it is," he said.

Luther answered quietly. "Gerdine's crazy."

"Maybe he just don't know Hugh."

They knew now that they would have to wait to see the drama played out, that they would undoubtedly have some part in it. Hugh was sure to insult Gerdine when he brought Elaine back. He was certain to say something that a man like Gerdine would be unable to let go by. Gerdine was a supervisor for an oil company with headquarters in Danciger; his job was a coveted one; he made good money; he drove a new Pontiac; and he was unlikely to give up Elaine if she gave him any encouragement at all. Dancing with him might be enough.

"Gerdine ain't no lily-white," Luther was saying. "And he's near about as big as Hugh."

"Yeah," said Matt, "but he ain't going to get that mad."

Gerdine was an honest suitor; a little drunk, so more honest yet. He had heard about this thing with Hugh, but he did not believe it. Hugh Littleton was too young for Mrs. Menutis. It was ridiculous. If she was willing to dance with him, to let him get near her, there was no reason to be cautious, not with a rich, spoiled youngster as her sole guardian. He figured that she was probably easing herself into the world again by choosing someone innocuous. He would be glad to take her off Hugh's hands, and as they danced to the easy rhythms of a slow waltz, he began to tell her so.

When Hugh lost sight of Elaine, he shrugged. In a euphoric state because of the alcohol and the loud and insistent rhythms of the country music, he had let himself sink into a luxurious and sensual hiatus, in which he meant to linger. He was not troubled. Let her dance. He raised his eyes to the lights on the ceiling, pale sulfurous blushes that barely illuminated the tables, and then looked around at the crowd. The candlelight rose and fell on Hugh's face, a throbbing illumination that high-lighted his fine eyes and the chiseled, hard aspects of his young face, changing continually the hollows and the ridges, so that he looked cast out of many molds, each more interesting than the last, all of them enduring prototypes of masculine excellence. Now and then he caught a glimpse of Elaine across the room; waited alertly for her to return to his vision as a sentry at a post monitors passersby who are unarmed and probably innocent, but who must be kept under surveillance all the same. Except for a thickness in his throat and a slight pain between his eyes, he was untroubled; he recognized the achievement in his composure, and he took pride in it. That devil Matt was in the corner with Luther, watching him. He would see this. He would think that Hugh couldn't handle it. Hugh would prove him wrong.

Yet when she stayed on the dance floor, disappearing once more behind the screen of couples as the band took up a new song, he drew his feet under him, sat up straighter, and leaned forward. His eyes lost their dreaminess, his mouth tensed, and

the skin of his face seemed to have tightened. Soon he poured the
last of the whiskey out of the pint bottle, half a glassful, and,
after a burning swallow, returned the glass to the table with so
much noise that it surprised him. There was no waitress in sight,
so he got up and went toward the brightness of the cut-out bar
window and bought himself a beer. On his way back to the table,
Matt reached out and grabbed his arm. "Who's going to drive you
home, Hugh?"

"You can, Matt. I'll let you know when I'm ready." He jerked
away from Matt's grip more easily than Matt expected and was
about to walk off when he stopped to glance at Luther. "Where's
your wife?" he asked. "You leave Lettie at home?"

"That's right."

"How come? She doesn't like parties?"

"She can't come out like she is, Hugh. You seen her?"

Lettie Kelly was pregnant. Luther no longer permitted her to
go into town to shop, and if she went in with one of the other
women, just for the ride, she would have to wait in the truck,
fanning herself with a piece of cardboard and wiping her face
with one of the white handkerchiefs that Opal Rude had taught
her how to embroider. The only place she could show herself
now was in church or Sunday school, and even then, it had to be
close on Luther's arm.

Hugh shook his head and smiled. "That's old fashioned,
buddy."

For a moment, Luther stared hard at Hugh. In general, his
temper was even: In fifteen years only one thing in the world had
ever seriously undermined his tranquility (even when he broke
both his legs, he attributed it to the will of God), and right now,
his boss's son was touching on it. "It don't have anything to do
with fashion, Hugh."

Hugh drank from his beer bottle, swallowed fast, drawing in
his lips. "She mind being left?"

"It don't matter what she minds." His expression stayed
steady, and so did his tone of voice. He had been sitting on the
edge of a table, but he was standing now.

"You decide, huh?"

"That's it."

Hugh laughed. "With her, that's not always easy."

Luther smiled, wide and pleasant; and as he might have said
himself, it didn't put him out none to do so. "No, it ain't," he
agreed. Luther liked Hugh, and although he didn't always understand him in the way that Matt did, he could appreciate any man

who was neither lazy, thick in his thinking, nor weak. And as for passing judgment on Hugh's relationship with Mrs. Menutis, his religion taught him not to pass judgment on anyone, and his past reminded him why.

Hugh nodded and, turning into the crowd, left them. Luther set down his empty Coke bottle and, after seeing that the boy had made his way back to his table without incident, observed to Matt, "At least Hugh ain't butting in on the dance floor. He's quiet now."

"It ain't going to last. If they stay out there too long, he's going to stop it; if Gerdine brings her back right now, he's gonna insult him. Watch it, kid. I guarantee you that you and me are going to come out of this bruised and hurting. And you might keep your eye on that slick-haired bastard, Lonnie Teague. If Hugh messes up this place tonight, Lonnie's going to peel the skin off my ass."

Lonnie Teague was the sheriff and, right now, he was sitting in a corner, behind a full bottle of Mexican beer. His black shirt and dark trousers pulled tight over the bulges in his oversized limbs. On his hip, in a holster so black that it looked greased, he wore a blued .38 Special. His hat lay on the table directly across from him, placed there to keep anyone from sitting down. When he was working, Lonnie avoided company, and he was always working on Saturday night.

The volume of the music was increasing; the hall was near full; people with young children began to talk about going home. Hugh slouched in his chair and straightened his legs, blocking the passage between his neighbor's table and his own. His arms were folded over his chest, his chin was raised, and his eyes roamed the crowd. His black head yielded to the darkness behind him, and the shadows of the dancers wavered continually over his outstretched, yet uneasy form. Someone behind him said Elaine's name, and he thought he heard a laugh. He turned quickly and, when he was unable to determine who had been responsible, had to fight back his irritation.

Two friends came to talk to him, but he dismissed them with a few absent words and then went back to watching for Elaine. He hated her now; she had hurt him; she had chosen to be away from him. All the sweet things she had done for him and said to him over the past month fled from his mind. As soon as she came back, he meant to take her out of the hall, and though he was too angry to imagine what he was going to do to her, he knew that she was going to see that temper which he had held away from her this long and with such incessant discipline.

His wave of fury did not last; like a boat coming about in the wind, it changed its objective when he caught sight of her at the edge of the crowd. Gerdine's hand had slipped down low on her hip, and he pulled her up against him. She turned to come back to the table, and Gerdine, following her, said something to her. Close to the table, within a yard of where Hugh was sitting, Gerdine took her chin in his hand to turn her face toward his. He was the type of man so unaware of the nature of women, so ill-suited for a complementary relationship with one, so oblivious to the occult system of attraction that determines the pairing off of individuals that he had failed to recognize the signals of her refusal at any level of his interest: Not only was he telling her that he was going to take her home, but he had even begun to stroke the side of her body.

As dangerous as was the instant collapse of Hugh's underexercised self-control at seeing a man lay claim to a woman whom he believed to be his, it was finally, more actually, Elaine's expression—her discomfort, confusion, and helplessness, heightened by the feminine error of trying to remain polite even when she was being taken advantage of (a practice that her upbringing had relentlessly encouraged)—that made Hugh stand up, push her out of the way without looking at her, and reach across the table and backhand Gerdine. The blow caught him on the cheek and spun him across to another table, where he fell over a chair, crushing its back.

The crowd reacted at once. Most of the women shrank back, some of them screaming. Many of the men, hoping to get involved, closed in. Gerdine would have been willing and ready to argue with Hugh, even to fight him over Elaine—fights over women occurred frequently on these Saturday nights—but the viciousness of the attack, out of proportion to his own assessment of the insult, caught him off guard. Wideeyed and blank of expression, like a rodent who has found the fox in a territory he presumed safe, Gerdine stared through his disheveled hair, fixing his attention on Hugh. His mouth was slack, and he shuddered in acknowledgment of the power in the hand that had burned into his face. He recovered himself, staggered briefly, bumped against the corner of a table hard enough to push it several feet, and then whirled around on Hugh with his right arm ready. Hugh ducked; the blow caught his face, slinging him backward, but he was able to shoot up his fist from waist level to catch Gerdine under the point of his jaw. Bottles and glasses shattered; the back of another chair splintered. Gerdine whirled, but before he could fall, Hugh, yelling for Elaine to get away from him (for an instant both her hands clutched the back of his shirt), grabbed him by the collar, jerked him upward, slammed down the arm that was rising to strike, and hit him again.

For an instant, the two men locked. When Gerdine fell, Hugh went down with him, straddling the side of the struggling man, turning him on his back and pounding him until he felt a bone in his right hand break; after letting out a yelp of agony—at the same time that Gerdine was reaching up for his neck to choke him—he switched to the left.

Luther finally managed to push his way through the crowd and come after Hugh from behind to grab his arms. Hugh shook himself free; then Matt, the only man in the room ever as vicious as his protégé, caught him around the chest, lifted him off Gerdine, and flung him sideways. Luther held on to him and raised him, pinning his arms. Matt yelled out to Jeffrey Mattox, a man who worked in the courthouse as court reporter for the circuit, and with whom he occasionally played cards: "Get Mrs. Menutis out of here, Jeff! You take her home and you see she stays!"

Furious at Matt's command—it was, after all, for Elaine that he had broken his hand on Gerdine—Hugh got clear of Luther, but Luther quickly grabbed him, and Matt slapped him so hard against the side of the head that for about five seconds, he was blinded. He could hear the beat of his heart; his knees were weak; blood streamed from his nose. He ducked his head and cried out in pain, struggling wildly against Luther.

"You just don't know when to quit, do you, kid?" Matt yelled, and when Hugh lifted himself for a new effort, he reached up to hit him again, this time slapping him just enough to sting him— what he would do to a bad child. Matt's efforts were directed half at keeping Hugh from killing Gerdine, and half at preempting Lonnie Teague.

Hugh struggled to turn toward Gerdine, who, at the sheriff's instructions, was being carried through the crowd and out of the hall. "You gone crazy, Matt? If you want to fight, hit that bastard!"

"You just done that, Hugh. You didn't leave me nothing."

Hugh tried to break Luther's lock on his arms, and would

have, except that Matt slapped him again. "You stay still, or I'll hit you a lot different."

"I'm going to break your goddammed neck!"

"Not unless you can bust loose from Luther." Matt was trembling from the exertion; the shirt that he had ironed that afternoon with such painful care was ruined, ripped out at the shoulder seam and soaked through with sweat.

A few years earlier, when they would wrestle on the cookhouse lawn, and Matt would get Hugh's shoulders pinned, Hugh would curse him with such hatred that Matt would end up by slapping him to teach him the difference between a game and a fight. Showing the same fury that he had always shown when he had lost a match on the grass, Hugh pulled his left hand free and nearly struck Matt; but Matt caught his arm as he lifted it and hit him with his fist. Matt grabbed one arm, Luther, the other, and with the crowd opening up before Matt's obscene admonitions, they dragged him outside, across the porch, and down the stairs, and shoved him into the truck cab between them while Matt yelled apologies back over his shoulder to Lonnie.

Lonnie wanted to arrest Hugh on the spot—assault and battery, disturbing the peace, and the illegal consumption of alcohol by a minor. "Give him to me, Matt!" he roared. "I warned you last summer, if you let that maniac loose again, I'd nail him."

Matt slammed the truck door and leaned out the window. "Hey, Lonnie . . ." He argued and made promises, as much for Hugh and Clarence as for himself.

"I'll be in to see you, Lonnie," Matt said.

Lonnie stretched his short arms toward the truck. "Give him to me, Matthew. He's mine."

"He won't go nowhere; I'll see to it. And I'll be in tomorrow."

Back in the hall, the volume of cursing and shouting rose, and Matt realized gratefully that another fight, set off by Hugh's, had probably started. Lonnie turned toward the hall and then looked through the truck window at Matt, his words shooting out like a link of firecrackers. "Tomorrow, I'm taking Mrs. Teague and my boys to church, Matt; but I'll tell you what you're going to do. You're going to be in my office first thing Monday morning, listening to my personal philosophy. Until then, you keep that bastard out of Dansville. You hear me good? I see him and that great big Chrysler on one of our pretty, shaded avenues, and I swear to God I'll lock him up and impound his goddamn car!" He narrowed his eyes. "One thing more, Matt: On your way over, you can stop by for Mrs. Menutis. There're some questions above and beyond this evening I'd like to ask her. . . . She buy him that whiskey, or was it you?"

In the sudden blaze of light—one of the children responsible for guarding the cars was shining a flashlight in his face—Matt had to shade his eyes. "Oh, no, Lonnie. Not her. You can't do that, buddy."

"I can do what I damn well please, Matt. You're just not aware of that yet. Somehow you think Clarence Littleton can buy you people out of this and every other damned thing, but I tell you, while I'm sheriff, he can't. Let's talk about Hinsley, or the other sheriffs this town's had. I'm ready, waiting, and willing. You start."

The frenzy in the dance hall was growing worse. "You'd better get in there, Lonnie," Matt said. "You're going to win the battle in this parking lot and lose the war. You forget there're some other adolescent killers in that room?"

Lonnie reached forward and pushed so hard on his hatbrim that his hat almost fell backward off his head. "You get smart-ass with me, Matt, and I'll lock you up too! Hear? You talk to me like that again, and I'll set your bail so high, it'll even make Clarence think twice about what you're worth."

"God Amighty, Lonnie . . ." Matt turned the key in the ignition and began to back away slowly. Lonnie followed after the truck, shouting oaths interpolated with orders and warnings, and when he had to turn his back on Matt in order to curse and quiet the small crowd that had gathered around him, Matt backed the truck jaggedly through an open space in the parked cars, slammed the gearshift down into first, and started home. Lonnie called after it, but the truck, boiling up dust, drowned out his shouts.

"Christ!" Matt had hit the railroad track too fast and had bumped his head on the ceiling of the truck cab. "It's Clarence or Lonnie, and I guess I got to choose Lonnie."

As the truck raced through the open land outside of town, Hugh groggily pulled himself up and demanded that he be dropped off at Elaine's. He cursed Matt for having interfered and for having hurt him, and he cursed Luther for having helped Matt. "Luther, you goddamn traitor. Why don't you think for yourself?"

"Matt and I think the same."

"The hell you do! Matt doesn't think. You ever see a cat pounce on a piece of string? That's Matt. Matt leaps like a tiger on any goddamned thing that moves."

Luther soaked the corner of his handkerchief in beer and began washing the blood off Hugh's face.

"That stings like hell."

"It's all I got."

Hugh closed his eyes, leaned his head back, and brushed vaguely at Luther's hand. "Leave me the hell alone."

"Stay still—don't make it no worse on yourself. You listening? You going to sleep?" Hugh's eyes were closing, and he jerked himself up, but gradually, as Luther continued to talk to him, his voice monotonous and calm, he relaxed against Luther's arm, until, heavy and limp, his weight on Luther's shoulder increasing, he fell asleep.

"He's got blood all over the front of his shirt, Matt." Luther spoke only loud enough to be heard over the wind and the pelting of the gravel under the fenders. "You think we should take him to Dr. Jackson? I wouldn't want no—"

"We got to get him the hell out of town. I don't need Lonnie changing his mind in no doctor's kitchen."

"I hope his face don't swell up. Clarence sees that—"

"Clarence sees nothing." Matt cursed and, without opening his teeth, spit tobacco juice out the window in a stringlike stream, wiping the corner of his mouth afterward with a brown-specked handkerchief that he kept stuffed between the dashboard and the windshield. "Better for him to look a little ugly than to be charged with attempted murder, and have Clarence yelling up there in Austin for extradition from Wharton County. Clarence don't care if he fights, just so he wins. If he gets hurt, so what? That teaches him something. Clarence is the smartest man I ever met, but he's got no sense about his family. It's nights like this I resent having to be responsible for his kid."

Feathery swirls of dry dirt spun behind the truck as it sped toward the Littleton ranch. The dome of the moonless sky was purple, almost black; the quartz planets shone steadily, as permanent in their places as shrines. Briefly illuminated trees rolled before the headlights like the unwinding of cloth; on the shoulder of the road, a cow jerked around and bolted at the sight of the speeding truck. When Hugh stirred and opened his eyes, Luther spoke to him softly: "You can sure be a nasty bastard. When you going to grow up, huh?"

Hugh turned his hurt head carefully. "Call off your dog, Matt. Get the hell off of me . . . both of you."

"Why?" said Matt. "So you can murder Gerdine and anyone else who bothers you and your—"

In spite of all his pain and the soporific effect of the alcohol and overspent adrenaline, Hugh's body stiffened dangerously, and he interrupted Matt quickly. "Look out, Matt! Stay off me! Not about her. I told you!"

Into the dark behind the spread of the headlights, Matt threw a spent wad of tobacco. It was hard to get an apology out of him, and when one was made, it was expressed less in his words than in the tone of his voice. "Okay, then, forget it. . . . Take it easy. Give me a cigarette, Luther. . . . Light it for me, huh?"

Hugh hunched his shoulders and lowered his head and soon began to relax. They passed a service station whose flashing neon sign was shy of two letters. In the picture window, a man in overalls frowned at a folded city newspaper in which he was working a crossword. Matt honked his horn twice. The man looked up and waved. A black dog, her hair erect along the center of her back, her throat contracted in rage, rushed into the swarm of dust in front of the pump and barked frantically at the blare of the horn and the vanishing twin insult of the taillights.

When Hugh was asleep again, Luther asked, "What in the hell makes him so mean?"

Matt shrugged. "He's got a woman loving him."

"Wouldn't you think that'd sweeten him? It did me."

Matt's eyes opened wide, and he threw a swift glance at Luther. "The hell it did! Don't you remember nothing, Luther?"

As they passed over a wooden bridge, the planks snapped like pistol shots. The water came alive under the fringe of the headlights, and Luther caught sight of a pair of coyotes running at a trot along the weed-shaggy bank. One of them, its eyes like nickels, looked back and shot the truck a glance of warning. "I still don't understand why Hugh done it," he said.

"He thinks he has to defend her."

"You think he's right?"

"It ain't no question of right."

"You'd have beat a man that bad?"

Matt looked up at the night as if he were remembering something. "I'd have killed him," he said.

Luther rubbed his hand against the slick door handle, his

amazement at Matt's vehemence showing clearly in the attitude of his tensed shoulders. "I couldn't hurt nobody that bad just for dancing."

"You don't dance, Luther."

"I used to."

Matt tossed the end of his cigarette out the window, watched the golden destruction of it as it splashed apart, and then laughed. "Yeah . . . well, you ain't sleeping with Mrs. Menutis."

"You ain't neither."

"Could be I imagine things stronger than you do, Luther."

Luther looked straight ahead. He had driven this route hundreds of times, but only once when he had been more acutely aware of every rut, every bump, anything at all that might be a source of annoyance or pain to the one who was riding beside him. The afternoon that he had found Lettie, he had brought her back on this road, slow and easy, praying not to hurt her any more than she was already hurt, nor by his carelessness or lack of attention to add to the agony she was already suffering. "I think I can probably match you for imagination, Matthew," he said.

Matt squinted his eyes, leaned forward a little, and flattened the gas pedal to the floor. A toy dog, a stiff rubber dalmatian hanging from the rear-view mirror, snapped to the left and then began a regular, jerking swing. Luther leaned across Hugh and turned on the radio. A man was singing a song about a girl angel in a honky-tonk café. The singer's voice broke with sadness at the inevitable faithlessness of cheap women. Softly, his lips hardly moving, Luther sang along with it.

When Matt came into the kitchen the following morning it was empty. He paced awhile, looking out the windows, listening for things, then sat down at the long eating table and opened a magazine; and when finally Opal Rude came in, he asked her to make him a pot of coffee. If Opal knew what had happened the night before, she kept it to herself, and when she handed him his coffee, she was careful not to interrupt his reading. As the ranch hands and their families began to enter the cookhouse, he was occupied and remote; if he replied to their greetings at all, it was perfunctorily. He kept his attention on the magazine, slowly turning the pages. It was only when he glimpsed Hugh's figure pass the window, moving quickly toward the trucks, that Matt grew alert, grabbing his toast and his mug of coffee and going outside, his steps deliberately taken.

As the screen door slammed behind him, one of the women complained, and under his breath, Matt cursed her. Lettie was the only woman on the ranch who would dare to criticize the way her husband's boss let go of a door. "Where you taking off to?" he asked Hugh, walking quickly to keep up with him.

"Elaine's." The dead white of the bandage shocked on the dark skin of Hugh's hand; a splint held two of his fingers. He kept moving toward the parking area without looking back at Matt, and he chose Matt's pickup. The tail gate of the truck was down, and he started to shut it.

"Don't take my truck," Matt said. "I need it. Take your car."

"You take the Jeep, Matt."

"No."

"Okay." He changed directions, but in doing so, he had to face Matt. The glance he received was harsh, and he had a difficult time steadying his eyes on the foreman. "You mad at me, buddy?"

"Not like you think." There was an edge to Matt's voice, and he was a little hoarse. "You go around the back way to Elaine's," he said. "Don't you think about going through the center of town. You take the back road. Stay out of Dansville and stay out of trouble."

"That's what I'm doing, Matt. I don't fight at Elaine's. You want to come along and see what I do?" Though it hurt his mouth, he grinned. "I sure as hell bet you would."

"Yeah, that's accurate. I really would. It's just in my line . . . except for one thing."

"What's that?"

"I'm too damned tired. I been up all night tending to your unfinished business." Matt waved the toast in the air to shake off a fly that had landed on the corner of it. It was deathly hot. The sun threw its golden shots through the ragged leaves and branches of the oaks; out in the pasture, near the canal, the wind lifted only small whirls of dust. "But, you know, one of these days, I'm not going to be around, and you're going to end up getting put in jail by Lonnie or some other jawbreaker who'd love to rough you up because of who you are and how you act. He's not a Mike Hinsley, Hugh. He don't sell." Hinsley had helped Clarence get rid of some undesirable neighbors—Clarence had considered them squatters, though most of the people around town had called them just folks who temporarily had no place to go. Clarence's move was unpopular, but Matt had to defend it, like he defended all of

Clarence's decisions, right or wrong. This one had lost him some friends.

"Probably not."

"Only the kind of man he is kept him from taking what was his last night: He knew what he wouldn't do to nobody else he shouldn't do to you, but he could have run you in. He's invited me to come see him Monday, and he's going to grill me good, and I don't relish it, not for something you done. You going to do anything about that temper of yours, kid? Having that woman ain't doing you no good, Hugh. When are you going to . . . ? Oh, hell. To hell with it."

Hugh turned back to him, his hand on the car door. A carpet of short brindle grass separated them, marred by a cattle path to the tank. "I'll go in Monday, Matt," he said, with the insufferable arrogance that Matt had been trying to work out of him for better than ten years. "I don't mind telling Lonnie what's on my mind."

Matt raised his voice and spoke fast. "I know you don't, Hugh. You don't mind nothing. You'll go in there and talk like a city boy, insult him, make him feel bad he ain't educated, give him some of your expert ideas about running this town, call him a stupid country bastard, and increase the trouble for every one of us."

Hugh looked down at the ground, his expression hidden in the shadow of his hat. He tapped the heel of one boot on the toe of the other. Behind him a pair of mockingbirds chattered in the willows; in the dry, powdery earth of the cattle path, a sparrow ruffled its feathers and fluttered its wings, as if it were bathing. Two girls, Mark and Opal's daughters, came out on the porch; the older one glanced quickly at Matt and Hugh, then nudged her sister sharply toward the path that led behind the house.

"I hope to hell she throws you out this morning," said Matt. "She got any sense, she will."

"Don't count on it."

"I'm so old I don't count on nothing."

Matt waited for a rejoinder, but none came. "Lonnie wanted me to bring in Elaine," he said. "I'm not going to have to do that, but she was with you, and theoretically you don't drink. You ain't old enough. You want her to have to go to Lonnie's and have him ask her about your living arrangements? I'll bet he's dying to rake her over the coals."

Although he hadn't meant to, Matt smiled; his arrow had

found its mark that time. He could tell by the shadow that crossed the boy's face that the idea of Elaine's going in to see Lonnie was intolerable to him, that he would protect her from that humiliation, and that he would go a long way to do it.

"People in town don't like it, Hugh. You can do what you please; you just visit Dansville when it appeals to you; you come around in good weather. But Elaine's had the respect of these people for years. They're her friends. They were her husband's friends. What the hell's going to happen to her when you leave her . . . because I imagine that's what you aim to do. Our fairest flower ain't going to be good enough for you one of these days, huh? Am I wrong? Ain't it true? Ain't you slumming?"

Hugh looked straight at him, neither averting his eyes nor showing any strong reaction. He was just tolerating Matt; Matt knew it, but he went on: "I know your staying around me and this ranch is kid stuff, and you're going to get over it; but what you're doing now, laying hold of a woman like that one, and busting into men who'd like to court her with the idea of giving her a home, ain't—You listening? You think Gerdine's a hick, but consider this, Hugh. He's one of them who would give his pay check to his wife just as quick as he gets it, take her to the movies on Saturday night, and to church on Sunday morning. He wouldn't never drink no hard liquor in her presence, and he'd give her something nice for her birthday without her having to jump through any hoops. He hadn't been in trouble of any kind here in town until he met you; and until last night, he would have been ready and willing to take care of that pretty widow in a way that just ain't never going to occur to no Littleton. You know what I'm saying? You got any idea at all what I'm talking about?"

Hugh was squinting his eyes though his back was to the sun. "What did you do for Gerdine?" he said. "Anything?"

"I'm surprised you asked." Matthew talked with his mouth full, the rest of his toast held carelessly at a slant. A spot of plum jam dropped onto the leaf of a cherry laurel to the left of the walkway. "Yeah, I did something after I got you quiet last night. I went back. They had to take him to the hospital, so I wrote him a check on your bank account."

"That's okay. How much?"

"Go to hell; I know it's okay. Two hundred."

"Good God, Matt, that's what the hospital charged?"

"Nope, they charged fifteen."

"Then why the two hundred?"

"To make Gerdine real happy, Hugh. I told him you were awful sorry about last night. I figured maybe that'd make him hate you less—he looked like hell—and decrease the possibility of him setting a trap for you and having Clarence kill me after your funeral. Anything happens to you while you're visiting down here, and I'm dead." He punched at his chest with the thumb of his free hand. "I don't care about you, I care about me! I'm so old your daddy'd probably fire me if I failed as a nurse-maid."

Hugh thumped on the brim of his hat to make it slip farther back on his head. Behind him, the willows shimmered gorgeously in a catch of the wind. "I didn't sign the check, Matt."

Matt finished his toast and set his coffee mug on a step. "Yeah, you did, Hugh. I'd forge any check of yours for your daddy." He closed his eyes partly and looked at Hugh obliquely, tilting his head to emphasize what he was about to say. "You strut around here long enough, making your debut as a stud, shacking yourself up with a respectable lady, coming down from the big city, or from that fancy school you go to, and whipping the residents, and you're going to get yourself gelded."

Hugh answered him quickly. "I'll tell you straight, Matt, something you seem to forget. Nobody's going to bother my girl. Not one of them is going to try pawing her, on or off a dance floor, or anywhere. That's the point I wanted to make, so when I'm not here this fall, everybody will remember it."

Matt watched him, knowing he was right: Whether he was in town or not, whether anyone knew where he was or not, as long as that affair was on, after last night, nobody would bother Elaine. Matt's face tightened into a smile, and two arc-shaped lines bit into his cheeks. "This ain't no summer romance, then? You didn't tell me."

Hugh kicked at something on the ground as if to loosen it. "I don't know what the hell it is."

Matt wanted to sit down with him then and listen; maybe there was something that he could say to ease things. The affair had to be broken off, he knew; but it didn't look like Hugh was going to be able to arrange that now, and to all appearances—her permitting him to move in with her, to take up every free moment of her time, and to squire her around town as if he owned her—neither was Elaine.

Hugh opened the car door. "Bye, Matt . . . and you can tell

Stephen that when my hand mends, I'm going to break it again on his jaw for the way he set it last night. Where the hell did he learn veterinary medicine?"

"The army."

"That figures."

Hugh turned back and rested his arms on the top of the car door. A wind rose into the lowest branches of the trees, a calf rustled through the shrubbery, and from the house came a woman's laughter. Matt turned his head as if he expected someone to come out on the porch, then quickly glanced back at Hugh and asked him the question he had wanted to ask ever since that afternoon when Hugh had grabbed a handful of steaks out of the freezer, gotten together some of his clothes, and not come home that night, or the one after. He tried to make it sound as if it had just come to mind, but the tone of his voice gave him away. "What are you paying Mrs. Menutis, Hugh? I ask myself what she's getting out of this romance with a kid ain't dry behind the ears yet and who can't even hold his goddamned temper. . . . That two hundred bucks I gave to Gerdine last night ain't nothing, is it? You must be emptying your pockets right smart."

Hugh reached into the car, picked up an empty beer bottle from the floor, and tossed it into the wire trash can next to the porch. As it exploded against another bottle, a young woman's face appeared at the window.

"Not yet . . . but I'm ready to."

Each knowing the question that Matt was prepared to ask next, but knowing equally that he couldn't ask it without creating a rift between them, the two men glared. Matt was the first to break into a smile, though Hugh followed an instant later. "What do you think, Matt?"

Matt's hands were low on his hips, and his shoulders, usually straight, were hunched a little. "I think you're going to hell, kid."

Hugh got into the car, rolled down the windows, and pulled away, leaving plumes of dust in his wake. Rocks were hurled against the trunks of the oaks and into the tufts of sunburned grass. When Hugh shifted into second and took the corner of the yard too short, the gears complained like deceived animals, and the stubborn twigs of the pyracantha scratched the side of his car. As the wind generated by the car's speed lashed into the field, a flock of grackles retreated to the blackberry hedges; crows shot up from the corn in the women's truck garden and scattered in the enormous pecan trees that shaded the corral like spread-wing angels.

Matt looked into the settling dust, struck a match on the heel of his boot, and lit his first cigarette of the morning. It tasted good; he pulled the smoke down to the depths of his lungs so there would be almost nothing to exhale. He watched the scene of Hugh's departure until some of the birds, having forgotten the recent disturbance, began to return. A dove scraped its pink feet in the gravel near him, pecking angrily at the things it found.

Tomorrow morning, Matt would get up early, dress for town, and prepare his mind, make it tranquil and steady for the nuisance of placating Lonnie Teague. He'd have to sit there in his jailhouse office, keeping calm, nodding his head in agreement; Lonnie knowing he could taunt him or tease him as much as he pleased, Lonnie knowing that at least for that morning he would have him toadying and apologizing—until Lonnie felt like releasing him with an insult and a warning. And Clarence? There didn't seem any point in telephoning and tattling on the kid. Clarence would only enjoy the story and congratulate his boy. That was the fool side of Clarence; it was a good thing that he was so much more. He just misunderstood what he was getting into when he begot Hugh. Matt cursed, spit against the boss of the black cauldron that held Lettie Kelly's petunias, and turning toward the house, raised his hand as if to wave away the landscape and all that had occurred in it.

Chapter 3

AT NEARLY ONE o'clock, four hours into Friday night's poker game, six men were left at the small folding table in the bunkhouse. All of them had their hats on, the brims hiding the top halves of their faces, so that their eyes, even when expressing shock, pleasure, or dismay, wouldn't give them away. Some were wearing spurs, and when their feet changed positions, they made music. Over them hung a cloud of smoke, its edges as regular and defined as those of the table. There was a minimum of motion and little conversation. Colored chips and green glass ash trays were scattered in front of each place. Once in a while, a man would leave to get a beer; another who chewed tobacco would have to go outside on the porch to spit. On the two long sides of the room, the windows were open full, and through the screens, specked with insects, a light breeze, cooled only an hour or two before, came up from the pasture. Still the men were uncomfortable from the heat. Their faces were damp, their shirts stuck to their skin in patches, and their sleeves were rolled up to the elbows. Occasionally one of them took out his handkerchief and dried his face.

After one of the hands had been played and Matt had increased his gain, Stephen said, "You think you got Hugh straightened out, Matt? Or are you going to have to keep watching over him?"

Matt shuffled the cards and leaned back in his chair. "Whatever I do, looks like I better keep it to myself."

"You better get you a spy to sit outside of Mrs. Menutis's place and tell you when he's going to a party."

"I'll send you, Stevie."

When Matt bent down to retrieve a chip that had fallen, Stephen looked around at the men and, sensing their enjoyment, continued: "If I was you, I'd ask Clarence for extra pay."

"You're not me. . . . I got extra pay."

"I'd sure get something nice out of it for myself."

Matt let his chair come down heavy on its front legs. "Get me a beer, Stevie. And don't worry about what Clarence does for me. I don't. I got no complaints."

"I thought you said you was too old and out of condition to tend a brat you didn't even have the pleasure of breeding."

"Well, I ain't worrying about it now," said Matt. "And you don't have to think about me and Hugh none."

Stephen hunched down to light a cigarette and rose up grinning. "I ain't thinking about you and Hugh. The one I like to think about is Mrs. Menutis. If I—"

Matt interrupted, cutting the cards and slapping them down so hard that his action seemed almost a warning. "Best not to concern yourself there neither. Didn't you learn nothing last weekend from what happened to Gerdine?"

Three swift hands were played, then a long one with the silence and lack of animation typical of the times when the stakes were escalating. The men who could see the door suddenly stopped looking at their cards; something had distracted them, and they were looking to Luther for an explanation. Matt caught his eye and motioned toward the door, and Luther twisted around in his chair. Lettie stood in the entrance, light behind her back, her features scarcely discernible in the vaguer light she faced. She wore a white flannel nightgown, full-length except that her pregnancy caused the hem to be lifted a few inches in the front. Her sleeves were closed with elastic at the wrists, the upturned collar almost covered her chin. She wore no slippers, and her small white toes contrasted precisely with the coarse dark wood of the floor.

"Luther," she said, her peculiarly pitched voice cutting through the smoke. "I need you to come to bed." Her face had the artificial whiteness of having been powdered after crying. She pushed back her carefully combed hair, as if making the halo it formed less apparent and the doll-like face more severe would make her look more like a real woman, so that she could not be refused.

C. J. Bedichek laughed, an untutored reaction—he was a visitor from a neighboring ranch—then cut it off short, since he found himself alone. Luther's eyes were shooting through him, and his body had jerked to attention, ready to defend the apparition in the doorway. Matt had never seen that expression on Luther's face before he met Lettie. Until then he had kept his emotions to himself; there were things in his past that hurt him, Matt thought. But after he got Lettie, he could hide nothing. It was awful for a man to have to expose his soul as Luther had.

The men looked at Luther, expecting him either to lash out at her, or to get up and drive her out of the room, talk to her for a minute or two outside on the porch, and then come back red-faced, fists clenched, and triumphant. This was the men's time, sacrosanct and inviolable, and it was inconceivable that one of the women would ask a man what this woman had. But Luther looked at his hand for a second or two and then put his cards down, pushed his chips aside, and turned to Matt. "I'm out," he said. "You count in mine when the game finishes, and we'll settle tomorrow."

Matt was sitting on Luther's left. He would not look at Luther, not even a glance out of the side of his eye, because he couldn't have done that unperceived, and to be discovered would be as bad as commenting outright. "Okay," he said.

Luther got up, took off his hat, ran his hand over his sun-streaked, curly hair, and replaced the hat exactly where it had been. "Good night," he said flatly.

"Good night, Luther," answered a quiet chorus.

As they had gone out, Luther had put his arm around the girl's shoulders; he was talking to her soft and quiet. When the hand was finished, Matt looked at Luther's cards and shook his head. A pair of queens.

C. J.'s eyes traveled fast around the lowered heads of the players. "That his kid?"

One of the men cleared his throat, but no one answered or looked up from his hand. Their eyes avoided Matt's especially. A full five minutes went by with nothing but the sound of cards and chips and bets, and the hiss of a beer bottle opening.

But C. J. was unable to let it go. "What the hell's the matter with Luther? Letting a woman, a little girl like that . . ." His voice trailed off.

On that Sunday morning when Matt had been thinking of Hugh and Elaine and the fight the night before, and all that turmoil kept crossing the well-lit path of his concern and making him want to stop it before it went a step further, he realized that his forebodings were not so different from the ones he'd had on

that spring afternoon when Luther had brought Lettie home to
Clarence's ranch and had carried her into Opal and Mark's house.

Matt's elbow rested on the table, digging in, and as he spoke,
slowly and directly, he beat out each word with a motion of his
smoking cigarette, held between two yellowed fingers. "C. J.,
that's Lettie," he said. "She has nightmares."

C. J.'s face relaxed, and he dipped his chin into his neck and
nodded knowingly. "Well, can't one of the women . . . ?"

"No. Isn't anyone else handles that. Luther sees to her himself. Better not to mess in it." He looked around at the men who
answered to him and took advantage of the opportunity to reaf-
firm his policy. "We leave Luther alone in whatever has to do
with that girl."

That policy had been honored by Matt and by all the men
under him ever since the day, nearly three years earlier, when
Luther had first seen Lettie in the courthouse square downtown,
her skirt partly unfastened to allow for the swelling of her pregnancy, emaciated, and whimpering at each movement she took.
Martha, a neighbor of hers, a black woman in a wash dress, a
cardboard patch over one lens of her glasses, and a shiny dust-
flecked wig, had lifted her off the slats of the truck bed where she
had been lying on a grease-stained mattress and was helping her
to cross the walk to Dr. Jackson's office. Luther could hardly see
the girl's face for the hair falling over it, and he certainly couldn't
read her features for the distortion there. From the color of her
skin, he thought that she might have been locked inside for a long
time. Her hands were dirty and scraped; her nails were torn, as if
she'd been digging away at something, ripping at the earth like a
fenced animal with too much spirit or fear to stay where it was.
The woman with her was as crippled by arthritis and bad food as
the girl was disabled by her suffering. They were like two
wounded soldiers trying to escape behind battle lines and nothing
to get them there but their capacity for suffering and their anticipation of relief. Their goal was at the end of a steep flight of
stairs, a ridiculous hurdle. Perhaps they thought that with what
was left of the strength of both their bodies added together, they
might climb it, but Luther doubted it. Things hurt as bad as that
girl don't get far unless an angel of mercy a lot more substantial
than that old woman breaks in and makes up the difference.

When Luther came near enough to give them help, he saw that
the girl was a mass of bruises and skinnings and swells. Her
blouse was almost torn off her body, so that the old woman was
using a good part of her strength trying to cover her with a blan-

ket from the back of the truck, which was in almost as bad a state as the blouse. He knew immediately that the girl had been beaten by a man. She might, from fear or love, lie and say that she'd fallen or had an accident, but he'd seen it often enough when he was a child to know all the signs, had seen his mother whipped periodically when he was helpless to do anything about it, and had to lie on a pallet in the corner of some one-room, windowless shack, smoky from a candle or kerosene lamp, outraged, frightened, and crying.

He had never known his real father, and his mother never talked about him at all; but he noticed that she wore a thin gold locket on a chain around her neck, and that whenever the chain broke, she labored quickly to fix it. He'd asked her if his father's name had really been Kelly, since that seemed to be her maiden name, too. She was vague and gave different answers, and it would be years before he would allow himself to understand why. When he was very young, he would imagine that his father was strong and good, and that only something too terrible to talk about could have caused him to leave. Thinking about him, he would let his imagination blow around his heart the way the wind sometimes sets in a windmill, light and steady on a mild summer day; but when the wind was gone, he wouldn't know where it had gone to, or where it had come from; and if he couldn't conjure it up again immediately, he would feel empty and bitter, and he would grieve and whimper in his dreams. Occasionally, when a man had lived with them for a considerable time, his mother would suggest that Luther call him Daddy, but he refused, figuring that he'd recognize his father without being told.

The men who did stay with his mother stayed a year or two at most, made love to her in the same room where Luther slept, spent the little money she had on liquor, and after getting drunk, would either sleep, talk loud, or torment some other woman in the labor camp where they had stopped to get work picking cotton or chopping corn. Before he was fourteen, he'd probably seen at least one example of every kind of cruelty that the human imagination can invent, so that, one day, when a rodeo came into the town near the farm where they were working (his mother had run off with a man, had been gone two weeks when she had said two days), he left with it. The rodeo superintendent had taken him on because he'd hung around, volunteering to take care of the animals, and because it was obvious to everyone in the show that he was better with them than anyone else they had ever seen. In three months, he could ride broncos and rope steers as well as their top stars, even though he had previously ridden only a few tired farm animals; in just over a year, he learned enough to serve as the rodeo medic, too. He was a natural at pulling down steers, calf roping, and riding Brahma bulls. By the time he was sixteen, he was on the entry lists; when he was eighteen, he was a champion, and his performances brought people out and filled the aisles and the backs of the stands. He simply had no fear of animals. He could always discover a reason for their meanness, and most often, if he worked at it—and he always did—he could change them and tame their ways.

It was people who gave him trouble. They frightened him with their perversions and meannesses. Animals always behaved in a way you could foresee and shield yourself against. He always knew how high a steer would jump and in what direction; he understood when to fall from a galloping horse onto a steer by the angle of its head. But people had to be watched and kept ahead of; it was only as he grew older that he learned to do that, too, to size up what they were like, and most of all, to determine what they wanted, what it took to calm them down and to get from them what they had that he didn't—not depriving them any, but giving them fair for fair. As he matured under the tutelage of men who reacted to the vicissitudes of life exactly like the sea reacts to gales, he had taken on a hard, tough, almost ugly maleness; but one that perceptive women were attracted to for its combination of self-confidence and competence, tempered by a deference to anything living that was weaker than himself.

For a cowboy he soon became rich. He spent little of his prize money or his salary, and since he had no relatives whose whereabouts he knew, he had no one to send his earnings to. He looked for his mother in every stop on the rodeo circuit, but, although for over five years his name blazed on signs and in newspaper headlines in most of the towns and cities of Texas, Oklahoma, Arkansas, and Louisiana, he never found her. His rootlessness appalled him; he felt very alone and, looking for a link to tradition and permanence, turned to religion.

He liked ritual, so Catholicism attracted him first. But in the small towns he traveled through, the Catholic Church was always on the side of the tracks where the Mexicans lived, and while they were good people and Luther liked their strong sense of family and their genial generosity, he found that they ate, talked, and lived differently from the people with whom he most easily blended. And he was too lacking in cultural identity to have the courage to search for the ineffable outside the experience of his own kind of people. He needed from the church more than just a place for airing his hopes and purging his fears: He needed a vow of affection, a pledge of continuity, and an assurance of stability —all that a good father might have given to him. He would be dutiful and obedient, but he expected (with all the pride of those who have been abused by life and dispossessed, yet risen above it) largesse and love.

As a young adult, he went to Sunday school, where he learned to read. And for three years, though he was in a different church in a different town every week, he never missed a Sunday. The rodeo stopped in places where there was always a Baptist or a Methodist church, and both of their Sunday schools satisfied Luther. The teachers were invariably patient and refined, and there was usually someone who would stay after the rest of the class had left in order to help him with his reading; and sometimes, when the rodeo wasn't performing a matinee, he could accept an invitation from one of them for a home-cooked meal and a discussion.

One December, after a rodeo he'd been working in Ft. Worth had been going on for a week in a heated arena, he received one of these invitations, and after dinner, the teacher had offered him coffee before a fireplace in which, instead of gas logs with their unwholesome smell and unnatural evenness of heat, a real fire was burning. The room smelled wonderful from that wood, and from the decorated spruce that was standing so high in the corner that its tip bent against the papered ceiling. The coffee was freshly made and steaming, and on a plate in front of him was piled a pyramid of flat white cookies in the shapes of Santa Clauses, double-humped camels, and stars; they were even sprinkled with hard silver candies. He had been told by the teacher's wife to eat them or they would go to waste, so, dipping the points and curves and feet of them in his coffee, he had done just that. He and the teacher had been talking about a three-year-old child in Plano who had been taken out of a trailer when her parents were sleeping, kidnapped, and later murdered; Luther had remarked, "That baby was innocent of evil; she was baptized, and she was pure and clean of sin. I don't see how, if there is any god, he'd have let that happen."

The teacher, a middle-aged man with a rim of graying hair around a shiny head, was thin and bent-shouldered, like someone who has recovered from a bad illness. His hands were long and white, but Luther could tell that they had been used hard. "You can think of it another way," he had said. "You're all Jesus has on earth."

The way Luther talked about morality came from the Bible; the way he acted on it came from within himself, and was independent of what he said, what he heard, or what he read. Baptized in a flooded arroyo near Ozona and having promised the minister to serve his fellow man in the manner of his savior, Luther was one of those rare people who understand the difference between superstition and revelation, without having an abject obedience to a creed he'd had no part in making; and since he had the ability to wedge his will into the kindly spaces between the surges of castastrophic random events, he was able to translate his belief into works. At the ranch, Stephen gave the shots, did the cutting, pulled and prodded; but Luther kept vigil during the torturous treatment and the time of convalescence, not only until the animal had recovered, but until it had seemed to forget. He was an able guardian, and no one dared interfere with him when he chose to stand watch over a creature hurt.

So Luther now stood in the path of the beaten girl, not to hinder her progress but, with his hands open and slightly extended, to be present before her, so that she might avail herself of his help if she chose to do so—which she did by pushing away from Martha and stretching out her arms to meet those that reached instantly to pick her up, raising her gently yet solidly against him. He carried her across the walk, past the people who had stopped to frown and whisper and give sensible though unimplemented advice, and up the stairs to the office. After the nurse had led them into the examining room, and had had Luther lay her on the table, the girl kept her head turned toward the blue window, as if she still thought she was imprisoned somewhere and she was listening for that moment when she could make her escape.

"You been locked up?" he asked, when the nurse had left them.

She shut her eyes.

"You going to tell me who hurt you?"

He pulled up the little stool on wheels that the doctor used, and sat down beside her. Hoping to gain her confidence, he told her his name and a little something about himself. Occasionally she opened her eyes, maybe to see again where she was, maybe to check on whether he was still in the room. Whenever this happened, he spoke to her, but she neither answered him nor acknowledged having heard. "You want me to get you anything?"

he asked. "You know anybody in town I could phone? You got a friend?"

After he'd tried to give her water from a glass and failed, after he'd tried unsuccessfully to get her to drink through a straw, Dr. Jackson came in from an emergency on the highway, a car wreck near Garwood. He was tired, panting from climbing the stairs; the cuffs of his pants were dusty from being so long on the highway shoulder; the front of his shirt was dotted with blood. Without paying attention to anything else, he went to the girl and pulled back the sheet that covered her. She looked away from him, but when he reached down to touch her, she caught his wrist with more strength than Luther imagined she had.

Dr. Jackson stood at the sink lathering his hands, straining his neck to look back over his shoulder at Luther. "You do this?"

Luther, stunned by the incongruity of the question, found no words to answer it. He shook his head violently.

Dr. Jackson yelled out the door for his nurse.

"I can help you," Luther said.

"Get out."

As the nurse came in, Dr. Jackson bent over the girl and began to question her. Luther picked up his hat and retreated like a shepherd dog who has done a good job and then been whipped for it. "He thinks I did it," he murmured. "But I guess there ain't a man alive wouldn't lie if he did this."

He stood in the narrow hallway, but just outside the door. He thought he heard what might have been her voice saying something, but then it hushed, and there were only the sounds of the doctor and nurse, the clink of metal falling against metal, a drawer opening and closing, and the squeaking hinge of a cabinet door.

When Dr. Jackson came out, he motioned Luther into a little office with a framed certificate on the wall. "I'll pay what she owes," said Luther.

"I don't charge the people in the settlement anything."

The girl lived in a camp of tin and plywood shacks behind the Macon ranch inhabited by people who had no right to be there, who had never had title to the land or to anything else, but whom the Macons, whose family had owned their place for a hundred and fifty years, had not the heart to run out. Naylor Macon let them poach deer and rabbits around the south fences, provided they stayed away from the stock, the houses, and the barns. Sometimes the women worked in Mrs. Macon's house, and she paid them a generous wage for the little they did. But they were

undependable; they would say they would come and then
wouldn't, and Mrs. Macon gave up counting on them. People in
town, even the best people from the two big churches, were
afraid to go out there, to have to see for themselves people so
weak-willed, shiftless, and unlucky.

There were no windows in Dr. Jackson's office, and the huge
desk, covered with patient files and forms, took up almost all its
space. Behind the doctor's head was a bookcase filled with worn
medical books and pharmaceutical digests. Luther felt cramped in
the hard wooden armchair; the rungs stuck in his back. In fact,
the chair was too little for him, so, as he spoke to Dr. Jackson, he
thought he must look awkward and hunched over, when he
needed to look strong. "I'll pay her bill just the same," he said.

"What are you going to do? You going to take her back
there?"

It was better not to look at Dr. Jackson then, so Luther looked
at the medical certificate. He knew Dr. Jackson would be suspicious of what he was going to do no matter what he anwered.
"I'm going to take her home to the Littleton ranch with me," he
said.

"Then you'll take her back to the settlement when she's well?"

"No," he said, picking up a paperweight and staring into the
snow that was shifting around a family of snowmen. "She won't
need to go back there."

Dr. Jackson rolled a pencil around the palm of his hands,
looking alternately at it and at Luther, who, having said what he
needed to say, no longer avoided his eyes. Dr. Jackson had figured out by then who this man had to be: the prize that Matthew
Kirkland had hired off a rodeo a few years back, the man that
Matt had watched with wonder ride and work with animals—
until he heard that Luther had been thrown, that his legs were
broken and that he'd need expensive help if he were to get back
the use of them even to walk, much less ride. One minute after
Matt had learned that news (he'd been sitting on a backless stool
in a café, finishing an order of apple pie and coffee, and listening
to some men who were shaking their heads and saying what a
shame it was about Luther Kelly), he was on the phone having
Clarence paged at a black tie dinner. A week later, Luther was in
Houston having a series of operations by a high-toned specialist
who lived in River Oaks, not all that far from Clarence, and who
did his work in an air-conditioned hospital twelve stories high.

With that, Matt had Luther. Dr. Jackson knew from being
with him for even these few minutes that because of what Matt

had done for him, Luther was in his permanent debt. "I'm sorry what I said awhile ago. I didn't know who you were."

"You didn't ask me."

"Clarence won't let you bring an unmarried woman in there. Jimmy Ferguson tried it and got fired."

"I ain't Jimmy."

"I've heard you're not. But Matt will have to go with Clarence."

"Matt owes me." And Matt did owe Luther, too. Matt had received free, the summer before, a wild horse that had been so badly mistreated that he couldn't work with it without losing his temper, and ending up by making it even meaner and wilder in addition to ruining its mouth. Luther had known that Matt would spoil the horse the moment he'd seen it; and on the second afternoon, when Matt was already in a rage after working with it for five minutes (both of them sweating, breathing heavy and furious, the horse stamping its feet, and Matt's body so rigid it was ready to break in pieces), Luther had taken hold of the rope and stared Matt down until he backed off. Luther didn't want him anywhere around once he started the tedious work, the first steps in establishing the confidence that would result in the horse's trusting a man; not only Luther but, later, Matt as well.

Matt had not offered to pay Luther for the long hours after work he'd spent with the animal, every day for almost a month, making it as beautiful a cutting horse as you could wish for, its mouth so sensitive that the horse would change its direction or speed so quickly that it might have anticipated the hand that guided it. Both men understood that Luther didn't want and hadn't expected payment, but that the favor would be returned when the moment presented itself. And it wouldn't matter how long it took for that moment to arrive because both of them would remember.

"You know who did it?" he now asked the doctor.

Dr. Jackson was too old to still be practicing medicine, but too experienced and too much a friend to the people he healed to retire in good conscience. He wore thick glasses, whose heavy silver frames, at the slightest movement of his head, flashed light from the overly bright bulb in a battered-looking gooseneck lamp. "Yes," he said. "She told me. I said I wouldn't treat her unless she did."

"Would you have?"

He nodded. "She didn't know that."

"Someone up there at the settlement?"

"Doyle Campbell . . . he's her uncle."

"That his baby she's going to have?"

"Yes."

Luther looked away sharply, trying to imagine how something like this could possibly happen, and knowing that his faith was being tested to the breaking point.

"He works on the roads sometimes, a redhead, maybe forty. He gets laid off for being drunk, but he's tough as leather and he goes back. When he's sober, he's good help, one of the few of them who works anywhere near regularly. But when he drinks, he's like a stuck bull." He motioned toward the room where the girl was. "He may not even know he did this."

"He will."

Dr. Jackson squinted his eyes at Luther in a way that was usually calculated to frighten his patients into getting more rest, drinking less, or paying their bill if he knew they could. "Don't you go out there. Better to report it to the sheriff, charge Campbell with a felony, and let the law get her in the county home."

As negligent as his own mother had been, even she had hidden him and shown some concern for him when the bosses or a representative from a committee from the town had come out to try to tell her that he'd be better off in a home. No, not even his mother would have accepted that, and she was a woman who had put up with things that were hard for many people even to imagine. He could still see her standing on the sagging porch of one of the better houses they'd stayed in, yelling at a peace officer, emphasizing her speech with her hand, the chipped red-polished nails moving against the austere backdrop of peeling gray shingles, like sparks in a dying fire. After the lanterns were out and everyone was asleep, they had left, his mother holding the handle of a big straw purse containing all they possessed in one hand and his hand in the other. They had hitched a ride on the road, put space between them and that man's suggestion. Luther must have been five or six—meek and skinny and always scratching at sores with the stubs of fingernails he'd bitten to the quick. "She ain't going to no home," he said. "Looks like she's done her time. I'll take her with me. That home's no place for her or nobody, them kids penned like dogs, looking out a wire fence. You seen it?"

So Luther paid her bill, carried her outside to his truck, and drove her around town while he did the rest of his shopping, wondering, each time that he made a stop, if she'd be there when he got back, or if she'd try to get away from him, too, like she'd

got out of that chicken coop, or whatever she'd been penned up
and padlocked in. If she really wanted to go back (experience had
taught him that some women love the men who beat them) he
was helpless to do anything about it. If she loved Campbell,
uncle or no, that was that. She'd return to him, and that was the
point at which trying to help would become interfering.

But she stayed. As he lifted his packages over the side of the
truck bed, he could see her in the cab, looking like a statuette in a
niche of a priory garden, her head bowed, her quiet hands folded
in her lap, her feet parallel and a bit apart in her overrun scuffs.
Her hair hung in damp curls, because the nurse had washed it to
get the blood off, and the white-blond pieces that had dried
wisped like the spun cotton that he'd seen at Christmastime on
decorated trees in the bellied windows of the big houses behind
the square in town.

"You want me to stop and get you a hamburger?" he asked
her. Although she didn't answer him, didn't even move, he went
to a drive-in and got her one anyway. He set it on her lap in the
napkin, but she never touched it. "Your mouth hurt?" He had
bought her a Coke, too. "Take a sip of this," he said. "You know
how good it is?" He pushed it toward her. "Try some, honey."
She took it from him, held it a minute, then gave it back, spilling
a little on the seat of the truck.

"It don't matter," he said, smiling at her as she made a weak,
ineffectual effort to rub out the spot. "This truck upholstery has
had a lot worse than that happen to it." On the way home, he
drank from the lumpy green bottle himself, offering it to her from
time to time with no result. "You been through too much, huh?"
She wouldn't even cry; and although once it seemed to him that
she was trying to say something—the swollen eyes shifted
slightly; her small mouth opened—the effort failed.

"I'm taking you to the Littleton ranch, where I work," he said.
She flinched when he pushed her hair away from her face to see
her expression. "But I won't bother you none." She leaned her
head against the back of the seat and looked at him out of the
corner of her eye. He smiled at her without getting a reaction.
"You can stay with one of the families. There's Opal, a married
lady, who can help you maybe to get ready. She has children of
her own.

"Is this truck bouncing too much?" he asked her. "You need
me to slow down?"

She neither looked at him nor answered. She cared about
nothing, Luther thought, only the way she was feeling, the fear

and maybe a certain humiliation, which right now, with trying to keep the truck wheels away from the ruts and bumps and to avoid any abrupt motion that might give her pain, he couldn't do anything about.

Matt had been in the bunkhouse, where he and Luther and the rest of the bachelors lived, when he looked out the window and knew that this time Luther had taken on a hurt human being rather than a bitch cur or a fox or a fawn, because Matt could see, floating between Luther's shoulder and the evening clouds, a mass of pale hair that almost had to be a woman's, a very young woman's. He ran out to meet Luther, appraised the wreck, quite obviously female, of what once might have been something promising, might have been able to smile or even giggle like Opal's effervescent daughter, Hazel, who had hardly even been punished, much less scourged like this child.

Though he had two reasons to be furious, Matt attended to the first because of his responsibility to his employer.

"Lord Jesus, Luther! I can't let you . . . Clarence won't . . ."

But then, canny enough to know when any argument would be useless, he stopped his protest in answer to Luther's face and his silence: Luther's eyes those of the initiated, his mind wise to and experienced in suffering, wretched now and miserable; Luther's expression advertising his commitment to the burden that he lowered onto a borrowed iron bed, then the sudden change of his expression when the girl bit her swollen lip and winced because he had failed to find any place where she wasn't bruised or skinned, any area of grace on which he could set her down; and the firming of Luther's jaw, his hard and indignant reaction; and finally a silent but unmistakable apology for his anger, and a setting of his thick shoulders and a sigh and moan of resignation which Matt read as an avowal to set himself once again to the task of aiding a broken and beaten living thing, and of restoring its faith.

Matt shook his head and looked away. "All right, Luther," he said quietly. "All right, then."

Matt turned and walked away, shaking his head, thumping his hat against his thigh, brushing off dust where, on this rare occasion, there was none.

When Luther had descended from the truck in front of the Rudes' house, and Opal had come out on the porch, when he'd explained what he'd done, and what he needed her to do—that he was asking her to make her little sewing corner into a hospital

room—she would not answer immediately, at least not before
she'd come around to the passenger side of the truck, and her
face had blanched at what her imagination had already told her
she would see, and she was unable to keep from covering
her mouth with her hand, or to hide at all what she felt at the
sight. She hadn't yet responded to his request, the unrepeated
request, though it was still on Luther's anxious face, when she
had turned her back on the whole unbelievable scene, then
abruptly stood straighter and motioned with her arm in an unequivocal gesture that meant that Luther could and must bring the
girl in.

She made up the bed in fresh-smelling sheets, then bathed the
girl's feet with a washcloth (the only part of her the nurse hadn't
seen to, because it was the only part that wasn't hurt) and slipped
her into one of Hazel's nightgowns.

When she refused Opal's dinner of steak, beans, and hot bread
—"It's real butter on the biscuits," Luther said, encouraging her.
"We don't buy none of that colored lard"—he gave her some soup,
which he had insisted on preparing himself, awkwardly mashing
the carrots and potatoes into the broth. He held her to his chest and
fed her, easing the spoon between her lips. Her body was rigid
against his arm, and she never looked at him or at anything else but
rather studied the inside of herself, studied something she still had
to comprehend. But in spite of the extremity of her isolation, she
was sane. He'd known that when instinctively she had put her arms
around his neck to be carried into the doctor's. She was surviving;
she had had her wits about her when she had taken the best chance
she had. Now that she had found sanctuary, it was as if she were
braced for trouble, as if she knew it was only a matter of time before
everything crumbled again, as if she had no reservoir of hope and no
belief in improvement.

It took her well over an hour to finish, but she did eat, and
after that, he left her with Opal and drove four miles to the gasoline station, the nearest place that sold ice cream. He hadn't been
able to get her to tell him what flavor she liked, so he brought
home a pint of handpacked chocolate. Coming back into the
room, he opened the door softly—if she was sleeping, he'd let
her rest—but he saw that she had shifted her position so that she
could lie on her side watching the door, and he saw her eyes, if
not eager, at least attentive. He spooned the ice cream into a cup
and fed it to her, and when she wanted more, he took up the
carton, and they finished it together as, little by little, she relaxed
against him.

"She never had ice cream before," Opal said later, when she and Luther were in the hallway. "Did you see how she jumped away from the cold?" Opal shook her head and smiled for the first time since she'd seen Luther's pitiful burden being carried into her house. "You got something there, Luther, but she sure don't trust nobody."

"She ain't had no cause."

He returned to the small room, crouched down beside the girl, asked her if she was comfortable, but still she kept her eyes away from him, looking at nothing, answering nothing, her hands holding tightly to the top of the sheet which Opal had arranged under her chin, her pale hair sprawling out on the faded blue flowers of the sun-bleached pillowcase.

Opal, entering the room with a glass of water and the bottle of medicine that Dr. Jackson had prescribed, shook one of the capsules into her hand, and offered it to the girl, but she refused it, turning away. "Maybe she don't know how to swallow one," said Opal.

"Get me a teaspoon and some sugar," said Luther. He leaned over the girl, who was facing the wall and shaking a little. "Come on, honey," he said. "Come on, turn around."

He took the capsule apart, poured the contents into the spoon, added the sugar and water, and then lifted her up. "Don't spit it out," he said. "It's going to help you sleep." But twice she pushed the spoon away, upsetting the contents on the blanket. "I'm going to outlast you, honey," he said sadly; and the third time, she took it.

As she gradually began to relax from the drug, she tried to change positions on the bed to avoid putting pressure on the bruises, but at last she seemed to give up. When he thought she was asleep, he eased himself off the edge of the bed as quietly as he could so as not to disturb her, and she said the first thing to him that she was ever to say, but he missed it. He kneeled beside her and begged her to tell him again.

She rose a little on her elbow. "Where do you stay?" she asked him.

He turned her head toward the window and pointed to the bunkhouse, a long, low building across the dirt road. "That's my room on the corner, with the light in it, just to the left of the trunk of that live oak. The room with the shade half down."

Her glance followed his finger, and she gazed so intently at what he was showing her that he sensed the importance to her of this knowledge. He expected her to say something, but as usual, whatever she was thinking she kept to herself.

Then he asked what he'd asked her a dozen times: "What's your name?" He smiled. "If you don't tell me, I won't know what to holler at you when you get well." When she didn't answer, he kissed her impulsively, like a father would kiss the cheek of a child, grateful for its return.

She looked straight at him, astonished. "Lettie," she said softly, in a childlike voice incongruent with her stature, which was willowy and almost tall.

He lowered his head a minute, rejoicing because, in that seemingly insignificant victory, he had learned more than he had hoped to learn. For the first time since she'd deferred to him on the sidewalk, she was making a connection, recognizing him, allowing the blurred edges of making a connection, recognizing him, allowing the blurred edges of her existence to fuse with the sharp edges of his. He told her to .send for him if she needed anything; one of Opal's girls would come for him.

"I'll bring your breakfast in the morning." He eased her down, and she turned her head, pulling her limbs close in to herself, and though, from this position, she could not see out the window, she was looking in the direction of where he lived, and it seemed to him that she was trying to hold her eyes open despite her increasing drowsiness. He tucked the covers around her shoulders, opened the window a little more fully, and then, with no little reluctance, left her.

But she never sent for him. Somehow she got off the iron bed. She did not reach his room or even the porch; she got only as far as the oak tree, almost as if she had misunderstood his directions, that her comprehension had stopped at the words *live oak,* as if the security that he offered her might come from that wide, scarred trunk.

He had been asleep a long time, from an exhaustion brought on by pity and worry; but when he heard her screaming his name, he sat bolt upright in his bed, and each repetition of it scoured his heart. She was screaming it through the night in a rhythm as regular as that of the pealing of a steeple bell; and by the time he got to her, she had begun to bleed, a long threadlike strip down the center of her gown.

Opal had arrived at the tree first, but Lettie had thrown her off. She flung her arms around Luther's chest and arms (she had recognized beforehand his shadow approaching her and had moaned an unmistakable cry of relief), her elbows thrust out with the saliency of saplings broken in the wind. She held herself to him as if he were all that stood between her and the agony that had begun, the misery that she seemed not to have expected but that was now crashing down on her, coming from this thickness in her waist, this mass of new blood and bone that sometimes in silence moved its foot or fist. It had hardly been in Lettie's consciousness before, but now it woke her, forced its way into her flesh, pulled her up, invaded her, stuck her again and again, disappeared, then roused her to repeat its cycle.

Lights were going on in all the houses. For some reason, she was afraid to go back to Opal's; and Luther would not torture her further by trying to argue with her. It was harder to lift her now than it had been that afternoon in town. She was terrified and fighting hard; Mark had to help Luther get her into his room, and Opal had to help him calm her. He tried to reassure her, but she was deaf to his voice; he let her scratch his arm or squeeze his hand, and turned her on her side to stroke her back in long, smooth strokes that seemed to give her relief in between the groans and finally the fierce screams.

He had seen animals giving birth, and he had assisted in their labor, but he had never experienced anything like this. Even in the war, in the field hospital where he had worked, he had rarely encountered such suffering. "It's because she's so young," he said. "She's nothing more than a baby herself." He wanted to take her in to Dr. Jackson, but Opal insisted that she was too far along to stand the rough ride, even in a truck with good springs. He cursed the doctor for not telling him to keep her in town. "Maybe he thinks she's trash, and it don't matter how bad she hurts."

Toward the last Opal sent him to wait on the porch, though she called him back quickly when the shrieking suddenly ceased, and the night was quiet, except for an occasional remark from the wakened hands and their families. When he entered the room, Opal was holding the silent child, whom she could not wake, and in whom there was no sign of life. It was underdeveloped; and neither he nor Opal could get it to breathe. "It wasn't big enough," Opal said. "You can't do nothing more." The baby, still warm from its mother's body, was covered with blood. Opal bathed it, wrapped it in a pillowcase, and put it in an old metal cashbox, and Luther went out into the woods to dig a hole deep enough to keep a wolf or dog from unearthing it.

When Luther returned, Lettie stared at him as if searching his face for some secret, and after her eyes had been shut for a time, she said resignedly, "I'm dying too, huh?"

"No, honey. You're just worn out."

"I sure feel like it. . . . I can't see far and I can't feel my feet."

He got her shoes and slipped them on her. "You feel them now?"

Her eyes remained closed, but she nodded, and for the second time that night, he watched her sink into sleep, her body so dangerously weak that he feared for her life, certain now that Opal had been wrong in assuring him of her recovery; his memory of her suffering remained so acute that he couldn't leave her but instead sat near her, disturbed by her shallow breathing, her weakened pulse, and the alternating symptoms of chills and fever. He stayed with her far into the next day, when, observing that these alarming signs had abated, and that she was resting more or less naturally, he slumped in his chair and slept.

She refused to go back to Opal's. After three days of sleeping, which Dr. Jackson had told Luther was normal, when she was able to sit up in bed with her hair combed and tied at the crown of her head with a shiny pink ribbon that Opal had saved from a birthday present of Hazel's, she pleaded with him to let her stay in his room. She hid her face under the collar of his jacket and started to cry hopelessly. Opal, who was standing behind Luther, knew from Luther's face that the battle was won, and there was no point in further discussion, that even Matt's protests would be useless.

Luther made a pallet for himself in the corner and eventually found a cot in the attic. Lettie got stronger and stopped looking out the window, vacant and lost; she began to eat and even to talk, though only to Luther, and never loud enough for anyone else to hear. At the dinner table in the cookhouse, there were never fewer than twenty people present, and Luther would have to bend close to her to understand what she was saying. Even when he was looking directly at her, she would nudge him or pull at his shirt sleeve before she spoke. If someone asked her a question, even one of the children, she would look at Luther, as if she had no voice except his, and she would wait for him to answer for her.

One evening, they came into dinner late, and the two places that remained were not together, but on opposite benches. Lettie blushed, backed away, stumbled slightly, and left. Luther took the seating arrangement personally; he thought the hands had set things up purposely to tease her and therefore to hurt him. He lectured them all, particularly Stephen's teen-age son, who snickered, and whom Luther jerked up from the bench by his collar and would have backhanded had Matt not stopped him.

He had calmed himself by the time he found her on the bed, face down and spread-eagled, the skirt of the new dress that he'd bought her in town crumpled around her pale child's thighs, her face smothered in his pillow, which she had taken off the cot. He pacified her with the patience and cheer with which he always talked to her when she was troubled, pulled her around and up to him, and held her until her gasping for breath and the flow of her tears stopped. He waited while she washed her face and smoothed her dress and then drove her into West Columbia, where they ate chicken-fried steak and Spanish rice in a café and looked at each other across an oilcloth-covered table which was so wobbly that even Lettie noticed it, and Luther had to put folded paper napkins under one of its legs. She glanced around in wonder at the customers: It was the first time she had eaten in a public place.

"Do you have to pay extra if I eat all the white bread?"

"No," he said, pushing the blue-rimmed plate across the table to her.

He let her order a piece of yellow pie that she had seen under a panel of glass; the golden, sugary bubbles in the meringue delighted her.

Because she was learning to read, it had taken a while for Luther to get through the menu. She had been fascinated by the way the names of food looked, and she asked the woman who ran the café if she might keep the menu. By the following week, she had mastered it, and read it aloud to Hazel and Opal and Mark, and anyone else who would take the time to listen to a menu.

Luther would read to her from the Bible, and then from newspapers and magazines. He was surprised that she knew almost nothing of the world, that she had never been inside a movie house, that she didn't know what a library was, and scarcely much more a church—the words *sermon* and *Savior* were not in her vocabulary. She had hardly been to school: During the war, the school bus service had been canceled, and afterward, when she had become the tallest in the class, the children teased her, and she never went back. Her grandfather never noticed anyway, she said. When she got tired of the reading, Luther would turn on the radio, and they would listen to music or to story programs or

to news. On Sunday night, Lettie preferred the comedians, and
Luther explained the jokes.

She wanted to be told about the ranch, and as soon as she was
able, he took her on walks to see the animals; he showed her the
two horses that were his and promised to teach her to ride Opal's
mare. She held lumps of sugar in the flat of her hand, shut her
eyes, and then laughed like a baby when the mare's velvety lips
rippled over her skin. Whenever she looked up at him, Luther
would be watching her, sometimes smiling, sometimes rapt and
serious. Both expressions she mimicked each time she noticed
them, almost as quick as a mirror.

Before the ranch women had felt comfortable enough to ask
her, she went to the cookhouse, sat down, and started peeling
potatoes and onions, badly, but with resolve. Nobody criticized
her or asked her what she had eaten at the settlement that she
didn't even know how to handle vegetables. She watched what
the other women did, and learned from them. Gradually, but with
a sure, steady progress, she worked her way into the close-knit
group of wives. She never joined the children for any of their
activities, not even Hazel, who in age was nearly her equal. She
would defer to Hazel and the rest of the girls as a cunning adult
defers to children for whom he has no time.

Lettie's other important field of discovery was Luther himself.
Little by little, as they sat in the room, or on the porch, or outside
under the trees, she would ask him about things he had never
revealed to anyone. One night when she was kneeling on the bed
and Luther was lying with his hands behind his head, the top half
of his cot bleached by the moonlight, his eyes glancing at the
ceiling or shifting toward her, she said, "Luther, you ever get
beat when you was little?"

"Not much, physically," he answered.

"It make you sad I ask you that?"

"Nothing you say ever makes me sad, Lettie."

"Why?"

"It just don't."

"You love me?"

"That's right."

She laughed, and he could see her small white teeth. "I love
you, too," she said.

He hesitated and cleared his throat. "Like a daddy, then."

The one aspect of his past that he refused to discuss with her
was the women he had known before her. No, he said, just no.
She was perceptive enough to see that that was an avenue on

which he would not stroll with her, and that by mentioning it she parted herself from him. After three or four tentative essays, each one weaker than the previous, she dropped the subject and never mentioned it again; nor did it bother her.

The emptiness and austerity of her own past made her a uniquely sympathetic audience. She lacked experience and point of view, yet her reactions soothed him and drew him to her, into the accepting aureole of her nature, where there was an unmistakable peace. They were orphans of disintegrated clans, castoffs from those who had not been able to serve them, not because of ill will or design, but because of weakness and failure. Lettie and Luther, both of them hardy, canny throwbacks, learned early that to survive meant to suckle at anything that would let them, though their parent surrogates were usually harsh and unwilling, and unable to cope with even their more direct charges, much less these destitute extras. As for herself, Lettie never mentioned either her uncle or her suffering at his hands. These details and recollections she seemed to have let Luther bury with her child.

She did visit the grave; he knew that. She would squat down next to the little mound, smooth the earth, and hum odd, abbreviated tunes. She would stay there motionless awhile, and when she would find that Luther had slipped away from her to lean against a tree or crouch over some flower or plant, pretending to be occupied, she would quietly go to him and touch his shoulder or his back to let him know she was there. He never saw any tears. He wondered how a woman felt about a child she had gotten the way Lettie had, but he never asked.

In the evening, when Luther returned from work, she was always waiting for him. She would watch for him out the windows of their room, or out the door of the cookhouse; and when she saw him, she would leave what she was doing and go out to meet him, greeting him with a strong hug.

She would follow him everywhere, and when she wanted something, she asked for it in a childish voice; what she wanted, she usually got. Each night, to make her happy, he drove her to the gasoline station four miles from the ranch—not counting the distance from the houses to the blacktop—and bought her ice cream, always chocolate and always a whole pint. She would lean over the store woman as she packed it, to make sure there were no holes or bubbles, suspicious of being cheated, unable to bear the possibility of any reduction whatsoever in the delicious dessert. This practice embarrassed Luther, but he let it pass without comment because he remembered that it had taken him years to stop counting every penny of change, to stop watching like a ferret at a rabbit hole for inequities, to stop taking for granted that he was being robbed, swindled, and flayed by anything and everything human. Once back in the truck, returning to the ranch, Lettie would relax again. Carefully balancing the carton on her lap, she would eat from it with a tiny, flat wooden spoon, feeding Luther a bite for every one she took. These daily ice-cream trips made the other children jealous, but Opal warned them to say nothing about it. "You've got nothing to do with Luther and Lettie. She's not the same. She wasn't brought up like you."

"She wasn't brought up at all," whined Hazel.

"Hush."

"Is she Luther's child or his wife?"

"She's a little girl," said the mother. "She's like you."

Opal's two girls looked at each other slyly. Under the sewing table, one ground the toe of her loafer into the ankle bone of the other. "She washes his clothes, and when he's late, she waits up for him in the kitchen. Ain't she his wife if she stays in his room?"

"You stayed with Dad and me when you was sick last winter."

"She ain't sick anymore. She's fine."

"That ain't our business."

As far as Luther was concerned, nothing Lettie did was wrong. He bragged about her, both in and out of her presence. People either said nothing or agreed. "For God's sake don't cross him," said Matt. He said that many times.

Lettie had never been required to conceal rage; she knew nothing of social customs, except those that were brutal. She knew that an insult followed a suggestion, and a slap followed a protest. When she was told no or reprimanded, she would lose her temper, yell, curse, or even fight. In silence, or perhaps murmuring her name over and over, Luther would take her by the hand or the arm and lead her away, either to their room or to the yard under a shade tree and talk to her. "You can't treat people like that, Lettie" or "No, I can't take you there now" or "You shouldn't have done that if . . ."

Sometimes her language was obscene, in a way that no one talked when the men and women were together. Matt disliked it: Bad language from an angry, distressed man was bad enough in mixed company, but from a young woman, it was intolerable.

"I can talk like I want," she told Luther when he warned her of Matt's anger. She pulled back her lips in a grimace and leaned forward defiantly. "No, you can't," he said. "You're going to talk like I tell you." The idiotic smile faded from her face, and she pinched his arm as hard as she could and held it; and when he neither flinched nor changed his expression, nor hit her, she fell against him. "You're going to take me back now," she cried. He grabbed her wrists in one hand and her chin in the other so she would have to look at him. She was trapped, but he did not hurt her. "No," he said. "I'm never taking you back as long as you need to stay."

What the ranch people could not ignore was that the mangled, swollen little girl whom Luther had taken in, so skinny that her pregnancy looked like a deformation, had, after a few weeks of pampering, feeding, and coaxing, turned into a girl as pretty as a storybook doll. Only a few days after her rescue, when she had sat up in bed and combed her hair in front of the mirror that he had taken off the wall, dusted with the shirt he had discarded the night before, and handed to her, Luther had seen that her eyes had opened again and were as bright and blue as two identical cornflowers on the same stem. Her mother had left years before, and she claimed ignorance of her age, since no one had ever celebrated any birthdays for her, but Opal said that she couldn't be a day over fifteen, because she was at the same stage of growing up as Hazel.

When Luther took her shopping to town, they went to the women's clothing store. He encouraged her to buy high-heeled shoes for church and a number of dresses, but he stopped her when she chose wrong. "That's too old for you," he said, and she returned a black tight-fitting dress to the rack, shaking her head at Luther's meanness, but hot with shame that she had made a mistake. "Get the yellow one with the full skirt."

Opal cut Lettie's hair to shoulder length and made bangs to curl over her forehead; she creamed her hands until they regained their natural softness, and when her nails had grown out, Opal showed her how to paint them with a pale pink polish. Luther didn't approve of lipstick, so Lettie used one that had little color, and she never applied it in his presence. Her thin, graceful figure made her look pretty in her new dresses, and in any other outfit that was appropriate to her coloring and youth.

"Luther must have seen through all that," said Arnold Sackett, a first-class wrangler that Matt had stolen off a ranch in Denton when he was supposed to be just shopping for a bull. "He just has an eye for things, knows by looking at anything that lives and breathes what it'll grow into. He can tell you about an animal, just sees it once and knows what you got—temperament, appearance, everything."

Arnold figured that Lettie was like Matt's wild horse that had been kicked around so bad nobody could come to terms with it, not even Matt (least of all, Matt!), though he fed it and gave it a scrubbed, straw-carpeted stall. It had not been enough for Luther, though, merely to come to terms with the horse. The animal had to be willing to look at him with anticipation when he approached it; willing to move eagerly under him, to respond to the subtlest of signals. It was not sufficient having that horse just tolerate him: There was a limit to how much you could enjoy spending time with an animal that didn't share the adventure; it was a certain dead end, and sooner or later the animal would have to be abandoned.

So Luther had begun slowly, approaching the horse easy, stroking its neck, its withers, moving his hand over its back in the direction the hair grew, then, finally, slipping the halter over its head, days before he'd slip the bit in, and days still before he'd mount it, letting his weight down slowly, holding himself up with all the strength in his calves and thighs so as not to startle the horse and so lose what he'd worked so hard to gain. If the creature was nervous, he might step away awhile, talking to it, keeping up a conversation, not because what he was saying meant anything but because the calm in his voice would reveal how patient and resolute he could be. That was what made the difference; and finally he had that horse perfect, cured of its shyness and craziness, even had it whinnying when he spoke to it from a distance. It was as if it had never been used falsely.

The first significant request Lettie made of Luther was that he let her fix up their room. "I want it to look like Hazel's room," she told him. Hazel had organdy curtains and a pink polished-cotton spread with matching pillow covers.

"You want to stay with Hazel?" he asked her. It was a blue day, almost summer, and she had been with him six weeks. "You don't have to stay with me. You want to move in there? Maybe it's more of a family."

She picked at the sleeve of his shirt, as if attending to an imperfection in the cloth. "No," she said, looking up at him slowly, her flower eyes shining through her light hair like the summer sky between stacks of hay. He smiled at her and ran his hand through her hair from her forehead backward so that for a second it would stay out of her eyes; it was soft and it smelled of perfume and soap.

"How come you wash your hair every day, Lettie?"

"Because Hazel does."

"It's pretty, honey."

They started to walk away from the bunkhouse, heading down to the end of the dirt entry road to the blacktop. "Then maybe you'd like to make my room into a little girl's room and have me move out. You want me to stay with Stephen . . . you have the room to yourself?" He often teased her about moving.

"No," she said, putting her cheek against his arm in the spot where earlier she had been bothering the shirt. "I just want it like Hazel's."

The road was broken, cut with deep, dry ruts from the trucks coming in when it rained, so they walked close together in the grass-covered middle. "You asking for money?"

She nuzzled his sleeve.

"How much you need?" He put his arm around her waist to keep her from tripping in the ruts. She slipped her arm under his, then around his waist, catching her thumb in a loop of his belt.

"Six dollars for the curtain material, and eight for the spread material and pillows, then two for the ribbon."

"What you need ribbon for?"

"The tiebacks."

"Tiebacks?"

She was afraid he was teasing her, so she answered with impatience. "To pull the curtains away from the windows in the daytime!"

"Opal teaching you how to sew?"

She squeezed his arm, almost a pinch. "I already knew some,"she said.

He frowned and brushed the hand away from him, swiftly, as if it were an annoying insect. "You didn't know nothing, Lettie." She lied when she was embarrassed, a habit he was trying to break her of. "You tell lies because you got punished, but I ain't going to hurt you. You lie, though, and you won't have friends."

"I'll have you," she said.

"Yeah, but we'd have nobody together."

"I don't need nobody but you."

"You might." He stopped, and she with him. "That calf over yonder ain't ours," he said, pointing to a corner of the fence. "I'll come back and get her in the truck, take her home. You want to come with me to Peterson's?" She nodded. She would have followed him to the stock truck and gotten in as a matter of course, but his asking her each time was a sign of the courtesy that Luther wanted to exist between them.

He reached into his pocket and handed her a twenty dollar bill. "Here," he said. She took it quickly and thrust it in the pocket of her skirt.

He laughed. "You think I was going to grab it back?"

This was the largest amount of money he had ever given her, or that she had ever asked for, although, when they were in town and she saw something she wanted, he always bought it for her. The first time something in a shop had caught her eye—a set of imitation tortoise shell combs in a dime store window—and she had asked him for them, she had been breathing fast, high in her chest, almost daring him, harsh as a weasel dipping her head in preparation for an attack, sure that he would say no. Without questioning her need or desire to have them, he had gone with her into the store, stood two or three steps behind her at the counter and let her ask the clerk for help herself (she had asked for clips instead of combs, and with her face as red as a struck flint had had to take the clerk to the window to show her). When he had given her the money to pay for them, then let her count her own change, she'd literally trembled with fear and pleasure. Afterward she had sat crushed against his side as he was driving home, pushing the combs into her hair, then taking them out, looking at them and rubbing her fingers over the surfaces, lambent in the low sunlight of the late afternoon, her voice equally lambent as she thanked him for them repeatedly.

"I can't take you into town now," he said. "You'll have to wait until this evening."

Her eyes darted sideways, bright blue, as she glanced at the clumps of primroses along the ditch, and then they came flying back to him. "No," she said determinedly. "Opal'll take me."

"No, Lettie."

"Why no?" she cried.

"You can't go into town yet except when I go. I told you that. And don't you ever sneak away from here with Opal or no one."

"But we want to get started. She has time to work with me tonight. Please." She brushed at something invisible on his collar, as if keeping him neat were one of her duties. "Doyle don't go into Dansville much. None of them do."

He had to look away from her, to pretend to see something on the far horizon, to be interested in the cows that were idly grazing in random patterns. If she had shown him her temper then, it would have been easy for him to be firm, but she had slid into her sweet wheedling. "He may be going in now," he said, not looking at her out of fear that something in her face might make him give in to her. "Lettie, you can't go in without me until things get settled down."

He started to walk away, but she stood in front of him to keep him from passing. She tried to push him back with her fluttering hands. "They are settled down!"

"What are you doing?" he asked, laughing at her, and took her hands in his. "Are these gnats or something?"

"Oh, don't tease me, Luther!"

He had hurt her: He quickly corrected his smile. "I ain't teasing, honey," he said quietly. "There's nothing been settled at all. Time's passing, but nothing's settled. There's a difference."

"That's dumb, Luther. Don't they know I'm staying with you? You think they may come for me after all this time?" She laughed nervously, stepped away from him, and pulled at a flower on the edge of the road. The stem was thick and fibrous and would not break though she stuck her nail through it until it had wet her finger. "Luther . . ."

He stooped down, cut the stem for her with his knife, and handed her the flower. "They'll come all right."

She turned to him then with the most blatant coquetry that a woman of her character can devise. "You going to let them take me, Luther?" she asked. It was a part of a familiar ritual, and if she had not spoken to him like this, he would have thought something was wrong. In another woman, such behavior might have evoked his pity or disgust, but in Lettie, it was right. Perhaps he was enough older than she to take pleasure in her efforts at manipulation and not to criticize her for them, not even to himself.

He pulled her to him, and she reached up around his neck, letting the petals of the daisy he had cut for her turn around and around over his ear. They were a quarter mile from the gate to the road into town. A truck passed, and a man Luther knew waved to him, but he did not wave back. The truck tires blew gravel up onto the shoulder, and then the horn honked the familiar code of greeting before disappearing in its own cloud over the crest of the bridge at the canal. "No," he said.

With a sudden pickup in the wind, the clouds increased their speed across the sky, and treetops yielded in green waves, dipping toward the white-blossomed shrubs. Lettie, complaining that the gusts tangled her hair, continued to collect flowers until she had a handful, then she looked up shyly at Luther and mentioned the stray calf and the promised ride in the truck.

The day that his room in the bunkhouse got white organdy curtains, a shiny pink spread, and pillows with pink ruffles six inches wide, Luther had left before dawn to go down to the branding. He would be away until late, giving Lettie and Opal the whole day to prepare the surprise. Luck was with them—the men even ate supper at the branding camp. Food had been taken there in the pickup, and the men stayed long after the sun went down to finish, working in an area lit by lanterns and the headlights of trucks.

Soon before she expected Luther's return, Lettie carefully placed a candle in a small holder in the window of their room, leaving the ceiling light on so that she could read while she waited. She sat up in bed with a magazine, slowly tracing beneath the words with her cured, polished index finger. From time to time, she underlined with a pencil a word she thought she knew. She was wearing a nightgown she had made out of what was left over from the organdy. The ruffles, matching those on the curtains, stood away from her neck and framed her face so that she looked like a child-duchess in a cameo. A bow of polished cotton was pinned to the side of her hair.

Luther was in one of the trucks at the rear, so Matt and Stephen were the first to see her through the window. They stood together for a moment under the oak tree wondering what Lettie was up to and then quickly ducked out of sight when they saw Luther come in, his head lowered, thinking hard about something and having no idea whatever about what had happened to his room or to his girl.

Lettie heard Luther walk into the bunkhouse, but she kept her concentration on her reading: One of his goals for her was that she be able to read at least as well as he could. "You can't get anywhere if you can't read," he had told her. Her face broke into a smile when she heard his boots on the hall floor, heard him say good night to Stephen or Ray. She could distinguish his walk from those of the other men who lived in the house because it was more thought out. *Luther's careful,* she thought with pride. *He don't make no mistakes.*

He knocked on his own door; it was his habit to do this since she had moved in. Their living together involved a set of very strict rules, all of which Luther had devised.

"Come in," she said, exaggerating the natural girlishness of her voice because she knew he liked it. The room smelled strongly of new material, unwound ribbon, bath powder, and Opal's cologne.

He had turned the door handle, walked in, taken off his hat, and started taking off his denim jacket before he realized what he'd walked into; when he did, he choked like a man who has been wading in shallow water and unexpectedly walks off the edge into the channel. "Lettie!" he said. "Pull down the shades, honey!"

She put the open magazine face down on the gleaming new spread, touched the pink bow with the palm of her hand to keep it in place as she moved, then eased herself out of bed, careful to leave the covers and the pillows undisturbed. Apparently it hadn't bothered her that the interior of her doll house could be seen from the outside, or that everyone walking by could see her in it, waiting for him. Lettie was so single-minded in her attachment to Luther that she thought of nothing else. She saw no need to account for herself to the whole theater when only the stage concerned her.

She was still thin, but by no means unattractively so; still on the whole a young girl and not a woman, but through the flat panel of organdy when she turned toward him, the woman in her asserted itself, because of the man and because of her belief that their time together had come, and that what she possessed under that cloth was adequate now to begin it. The candle glowed behind her, making the organdy nightdress perfectly transparent. Luther had not seen her body since the night the dead child came, and he had never seen it peaceful, gentle, and composed. He sat down on the cot and put his face in his hands. In a second, he felt her breath on his neck. "Don't you like it?" she asked, savage as a hurt child.

He looked up. "Lettie—like what?"

Instantly her tone of voice changed. "The room," she said. The bow, which had progressively been freeing itself from the bobby pin, now bounced loosely on the side of her head. "Ain't it pretty, Luther?" Her question dazzled him; he loved the sound of her. She put her hand on his shoulder, and though it was practically weightless, he thought he might collapse under an insistence that was hinted at not only by the gesture but also by the question.

"Don't touch me, Lettie. I've been out all day. I'm filthy dirty. You don't understand what I do." She removed her hand, and he realized immediately the absurdity of his statement. He knew that because of the white organdy and the silvery hair with the light behind it, she looked like a madonna, a Bible illustration of a saint, and that he had been fooled into forgetting who she was and where she had come from. She had been tortured; she had been abandoned for fourteen or even fifteen years to the vicissitudes of an environment that was out of her control or anyone else's; she had then had to put herself at his mercy, to come out here into the unknown and trust him. In one day, with less than twenty dollars, she had created a slice of heaven for herself and included him in it. With her sure female instinct, she had made a home for them. Before that evening, it had been a room that might have been any kind of room at all. It had an oak floor, cedar walls, four windows, and a closet. The overhead light was covered now with a white globe; he had been satisfied with a naked bulb and a string pull, never having thought about it or cared, because it was not the habit of a man who had been in the rodeo to notice such things. He had made good money, but he had never stayed in fancy places; and if he hadn't longed for their luxuries, it was because he was preoccupied with thoughts about the next day, when he might break his neck or his legs, throw out his knees, fracture his skull, break his hands and his feet, or get his chest crushed, so that, like friends of his, he would be forced to panhandle in towns where he had used to be famous and drink cheap whiskey to ease the pain.

He wiped the tears from his eyes on the stained sleeve of his shirt. He couldn't remember when he had last cried. He had been inhumanly stoic when his legs were broken. (In the rodeo, where men were hurt every day, an injury was not a thing to grieve over: Complaining or, even worse, crying worried people, and they had enough of that as it was.) Certainly he had not wept since that evening when he had sat in the front seat of the rodeo van, driving away from the room where his mother had left him two weeks earlier. He remembered the truck jerking along the dusty road, and he remembered the cowboy who came for him, saying nothing to him at all.

"I'm dirty, Lettie," he said. "And I'm tired."

"It's all right."

He had come home angry; he hated the branding. The registered cattle were left alone—only their ears were taped—but the beef herd had to be marked with hot metal. He never saw the sense of it and damned Matt, who refused to let him off, even knowing how he felt. Matt had insisted that he, Luther, was the best with the young animals, flattering him and telling him he could get the calves to be still without hurting them; with Luther there, setting the tempo, yelling at anyone who went too fast, cursing anyone who threw a calf too hard, there were never any broken bones or pulled muscles or torn-up anything. Yet Luther realized that with his gentleness and coaxing, his remarkable talent for drawing frightened animals to him, he in fact deceived them and took advantage of their trust. He imagined he could see the resentment in their eyes afterward when they and he simultaneously smelled the singed hair. They rolled their crazed eyes at him and hated him the worst.

Lettie sat back on her heels on the rug beside the cot. "You want me to rub your back?" she asked. She had infinite patience with disappointment, and infinite pity for him because he had cried. She handed him one of the handkerchiefs that she kept ironed for him, and he dried his eyes and was finished. Lettie untied the dust scarf he had around his neck and pulled off his boots.

Exhausted, he lay down on the cot. The white curtains made the room brighter, illuminating even the ceiling with their reflection. *It has to be right,* he thought. *It's not time. Does she know what she's doing herself? Am I understanding? Does she know what she has done to me?*

She got up, went to the closet, stood behind the door, and put on her dress. She laid the nightdress on the bed and smoothed the skirt; it had taken her a half hour to press it, to get the seams flat and the ruffles to stand out, and it had already become wrinkled while she was sitting up in bed reading and waiting for the men to come down from the pastures.

"Where are you going, Lettie?"

"To the cookhouse."

"What for?"

"To get you a Coke." She paused. "You rather have a Pepsi-Cola?"

"A Coke's fine."

Their relationship had been founded on his taking care of her, never the other way around. Now she was fixing up the room, wanting to rub his back, and getting him things to drink.

He went to the bureau and removed the pajamas she had laundered for him.

"What you doing, Luther?"

"I'm going to take a bath," he said. "I'm going to stay with Stephen tonight, Lettie."

"Come back here for your drink, though," she said softly. "Talk to me awhile. You know I've been alone all day."

But when he returned to the room, dressed in the light blue pajamas, his wet hair combed back flat against his head, he remained silent and reflective, lying on the cot, sitting up at intervals to drink, then lying back to look at the ceiling. Lettie went to the window, adjusted one of the tiebacks, and pulled at the curtain to make it hang fuller, then stepped behind the closet door and put her nightdress back on; and again, on her way to bed, passed in front of the candle. He rose on one elbow. In the organdy gown she seemed to be a spirit walking through a mist, fascinating him and urging him to follow.

If she was aware that he was watching, she kept it to herself. She got into bed and resumed her reading, as if he had never come back into the room. Looking at the magazine with the pencil poised over the page, she said softly, "You still going into Stephen's?"

"No." There was a sick irritation in his voice that she had never heard before.

"Oh," she answered strongly, yet hollowly.

"Blow out the candle," he said, with the same irritation. "I'm going to sleep."

"I'm reading."

He turned his head sharply toward her: "Lettie, you can't read!"

"I can."

He sat up in bed. "You couldn't read the story out of that magazine last night. How can you read it today?"

"I—"

"Tell me what you just read, Lettie."

"I can't do that because I only know some of the words. But Opal says if you can read one word, you can read, and I read a lot of them. I have the ones underlined that I know." Her voice slackened. "I don't know the whole story yet."

He sighed and placed the empty Coke bottle beside the leg of his cot. "That's right. That's good. I'll help you with it tomorrow, honey. Now blow out the candle."

He heard her breath; the candle went out, and the room fled into darkness.

From across the road, Opal saw the light extinguished, and she shook her head, rearranging the sweater she was knitting for

Hazel on her lap. "I hope I did right in helping her," she said to
her husband.

"She's lucky as hell. He's a good man."

"But she's been hurt so bad—it'll take a long time."

"He'll be careful."

"I hope so."

"Luther ain't no Doyle, Opal. Ain't you forgetting that
women like men?"

"But Doyle—"

"Luther ain't Doyle, Opal!"

"She—"

"What the hell you think she fixed the room up for?" he said.
He leaned back in his chair and put his stocking feet on the porch
rail. "She wants to play house."

His wife held her arms tightly around herself. Mark looked at
her. "If you're cold, go in and get your jacket."

"I ain't cold, Mark."

He spoke so slowly that you wondered whether or not he'd
finish each syllable. "Little stray bitch picked up in the street . . ."

Luther lay still. The organdy nightdress rustled between the
sheets; he knew she was awake. A little wind was blowing on the
other side of the open window, and he could hear its low hum-
ming clearly.

In his mind, he kept seeing the branded calves, smelling the
burning and hearing the cries of pain, feeling the hide squirming
under his hands. He had held them down so that they wouldn't
hurt themselves, but he had imprisoned them as well. *Any day
but today; any time but now. Out of all the year, she picks this
day to make up the windows and the room and herself. I could
have waited months for her. I was all right.* He heard her shifting
in the bed.

He dozed off, sleeping lightly as he always did since she had
come, until above his sleep, he heard an unmistakable sound. For
a few seconds, to clear his head, he sat on the edge of the cot, but
then he stood up and went to her, as he had always gone since the
first time on the sidewalk in town, when she'd looked at him and
he had realized that whatever future problems the girl had, he
would share them with her. He answered her, let himself be
drawn to her, into her misery. At her back the two pillows were
arranged—Lettie always slept half-sitting so she could watch the
door. He smelled the new cloth, the ribbons, and the odor of
sweet cologne, the effort a woman makes for a man. He gathered

the limp, sobbing contents of the bed into his arms, the rough organdy ruffles of the gown scraping roughly against his face. He calmed her in his usual manner, repeating a formula that seemed to chase the devils out of her mind and soothe her and let her go back to sleep.

"What did you dream, Lettie? Tell me what's wrong. What is it, honey? Tell me the story of it." Luther believed, and he had told Lettie this, that telling a dream exorcised the evil in it. "Tell me," he said.

"I ain't been asleep," she answered, catching her breath to say it; yet despairing as she seemed to be, she moved against him then in one perfect motion, flesh on flesh, in what was unmistakably an invitation.

His arms tightened around her. "What you been doing then, Lettie?"

"Waiting."

When he kissed her, he seemed not to be himself, and for the first time, he let slip away his near-perfect guardianship. He kissed her as he had not kissed any woman since his conversion and baptism, when he had made a decision to put his sensuality in abeyance, reserving it for this moment. Over these long weeks, when he was working and he would think of her, a flash of anticipation would go across his heart like a feathered pinwheel; but every time he had looked at her soft face and heard her toy-doll voice, he had told himself, *That wouldn't be fair. No. There's even something wrong with me that I want to. A full-grown man almost three decades old cannot mate with anything that looks and talks like this. It would be a sin.* The paradox, that she had already not only been mated with but borne a child to a man much older than himself, had no relevance for him because it had been an outrageous anomaly, and he knew it. Maybe he was no better than Doyle. Wasn't he taking advantage of her trust? "You know what you look like in that gown?" he asked in a quiet, quickened voice, more baritone than was normal for him.

Less careful of her gown now, she wiped her tears on one of the ruffles. "Yes, I know."

"How do you know?"

"Opal told me."

He kissed her again. After that, she did not really move her mouth away from his; the rhythm of her quick breathing was synchronized with his, and when he spoke, he spoke against her lips. "And what did she tell you?"

"She said I looked like an angel in the Christmas pageant the

Sunday school gives, that I would have been better than Hazel
because of my hair. . . . Is that what you think?"

"Not exactly."

He struggled to continue talking to her in order to keep himself civilized and distracted. He would resist for a moment longer
the desire that was about to overcome him, but to which she
seemed already to have relinquished herself, such was her softness and the insistence of her consent. Then, as suddenly as if he
had been pushed to earth, his body leaped ahead of his intellect,
and it no longer occurred to him to stop himself. The orphan
child disappeared for him, and the woman materialized.

He reached for the sheet that covered her. "What are you
going to do about that gown now it's done its work?" he asked.

She pulled it over her head and threw it carelessly to the foot
of the bed.

He offered her one last escape. "You don't owe me nothing,
Lettie."

"You don't owe me, neither."

He was beside her; up against her, full length. "It's got to be
equal," he said.

"It is."

"It never is."

"You going to argue?"

She knew that he couldn't. She laughed because it was the
first time she had ever dared to tease this austere man who had
placed himself between her and evil. She laughed because she
loved him and because she was ecstatic in the celebration of the
success of her plan. She laughed at him until he stopped her voice
and the orderly progress of her thoughts by the complete, unintended, violent impulse of his love, and by his success in engaging her in it, thus confirming her faith.

The next day was a full workday, but no one who had seen or
heard about the room the previous night was going to disturb
Luther. He was first sighted in the afternoon a little after two
o'clock, taking a package of cinnamon sweet rolls and a pitcher
of milk from the refrigerator on the cookhouse porch. He said
nothing at all to Imogene, who was cutting out sugar cookies on
the floured kitchen table, though she had looked up from her
work with uncommon interest. He reappeared about two hours
later accompanied by Lettie, her hair pulled back in a ribbon to
make her look older, her ears adorned with pearl earrings that
Luther had surprised her with a week before. They went straight

to Luther's truck, deadly serious, Luther guiding Lettie by the arm as if she were a glass figurine, neither of them looking at anything but the ground, and certainly not looking at each other. They drove straight into town to the jewelry store. Lettie picked out a wide gold wedding ring delicately engraved with flowering vines. She said it looked like honeysuckle, but the woman behind the counter, a large, pale matron with a starched white jabot just under the fold in her chin, told her the ring was made in England.

"We don't have that vine in this part of our country," she said politely, her chin disturbing the jabot as she spoke. "It's called a clematis." She reached behind her for the catalogue and showed the couple the printed word.

Lettie's eyes raced nervously over the page like waves being pushed too strongly from behind.

"You still want it?" Luther asked. He was shy with Lettie now; he did not like to look directly at her.

Lettie nodded. "Can I wear it?"

"Not yet, honey . . . pretty soon." On the way out of town, he stopped by the florist and bought her a bouquet of white flowers.

At supper, although everyone saw the wedding ring (Lettie kept her left hand on the table), no one commented on it; it was understood that it couldn't be discussed unless Luther mentioned it first, and he said nothing at all during the entire meal. But when Opal and Lettie were alone finishing up the dishes, Opal asked, "Everything work out okay last night?"

"Yes." Lettie put the cup she was drying on a hook and steadied it so it would not hit against the one beside it. "It was just fine."

"He liked the room all right?"

"Not at first."

Lettie picked up another cup, her favorite, the one with blue roses that Ellen Khinsky had ordered from a coupon on the back of a soap package but hadn't been there to receive because she and Jimmy weren't married and so Mr. Littleton had run them off. The cup had a beautiful shape, Lettie thought, and she liked the way it felt in her hand. Luther had told her that afternoon, just as they were getting into town, crossing the bridge over the Colorado, that if she liked, they would buy a house in town and a set of dishes and whatever else she wanted from the money he had saved, but Lettie had declined. She preferred being one of the wives at the ranch—and wasn't it true that if you were married, Mr. Littleton provided a house? Couldn't they have the place behind Opal's house that had been empty since the Hammels had

left for Oregon to be in a milder climate? Mark and Stephen and
Arnold could help him fix it up, and she and Opal could make the
window coverings and upholster the old sofa that was still there
and not moldy because the house was well sealed.

Opal let the water run out of the sink. As the sucking sound of
the last of it being pulled through the copper pipe ended, she
asked, "You get married this afternoon?"

Without looking at Opal, her close attention on a plate she
was drying, Lettie nodded, and then she placed the plate on a
stack of dry ones.

"How did you get your blood test so fast?"

Lettie somehow expected that Luther Kelly's ring on her
finger would keep her hand from trembling, but it didn't.

"Who married you?" asked Opal. "Mr. Frazer?" Mr. Frazer
was the justice of the peace.

"No." Lettie was looking down at her ring; Opal's questions
made its design blur into the pink polish on her fingers; everything she looked at was blurred.

"Who, then? The preacher? Dr. Mengden won't generally do
it so fast."

In the dying light of the happiest day of her life, Lettie was
silent. She looked out the window into the blue of the fast falling
twilight, but all she saw was one of the hunting hounds, who had
nothing to do until deer season in November, rolling in the dirt.
She wished Luther had had no business that evening so that they
could have stayed together in their pretty room. Right now he
was talking in Matt's office, going over the work schedule for the
following week.

"Who, honey? Who married you?"

It would be impossible if her eyes met Opal's. Opal was five
years older than Luther, and she understood women and how they
thought, something that Luther did not know completely.

"Who, honey? Who performed the ceremony?"

"Luther," she whispered. She had to tell the truth now; married women were never liars. "He knew the vows and he taught
them to me over to the lake, out by the China bridge." The
bridge, a surprise Mr. Littleton had built for his wife, passed over
the narrow neck of the lake and had been prettified by the addition of weeping willows and a pair of swans.

Opal polished the bottom of the sink and the new chrome
spout with a dish towel and then reached out for Lettie's hand and
rubbed her damp, wrinkled finger across the pretty engraving.
Tears had caught in the rims of her eyes, but she swooped down

and blotted them on the tail of her blouse. She kissed the girl's warm cheek. "Well, that's just fine," she said.

For the next three days, Luther stayed with Lettie in their room, where they snacked on leftovers, fruit, and packaged things that Luther took out of the cookhouse at intervals when no one was around; not because he feared criticism for taking the food, but, rather, because he wanted to have those three days completely separate from the company of others. In the evening, after dark, Luther's truck would start up, and he and Lettie would leave the ranch, traveling into one of the towns, eight, fifteen, twenty miles away to have supper.

On the fourth day, at six o'clock in the morning, as if the three days of truancy had not intervened, Luther arrived in the cookhouse to have breakfast, and Lettie was cooking and washing with the women, just as she had been the week before. But to everyone's confusion, Luther was touchy and irritable. It wasn't until two weeks had passed, when Arnold Sackett came in during lunch to tell him that a colored person named Martha was waiting for him outside in a rusted, broken-down, wood-bed truck, with an engine like a sewing machine, that the ranch hands realized what they should have been aware of the entire time.

"They want her brought back," she told Luther when he came out of the cookhouse, still wiping his face on a napkin. He had jumped up from his meal, jarring Lettie's arm and causing her to spill a spoonful of soup when Arnold had given him the message. "They gave me five dollars to come out here and tell you, Mr. Luther." Martha wore a silk dress that had once belonged to a white woman, but her purple head scarf was new. She had fixed herself up as carefully as if she were going to church. She was clearly tired of standing, and though Luther had asked her to sit down, she was unable to do that in the company of white people, so, with Luther following, she walked back to her truck, got in, and shut the door.

Luther tipped his head backward so that his eyes could clear the brim of his hat. "Who gave you five dollars?"

"Her uncle, Doyle Campbell, who kept her. He sent me for her, to bring her home; said it was me who should bring her back because it was me who got her lost."

Luther shook his head. The shadow from the brim of his hat shaded the upper part of his face and fell sharply over his nose. "I'm not sending her back," he said. His lips hardly moved, and his eyes, because of the shadow, were hidden from her. "There's no way I'm going to do that." He spoke automatically, with no inflection.

Silent and troubled, Martha stared ahead through the scorched glass of the windshield, which was pocked in a dozen places by gravel shots. "They say if she don't come back, they can get the sheriff to bring her back, because they's the legal guardians."

Luther put his hands in his back pockets, hunched his shoulders, and looked toward the ground. *Why does this keep being so hard?* he thought. *Why doesn't it get easy?* Martha watched him warily, the whites of her eyes stained and yellowed, the dark centers diffused and tired.

"Wait for me," he said finally. "I'll follow you back."

While Luther went inside, Martha sat in her truck, fiddling with a pipe that was still warm. She puffed at it once or twice, and when it did not draw, she turned the bowl over and tapped the contents into a tin can that was fixed to the dashboard.

Lettie had been running when she came up to the truck; her forehead was moist, and she was shaking. She appeared from behind the hawthorn hedge, swinging around the vehicle's dented fender, leaning on the door to get her balance, then reaching for the partly rolled-down window, her hands turning white as she clutched the top edge of the glass. When she had rushed out of the cookhouse in pursuit of Luther and had seen the truck, she had run into the woods, planning to go the fifteen miles to the settlement—all alone because she wanted to keep Luther out of it; she had planned to do this ever since she had gotten well. But as she reached the fence, she thought better of it and decided that she would try to talk Martha out of taking her; doubling back, she waited for Luther to leave and then made her move.

"Martha," she said, "I'm grateful for what you did for me." She made forceful and adamant sounds while the black woman watched her with the scuffed, benign features of an idol. Her words, practically incomprehensible, rolled one over the other like dry weeds in a fast wind, some of them fastening together, others floating helplessly adrift, finding nothing on which to anchor. "I lost my baby.... Don't Doyle know? I lost him the day after Doyle whipped me! It came too early, the whipping was what done it." Her voice had risen progressively in pitch and volume until at last she was yelling, and her fingernails were digging at the rusted, eaten-out metal on the truck door, as if to destroy the vehicle that had come for her.

Martha shouted back, not out of harshness but because Lettie had frightened her. "Doyle wants you back. He say he won't hurt you no more."

"But Luther and me's married, Martha!"

"You ain't married. Mr. Luther may have told you some story, but you ain't."

"I got my ring!" Stepping up on the running board, she thrust her left hand into the truck cab for Martha to see. She turned it back and forth so that its surface would jump in the sun and blind Martha with the truth, as the prophets Luther read to her about were sometimes blinded.

Martha raised her hand and, with antipathy toward this symbol of Luther's guardianship, which so particularly seemed to place her and Lettie at risk, turned her head away in disgust and pushed the ring roughly out of her sight. "It don't matter how many rings he give you. You ain't married 'less you have your grandpa's signature from the courthouse, and you ain't got it. He told me that this morning. He heard you think you're married, and that's why he and Doyle come to tell me to get you back in this truck. He say you was spoken for first by Doyle anyway, and you ain't nobody else's till he say so."

Martha's words made no sense to Lettie, and she began to shriek. She turned on Matt now, whom she had seen, out of the corner of her eye, coming toward her from among the lawn chairs. He was poised to grab her, and so she attacked him first, in the same spirit in which she had attacked the truck door. "Don't let him go!" she screamed. "You can order him!" It was the first direct statement she had ever addressed to Matt. She was terrified of him; he was the boss—like her grandfather, the symbol of authority and, therefore, of injustice. She did not know him at all, had never tried to know any of the men except Luther, but she distrusted and hated Matt.

Some of the women had run out onto the road to try to quiet her, but it was finally Luther who grabbed her from behind, pulled her off Matt, and dragged and then carried her to their room. He held her tight against him until she wore herself out thrashing and shouting. Pinning her arms to her side, he restrained her until her fury was spent, and then stayed with her, sitting on the side of the bed, drying her face and straightening her hair. He helped her sit up and supported her against his side. The shades were up, sun was coming in the south windows, and the shadow it formed of them was a solid and single mass against the cedar planks of the wall.

"I'll go back, then," she whispered. He touched her face with his handkerchief because tears were mounting in her eyes again. "I got to do it. They have all the right to me." She was panting, and she struggled to speak over her exhaustion.

He told her he was going.

"You ain't! I—"

"Hush, Lettie."

She looked at him sideways, savagely, but kept silent.

"You're going to stay here with Matt and Stephen," he said. "You can't go. You know what has to happen. You're not mine until I go out there, tell them you are, and settle. I always told you. And, Lettie, don't go sneaking off neither, because I'll have to come get you, and then I'll have two things to do instead of one."

She looked at him again as if she would cut him down. Exhausted as she was, she prepared for a new onslaught, this time on his despotism. She began to reach for him; when she caught him off balance, he slipped and almost fell.

He shook her viciously then, something he would never have done had he not grown somewhat resentful of the fact that getting a woman was so easy for some men (a few visits to a farm or a cottage in town with flowers and an invitation to the movies; you just had to sit in whatever room the family used for a parlor and talk to the daddy more than to the girl), yet so difficult for him now.

"Hush, you hear me?" he said. "And don't you ever think to turn that temper on me." She started to say something, and he shook her again. "Hush!"

"I am!" she said angrily.

"Sometimes I wonder if that temper ain't responsible for all the trouble you ever got, Lettie."

She howled as if he had struck her. He realized the unkindness of the remark and immediately regretted having hurt her with it. "Don't divide us up, Lettie! Everything we do is right together! You hear me?"

"Yes! If you'll stop shaking me and ruining my teeth!"

He tried to smile, to joke with her, to breathe quietly; she listened to him, though she refused to smile back. "It'll be easier to tell them you're staying with me if Doyle don't have to be looking at you while I say it. He'd figure on putting up a real fight to keep you there, if he saw you now. You're pretty, honey, and he won't never have seen you like this." He touched her cheek. "Now, stop crying. Riding over there, I don't want to think of you crying. Stop. Stop it, Lettie."

"I'm trying, damn it."

He overlooked the cursing; only one thing at a time; he couldn't give her lessons when he was upset himself. He went to the chest of drawers and opened the top drawer.

She ran to him and grabbed his arm. "You ain't taking your gun?"

"No, I'm not taking my gun, Lettie; I'm taking my money."

Her huge eyes, magnified by her fear and disbelief, searched his face. "Goodness, Luther, you going to buy me?"

"Sort of, but that don't bother me none." He kissed her wet face. "That bother you, Lettie . . . huh?" He smiled; he knew it didn't.

"No . . ." she said slowly. "I don't care how you get me."

"I didn't think so."

She clung to him, closing her eyes and trying not to think about what awaited him. "Don't get hurt," she said.

"You think I will?"

She looked around their room, bright and shimmering with the noon light. "No," she said. "I know you ain't the kind who does."

She tried to come with him to the lot where his truck was parked. "You wait for me on the porch," he told her. "Get Opal to sit with you."

"I love you, Luther," she said. She was hanging on to the sleeve of his shirt, almost running now to keep up with him.

He stopped and turned to her. "I hope you know, Lettie."

"I love you, I said!"

He took off his hat and, after making an effort to smile, kissed her and held her a moment with his head buried down in her neck. Turning her around, he said, "Now, go on up to the porch. Hurry! Let me talk to Matt a minute."

She looked over her shoulder once, and he waved her forward and then walked quickly away.

Matt had been in the yard talking to Stephen, but when he saw Luther, he moved toward him, motioning for Stephen to stay where he was. "We're going with you, Luther."

"No, Matt. It'll confuse them if I bring help. I want it to stay even and easy. I got to see what they want."

"They damned sure want Lettie."

"Maybe. They want something. But remember, it's them doing the asking, not me. I got what I want." He touched the brim of his hat and shifted its angle. "I found it, Matt, found their leavings, what they forced out." He motioned toward the porch where Lettie stood beside Opal, holding his big white handkerchief to her nose. "Take a look, Matt. She's pretty, ain't she? She looks like a picture. And she's getting sweet. I'm getting her sweet. One day she'll be a real good mama."

Matt grinned. "She ain't pregnant already?"

"She will be spring after next, and she'll be just fine."

Matt had stepped back into the dappled shadows of the trees while Luther remained in the sun. "Maybe they'll pay you for your services," said Matt.

"Nope. It's me buying."

A breeze fled by and shook the limbs and the mottled patterns. "If you're not home by dark, we'll come out there."

Luther shook his head. "No, that might scare them just at a time when I'm getting somewhere. I'll be O.K."

When he got to his truck, a Mexican boy who'd just signed on, and whom Luther had been teaching to use a cutting horse, was sitting motionless on the rider's side; his hat was pulled low over his eyes.

Luther put his hand on his knee. "I thank you," he said softly, "but I got to go alone."

"I could help you."

"I know. Now get on out," Luther said gently. He was looking straight ahead, concentrating on his task and, in his mind, outlining his method. "I got to hurry before they plan too much against me or I lose my nerve."

That afternoon Luther saw the place where Lettie had been locked up: a shed behind a shack, leaning against it as all the five or six structures leaned against some support, as though they had been propped up after an earthquake. She must have managed to dig her way out from time to time but was always caught, until that final effort when she had made it to Martha's. Martha had seen her coming across the ridge of the hill that had once been the bed of the railroad track, had gone for her, had lifted her up to the back of the truck, and made her as comfortable as she could, hoping as she latched the truck bed shut, her fingers trembling over the hard metal of the poorly installed latches, that these same men whom Luther was now looking at would not decide to pursue the girl over the hill.

The five men who came out to meet Luther had been watching for the return of the old woman but hadn't been at all surprised to see Luther following behind her, no more than Luther had been surprised when they had finally sent someone for Lettie. Luther

had decided, after their ceremony, to advertise the fact that he
was calling himself her husband by letting her exhibit the gold
ring as a beacon—knowing that Lettie was so eager and proud
that she would extend her hand and display it for everybody she
saw. When she had run out on the road to show it to Josh Killian,
who also delivered the mail to the settlement, the confrontation
was guaranteed.

Luther was not a particularly tall man—less than six feet—
but he was strong and seasoned. As a boy in the labor camps, he
had fought often and hard; and occasionally, while he was in the
rodeo, and before his conversion, he had quarreled with his fists
because it came easily to him. Once, in a café, he had beat a man
senseless over a woman neither of them knew very well or even
much wanted (she was already married and a little too fast); they
had fought because a fight was in the air and because neither of
their young bodies, once braced for combat, had been able to
renege.

He knew what kind of men these were to have let one of their
own tribe torture a child, and do nothing about it. Drugged,
drunk, underfed, the world against them or not, that they had
allowed that to happen—and not only to see it once but to let it
continue—gave him a feeling of power over them, no matter
what their numbers.

The houses stood in a deep shade where nothing grew but
stunted weeds and the kind of wild flowers that develop hard
little buds but never bloom. The common yard was filled with
broken trash; at its center was a hill of cloth and rags wet by rain
so often that its components were indistinguishable by either type
of cloth or color. The only amenity, a rubber tire hoisted to a limb
by a chain, was occupied by a boy who fled at the sight of a
stranger. There was always trouble when people like this one
came: Maybe they would have to move.

The settlement reminded Luther of places where he'd lived
when he was little, when he was hungry all the time, and his nose
ran until his lip was sore, and his throat burned so he couldn't
talk, and every winter, he came down with a fever that he
sweated out and cured alone, lying on a bed for days, looking up
at the inverted arcs of spider webs and throbbing clumps of
daddy-longlegs. He dreaded walking into that shade, not because
of the five men and what they might do to him but because of the
pain the place caused him. He would never have done it except
for Lettie.

He waited for a long moment in the cab of his truck, assessing the rapacity of the group, determining quickly what kind of men they were and what they would want in exchange for one of their own. *They'll have an easy price, maybe not low, but easy,* he thought. *I just got to figure out what they're going to ask.*

He slipped quickly out of the truck and began to walk toward the group with his shoulders up, his back straight, his stride even, neither cocky nor ruthless. He had considered wearing his hand-tooled boots, the new ones that he saved for town parties and church but had decided in favor of an old pair that were soft and nicked and hugged his feet, the ones he wore for visiting prosperous neighboring ranches, or for when Clarence came asking his advice, or for playing poker and pitch. On them his spurs fit best and made more noise. By the time he had stopped walking, he knew everything he needed to know about the men he was facing. "Who does the talking?" he asked. "Who'd she belong to before me?" If Doyle was going to kill him, he figured he would do it then for that last comment.

A skinny man with stiff gray hair covered by a dirty cap, and wearing overalls with the knees out and no shirt (since it was still cool enough to be wearing a shirt, Luther knew he'd been asleep, that someone keeping watch had wakened him) stepped forward half a step. "I was coming to get her this evening," the man said. The deep creases in his face and neck were dirty, and a recent scratch on his cheek reddened under the flush caused by his effort. "But I saw Martha and told her to get over there." He paused and looked past Luther to the truck. "You bring her?" He was either chewing on something or he had a tremor in his jaw.

Luther waited briefly before replying. "No," he said. "I came here alone. You her grandfather?"

"Her legal guardian." This sounded odd from his mouth; someone in town had probably told him what to say. "You Kelly?" he asked.

"That's right." Luther hung his thumbs in his belt. He didn't let his eyes stray to the other men, though he had seen the redhead, knew he was in Doyle's company, knew at once that fighting or not fighting Doyle had nothing to do with acquiring Lettie because it was Doyle's father who made the decisions. He hoped he'd be able to bargain with this old man, who knew he had a commodity the winning or losing of which vitally touched his petitioner's heart. He'd seen a similar confrontation years before, but the details were blurred—though not the aspect of the man who had succeeded, nor the cadence of the exchange, the lack of motion, and the economy of talk.

Luther kept his eyes on the old man. "How much you want for her?" he asked.

"I wouldn't take nothing." The old man had answered fast and correctly, if a little drowsily, as a man who is not yet over the effects of alcohol.

Luther took out his wallet and emptied it of ten new twenty-dollar bills. He'd gone to the bank to get these just three days after he'd found Lettie, and they'd been lying for almost two months in his drawer under his socks. From the first he'd meant to keep her—going against Clarence, against Matt, against good sense if necessary, but keeping faith with humanity, he thought, with his religion, and with his passion for Lettie.

A woman stepped out of one of the houses onto the porch. Behind her scuffled two scrawny roosters, whose red, fleshy wattles hung raggedly on the scabrous skin of their necks. The woman was fat and oily, as if she'd never had a meal in her life that consisted of foods other than fried pork fat and grits. She was well over thirty, but still she had the blemished skin of a pubescent child. When she cleared her throat, the old man waved his hand to silence her.

"Am I supposed to give her the money?" asked Luther. "She the one handles things?"

The old man spit on the dirt. "She don't handle nothing."

"What she want?"

"She ain't doing the asking."

Luther crushed the money in his fist. "What does she want, Campbell?"

Lettie's grandfather swayed slightly. "One of them Littleton cows. A young one with a good calf."

Luther let his eyes wander over the littered yard with no fencing and hardly a blade of grass. The dirt was packed up as shiny as a government road in a poor county; bitterweed and sedge clogged the ditch. "You ain't got no way of feeding a cow proper," he said. "You get one and her milk'll stop in three days. The calf'll die of starvation when his mama quits eating. You ain't got grazing space, and you sure ain't going to buy feed with the money I'm giving you."

The old man glanced at the woman, then at Luther.

"Think of something else," Luther ordered.

The woman made a noise in her throat, loud, raucous. It might have been speech; at any rate, the old man seemed to have understood it. "You butcher me a steer then," he said, speaking with more authority than he had previously. "And you bring it here cut up and on ice."

The woman wound her hands in her skirt and tipped her chin in what must have been a nod.

"A steer's worth two or three hundred dollars," said Luther. "That's too much if you want the cash, too."

The red-haired man went down on his haunches, took up a stick, and began to draw it across the earth in straight lines all going the same direction until the stick broke under the pressure and he threw it sideways into a pile of metal, all that remained of a red Ford coupe that he'd given up trying to repair. Lettie's grandfather pointed at him with his thumb, and for the first time, he and Luther exchanged glances. His eyes were the same color as Lettie's and had about them a similar watchfulness, but the whites were marbled like those of strong, brutish people too long troubled by overwork and dissipation. "He wants her home here," said his father. "He don't want me to take nothing for her; he thinks she's his. And he's right."

The hair on the back of Luther's neck bristled, and a wave of anger washed over him; his eyes became instantly colder, and he took a big risk in what he said, snapping out his words like something heavy walking across dry sticks. "He ain't getting her back, not ever, Campbell. Either I keep her, and you get your pay, or the county home takes her. You send the sheriff, and Littleton and me will go to court against you. She ain't but fifteen or less, and the doctor in Dansville seen what you done."

He corrected Luther immediately. "I didn't do nothing. Doyle, he—"

Luther interrupted. "Where was that woman up on that porch? She can't protect nothing? She don't look like no man lays hands on her."

Campbell hesitated, looked dodgingly at his son and then at Luther. He shrugged. "The cash ain't enough," he said. "What you offer?"

Luther set his mouth, and his eyes took in a discarded wagon wheel with weeds that were struggling to grow through the spokes. One of the men had kicked at an ant bed, and it was sending a black-pepper crest over the iron rim. The swell of tiny ants spread over the oil-stained earth. Luther watched the ants, some of them with white particles in their jaws, staggering under their burdens, reeling like burlesque drunks. He had never seen an encampment like this without ants, so many that they came through the floorboards and stung you even in bed, and got into the flour and sugar, so that the women had to pick them out and rub them dead between their thumbs and fingers. His mother, or some woman she had left him with, was always opening a package of something and yelling about the goddamned ants. At the ranch, they were quick about controlling the ants because they couldn't have them around the newborn stock, or killing the fawns that in a year or two one of the Littletons would shoot. "I'll give you the cash and half a steer, butchered, wrapped, and marked," he said, looking up from the swarm.

Pleased with his success, the old man put his hands on his hips; in another moment he would have smiled. "You bring Lettie back here until I get it."

Luther turned his head quickly. "You don't see her no more," he said. "Let me spell it out for you real good. She's mine, or she's the county's—but I figure any man who finds a woman in the condition I found her, and nurses her back, has got the right to her. No one would give you no surprise judgment on that, Campbell. The fact is, I don't have to give you nothing!"

Doyle got up and walked behind the house. He was a big man, heavily muscled in the shoulders and thighs; but his skin was peculiarly splotched, which made him look unhealthy. Luther wished for a pistol then because he sensed that Doyle might rather use a gun than fight him. "I'll give you the cash now and bring the meat tomorrow," Luther said.

From behind the house, he heard what he thought was a clip going into an automatic.

"Don't think of killing me, Campbell. There isn't anyone at Littleton's don't know I'm here. That son of yours will get his neck stretched, or he'll rot at Huntsville, depending on how much Clarence decides to spend on a lawyer."

The gray-haired man extended his hand for the money, but Luther drew it back. "You call the sheriff claiming the girl after I give you this, and I'm going to do like I said."

Campbell spit to the side of him, then wiped his mouth on the back of his hand. "You bring the meat before five tomorrow. And don't bring me no half-year bullock, neither. I want a grown steer, grade-A meat, one of them like I seen through Littleton's fences, Mr. Luther Kelly. And not a tough one. We want"—he looked back at the woman for approval, but her face was unreadable—"a two-year-old."

Luther stepped toward him and pushed the money into his pocket.

He could turn his back on them now and walk to his truck in

surety. The deal had been made, and they were satisfied; at least, the old man and the woman were, and probably thought he was a fool for paying so high. He wondered if there was anything in the old man that was a bluff—if he was glad that Lettie was gone.

When he arrived home, Lettie ran up to him and helped him out of the truck as though, in the time he had spent away from her, he had become an invalid. She kept looking him over, searching for wounds; she touched him carefully and then examined her fingers, as if she expected blood.

"He take the money?" she asked. She trembled a little and took in occassional long draughts of air. Her face had a high red color, and her eyelashes were wet from having cried the whole while he'd been gone.

"Yeah, he took it. That pleases you, don't it, Lettie?"

He put his arms around her and drew her close. "Lettie, you're pretty this evening," he said and told her that she had cost him the price of half a steer as well. She walked with him to their room, touching him softly, circling him and staying with him like a moth stays with a slowly moving lantern.

Before dinner, he went to Matt's office, knowing that he was waiting to hear what had occurred at the settlement. He talked to Matt, and together, by dark, they had the steer: a fine two-year-old that would have marbled steaks and large, firm roasts. There would be no more than twenty pounds of stew and hamburger on it. When the bleeding meat of the slain steer was stacked in piles, the arms of the men still red and smelling sweet from blood, Matt said, "Luther, you're a real fool. You married one of them girls owns a farm, her daddy would have been giving you the steer, and more. Men don't buy women. It's the other way around."

"Sure they do," said Luther, in full possession of the uninhibited mental clarity of a man who has recently been made wiser by an experience that has required and tested all of his strength. "It's just that the way they pay isn't so obvious." He shrugged.

The next day, he made the same trip down the mud-clogged roads to the settlement; again, he went alone.

When the meat was unloaded and the pieces counted (some of them unwrapped and appraised) and found to be in the amount and of the quality agreed on, the old man stepped forward, as if offering to shake Luther's hand, a gesture which Luther rejected. With a quick glance, he searched the now-empty yard, his arms at his sides, restive.

"She's mine now."

"Yep." Having been refused a handshake and believing that any other conciliatory gesture would be refused as well, Campbell started to go inside.

"There's one more thing."

"What?"

"You call for me the one who done it." Luther had thought long and hard about this request, and he had decided that whipping Doyle would not be incompatible with his belief in turning the other cheek.

Campbell took a step toward Luther and held out his hands palms up as though to show he had no weapon in them, any more than he was now going to have a lie in his mouth. "Doyle ain't here," he said.

"Call him."

"He's gone."

"He ain't gone. He's hiding."

"No, I told you he's gone."

"I paid you for the right to settle with him. I can't be calm with her until that's done." He was tense and breathing fast. "I didn't buy no whore from you, Campbell," he said. "I bought the woman who's going to give me my family. You understand?"

The old man nodded; he stood with his hands in his pockets and pretended to think.

Luther looked around the settlement. The place seemed deserted except for the old man, as though once the price had been paid, the others had fled. He stared hard at Campbell and made a statement that betrayed his heart—it was the only time in his life he would allow himself to be so dishonest, but it was the only way Doyle would be delivered to him. "There ain't no girl from around here worth what I paid you. Call him."

"Maybe not, but all we talked about was the girl—my son wasn't throwed in."

Luther watched him for a minute to see if he would break down, but he was resolute. He had the same sharpness in his eyes that Lettie sometimes had; and if she had decided on something, you'd have to trick her if you needed to change her mind. Luther straightened his hat over his hair and looked up, as if he were trying to locate the sun through the opaqueness of the trees. Then he turned and went back to the truck, walking at a moderate pace, so that the old man would know that he was not leaving. Campbell, barefoot, the white hair on his chest curling around the bib of his overalls, waited in the yard.

When Luther came back with a large paper sack and opened it

before the old man, the patriarch of the Campbells drew in his cheeks, looked at Luther gravely, and nodded his head up and down, as if the muscles in his neck were tight and partly paralyzed. He turned abruptly, cupped his hands around his mouth over the bristles of a week's growth of beard, and bellowed.

"Call him again," said Luther when there was silence and not the least sign of the man.

Campbell repeated the bellow, and a minute later, Luther saw a mop of red hair begin to move through the eight-or ten-foot weeds, like a bird flying low to land on a lake or in a field of grain. The desire to have a shotgun and to use it scalded Luther's mind. *That's it,* he said to himself. *I'm going to kill him. That's what I knew.*

When Doyle saw Luther, he threw his head back toward the safe pastures, as if, like a wild horse, he would break and run. The glance was brief and without resolve. He turned again to his rival and smiled; or, at least, rolled his lips away from his teeth in a way that was neither ugly nor brazen, but merely an acceptance that the time had come that he had expected since the night he had overheard in the drive-in grocery (outside of which he spent most of his evenings drinking) that a bastard child of one of the settlement people had been born dead at Littleton's, and that a self-appointed knight had taken charge of the dead baby's mother, so that in order to see the girl, a man would have to go through Luther Kelly.

Luther looked at the old man, who nodded again and, stiff-legged, walked into the house with the quart of Wild Turkey. He turned to Doyle, who came toward him, his splotched skin suddenly drained of color, his muscles contracting, with exactly the right amount of nervousness, no fear, and with the insensible single-mindedness of a man who has never known either gallantry or cowardice.

Luther hit Doyle first. A muscle in his back tensed, then one in his shoulder; he lifted his arm, yelled in a voice he thought he had buried when he had repented, and smashed Doyle to the ground. Reacting as quickly as a mechanism on a spring, Doyle rose, lowered his head, and crashed into Luther's ribs, knocking him backward into the side of a shed. Luther rebounded, breathless, jabbing at Doyle in quick, hard blows. Doyle heard Lettie's name repeated by this furious man many times, but his curses and accusations were drowned out by the cries of pain that came from both of them.

Luther's face was cut; his hands bled. He had to breathe

through his mouth now because his nostrils were filled with blood, and a flow from a cut over his eye made it difficult for him to see. The two men circled each other striving for the best position—then suddenly Doyle dived into Luther, and Luther fell sideways, his arms outstretched, his feet tearing at the weeds and rocks on the slope of a ditch. Doyle followed him down; Luther ducked Doyle's right fist, yet took a blow from the left, then Luther's fist crashed into the short bone of Doyle's nose and the longer straighter one of his jaw. Standing ankle-deep in water, Luther brought his fist up from his knee, hit Doyle once on the side of his face, and as Doyle went down, Luther struck him again with the side of his hand on the base of his skull.

Doyle lay motionless; his legs half submerged in the shallow water, his arms and torso spread out in peculiar angles on the broken stems of the jimsonweed and brome. With each breath, he moaned; his left arm seemed broken; his face had begun to swell. Luther bent over him, his hands on his knees, his lungs ready to burst, not only from the repeated blows to his chest, but because now each breath he took brought with it a razor cut just above his heart. At last, catlike, he dropped to his haunches and watched the suffering man. He thought of the first time he'd seen Lettie and then of her long labor; how even now when he slept beside her she sometimes woke screaming in her dreams.

On the other bank of the ditch, the wind lifted the tattered leaves of a stunted mesquite toward the drift of clouds, while a summer tanager flitted delicately among its branches. Beneath the tree Luther noticed a scattering of dwarf dandelions trying to raise their yellow heads out of the mashed tin cans and rusted parts of machines. Lettie always kept jars full of flowers in their room. The room itself she kept spotless and neat; any kind of disorder disturbed her.

Doyle opened his eyes but seemed unable to focus on anything. "Why don't you finish it?" he whispered; and it seemed to be a dare.

Luther spit blood in the grass, held his nose to the sleeve of his shirt and observed the widening stain. The razor-cut in his chest tempted him to relax and take care of himself; the ache in his head urged him to lie down, but he did neither. Doyle's lips straightened, his head drooped, and then he seemed to sleep. "I done it, Campbell," Luther answered softly.

* * *

No one knew for certain whether Luther had killed Doyle—
people in town said Doyle had either been buried real deep or had
run off—but Luther took a heavy punishment for his vengeance.
The people at the settlement were quiet about the bargain, the
fight, and Doyle's fate, just as they had been quiet about Lettie,
and Luther was quiet, too, but when he came home after delivering the meat, his clothes were soiled with grease, dust, and
blood; the skin on his face and hands was raw to bleeding; he had
a side full of cracked ribs; and his nose was close to broken.
When he bent over Lettie and showed her the paper that her
grandfather had signed giving permission for her to marry (he had
told Luther that she was born after it got cool in 1930, so she had
to be fifteen), she was sitting in a red lawn chair beside Opal,
waiting for him. He kneeled and put his head in her lap. His shirt
was ripped in two places; there was blood on his neck and a
wicked cut over his eye, which Lettie bathed for him, but which
he refused to allow her to tape, saying that he wanted to keep the
scar to remind her of the price he had paid.

Matt, from his place on the cookhouse porch, sighed to see it:
the best cowboy he had ever had, as fine a man as he had ever
known, kneeling half-dead and bleeding before that little girl who
was responsible for his condition. She had never done one thing
he knew of to merit what she was getting, and she probably
would never have the sense to appreciate it. A strange world
where Luther Kelly would be stung helpless by a forsaken and
wretched girl who before he'd found her, had already been broken into by another man, had never tasted ice cream, had never
been inside a picture show, and had hardly even worn shoes. Matt
hoped to God that Luther would finally get some happiness, since
he'd paid so heavy.

Luther refused to go to the doctor, but that evening, after he
fainted at the dinner table, Stephen and Matt took him into town,
and Dr. Jackson put him in the hospital. The trouble was a broken
rib bone poking a lung and forming an abcess: It was bad, but the
doctor fixed the rib, dosed him heavily on sulfadiazine, and said
he would probably get better—no guarantees. It was a lengthy
confinement, and Lettie stayed with him, sleeping in the wood
and leather lounge chair beside the bed. The doctor tried to be
strict with her, saying that there was nothing she could do, the
nurses would take care of everything, but Lettie stood up to him
and got her way. While Luther slept, Lettie held his bruised

hands and cried. When he was awake, she tried to read to him from magazines she found in the waiting room. If he grimaced or groaned, she rang for the nurse.

"Don't you bother him at night," Dr. Jackson had warned her, and she slept in the chair, never stretching out beside him on the bed and pulling up her blouse to feel his chest against her breasts, or kissing him in the special ways that so quickly aroused him when he was well. She also hid from him her impatience at his slow healing.

She had thought he was asleep one night when he called to her.

"You can't," she protested, breathless and leaning over him tensely. Only a dim red light shone in the hallway, but it was enough for her to see how he was looking at her—a little out of his head, but this had nothing to do with the rib.

"Yeah, I can, if you'll just . . ." He showed her what to do.

It seemed strange to her, new, maybe wrong even, but it turned out fine, though a little better for Luther than for her, she thought.

Occasionally during the day, if Luther was sleeping, she would stand at the window looking out at the tidy lawn, the neat cement walk, and the little square flower bed of roses, where none of the grass was allowed to creep over the borders and ruin the carefully tended edges. When she and Luther got their house, they would fence off a lawn and raise roses from cuttings. She was tempted sick by those flowers, and finally, on the day before Luther was to be released, she went outside and picked the largest of them, the one that for so long had made her dizzy with its loveliness. She had broken it off carefully, twisting the stem gently, but before she had even been able to bring it up to her nose, it had shed its petals in her hand. She looked down at the ruin, knowing that it had destroyed itself because she had disobeyed the hand-painted sign at the corner of the rose bed prohibiting her from picking the flowers. To punish herself, she looked up directly into the sun; but it shut her eyes, and its warmth pleased her so much that her penance was as spoiled as the rose, and she began to laugh. Luther was better. He was so much better.

Chapter 4

ELAINE WAS STANDING in front of the stove cooking her breakfast when she heard Hugh's car pull up. She had planned to eat and then to leave the house. It was better not to see him until she had made up her mind about what she wanted to do. Instead of turning around, she looked out the back window, and the sunlight centered in her eyes and glanced off her hair like the reflection on a piece of contoured brass. She tightened the sash on her dressing gown, a little more harshly than necessary, then removed the skillet from the burner and turned off the fire. When she heard her name called, she moved away from the stove and looked out the window on the far side of the living room to see him start up the walk, leaving the gate open as he always did. She knew she should break with him now; he was vicious and too young—the fight in the dance hall the night before had made that painfully clear. She had to tell him that it was over, yet she feared doing it, not as much because of what he might do to her as because of what she was doing to herself.

When Jeffrey had let her off after the dance, Elaine had lain fully clothed on top of the bedcovers, expecting to cry. She was surprised that she had kept calm on the ride home, that she had concealed her feelings from Jeffrey and, therefore, from anyone in town who might question him. Had she been less disturbed by what had happened, she might have wept out of frustration or self-pity; as it was, she could only think. Over and over she asked herself what she was doing in a relationship that was alien not only to her upbringing and her past life but also to her moral vision. She must stop this thing with Hugh. It had run its course.

What he had done that night would cost her dearly, and she knew it. She should renounce him while she was still strong, while the investment of her time with him was short, and while her heart was still on the frontier between the mindlessness of an unreasoning passion and the captivity of love. She imagined that she could accomplish it if she did it quickly and with a certain harshness.

The previous night she had slept, wakened without having rested, thought again of her situation, and fallen back into sleep. Her eyes had opened again to see the sun coming up, the first shallow waves of gold blushing the rim of the earth, turning the sky's purple to lavender, to rose, and to blue while the leaves of the roses and the trumpet vine flattened out and silvered. Finally the light had grown so strong that she had had to look away from it into the plants that were swaying in the steady and agreeable breeze. She had not noticed them in the moonlight during the nightmare in which she had kept seeing the look on Hugh's face as he lifted his arm to hit Gerdine, kept hearing the roar of his rage over the sounds of skidding chairs, people running into things, the breaking of bottles, screams of excitement.

She had tried to stop it. She had pulled on him; he had shouted at her to leave him be. She had become accustomed to his gentleness with her, to his gathering her to him, keeping her close, wanting her with him, never forcing her away. She disliked what he had done; she disliked him, and she reasoned that, last night, when he had shouted her away from him, he had disliked her, too. As she had sat up and watched the spectacle of the morning, the colors being relentlessly absorbed by the sun, she had felt that she understood something for the first time since they had come together. Hugh was unmanageable even to himself.

"Good morning," he said. His tread as he came across the living room floor was so heavy that the chain cups rattled in the corner cabinet. His face was neither flushed nor drawn, and he showed no signs of dissipation. His hand was bandaged, but he managed it with no particular caution. Nothing seemed to have happened to him at all. He had wakened regenerated, and he was now standing in the kitchen doorway, the crest of his hat not an inch from the lintel.

"You're a crazy bastard," she answered easily, quietly. She had not planned to say that; it was the only response to the way he was looking at her and the way he looked: the bandage, the bruises, the slightly swollen lip. There was no anger in her voice, and it caressed him as it always did.

"Okay." He assumed he had passed the test and laughed carelessly.

She lowered her head a bit and, glancing up at him, frowned. "I don't think it's funny."

"All right . . . it's not funny."

"Maybe you just wanted to fight. You might have hit me instead of Gerdine."

"I thought of that."

She glanced at his hand and made a motion toward it with her head. "You broke your hand. Why would you want to do that?"

"You like being taken care of, Elaine."

He came to her, and she made no move to resist him. She returned his kiss, winding her arms high around his neck. "When did you decide that?" she asked. Now that he was here, standing before her, she forgot her fear of him, her desire to be free of him, her anger. He was neither contrite nor boastful but regarded his behavior of the night before with all the indifference of sea water sliding into the sand. He did not understand or appreciate the concession she had to make to allow him to be in that room, or that his obtuseness in this matter was part of the reason for his success with her. She was slightly ashamed of showing him so much love and so little disapproval. Loving Hugh and living with him was like getting more and more into debt for a luxury, the cost of which was increasing in direct proportion to her pleasure. *But he's changed me,* she was thinking, *and I can't go back. It isn't happiness he's giving me, and it certainly isn't security; it's an enchantment.* And that word reminded her of the stories she had read as a child, when the gentleman-warriors had seemed so reasonable.

"The first time I saw you."

With his good hand, he took off his hat and flung it from the kitchen door toward the sofa in the living room, exactly as Matt or Luther would have done on the plaid sofa in the main room of the bunkhouse, where Lettie would have quickly picked it up and hung it on the hat rack at the door with a shaking of her head. It landed in the corner, on a pillow with a crocheted cover.

"You can take off your dirty boots, too," she said, "though I guess it doesn't matter, now that you've come through the living room. One of these days, I'm going to make you clean my house, make you neater, like your mama didn't."

He was leaning against the doorframe between the living room and the kitchen. She knew that he was absorbed in watching her, half-listening to her. She moved before him nervously, feeling the power she had over him, wishing that it were more deserved from the point of view of being what she could plan on and control, rather than what was innate in her and ephemeral in their relationship.

"I'll never clean house," he said. "You can't make me do anything."

"I can make you do plenty, Hugh. You sure forget easy."

He started to light a cigarette but then stopped abruptly, letting the match burn down in his hand. "You're smart this morning," he said.

"I'm a lot smarter when you're not here."

He sat in a kitchen chair, reached down and pulled off his boots, threw them one by one in the corner behind the table. "Elaine, how come you cook breakfast in high-heeled shoes? Is it because they make your legs pretty?"

She turned to him, suspicious of this line of conversation, and asked, speaking softly, wary now of herself for wanting to draw it out. "It must work."

He leaned across the table on his elbows, pulling at the tablecloth so that the salt and pepper shakers fell over and he had to set them right again. He smiled. "Yeah, it works. . . . How come you didn't drive out to the ranch last night? I thought you might want to thank me. I'm sorry to have missed that encounter."

His remark annoyed her; he really had no idea at all of how she felt about what had happened. She would not give him the satisfaction of a reply.

The sun was high; it was nearly eleven o'clock. As she walked back and forth in the kitchen in the loose cotton dressing gown, the breeze from the fan fussing around her skirt, rippling it at regular intervals, Hugh was overtaken by that mood of languor and peace that he now always felt in her house, a voluptuous complacency between the times when the stirring of his blood propelled him toward her. At first, he had wanted to hush something in her that seemed to need silencing, something too menacing for a beloved woman to possess; yet Elaine would never be hushed because she never remained the same. He had given up trying to deny her her pride because it was so richly confused in the melange of attributes that attracted him. He wondered when they would stop fighting each other for what they both wanted, and he questioned whether he might even wish to.

Elaine was looking out at the roses. This summer they were the prettiest they had ever been, and their reds and pinks and yellows bled into the larger area of color in the lilac bush. In the breeze, the zinnias jerked apologetically before the perfection of the roses. "Who hit you?" Elaine asked. "I know Gerdine didn't do that. I mean, the bruise."

"Hit me?" he said, as if her question were ridiculous.

"Your face is bruised, Hugh. Did Gerdine do that?"

He put his hand to his cheek and touched his mouth. "I don't remember."

"Sure you do. You weren't that drunk."

"Matt."

With a fork, she turned the hissing bacon she was preparing for him. She put one hand on her hip. Through the triangle of her arm, he could see the clock mounted on the stove. "What about Gerdine Bowen?" she asked. "How bad did you hurt him? Does Matt know?" She knew Gerdine's injuries were not serious—two of her friends had telephoned that morning—yet she allowed this conversation to drift on to fill a space, to give her time to settle her emotions and bring them into harmony with his. She opened the refrigerator and handed him the glass of orange juice she had squeezed for herself.

"Matt knows," he said.

"Is Gerdine in the hospital?"

"No, but they took him there last night."

"You don't mind Matt picking up the pieces for you?"

"How was I going to stop him, Elaine?"

For a moment she felt a flicker of her earlier anger—but she was not prepared to fight with Hugh. If he had been harsh last night, she had been careless. Hugh would not have known how to behave differently, and she should not have expected him to. If he was dangerous, she had accepted that long before she had walked into that dance hall, and if the townspeople were critical of her, she had only herself to blame. And although she drew back from acknowledging it, she had perhaps not been entirely innocent in agreeing to dance with Gerdine.

"What are you going to do for Gerdine?" she asked him.

"Nothing. Why should I do anything for him?"

"Because you hurt him."

"He asked for it."

"He was drunk."

"So was I." He was leaning back against the wallpaper, a shiny, glazed print of windmills in a Dutch garden, regarding her as he always did, suspicious of her existence apart from him, hovering as if he were stalking something to catch it.

She took the bacon out, holding up each piece, and letting it drip back into the skillet before laying it on the paper towels; she dropped two pieces of bread in the toaster and broke the eggs into the hot grease. There was no reason to ask him if he had eaten; he would be hungry anyway. Like the mother of a precocious child far out of her control, she frowned.

"What do you think, Elaine?" he asked after a few minutes. He rarely remembered what she said, but she was wise enough not to attribute it to indifference.

She put the toast on two plates and then slid the eggs on top. "I told you, Hugh—I think you're mean." But she turned her head to him, and he knew that was not what she was thinking. "I love you," she said.

Outside, it was never quite still, even when the breezes had died down. In the window, a little shadow of leaves, reflected twice, floated at the side of her hair.

He took the knife and fork she handed him, sat up straight, and pulled her down on his lap to kiss her, but she pushed him away. "Eat your breakfast," she said. "I cooked it for you."

He kissed her again, partly because it pleased him, but also because she had resisted him. "Did you know I was coming this morning?" he said.

She framed his face in her hands. "Where else would you go? Who else wants you? I was having fun, and you spoiled that. Now, let me go. I'm hungry. Let me go, Hugh."

"He was treating you like a whore."

"You do that."

"You love me."

"If you know it, why did you hit Gerdine?"

"What he wanted is mine, hmm?" He released her, and she went to sit before her plate. "Okay, you think I'm mean. I'll live with that," he said. He cut through the toast, soaked through with the warm, salty yellows of the eggs. "Go make me some coffee," he said after a few mouthfuls.

She smiled and moved her head lazily, stretching her neck like a cat. "Not until I've eaten."

He frowned and nudged her, then motioned toward the stove, where the coffeepot sat empty, but she shook her head. She was sitting so close to him that he felt the movement of her arm as she ate. "Do you have to go to work this afternoon?" he asked.

"At two o'clock. And I'll be out all afternoon. There's some land . . . You don't have to go to Houston, do you? You'll be here tonight?"

He stared at her, and she met his gaze evenly. "What is it?" he asked. "What land?"

"The McKinney property."

"Ashwood?"

"Yes."

"Tell Felix to show it," he said.

It was done, the pieces shattered; his tone was like that of a hammer hitting a pane of glass. She knew he meant it, that he was not making conversation, that he was going to try to keep her from doing what she should do, this time, and then many times more. She had to make her living. She must resist him now; there must remain a part of her life that he would be unable to absorb and use up. "I'm not showing it," she explained, quietly. "I'm going out to talk to Alan about selling it. He's putting it on the market. I can't send Felix. Alan is old and set, and I don't want him to change his mind on me." She paused and put her hand on his arm. "Hugh, listen. You've got to quit trying to . . ."

He looked at her sideways without turning his head. "I want you to drive down to Refugio with me. I've got to talk to Harold about the pipeline. I'm not going to give the easement. I talked to Dad."

She spoke slowly. "You told him you would. What made you change your mind?"

"I'd have to lose fifty feet of timber on each side of the right of way. It's not worth it. The alley's wide enough already, and the timber's young. I hadn't looked at it carefully when I talked to Harold."

"Do you want more money?"

He set down his fork and placed his hand over hers, pressing it to the table. "No," he said. "I don't want to do it, period. Call Felix." He was speaking louder. "I need you with me."

"To talk to Harold? What would I—"

"For Christ's sake, no!" He waved away her question with his uninjured hand. "I'll talk to him alone. I want you with me, that's all!"

She shook her head.

He took her by the arm and said with annoyance: "Make me some coffee, and then call Felix."

She looked down at the hand that was restraining her. "You keep it up, Hugh, and we're going to be fighting."

"We're fighting now."

"I have to make a living," she replied vehemently. "I am not going with you to see Harold or anyone else."

He blinked rapidly, his jaw tightened, and he smashed his fist on the table. The soiled plates jumped, and the water sloshed out of the glasses, leaving spreading pools on the tablecloth. The light had gone from his eyes, leaving not a glint of the extravagant brightness of midsummer. "I like you with me. I want you with me. Do what I ask you, Elaine! Why don't you want to? If you're worried about money, I'll take care of you. I've told you that." He took her chin in his hand and squeezed it until it began to hurt her. "Christ, Elaine—I'm the goddamned fairy prince. Why the hell don't you take advantage of me? What difference does it make how you pay your bills?" He stood up, knocking against the table. Everything fell over, and a plate shattered on the floor.

She cursed him as much for losing his temper in her house as for his attempt to reduce her, to push her into a position where she would be asking him for things. That must never happen—not with anyone, but particularly not with Hugh.

He wanted to hit her, and had she spoken to him defiantly again he would have. Answering her curse with a much more damaging one of his own, he reached into his pocket and threw his money over the table; then he lifted her to her feet lowering his head to look into the face that would not raise itself. "Take it!" he yelled, shaking her so that she would have to look at him. "Pick it up and keep it!"

There was a defensiveness in her eyes that he had seen in them only one other time, the morning he had wrestled with her in the swale. Then the expression in her eyes changed, and so did the contour of her mouth. "Get out of my house," she said softly.

"Elaine . . ."

"Get out." The color flared in her cheeks, but she would not cry. She knew that he was angry enough to raise his hand against her, that he well might. And she wanted him to strike her, hard enough to make her hate him, to end it, as it would one day have to be ended.

He released his grip on her arms, then held up his hands and turned his head. She repeated what she had said, and when he neither looked at her nor moved, she walked into the living room and returned with his hat. "I don't want you here," she said. She waited a moment for a reply, and when none came, she set the hat on the kitchen table in the midst of the ruin, poured herself a glass of water from a plastic bottle in the refrigerator, went into the bedroom, and shut the door. She started to lock it but decided that it would be better were he not to leave angry, merely disenchanted.

For a moment, Hugh stared down at the table, surveying the mess. Both the orange juice glasses were overturned; the bowl of strawberry jam had been upset, and bits of red were dropping from the table's edge. The napkins had fallen to the floor, the sugar was spilled, and the checkered tablecloth was wet and pulled to the center of the table. He picked up his hat but let it fall in the chair beside him and then removed his watch and laid it on the window sill at the end of the row of ripening tomatoes. Under the sink he found a yellow dish pan. He filled it with scalding water and poured in a stream of powdered soap. He had never washed dishes before, but when he was young, and would be playing at the kitchen table, he had watched Cana at the sink, and more recently Elaine. He took care not to chip the china as he held it under the driving hot water to rinse it, using only his left hand since he had been told to keep the right one dry. When the plates, the silver, the glasses, a spatula, and a skillet were clean and stacked in the rack beside the drain, he wiped off the table with a sponge, restored the tablecloth to its place, and swept up, gathering the pieces of the plate he had broken in a dustpan and letting them slide noisily into the rolled-back paper bag that Elaine used for the trash. After putting away the food left over from the meal, he took the scissors off the hook by the back door and went outside to cut a half-dozen huge pink roses, so ripe and heavy that their petals hardly held to their crowns. He put them in a widemouthed vase that he had seen Elaine use, ran a comb through his hair, dried his good hand on his jeans, and turned off the noisy little oscillating fan.

When he opened the bedroom door, Elaine was sitting at her dressing table on a cloth-covered stool. She had arranged her hair, he noticed, not more beautifully but more neatly.

"I thought you were gone," she said.

It was a feeble lie; she would have heard his car. He saw the flicker of a frown cross her face. She hated lying, and he knew that she must have been especially ill at ease to have done so. "Then who are you fixing your hair for?" he asked.

"I thought I might go to church."

He glanced down at the tiny gold clock in the porcelain saucer at the base of the mirror. "Isn't it too late?"

"There's Sunday school yet, and I haven't been in a while."

He held the roses out to her. She looked up at him for an instant, but she did not smile or indicate in any other way that she

was granting him a pardon. She just took the vase and put it on
her dresser in the place where she always kept flowers. She
seemed to expect the offering, as if he had merely brought her
something she had requested. The big blossoms sagged close to
the dresser's glass top.

He moved back a little, curled his hand around the bed post,
and stared steadily at Elaine's reflection. The morning light fell
on one side of his face all along his cheek, but his dark eyes and
the crease of his mouth remained in shadow.

Elaine knew that this peace offering was motivated not by
guilt but by a sense of loss, yet understood the danger in which
she placed herself by accepting it. "I'm not going to let you pay
me," she said to him. "I'm not going to let you or anyone else do
that. I don't have to. I've made a great effort to arrange my life
so that I never would."

"All right," he said.

She opened her jewelry case, picked up a pair of small loop
earrings, and began putting them on. "I'm not going to play that
game with you. I know that's what you want, but it isn't what
we're going to do."

He pulled a chair up behind her and put his chin on her
shoulder. Her eyes shifted; he felt her shiver; she did not return
his tentative smile. He moved his cheek to her back, rubbing it
against her blouse. "I could help you," he said.

He had started kissing her arm, then taking the skin between
his teeth, leaving little marks.

"Are you listening?" she asked. She turned halfway around.
"Do you ever listen to me?" She took his face in her hands. He
wanted to feel her affection, but these were not the hands that
made love to him, encouraged him, and sometimes sought him
out. "I don't think you do," she said.

He slid her onto his lap, trying to return to some time during
the last few weeks when she had seemed to love him no matter
what he did, but she pushed at him uncomfortably.

"I do listen," he said.

"Are you getting ready to laugh?" She would not make it easy
for him. Pulling away, she rose and went to the window. He
followed her immediately and stopped behind her, watching the
butterfly that had her attention. Its great yellow and gold wings
came together at the apex of an arc, drifting apart slowly to reveal
their extraordinary pattern. Because the butterfly never quite
touched the creamy velvet spathes of the lilies, its errand seemed
purposeless, entirely aesthetic.

The day was lovely; the scents of vegetable gardens and pear orchards and fig trees were heavy and hot and sleepy on the wind. The honeysuckle, strengthened by the sun, made Elaine close her eyes, and tempted her to smile.

He had said nothing, and at last, she had to turn to him. "What were you doing so long in the kitchen?"

"Go look," he said, giving her a gentle push in that direction.

She reached up and pulled the string on the ceiling fan, picked up her empty water glass, and left the room. From the center of the kitchen, she looked back at him. "Why did you do this?" she asked. She was almost scolding.

"So you'd like me again."

"I like you."

"So you'd have to go with me." He winked at her and smiled. "So that you'd feel obliged. It looks nice, huh?" He rocked backward on his boots and slipped his hands into his back pockets.

Outside, the camphor tree shivered under a new thrust of wind, and the flowers shook beneath it. It was not cool, but the garden gave that illusion. "You think I will?" She opened a drawer and replaced the long kitchen fork that he had dried but neglected to put away.

"I don't know, Elaine." He reached for her, but she stepped back. "You're sweet," he said ineptly.

"I've never been sweet," she said, "and I know you don't think I am. That's not why you come here."

"Why do I, then?" He rubbed her arms in response to seeing her tremble, going along with the fiction that she was cold.

"I missed you last night," he said, inept again when she gave no answer.

She might have been able to deny him forever had he come to her at that moment in his usual perfection, but his awkwardness allowed her to pity him a little; his flaw won for him his case. She pursed her lips, lifted her chin, and made the sound of a kiss. "You had Matthew," she said.

As she turned away from Hugh, she wondered what kind of stolid heroism was making her go with him that afternoon, why she was jeopardizing her career this way. What was she doing running out with him this afternoon, risking losing a commission on an important piece of land? Would she one day have to go back to her father holding out a begging bowl, whimpering that she had let a rich, beautiful, and very spoiled young man from Houston rob her of what little security she had? More and more, she was crossing into an uncharted zone in which she would have no other companion than Hugh, but the choice she now made seemed to testify to her willingness to do so.

She tried then to imagine that she was going to be punished, but she was unable to believe it. *By whom?* she thought. *Not by God. I have already suffered. I am free of that.* She had not gone to church that morning; the night before, her prayers had been interrupted by random sounds outdoors, any of which might have been the first indication of his car taking the turn before the creek bridge.

She left the kitchen, the heels of her shoes clicking on the wood floor and then falling silent on the flowered rug in the hall. "I don't guess anyone's going to bother me after last night— speak to me, either," she said. She was talking back into the room.

"That's all right with me. That's fine. I'm all you need." He sprawled in a chair, lazy again and comforted. The toe of his boot played with a coin on the floor. He picked it up. "Jeffrey didn't come in here last night?" he asked. He turned the coin over in his hand, then threw it up and caught it left-handed.

"I told you, Hugh, no one's going to bother me."

He looked at his bandaged hand. It still hurt him, and he held it up to stop the throbbing. "I wouldn't have wanted to fight him with my left hand," he muttered in the direction of the hallway, where it was too dark even to see the wallpaper. "He's bigger than I am."

He heard her dialing the telephone, and then the receiver hitting the cradle as the clock began chiming twelve. As the last note of the clock echoed, the dialing began again, now more slowly. She spoke as strongly and as directly as if the decision had been one she had made, the idea hers and not his. He got up and turned on the little blue radio on the counter next to the toaster, waiting for it to warm up, for the noon news broadcast to begin, then turned the volume down, listening to the last of Elaine's instructions.

Luther had been staring steadily toward the several houses among the dark umbrella shades of the live oaks. As he and Matt neared the corral, their horses pranced and whinnied. It was almost seven, and the sun had just fallen behind the high-pitched roof of the barn, shooting a flare of orange and gold to the center of the sky as the corral was plunged abruptly into shadow. Luther and Matt had been talking as they rode, but it was evident to Matt that, though the conversation interested him, Luther was preoc-

cupied. His hat was pulled down so low that he had to lift his
chin to look out under the brim with his large blue eyes. "A
summer's too long and hot without two men getting real drunk
and nasty," he said, "and one of them giving the other a busted
head over a good-looking woman."

"Too bad it had to be her, though," said Matt. "I mean, Menutis's wife."

"Better than mine," said Luther, and then he suddenly
straightened in the saddle, seeing in the distance what he'd been
looking for ever since they'd left the pasture for the dirt road. He
urged his horse into a lope so quickly and gracefully that Matt,
left behind, thought, *Luther rides like a goddamn knight*. It was a
source of pride to him that after the accident and after his long
vigil in the hospital in Houston (bothering that great surgeon,
following him down the glaring white halls, asking too many
questions, refusing to be beaten back by the stiffly flapping wings
of his splendid white knee-length coat), he'd been able to coax a
man like Luther to work for him, and also that he'd been shrewd
enough both to keep him and to keep Clarence from firing him
when he was going through all that hell with Lettie.

Luther left the road and crossed the small pasture to the gate,
where he pulled up, not harshly but deliberately, and with an
assurance that reflected nearly twenty years of skill. Lettie, tall
and blond and barefoot, in a billowing voile smock, had come
out onto the porch of the house. She ran to the gate to meet him
as fast as she could despite the awkwardness of her pregnancy.
As he reined in his horse, she reached her arms up to him; she
was talking rapidly and smiling. He bent down to kiss her, easing
himself off his horse in a motion so fluid that not for an instant
did his mouth separate from hers. She stayed with him as he
unsaddled his horse and turned it into the corral, then they
walked together toward their house, Luther listening to something she was saying, one arm holding her tight, while with the
other he reached out from time to time to touch her face, her hair.

"There goes another one," whispered Matt. "He's looking at
her like she's saying something worth listening to, and she ain't
saying a damned thing." It was too bad what had happened to
Luther, though he didn't see it that way. Matt left his horse in the
corral for the two little Mexican boys to unsaddle, and while they
chattered in Spanish and stroked the beautiful animal's thick neck
and bathed in the warm breath from its soft, flared nostrils, he
walked through the kitchen and its doors of frying meat, yeast
bread, and ham hocks and chilis boiling in red beans and went

into his office. He took a bottle of whiskey from behind a row of ledgers, drank a long drink, recapped the bottle, and settled down on the rough plaid covering of his daybed for a rest before dinner, though not before turning the photograph on his desk toward him, relaxing his mouth, and letting his eyes go soft on the image of Hugh. He had been thinking a great deal lately of Hugh and Elaine; if Lettie and Luther were an unlikely couple, what about this? And how would it resolve itself after that beating Hugh had given Gerdine?. . . . But then, Luther, even Luther had seen fit to beat a man. Why the violence? Why was it always like this with a man and a woman? And if the violence was not on the surface, it was always underneath, waiting like a sharp rock under dark water. Why couldn't it be easy, like some of those movies with music, where the girl was so quiet and good, and the man was a well-dressed gentleman in a big town with taxis and hotels?

Hugh's picture reminded him of how the boy had been when he was young, of Clarence, of all of them; of how he himself had first come here, how dazed he had been, not only by the huge budget and salary that Clarence had given him but also by the man himself. "Fix it up, Matt," he had said one night as he was leaving, losing his balance a little from the brandy he'd had and having to catch himself on the edge of the opened door. He had stared at Matt, still hard-eyed and certain, no matter what he'd drunk. "Make it perfect."

And then there was Clara, that woman whom Clarence had married, and who, Matt supposed, had never for one moment in thirty years shown gratitude for the sinecure she had received from him; that woman with whom he had made his son, who was as fragile as the diaphanous wing-sails of a sloop, so frail that the thought of a man of Clarence's stature mating with her at all seemed obscene, even to a man like Matt. Her producing a boy like Hugh, who must have got half of all he had from her, was nothing short of a miracle—a miracle that had demonstrated to Matt, once and for all, the indomitable potency of this particular man, whom he admired in all things—except his choice of a wife and his obsequiousness when he was face to face with Hugh, whom he loved too deeply to correct, much less to punish. "I was nearly forty when he was born," he had said to Matt once, as if that were an excuse.

Clara, who had nothing in common with Clarence, came out to the ranch once a year, usually in midwinter when the hardwoods were stripped naked of leaves and nothing but a few cedars stopped the wind. She would be dressed for the opera, and

Cana, her black maid, would have to help her slide off the white chamois seat covers of her white Cadillac. Clara was certainly able to get out of a car by herself (she was less than fifty, a whole ten years younger than Matt), but Cana's attentiveness made it possible for her to be transformed from a personal maid to a lady-in-waiting. Cana was also the coachman, because Mrs. Littleton was usually unhappy with the real chauffeur, Jesse, who, even when he came out to the country, had to wear a black suit and a shiny black-billed cap. He drove too fast, she said. Jesse's driving frightened her.

When Mrs. Littleton arrived at her ranch, speaking with puffs of smoke in the cold air, her little gloved hands like the busy paws of a squirrel, clutching at her full-length sable coat, picking at the buttons, but never opening the coat fully, she would ask Matt and Stephen to unpack her trunk. In the house, she would touch everything tentatively. She had no familiarity with these objects; her husband selected them, and her activities at home had prevented her from participating in arranging them. The decorator had come from the city with his team of artisans, and spent the better part of a month working on the house, keeping the radios playing and the lights on half the night; even on Sundays, the only mornings Matt's cowboys could sleep, the hammering and scraping began before the roosters had awakened.

Clara would have Cana slide all the sheets off the exquisite furniture and would then launch into a litany of complaints to the effect that she was unable to stay because the house was too damp or too cold or too unkempt or too savage—though it would have been painstakingly prepared for her arrival: the floors and stairs mopped and waxed, the brass polished, the bathrooms made immaculate, the rugs beaten, the bedding thrown out onto the porch roof to air, the windows washed and even dried by the children. The leaky window would have been caulked, the fire laid and lighted, and the pillows fluffed. But with her fur coat still half-buttoned, Clara would leave before the moon rose or before supper, whichever came first. She would have Cana replace the furniture covers and return the long-stemmed red roses and ferns, which her husband had had sent fifteen miles from the florist in El Campo, to the noisy grass-colored tissue paper. Then, while her hands fussed at the pearls on her necklace, she would ask Matt and Stephen to repack the trunk. Standing at their elbows, small as a child, speaking almost too softly to be heard, she would tell them precisely how this should be done, as if they had forgotten in the short time since her arrival how the trunk had been arranged. When the box of flowers had been carefully slipped into the car, Cana would help her into the back seat beside them. Without looking at anyone in particular, Clara would wave a gloved hand; and the car would rush off in a cloud of dust and clattering gravel, as a genie leaves in the smoke and music it has conjured.

Without a glance backward, she would allow herself to be driven away from her thousands of manicured acres, her finely planned orchards of paper-shell pecans, her registered cattle, her herd of lazy steers, a thousand tons of marbled beef—all of it paid for out of timber, sawmills, liquid gold, and the fornication of animals. She would leave without having passed the time of day with any of the hands, and worse, without having seen the three or four wives who were responsible for the big house— these wives who feared her so, yet who put great value on meeting her, on shaking for the first time in their lives the hand of a woman who had never washed socks or hoed or held plow lines or milked, who had hoped to get a glimpse, just once, of the enormous diamond solitaire that some of the men had described, and the gold ring on her other hand, with diamonds and rubies lined up one after another like ducks in a shooting gallery.

On Mrs. Littleton's last visit, the women had, in her honor, put on fresh dresses, stockings without runs (even during the war), and open shoes—though that made their feet cold—and had done their hair as if they were going to church. The night before, after the dishes had been washed and the children put to bed, they had polished one another's nails. They had hoped she might ask about their children; even want to see Imogene's boy, who did so well in school that, next fall, he was going free to college; or Alice's baby, who could take three steps if you held out your hands to her and crooned her name, Lydie—"Come to me, hon. Lydie, show Miz Littleton what you can do. . . ." They had put up extra jars of pear and blackberry preserves, prepared venison sausage, plenty of beef, and a dozen cured hams. Opal had even thought to make her a gift of the red wool shawl she had just finished crocheting for her mother-in-law in Shiner, telling another of the ranch wives, "If she likes it, I can do another one for Alma Rude."

The women waited, nervous, in the cookhouse for Cana or Matt or Luther, maybe even Stephen to come and get them; afraid Clara would call for them but, worse, fearing she wouldn't. It disappointed them awfully when she did not. After this last visit, it was only Lettie, in awe and wonder at the turn of her own life, at the preeminence that her condition gave her, who did not complain. But the others were angry, justifiably so, and since, axiomatically, Miz Littleton was perfect, and no one here was, the wives blamed Matt or Luther or Stephen or whoever had access to Clara. They made trouble for the next couple of days: The food was bad, the eggs went half-collected, nothing was ironed smoothly, the starch was too thick, and the children, slapped for nothing, made up for the injustice in dozens of ways.

Nor did Clara ever remember Matt's name, though he'd been here for over a decade and had made a barbarous and uninhabitable wilderness into a show-place ranch for her. No, not for her, but for Clarence, because it meant so much to Clarence to please her. She would poke Cana in the ribs with her skin-and-bones elbow and put her hand over the maid's ear, the five or six gold bracelets (she never held her hand still long enough for you to count them) clanking down her arm as she whispered, "What's that older cowboy's name?"

And then, after Cana's reply, he would hear her say over the click of the closing gate: "Oh, yes, Matthew!" Though, of course, Cana had said, "Mister Matthew." Shit.

Matt heard the bell ring for dinner. He rose and stretched and shoved the tail of his shirt into his pants. One thing was sure: The elder Littletons would want none of Mrs. Menutis. She was better out of this romance. God knows, Hugh was. The arguments that had failed to persuade Hugh might work on Elaine. He took another long swallow of whiskey and put on his hat. "That's next," he said. "That's next on my list."

Two days later, on an afternoon when he knew that Hugh had gone into the city for a cousin's wedding, Matt took the road behind Dance Creek and saw that Elaine's truck was parked in her driveway. He realized, as he pulled the Jeep before the house, that he was slightly afraid of her. He'd watched her, as many of the other men had, since her husband's death, but she'd had nothing to do with any of them. If a light was on late in her office, they might drop in to talk for a while or ask her to go for a drink, which she would sometimes do, but not for more than an hour or so. She would refuse to let them pay and would never go home with one of them, or invite them into her place, even when her boy was away. Their attentions seemed to embarrass her, and unless it was business, she avoided them when she could. They talked about her, though; in the pool hall on smoky summer nights, or in the bar at the hotel, after a man had drunk more than was good for him, his remarks, bawdy, vicious, or both, were, as often as not, aimed at Elaine Menutis.

Matt had known Foley for years. Foley had never been a drinking man, so, at the end of the day, rather than stopping off somewhere for a beer or a whiskey, he would close the office on the street that ran into the courthouse square and walk the two blocks to his house on the corner of Boling and East Second streets. But at about ten o'clock in the morning, unless he was out in the country with a client, he did go for coffee in the drugstore, and there Matt had occasionally sat with him, discussing finances, taxes, property, politics, and women, though on that subject, Foley talked only about Elaine. Foley's greatest asset and interest was his wife, and Matt had not known Foley long before he'd realized that this was so. Foley was a pleasant, congenial, hard-working man who sold land, had an accounting office, and owned a few small pieces of acreage. The only time Matt had ever seen Foley unhappy, breaking his work routine and avoiding his friends, was right after they had lost their baby girl, Laura, when he had stayed shut up in the house for several weeks. Otherwise, he was someone who pulled up everyone else.

But the Germans had killed Foley. That puzzled Matt: He was the last man you'd have thought they'd get. Had he lived, Foley would have had a hundred stories, which he'd have told quietly and without passion, and Matt would have liked to hear every one of them. A cousin of Matt's had been killed, too, a man who had made it through medical school and had a baby he'd never seen. But war was like that; it took the best men . . . just accidents, a series of accidents begun by a misunderstanding between two parties, and when the insults got too raw, it was easier to hit than to think long and careful.

Elaine had sold their big house in the center of town to a rancher whose young wife disliked the isolation of the country, and with that money she had bought a cottage on the outskirts. The air was fresher, she claimed, but the truth of it was that she had less income than she'd had when Foley was alive, when he, with his great reserves of energy, had worked over ten or twelve counties rather than the four or five that were for her all she could manage. But it must have hurt her to sell the house that she and Foley had moved into and fixed up. Matt had once seen her standing with Foley in front of it, one of her hands around his waist, the other pointing to the day lilies, the round, rock-bordered bed of zinnias, petunias, sultanas, and ferns. She had looked up into his face, and Foley had bent down and kissed her.

Another time, on a heavy summer afternoon at about five o'clock, Matt had watched her in the yard, teaching her little boy to play catch, both of them turning occasionally to look up toward the square for the first sign of the father and husband coming home. Jimmy had broken into a run when he had finally caught sight of him; and then Foley had swept the boy up and tossed him a foot or two in the air, and when he came down, gurgling with pleasure and hollering to fly again, Foley had mussed up his hair and delivered the laughing child to his mother.

After Foley's death, she had kept to herself, playing bridge now and then with someone who needed a fourth, going to church or to the movies with her girl friends, and working the rest of the time. While no one in town was surprised at her desire for solitude, many of the people who knew her well were puzzled when, in the course of her work, she began to adopt a number of masculine mannerisms, as if she thought that she would have to be part male in order to succeed as Foley had succeeded. When visiting a prospective seller, she would stand with one foot on a chair and lean forward, her arm resting on her knee, her hand opening out flat to emphasize her speech; when she smoked, she might take the cigarette out of her mouth between the thumb and forefinger of her left hand to crush it in the ash tray, having inhaled deeply, so that the smoke came out of her mouth and nostrils in a slow stream, wisping upward until her entire face was veiled. She drove her pickup almost too fast for the country roads, keeping her left hand hooked over the steering wheel, her right hand flipping through the maps and papers that she kept beside her. She wore only wool gabardine slacks or jeans, and a western shirt with snaps, a scarf around her neck, and boots, always boots. On a rather delicate wrist she wore a heavy watch, not quite a man's model, but the last word in feminine utility—a Bulova that had been developed during the war for women factory workers. When she was in her office, talking to a client, she would lean back in her swivel chair and challenge the person across the desk with a businesslike, if not cold, stare. She rationed her emotions, she rarely smiled, nothing she said or did was conciliatory, and she never apologized to anyone for anything.

Her incongruous behavior remained a subject of discussion until, at last, the conclusion was generally drawn in the small community, particularly by the men who liked her most, that the loss of Foley had ended her interest in men altogether, that the tragedy had been too great, that she had taken on the inner austerity of a nun and the external trappings of a small but capable man. To want to be a woman, she would have had to be in love. As much as the change shocked people who had known her prior to August 1944, it was complete, and she could not be tampered with. She refused advice from any quarter, she kept her troubles to herself, and attempts on the part of her friends to "fix her up," to have her meet their male friends, ended in failures so absolute that her indifference was inevitably construed as rudeness.

Then, when the man finally appeared whom she allowed to approach her, people asked, But why Hugh Littleton? Why would this woman, three years a widow, make her alliance, so long in coming, with a man so many years her junior? And why would a woman who had been a model of propriety since she and her husband had moved into the town have a liaison with anyone? Hugh was rich, that was true, but she was apparently neither interested in his wealth nor amenable to profiting from it. She seemed unwilling to permit him to do anything for her that changed, in any sense, the way she lived, though people close to him claimed that it was not because Hugh had not offered. Whatever bad qualities could be attributed to Hugh, being ungenerous was not one of them.

Matt had all this on his mind as he walked up Elaine's front walk. Hugh was going away; in only a week, he would return to school on the East Coast. If he told her good-by, finished it before he left, that would be just fine; if he didn't, Matt would have to worry about it until his next trip home. Better to end it now. The screen door rattled angrily against its frame each time he rapped it with his knuckles; he heard footsteps, then moved back a little. When Elaine stood before him and lifted the latch, he saw by her expression that, though she didn't seem particularly glad to see him, she wasn't surprised. She seemed to have expected his call, and after he entered the room, she was friendly.

Her house was dark and cool, and it smelled of an iron and sprinkled clothes. Matt had come into the house carefully, looking at the rug, as if he were calculating his every step in terms of the resistance of the pile, like a man who has always walked on grass or bare boards. He took a seat on the sofa; she sat at an angle to him, fairly close in the comfortable straight-backed chair that she always chose for herself when the situation was going to be difficult and she wished to be more than alert. She offered him a cup of coffee, but he refused, not wanting to accept anything from her, planning to say what he had to say and leave. He had already been discomfited by the smoke screen she had thrown up,

treating his visit as a social call when he was certain she knew
he'd come on a mission. He sat on the braided edge of the sofa
cushion, his knees tight together, his elbows on his thighs, his
hands turning his hat around and around in the fingers of his
broad, shapeless hands. Mostly he looked down at the rug or
made a quick search of the walls, stopping briefly at a picture or
a lampshade or a light switch. He noticed that Hugh's boots were
standing right inside the door of the bedroom, and that one of his
jackets hung from a hook.

It was a glary day, almost September and still too warm. His
hatband and the dusty gray felt around it were wet, and Matt's
tarnished hair was plastered to his head, indented where the stiff
rim pressed on it in a continuous circular track. The hat smelled,
but it was an odor that Elaine had been around all her life.
Foley'd had it. It was the smell of a man who worked for what he
had, who lived a little beyond himself, who had something that
bothered him and drove him too hard. The presence of this smell
in the cottage, a house in which her husband had never lived, was
strange and disturbing, though not unpleasant.

Matt talked to her for a long time about nothing—weather,
crops, cattle, prices—and his words, spoken in a soft, breathy
baritone, spun out slower and slower. He repeated his thoughts,
missed an important conclusion a time or two, used a word incorrectly (he didn't know it), and then, when he couldn't stand
himself any longer, or his reason for coming, he jabbed out his
cigarette in a glass ash tray, cursed without meaning to, and got
up to leave. She was too difficult to talk to. She had crossed her
legs, one leg swinging gently in and out of a patch of sun. Pushing her hair away from her face, she would clear her throat with a
high little note that was as delicate as that of some small bird.
She tipped her head back and sometimes rolled it around slowly,
as if her neck hurt, or as if she had a headache at the base of her
skull. *I'm not that old*, Matt was thinking. *No, God*.

Yet he must say it; remembering Clarence, he rubbed his hand
once quickly over his thigh, as if he were cleaning it, and blurted:
"What are you going to do about Hugh?"

It was awkward, too short, crude, not at all what Clarence
would have said, not smart. But he had looked her straight in the
eye, and his voice had remained steady.

She responded with a laugh, yet she was alarmed because she
feared that the question might have come from the source, from
Clarence. Hugh had not spoken of his relationship with his father,

and she was unable to guess how persuasive his disapproval might be.

"What do you want me to do about him, Matthew?" She opened the palms of her beautiful hands upward toward him in a gesture of surrender. "Is asking me about Hugh part of your work nowadays?" She paused, drew her chin downward, and looked at him obliquely, as if she might deflect his answer. "If it is, you're underpaid."

"It's part of my work, in a way." The hat started around again in his stubby fingers.

"Did Hugh's father send you?"

"Indirectly." A bead of sweat rolled down his temple; he caught it with his finger.

Elaine went to the corner and turned on the electric fan. "Then he didn't send you specifically?"

"No, Clarence never asked me to come. I'm here on my own." He looked up from the hat, his eyes moving around quickly, showing more of their yellowish whites than was normal for him. "Hugh's just a kid, Elaine. He don't know what he needs, or what's good for him."

She lifted her eyebrows and laughed without opening her mouth. "I don't think he's ever been a kid, Matt. I don't know that side of him. He gets out of control sometimes, but it's not because he's a child."

"There's nothing in this for you, Elaine."

"You're not talking about money?"

"No," he told her. "I know you don't want money."

She smiled, and she had never been prettier. "How do you know that, Matt?"

"Because I knew Foley. Remember, Elaine? I knew you both."

Her head turned to the side, and her eyes lost a lot of their fire. "Don't hurt me, Matt," she said quietly. "I'm sure you didn't come here to talk about Foley."

"I don't know how the same woman could be interested in Foley and Hugh. I just don't see it." He was silent for a minute, and then his eyes narrowed shrewdly. "He's different from Foley, Elaine."

"He's like Foley."

"I can't understand it."

She hesitated. "Foley would." The words were spoken almost too softly to be heard.

He had to leave; staying any longer would just be repeating

what she would not hear. He moved around the coffee table toward the door; she was out on the porch ahead of him. He followed her and touched her arm, which was quite cool in spite of the stifling heat of the afternoon. "Let it alone, Elaine."

She turned around so swiftly that his hand was roughly disengaged. "Do you mean, leave Hugh alone?"

"Yes, that's what I mean." As he moved back slightly he hit the corner of the porch swing with his leg and turned around to steady it, not because he was fastidious but because he needed to look away from Elaine.

She leaned against the fluted wooden post of the porch and folded her arms under her breasts, pulling them in tightly, as if she suddenly felt cold. "Listen, Matthew," she said, shivering slightly, yet smiling at him now because his request seemed so absurdly naive. "Do you really believe that Clarence's baby boy was lured into a trap, that I enticed him and then tightened my net? If you know him at all, even that much"—she held up her thumb and forefinger, measuring out a tiny space—"you know he wouldn't be taken in by the likes of me. You think I went after him? Who do you think is being taken advantage of, Matt? Oh, Matt . . ." She laughed again, but nervously and out of tune. She changed her position, taking a step off the porch onto the grass, and then turned around to him, her back to the bed of roses, a flood of afternoon sun falling on the crown of her red hair, as if it would melt the coming sunset colors out of it. "If I told him that his daddy didn't want him to come here anymore, he'd laugh at me and you and everyone, and he'd come anyway. If I told him I didn't want him to be around me anymore, he'd know I was lying, because I'd be holding on to him, keeping him in my arms to tell him something like that."

She paused for him to respond, but he only watched her, his eyes softening, becoming still, his face settling. "Maybe later on, Matt. I'll try. But please, not yet. I can't." She reached up to touch the gold heart she wore around her neck, as if some recent thought or action might have disturbed it. "He does as he pleases, and that includes what he does with me. Give us time. Maybe he'll get tired of me. Maybe he'll cross me up some way and make me hate him."

At once, she was thinking of the afternoon when she'd driven with Hugh to Refugio, and he had pulled up in front of Elizardi's Drugstore, leaned across her to open her car door, and told her to wait for him inside while he conducted his business. She had hoped to accompany him, to justify her trip to herself at least by

observing an unusual property transaction, but capitulated for the
sake of keeping peace between them. She waved as he sped off
and went into Elizardi's, where she ordered a cup of coffee and
discussed with the druggist's wife the changes in the real estate
market since the war. It was Sunday afternoon and, most of the
time, she was the only customer there. The store was filled with
faded items of every description, and except for the three week-
lies, the magazines were out of date, and the pictures, like people
too long out of touch, had no information to convey. A fly sucked
at a sugary spill on the counter. Ice cream cones, brown and
waffled, some of them chipped, were in two dusty glass jars. In a
can of cloudy water, an aluminum scoop waited for the next child
who, with a damp nickel in his clenched fist, would order its use.

Mrs. Elizardi knew Elaine and had known her husband. Foley
had sold her son a small farm, one of his first sales after he had
set up the business in Dansville. Elaine had eaten lunch at that
farm, a big Sunday meal with fresh pork and homemade pastry,
followed by a coarse and highly potent pear brandy. All the relatives had been invited, and there had been singing around the
piano; after the dishes had been washed, someone had suggested
a game of softball, and she and Foley had played on opposite
teams. They had teased each other, criticized each other's playing, both screaming with laughter. Many times after, Foley had
talked about those people; he had particularly liked them.

While they chatted, Mrs. Elizardi spoke so often of Foley,
shaking her head and using her handkerchief, and seemed so
relentless in reminding Elaine of her marriage that Elaine wondered if she had heard of her relationship with Hugh and disapproved; and when, two hours later, Hugh finally came for her,
when he walked into the store proprietarily, pulled her off the
counter stool, put his arm around her waist, and threw a folded
dollar on the counter (not waiting for his change), Elaine was
ashamed. She had introduced them hurriedly, and Mrs. Elizardi
looked back and forth quickly between their two faces—Elaine's
now flushed, Hugh's bruised and a bit swollen—not as if she
were judging them but as if she were reaching a conclusion that
she wished were different. Elaine sensed her discomfort, and it
caused her to say good-by a bit vaguely and to hold her lover's
hand more tightly than was her custom in public.

Reacting to Matt's silence and avoiding his critical glance,
Elaine reached down and pulled up a stalk growing out of a tuft
of Johnson grass and ran the end of it along her lip. Her eyes
were the color of the leaves of the morning glory vine that hung

so thick on the side of the house, looping down heavily toward the railing of the porch. "But let me tell you this to make you feel better, Matt: He'll leave here; it won't last too long, maybe not even until his first vacation. He'll see someone he wants more than me, and that will be that. I'll be twenty-eight next winter; that should be a relief to you. He'll want a family someday. I've had mine."

"And if he wants to marry—"

"He won't. He won't want my babies. I know what he is."

She waited. Matt was putting on his hat, looking down at the walkway, fixing the brim of it just right, just the proper distance from the tops of his small ears. He looked up quickly. "I'm going to try my best to break it up. It ain't good, and I'm going to stop him coming here if I can."

She was nervous, and her composure was beginning to fail. "You can do as you please, Matt."

"I intend to."

"You can go home," she told him. "You can discuss it in the bunkhouse with Stephen, Martin, and Doug, and whoever else is out there now, and then you can telephone Clarence and tell him this: As long as I'm here and Hugh wants to see me, I'm available—just as long as it pleases him to come to me. If his father can talk him out of it, or you can, or Stephen can, that's fine, but none of you will get anything out of me."

"Starting today?" Matt was confused; while she opposed him, her expression remained soft and gentle. The sun was behind her, shadowing her face. Just as her relentless sensuality made Matt ill at ease, so she was troubled by his tenacious hold on a line of wisdom that she knew was sound. "No, starting July 9," she said. "The first time he stayed with me."

"Apparently he has what you want."

"It's reciprocal."

"He's teaching you big words."

"I already knew that one."

He started down the porch steps; she was standing on the path now, between him and the Jeep. "You're right to think he won't stay permanent," Matt said. "He can't. He'll have obligations. This is just recreation for these people. We don't count none. He's going to leave here and never come back, except once in a while to sit in a duck blind and kill things. Where're you going to be then? You're going to have to stay in this town. You understand me? Clarence is going to—"

"Fine," she interrupted, snapping off bits of a dry twig of

mimosa, an inch at a time. "Then you'll have the pleasure of seeing my grief—but that's all. And until then, you can leave me alone. Clarence is okay, the little I know of him from the few times he's sat in my office drinking coffee and smoking and picking my brain for information about real estate values that I think he already knows. Are you aware that Clarence telephoned me to say that Hugh was coming down here to look at the Greeley estate? He sent Hugh to me all by himself. I think he almost told me to be good to him. Fine. If a little finesse will be an asset to him later..."

"That had nothing to do with you."

"Maybe Clarence wanted his boy broken in."

"You didn't break him in."

"Maybe not," she flared. "Or maybe it depends on what you mean."

"Hugh didn't tell me nothing, Elaine."

"I know damned well that he didn't tell you. I know that, however much you or I might disapprove of him, he doesn't talk, not about me, not about what he does in my house... right, Matt?"

Matt took out a pack of cigarettes, but when he offered her one, she refused it with a solid shake of her head, and he returned it to his shirt pocket. "Don't it bother you, bedding down with a youngster?" he asked.

"Didn't it bother you getting him bred in Mexico when he was a baby?"

"You were married then," he shot back. "You weren't available. Don't you think about what the hell you're doing?"

Her eyes were filling up, and she was biting her lip white. He had never meant to make Foley Menutis's wife cry. He recognized the error in that. He scratched roughly at the inside of his hand, and he spoke quickly. "I don't mean nothing..."

She sighed, a touch of exasperation in the gesture, her nerves tight from fighting from her lonely corner for too long. "Nobody means anything. It's okay. I'm enjoying it, Matt. Even at its worst, it's fun. So don't worry about it, and don't worry about Clarence's boy. He's in good hands."

She glanced at the sun impatiently, as if she were in a hurry for it to go out. It was all right; she'd better get used to it; she just hated for Matt to see. "I love him," she said.

He looked at her squarely then, realizing that those last three words had put him back in the offensive position. "That's too bad. You're not lucky to have hold of Hugh."

"As it turned out, I wasn't lucky to have hold of Foley, either."

"It's still too bad."

She opened the clasp on the gate, put her hand over the metal loop, and pulled the gate back for him. As she stepped out, she reached down into the flower bed that bordered the fence, broke off a zinnia, and began twirling it between her fingers against her neck. "I guess so," she said, "but that's sure how it is."

He played his last card. "What does Jimmy think of his mama?" he asked.

"He doesn't know."

"He will. The other boys'll tell him. Be sure of it. He coming home for school, or staying up there with your folks? You going to kick out Jimmy for Hugh? That's going to be right on the line, ain't it? They're both kids."

She stood still, looking back at the double distortion of her face and neck in the lenses of his glasses. Matt touched the brim of his hat in the convention of country deference, as Foley would have done, as Hugh would never have done, and went toward the road, disturbing the gravel ahead of him with the frayed toes of his boots, which the rain and dew had molded to the shape of his feet. "All right, Elaine," he finally called back at her, leaning out the window of the Jeep, pulling at a plug of tobacco. "It's your funeral. Hugh? He's going to get off."

She kissed the palm of her hand, waved it toward him, and then watched him disappear before she lost her nerve and began to shake. Across the street, the bare branches of a willow tree made a mesh of copper quadrilaterals against the dying sky. A car stopped before her neighbor's house. People got out, and one of them waved at her. She waved back, but the person had already turned away. Her neighbors weren't as friendly as they used to be. She went indoors and began ironing through a pile of laundry, both hers and Hugh's, until she felt a stinging at the end of her nose and a flood of tears in her eyes. The sleeves and the cuffs of a shirt blurred. She was trying to focus on a little bluebonnet oil painting that Foley had given her when Laura was born when she started to cry. She set the iron upright, jerked out the plug, collapsed on the sofa, and sobbed.

They would get him. Somehow, someway, they would take him from her, tether him, cripple him, neuter him. *They do that or kill you,* she thought. It was just a matter of time, but the world he was a part of would get him, just as sure as the war had gotten Foley.

On the coffee table, Matt had left his cigarette lighter. It was Mexican silver and had been etched, but Matt's hands had worn it smooth, until it was like a stone under water. While he had been lighting a cigarette, he was shaking so that she'd had to get up and steady his hand. He had not thanked her.

Let Hugh return it to him, she thought bitterly. *Let him tell Matt to go to hell for coming here!*

But after a while, knowing that she would return the lighter herself, and that she would not tell Hugh about it, or about the visit, she tucked it in her bureau drawer, not far from the picture of Foley, which she dared no longer see.

Chapter 5

MATT NEED NOT have concerned himself about keeping the news of Hugh's affair from the Littletons, for they had known about Elaine since that first afternoon in July when Hugh had driven from the ranch with a small suitcase, a sack of steaks, and a package wrapped in gift paper, and left his car parked in front of her house well into the next day. A friend in Dansville had telephoned Clarence in Houston and given him the information in a manner more appropriate to disclosing news of a death than to revealing an illicit mating, and Clarence had had the composure not only to receive it calmly but to thank him. However, when Clara, who had been reading in a lounge chair under a shade tree in a far corner of the garden, had learned of Hugh's liaison from Cana, she had flung down her book and run to her room with Cana following behind her, shaking her head, regretting her role as informer (she had imparted the confidence with eyes averted, and so softly that Clara had had to ask her to repeat it), and knowing that she had told her only to save her from hearing it outside her home, and maybe from a malicious acquaintance.

Clarence was not troubled by the relationship. True, it was annoying, and it would cause him trouble with Clara, but it was something he might have expected. Men of Hugh's age and temperament had experimenting to do, and as a result, they often got into trouble. Hugh could do far worse than to take up with an experienced and, as far as he could find out, kind woman in an oak-shaded, lazy river town like Dansville. Better to get on with this first romance than to pine away, idealizing some well-bred city girl, too closely guarded to remedy his problem. And Hugh was bound to have one. As a child, he had been difficult, disobeying everyone Clarence left in charge of him, including his mother, disturbing the neighbors with pranks, and incurring the enmity of all the servants except Cana. Nearing adulthood, he was tense and aggressive, and he could be dangerous. Maybe Elaine would calm him, settle him down, discipline him a little, and make him happy.

In addition, Clarence had seen no reason to interfere with a son who was capable, and who had, since he was fourteen, gone away to school—first to Gilman, an Episcopal school in Baltimore that Clarence had chosen for him, and then to Princeton, which he had chosen for himself. Despite his temper, he had never really been in the kind of trouble that Clarence would have considered serious—only an occasional fight in which Clarence had naturally enough taken his side; he was astute; he had a feeling for business; and he need not be treated as if he lacked good sense. Personally Clarence liked him. He would have, he thought, even if he had been another man's son. He could admire Hugh's recklessness; he understood it. Hugh might be something to reckon with now, but he would come around. Clarence was certain of it. This thing with Mrs. Menutis would probably serve to speed things along.

By way of a formality, a checking in with his own conscience, he had gone down to consult with Luther because Hugh listened to Luther—at least, he had listened three years before, when Hugh had announced his decision to become a rodeo rider, to go on the circuit, and Luther had talked him out of it, not because Clarence had asked him to (he had not), but because he himself believed it was wrong. Only a man who lacked the privilege of choice should take such a personal risk, Luther had said. "First priority is staying alive; second is not getting broken up so bad you can't do nothing with the rest of your life."

Luther had come out to speak with Clarence, followed by his pregnant wife, who was lovely in a huge blue dress with white smocking. In the end, it was Lettie who had the most to say, her advice being that Hugh should marry Elaine: Marriage was her solution to the problems of all troubled couples. She talked spiritedly, unaware that she had no right to talk at all until Luther told her patiently to leave them. She obeyed him, as far as the cookhouse porch, where she turned, leaned her heavy body on the balustrade and watched the two men—one blond and rugged, the other dark and commanding—while they conferred, and while she came to her own wiser and less complicated conclusions.

As the months passed and the relationship endured, Clarence decided that Hugh would be safe in continuing it—and protecting his son was his sole concern in the matter. If the woman did not trifle with Hugh (and Clarence felt that she would not), it would be fine; the situation, one of need and accommodation, was clear-cut. Sleeping with a woman like Mrs. Menutis would have its salutary effects for Hugh; and that he had arranged to do this on a regular basis showed that he was capable of coming up with a shrewd solution to a not uncommon predicament. Clarence had talked to Elaine several times in her office and remembered that she was beautiful and competent and, moreover, as cold as ice. He admired that in a woman; but, more particularly, he admired the man who could break into it. And though Elaine was very much a country girl, he felt that she was perfectly capable of taking care of herself, even in a relationship with a young man as obstreperous as Hugh. He was certain that Hugh would never marry her, and almost equally certain that she would never be so foolish as to bear him a child or abuse him in any other less serious way.

A friend had reminded Clarence that these situations were usually expensive. Yet this one had not cost much more than a few presents and some small amounts of money. It had come to his attention (his banker had telephoned him one morning to report: "Mr. Littleton, a Mrs. F. D. Menutis has—I thought that I might just tell you—a woman in Dansville has received . . .") that Hugh had seen fit to pay for a new roof and screened side porch for Elaine's house, plus what must have been a very fine silver-gray Persian cat, and several short vacations. None of these gifts was so large, however, that he could not take care of them out of his own funds, which, now that he was past eighteen, were considerable; in any case, the presents he made to her were such tokens that it was obvious that she was not permitting him to take over her keep in the traditional way of these things. She retained her independence; so much to her credit.

When, one Saturday afternoon in the locker room of his club, after playing eighteen holes of golf, one of Clarence's friends, a man who owned property in the area of Dansville, mentioned Hugh's involvement with a woman older than he was and probably not of his class, Clarence replied, "I'm not going to seek to punish him for getting itchy because he has red blood in his veins and for doing something about it, especially if he can find some woman crazy enough to let him." He raised his black eyebrows and rubbed a twisted towel hard against the back of his neck. "By the way, Dillard," he went on, just before he began to laugh, "have you ever seen Elaine Menutis?"

"Yes." The other flushed and turned away.

"Well, what do you think you'd do if . . . ? Huh? Hey, Dillard!"

That incident made Clarence acknowledge one aspect of Hugh's affair that he had been unwilling to admit to himself, fearing that it would seem a condonation: Namely, that he was proud of his boy, and though what he was doing might be wicked, it was alluring all the same. Hugh's was a situation that he himself had sought when he was young but somehow had never quite managed to make happen. His love affairs had been fast, furious, widely broadcast. He had lavished presents on his women, loved them as fiercely as they would permit, and left them after a day or after a few weeks, not because he had had a change of heart, but because he was distracted or separated from them by distance, usually by the demands of business. He had not been a Don Juan: There was no stealth or guile in him. He had had no time for clandestine affairs; he had never gotten mixed up with a married woman. The women he knew had been either "of the trade" or from that very different social class that lived north of the bayou, so that gossip in no way affected them. It had not been fickleness that motivated Clarence but convenience; he had been a very busy man. He had picked up women as they came to him, as casually as a beachcomber picks up what catches his eye if it happens to be in the direction he is going.

The woman he finally married—he was thirty when he decided the time had come to take that step—was now the one intractable party in the matter of Hugh's relationship with Elaine. He had tried to talk to Clara; he had tried long and seriously. He understood her hysteria, and he forgave her immediately for blaming him. It was natural for a woman to feel the way she did about a thing like this: It reminded her all too clearly of her own situation. He attempted to convince Clara that this was only a temporary state of affairs, and not a particularly serious one, since it would have no bearing on their son's choice of a wife, but Clara was adamant. She thought of Hugh as Clarence's child; he had never been hers. From the time he was born, from those first few days when Clarence had held him in his arms, quieting him when no one else could, Hugh had been his father's. And why wouldn't she have wanted the shrieking child away from her after her sufferings? What remained of her to give him attention then? And how dare Clarence plead with her now?

After the call from Dansville, it was only Cana who could get close to Clara. Only Cana, the black maid, Hugh's nurse, who could quiet Clara, urge her to bed, get her to slip between the sheets—just as she had done thirteen years earlier when Clara had come home drunk from the Art Forum luncheon, had gotten sick on the hall runner, and started talking; two hours later, she was still talking, and Cana heard for the first time the story that Clara could never tell often enough.

Clara had not cried hysterically nor had she been difficult to manage. She had been calm and her voice steady as she told Cana of that afternoon, a few months into her nineteenth year, when her father had found her and her cousin in his apartment, the bed rumpled, Clara wearing Ben's robe, Ben sitting in the sunlight of the window, reading a passage to her from a favorite book. Her father was not a man to raise his voice; he told her to dress, that he would wait for her in the vestibule. And when, the following evening, her family spoke to her again, when they allowed her out of her room, called her downstairs to talk, it was to tell her of Ben's illness, which they called tuberculosis, though Ben's doctor had said it was pleurisy, aggravated by the damp climate of the Gulf Coast. Her mother said that she would be nothing but a nurse to him; having children would be out of the question—he couldn't even support himself. Then her mother berated her for her shameful secrecy and for having deceived them. Clara suffered for herself and for her lover; she was miserable; vainly she sought expiation, and she tried to think of ways in which she might restore her parents' regard for her. She cried and kept to herself; often she couldn't complete the day at school. Some weeks later, reacting to her despondency, her parents decided to distract her with a trip and a course of study. She wanted to be an artist; her sketches and water colors showed promise. They would send her to Philadelphia to the art school at the university. They bought her things for the trip, treated her with fondness; they were solicitous of her, indulgent in all things except one: They forbade her to see her cousin or to communicate with him in any way.

A week before her scheduled departure on the train, at a party at the Brenners' estate on the bay at La Porte, thirty miles from Houston, the first real party of the season, she met Clarence Littleton. As she was crossing an anteroom, her corsage loosened and slipped down her skirt; Clarence, without either bruising the flowers or pulling their ribbon loose, retrieved it and, with surprising gentleness for a man of his type, repinned it to her dress.

His hair was black; he dared to wear it longer than most men; he danced well, but he seemed ill at ease. "I don't go to many parties," he said. "Neither do I," she replied with a sigh and a look of contempt for all entertainments.

Later, as they walked out on the pier, he told her that he was in the oil business, and then as they watched the lights of distant ships making their way into the channel, he talked about the value of the new waterway, praising the foresight of the men who had underwritten its construction. He knew many things, and knew them as a pragmatist who searches out secrets and uses them for his own purposes. As he spoke, the water slapped against the posts and the underside of the pier, and a meadow of silver fluttered to the lighthouse and to the ships on the channel, for as far as Clara could see. On the way back to the party, her hand disappeared in his, and she made no effort to retrieve it until it was time for her to leave with her friends.

During the next several days he saw her at home in her parents' tiny parlor, messy with books and bibelots and dark with family portraits, but she made excuses and never let him stay longer than the time it took him to finish his glass of sherry and eat his cake. She refused his invitations to dinner, explaining that she had to prepare for her trip. But she received a long telephone call the night before she left, and when, on the morning of her departure, he came to the train station to see her off, he brought her a white octagonal box that held a huge purple orchid, whose fine head would later shiver among its tissues on the seat beside her.

For several weeks there was an exchange of letters between Houston and Philadelphia, until one afternoon the maid announced that a Mr. Littleton was waiting in the downstairs parlor. He was not there on business but had taken the train to see her; he had a room in a hotel downtown and had no idea how long he would stay. He was with her whenever she was free, and every visit, he brought her so many flowers that her bedroom soon became a jungle: Under the tendrils of the ferns and behind the dark green vases, she would lose her hairbrush, her lilac water, her fine drawing pencils. She could hardly breathe for their scent, and though frost was on the trees, Clara opened her window to let in the cold air.

She would sit with him on the sofa, showing him her charcoal drawings of arranged flowers and fruit and imaginary landscapes. On one of these visits, he kissed her, gently at first, but when she put her hand on his neck, he pulled her to him so forcefully that her drawings fell out of her lap and scattered on the floor. He kneeled on the rug to collect them, handing them back to her in a stack that he took the trouble and time to make neat, and then, after telling her of his feelings for her and all the ways in which he thought she was perfect, he asked her to marry him.

Certain that he would find out, that when their engagement was announced in Houston, someone would inform him, she told him immediately about her affair with her cousin, and she made it clear that if her parents had allowed it, she would have married him. Clarence's eyes traveled the room without objective, confusion and grief marking every feature of his face, and when she tried to touch him out of sympathy for his disappointment, he avoided her hand. He stood up, began speaking to her courteously about trivial things—he might never have proposed marriage. Then, in a few minutes, he picked up his coat, told her good night amicably, and left.

She imagined that he would not return. Clarence was the kind of man who would never go contrary to his principles, and surely one of his beliefs, the cornerstone of his understanding of marriage, would be that society owes a hardworking, productive, and successful man a virgin bride. At the hotel, he would pack his bags; if a train was leaving that night, he would be on it.

She was writing to her mother at the little desk in the alcove of the parlor when, two nights later, she heard his voice in the entryway, boisterous, demanding, and rude. She went to him quickly, hid him in the alcove, made him sit down and stay silent, then pleaded with the astonished maid not to report his presence to the housemother, to bring him some black coffee, and then to leave them alone.

The next morning, when the sun was just up, glistening on the snow-covered porch where she waited, her suitcases in the hallway, her coat securely buttoned against the bitter cold, he came for her in a taxi. They drove through the streets of the famous city, ice floating on the shadowy waves of the river, an overlay of snow on the lance tops of the iron fences and on the bronze figures of patriots in the courts of ancient buildings. They were married at the city hall, made love in the bridal suite of Clarence's hotel, then shared a long champagne lunch, served in their room on a linen-covered table with wheels.

Clarence had nothing in common with her professor-father, or her intellectual, Virginia-educated mother, but he was rich and well thought of in business circles; his manners, though acquired rather late in life, were more than adequate; and he belonged to the two best clubs in town. Her parents, having feared that their daughter's ruined reputation would spoil her chances of marriage, were amazed and pleased.

Clara learned quickly that her husband didn't work an eight-hour day or a five-day week; he worked constantly. No sooner had they returned home than the telephone began ringing: Money was needed immediately for the Swenson field; would Clarence advise his banker? An investor had backed out of a land purchase in southern Louisiana; did he want to pick up his equity? A fire had started in the field near Beaumont; he'd better get down there quick. Often he stayed away for weeks at a time, and when he returned and Clara was tearful and hurt, he lavished attention on her, bought her expensive presents, and told her repeatedly that he loved her. Yet he was simply never with her. Even when he was in town, which was little more than half his time, he was at the office or at one of his clubs, talking to investors, field managers, colleagues.

Years passed with little change, and Clara stopped grieving aloud. Gradually she planned her own activities, joined a writing group, painted in the studio Clarence had built for her at the back of the property, joined the Tuesday Musical Club, and entertained her friends. At first, she imagined that it would be wrong to go out at night without her husband; later she broke that rule, going to the homes of her closest friends, then venturing steadily into wider and wider circles. She was lovely and rich, and her loneliness showed. She attracted attention, and at last, when gossip linked her name with that of a prominent lawyer whose brilliance was well known and who possessed a notable collection of paintings and rare books, Clarence got wind of it and acted.

He hired a full-time production manager for the field west of Kirbyville and spent more time at home. And Clara stayed at home with him. If he had to be gone overnight, he took her along. She kept track of his schedule so that she would be prepared when it was time to leave; she soon was able to accommodate even a departure for a last-minute emergency—a blown cap, a cave-in, a collapsed derrick. She learned about all the better boardinghouses and clapboard hotels in East Texas; about rooms where the bathroom was shared; about bathtubs that were a yard high and had lion-claw feet; about thick white plates, batter fried foods, collard greens, chitterlings, and grits; she discovered that everything served warm was covered with a thick, white flour gravy or with a hot sauce made by pouring boiling vinegar over tiny red peppers; and that everything served cold was covered with sugar. She heard country accents, most of them crude. She watched her husband blend in with everyone: black, Mexican, white; farmer, oil-field worker, storekeeper. She watched him stand as they did, hunching his shoulders, speaking slowly with their intonations, squinting while he smoked an entire cigarette without removing it from his mouth until it had almost burned his lips—just as they did.

Clarence enjoyed this life: The blood of the Irish peasant farmers that flowed in his veins filled him with affection and love for these people, these little towns. But Clara, a true descendant of Alexandria, soon found that she hated it all. In dusty rooms where there was nothing to do but wield a fly swatter and try to find out how the flies got in, Clara spent days at a time alone. Clarence would not come in until she was asleep, waking her accidentally by dropping his boots or walking down the hall to draw his bath. He would wake her intentionally, though, when he got into bed, saying both her names—at these times, she was always Clara Fay—shaking her gently, ignoring her soft complaints, turning her to face him, and then kissing her and loving her and promising her things until her voice was swallowed up by his quickened breathing, and finally his expression of the pleasure that he sought. Clarence had told her that possessing her body eased the pain in his muscles, wiped away the glare of the sun, erased from his memory the filthy and brutal work.

This new life of Clara's lasted only for as long as she could endure it; After slightly less than three months, she became too weak to accompany Clarence, too sick to go anywhere, and Clarence had to hire still another assistant so that he could stay with her at home in Houston. She was pale and worried, she kept to her bed until noon, she would eat only in the evenings, and she no longer read or listened to music. After supper Clarence would sit with her on the sofa, playing board games. She refused to see a doctor, yet one night when she had a violent attack of nausea and a headache so severe that she cried, Clarence telephoned one. Clara was pregnant with Hugh.

In the ensuing weeks, something disturbed her deeply, perhaps the news that her cousin Ben was critically ill in a sanitarium in Denver. She grieved for him, despondent and dejected, and then she became anxious for herself, certain that she, too, was in serious danger. She stayed at home, she refused all invitations, nor did she entertain. Clara had never been vain, but now she complained that her pregnancy made her ugly, deformed her body and discolored her skin. She was consistently unkind to Clarence, and when he urged her to begin preparations for the birth, she answered him disinterestedly or did not reply at all. Her apathy obliged her mother to make the arrangements for the nursery, to buy the layette, and to hire the trained nurse, who would stay with Clara for the three weeks of the lying-in. Near the close of the sixth month, when she began spotting blood and the doctor ordered her to stay in bed, she ignored his instructions, even after twice starting into labor at a time when this could have caused the baby to be born dangerously premature.

The birth shouldn't have been difficult—fragile as Clara looked, she was reasonably well built for having children, and her muscles were strong—but her refusal to relax during the first hours of labor or to make an effort to expel the baby during the last caused her extreme suffering, and afterward, she went into a depression so alarming that the doctor warned Clarence that unless she was brought out of it soon, he could expect permanent damage. When Hugh was six weeks old, they left him with the nurse, and Clarence took Clara on a vacation to the Virgin Islands, rented a villa on St. Thomas, and encouraged her to sketch and paint the hedges of hibiscus, the palm groves, and the tropical birds. Despite his guilt over leaving his son, it was a good time for the couple: It renewed and strengthened their relationship and restored Clara's health.

When they returned home, she took an interest in the child, though mostly in his schedule and health, usually leaving the nursery after she had given her instructions, and when Cana was hired, she abandoned even that. She returned to her clubs, attended concerts regularly, and worked as a volunteer fund raiser. She was active and happy. It wasn't that she didn't love her home; it was simply that domestic duties bored her, and she was rich enough to delegate them to others.

As Hugh grew older, Clara established no relationship whatsoever with him, for which she blamed the child, since he avoided her. He was intractable, she said; and he was mean; he did not enjoy his family as other children did. She remembered the closeness of her own family, how she had loved her parents and always obeyed them. Hugh was cold, she claimed, and he disliked her; the only kind thing he ever did for her was to make good grades.

In fact, it was clear to everyone who had observed the boy's upbringing that the failure was on the mother's side: She had neither prepared his meals, nor pasted photographs of him in albums, nor driven him to school, nor taken him on outings, nor listened to the strange troubles and fears that young children

have. Birthday parties she arranged by making a single telephone
call to the manager of the country club, and these were marvel-
ous, complete with Mexican musicians in native costumes, gypsy
dancers with real ebony castanets, helium-filled balloons, magi-
cians, and clowns. Only when he was sick did he engage her
sympathies, and then nothing could take her from him. When, at
six, he had the measles, she sat a week with him in a dark room;
when, at nine, he nearly died of the flu complicated by an ulcer-
ated throat, she dismissed the professional nurse and cared for
him so diligently that she became ill herself—Hugh was back in
school before Clara was even able to come downstairs.

But for the most part, she was busy. She went to lectures; she
was an officer in a literary club. She wrote short stories and
poems and read them to special friends at salad luncheons on
shaded porches or at afternoon gatherings in living rooms that
smelled of silk brocade, Bristol Cream, and exotic wood, leaving
the duties of tending to her child to relatives and servants.

By and large, the responsibility of raising Hugh fell to Cana.
The day she had come to the back door looking for a job, told by
the neighbor's cook that the Littletons needed a nurse, he had
been playing in the sand pile. When she had insisted that he clean
his hands before lunch, he had kicked at her, and when she had
made him eat something other than Jell-O and Oreo cookies, he
had shouted that she was too fat and too black. But gradually she
gained his confidence by pushing him in his stroller along the
wide, shaded sidewalks before the sloping lawns and by reading
his big picture books to him, her soothing voice causing him to
leave his toys, to rest his elbow on her knee, and finally to crawl
into her lap, leaning against her, sucking his thumb, looking up at
her occasionally to study her wide, broad-boned face. At night,
she eased him into bed yet stayed with him as long as he wished
her to, and she left the light on in the bathroom at his request.

As a boy, he had arms and legs that were long and straight and
brown, and he laughed with pleasure when people said he looked
like an Indian. Except in hot weather, under the sprays of the
sprinklers, he refused to take baths; he screamed at the barber and
circled under the chair, so that Cana let his dark hair grow until it
almost covered his ears and eyes, then cut it herself while she
distracted him with stories about cowboys and pirates. In summer, he shed his clothes and wore only his swimming trunks and
a beach towel tied around his neck with his dog's rope. He ran
around the huge yard carrying a cap pistol, the towel cape flying
horizontal behind him. By lapping slices of meat over each rung

of a ladder, he had taught his father's hunting dog to climb to the roof of the servants' quarters, where, when he removed the ladder, the dog would raise his head to the white, fist-tight summer clouds and howl; and then, while the child sat in stubborn silence in a chair in the kitchen, Cana would send the yardmen to look for the ladder behind the garage, in the cellar, in the neighbors' shrubs.

Cana was an indulgent guardian; she loved Hugh and saw to it that his needs were met, but by the time he was a teen-ager, her influence had waned, and she couldn't control him. She discussed this with Clara, but Clara either evaded the issue by saying that she would consider what to do, and then did nothing, or she deferred to Clarence. She seemed to have accepted her boy as impossible and a problem, and since she had never erected for him a pedestal from which he could fall, she suffered no disappointment on account of his behavior. It was his affair with Elaine that suddenly forced her to think of him as grown-up, and while she reasoned that a willful and insubordinate child was one thing, an immoral and conscienceless adult was another. She spoke of her feelings heatedly to Clarence.

Criticizing Hugh made Clarence uncomfortable, particularly now in the matter of asking him to give up a beloved woman, but he promised Clara that he would talk to him and set him right if he could. One night, when Hugh was leaving for Dansville, Clarence asked him into the library and offered him a glass of something strong. He sat in a desk chair that tilted, and made it clear immediately that he was more interested in his son's welfare than in disapproving of his behavior. Hugh remained standing, not because he was ill at ease but because he was in a hurry. Clarence asked him to be careful and, of course, to be discreet, never to talk about Elaine to anyone at home, or to friends, and particularly never to his mother.

"I never talk to Mother about anything," Hugh answered. There was no bitterness in his remark; he was just stating a fact. He was able to remember hugging her around the knees as a very young child, and having her ease him away from her with her soft, determined hands—she had something else to do, she was always rushing somewhere. He remembered, time after time, running to her car to ask her to take him with her, but always she refused him. He remembered that he'd had no pride before her, that he had known incredible humiliation, but he had struggled on, as stolid and stubborn as any young animal must be, who strives for attention and recognition from the adult centers of power—particularly the maternal one, the fruit of whose nurturing is equanimity and peace. For whatever reason, he was of no concern to her, and she had let him know it every day of his life. Her face had stayed behind a book every time he had tried to tell her something; her eyes had slanted towards his activities without her ever engaging her attention in them fully; she had left the house whenever anyone telephoned her, yet never to go anywhere with him; she had sent Cana to tell him good night, when he had repeatedly asked for his mother. He had given up the idea of interesting her in his life so long ago that the impulse to do so now was as absurd as would be the impulse to climb on Cana's lap, put his arms around her stout neck, his head on her breast, and ask her for a story or a song.

At the end of a very agreeable interview, in which Clarence had found out absolutely nothing and had never meant to, he stood up and put his arm affectionately around his son's shoulders, which were as broad and heavy now as his own. He didn't have to worry; what Hugh wanted was what he himself had wanted. They were very much alike. Hugh's ambition would serve him; he would have a strong, solid plan from which he would never let an unsuitable love affair distract him. He would enjoy the woman and the adventure, but when the time came to finish, he would know it and break with her. Clarence walked with his son to the side door and stood in the doorway, nodding his head affirmatively as Hugh walked to his car. He found himself reassured, not at anything Hugh had told him but at the conclusion he had come to himself.

A misty rain in the early fall morning had left behind a coolness that would stay for hours. In the side yard along the driveway, the leaves of the tallow were beginning to color, and with each gust of wind, Elaine had heard flutters of leaves in the thick wet branches. By afternoon, the wind had cleared the sky and brought brilliantly figured, feathered clouds in its wake. Elaine was sitting at her desk in the living room, preparing to write a letter to Hugh at school. A box of stationery was open to the thin blue sheets; an envelope, pulled out from beneath them, was already carefully addressed in a slightly self-conscious but graceful script. Considering for a moment what she wanted to say, she let her hands slip off the desk into her lap and stretched. She looked like a Petty girl on the page of a calendar, the length of her white legs exaggerated, her sleek red hair turned under. She even had the round, doll-like stare of incredulity, suggesting a willingness to be loved.

It was an odd time: Hugh might have been in the military as Foley had been; eventually he would come home on furlough to love her, to pick up their lives where they had left off, and then to go again, leaving her on the porch or standing in the doorway of her office downtown, strained by the fear that their union would end in an unimaginable grief.

But more and more, it seemed that he was hers. Since he had left her, she had at last had the time to ponder those last weeks together during which both of them had been reluctant to let the other out of his sight, when every activity was planned together, and every thought overlapped, encouraged, and caressed the thought of the other, and she was able to convince herself that she need not fear losing him. It even seemed that his family was going to leave her alone, that the irascible Clarence had given up trying to wrench his boy away from her, either by sending his envoy, Matt, or, perhaps, by urging Clara to find for him, among her friends' daughters, a match, sweeter, younger, and purer than she.

There had been times during those hot, dreamy weeks of summer when she would forget how Hugh had come to her. His big hands seemed always to have been holding the steering wheel of a car in which she was riding, and she seemed always to have been sitting beside him in a way that was so natural that it had no beginning and could have no end. She had gradually stopped trying to discover why she loved him; her feeling for him had become too strong to be subjected to such an examination. She had always been ahead of him somewhere, thinking about how she might be able to keep from expressing her emotions so directly that even he might be frightened by them. *I'm older, but he's smarter,* she had said to herself. *I've learned a lot, but he knows more. One day he may push me away scarcely remembering his infatuation, much less missing it. But he'd be wrong to do that.* She sensed that he must feel ill at ease when he was away from her, and that like any healthy animal who has found its way to an elemental satisfaction capable of nourishing a vigorous system, he must have stopped thinking about why.

Since Hugh had left for school four weeks earlier, she had written to him almost every day; he had written less frequently, but he telephoned on weekends, blaming the lack of letters on his heavy schedule of classes and on two of his history professors, who demanded weekly papers, detailed and carefully researched.

Weekends he spent in the library, he said; week nights he fled the noisy dormitory to study in the quiet of an empty classroom. Elaine hardly went out at all. Movies, a game of bridge, a Saturday lunch with women friends held no interest for her; furthermore, since the beginning of her liaison with Hugh, she was less often invited. She attended church, making an effort to make up for the Sundays she had missed in the summer, when Hugh had not only refused to accompany her but had prevented her from going. One morning in the hallway after a Bible class, when the minister mentioned something about a family at the Littleton ranch, and she sensed that the conversation was drawing around to her relationship with Hugh, she welcomed the interruption of one of the teachers to ask a question, and she left as the two of them discussed the answer.

When there was no work to keep Elaine at her office, she stayed in her house, comforted in her isolation by this cottage on the outskirts of the small, old town. Six trees stood on her land: one sycamore, one water oak, two live oaks, one tallow, and one mimosa. She had planted a vegetable garden in back, and a tool shed and a white-washed garage stood in the far corner of the back yard. Up against the front porch were two flower beds which a black man, who had kept a few dairy cows on a piece of property that she and Foley had owned, came to cultivate twice a year. Four oblong rose beds faced each other in pairs across the walk. A swing hung suspended from the porch ceiling by four thick brass chains—the same swing she had had in her house in town (she had asked for a clause in the contract of sale enabling her to keep it), a heavy, well-made, well-proportioned swing, which Foley had built for her in the garage on a spring weekend, slow for showing property because it had been raining. She never walked past it without running her fingers gently over its smooth and carefully sanded surface. In the days right after the war, she had sat in it and cried until she was exhausted, until what had been a clamorous and clear image of her husband, bending over a worktable, looking up from time to time to respond to what she had said or simply to exchange a smile with her, had retreated for a while into a misty recollection. Her grief for him would collect safely in the silence of her inattention and then break out unexpectedly at a time when, because of fatigue or solitude, she was unable to defend her mind.

She had lost Foley, and she knew that because she would be unable to offer him a varied and rich enough experience, she would probably lose Hugh. Her role in their relationship was clear, and it hurt her to think that he might spend himself on her until, practiced and grown-up, he would finish and be gone. She would keep him as long as she could, enjoy him while she had him, and never spoil it with her fears. She had no control over what he did, but she loved him as he was, and her happiness was in the present. The best she could do was to make time stand still, like a drop of water that has slipped down a leaf to be held in a prolonged and agreeable suspension.

Sometimes, Hugh's youthfulness startled her. He would do or say something to remind her of it, and she would realize that she had stopped thinking of him as either a boy or a man, that she had, in fact, stopped assessing his attributes and qualities long ago. He was simply her lover, and she responded to him with all the unquestioning respect she would grant a superstition. She recognized his innate power, despite his youth, and the power behind the tradition from which he came. Yet she was as suspicious of that tradition as her farmer father had taught her to be; and though her livelihood depended upon it, she resented it that city people bought out the farmers and invited the lumber companies in to clear away the hardwood, made pastures for the cattle they had shipped in to fatten, planted even-rowed pecan orchards, mowed the wild flowers, dug up the milkweed, the Queen Anne's lace, the sedge, the palmettos—treated them as if they were worthless, had never glistened with dew in the early morning, had never given pleasure and peace. The old families in the area complained that the landmarks of their counties were disappearing, and she knew that was true.

She looked up from the desk, where the sheets of letter paper were still blank before her, wishing that she might see his car pull up in front of her gate, as it had during the summer, wanting to see him walk between the beds of roses, then, before coming up the steps, remove his hat, call to her or keep silent to surprise her, then take her into his arms, demandingly or affectionately, holding her close to him, telling her in exaggerated phrases how much he had missed her. Sometimes she wished for someone with whom she might share these reminiscences, yet she knew she couldn't speak of them. The joy she felt in his presence, the insistence of her love, her anticipation of seeing him, must be kept in her own mind; the pleasure of the accumulated memories must remain exclusively between the two of them, and she realized finally that this forced privacy pleased her and gave to their relationship a secret sweetness.

Behind the windowpane, the sun had just come out, shining in the raindrops on the varnished leaves of the ligustrum. A sparrow was rustling its wings in a puddle of water on the shell drive. Scored underneath with swatches of gray, glaring above with an intense white from the freshness of the sun, the clouds stood still over the pasture. She sat up then and quickly wrote a cheerful and pleasant letter, a long one, filled with news and sentiment, without anxiety or the least hint of sadness.

When she was finished, and the letter was sealed and stamped, she turned off the desk lamp and put on her sweater in preparation for going to the post office in advance of the pickup at five o'clock. Before leaving, she glanced around the living room, where they had been together so many times, where, after supper, she had seen him stretch out on the sofa to read, watched him reach behind him to do something about the radio, light a cigarette and then forget about it in an ash tray until she called it to his attention or got up to extinguish it herself. She smiled at the memory of their last day together, when he had wanted her to stay with him in the house, hardly willing to let her leave him even to answer the telephone, then delaying his departure until the last moment; and after twice saying good-by, leaving the car motor running and coming back to embrace her again and to speak to her so lovingly that even now she seemed to hear his voice and feel his kiss on her mouth. Except for the solace of these memories, every moment was one more to check off quickly, to encourage to pass, to place herself into tentatively and begrudgingly, until he returned to her. She reached for her keys on the hook by the door, let the screen door slam, and with her letter to Hugh in her hand, hurried across the yard to the garage.

In this way she passed her time: She worked hard and for the most part avoided social contacts outside of her job, thought continually of her lover, and somehow managed to get through the tedium of the summer's end and the fall's slow beginning. By early November, her agitation had settled, since now she could begin to prepare for Hugh's return and arrival.

A few days before Thanksgiving, unable to sleep, yet unwilling to leave her bed to begin the tedious waiting, Elaine turned on her side and brought her hands under her chin. All night long, thoughts of Hugh had nudged her awake, playfully or insistently, much as he himself might have done. She believed in the necessity of imprinting on her mind every one of their experiences together; she had hoarded every detail; nothing was insignificant. When her inventory was complete, its contents neatly arranged and in the order she remembered, she smiled and uttered an expression of satisfaction. Stretching, she turned over and looked at the ceiling, noticing traces of dust on the edges of the ceiling fan. How had she missed that? She looked around the room . . . No, the rest was perfect. On the dresser, white chrysanthemums floated in a low dish; an enlargement of a snapshot of Hugh holding mallards and teals, which Matt had taken the year before, stood in a dark leather frame she had picked out herself and which, as yet, he had not seen. Everything was done; her preparations were made; all she had to do was wait for him.

"I'll be there tomorrow before lunch," he had promised.

"Early?" she had wanted to know. "When?"

"I don't know, baby." He had been using an airport telephone; there was no time to talk.

At nine o'clock, she finally rose, dressed herself carefully, and ate a small breakfast of toast and fruit. By eleven, she was so restless that she stood in the doorway shivering with cold, her arms folded across and clamped to her waist, looking out at the platinum sky, pale as it left the horizon, wondering if there would be any sun at all while he stayed with her. During the last week or so, her increasing anxiety over his return had surprised her. Questions she knew were unanswerable until she was with him again had unsettled her usually reliable and reasonably well-ordered mind. How would he have changed? How would he feel about coming back to her after almost three months? On the telephone, his voice had seemed that of a stranger. And what was Hugh anyway when she was unable to touch him or see him? The things he would say to her, the way he would look, his closeness, his presence must yet arrange themselves into the gift to her which she remembered.

At the end of the road, she saw his car slowly approaching, watched it pull up in front, take its habitual place before the gate. He stayed still a moment, possibly waiting for her to come down to him, and when she did not, he took the suitcases off the back seat, set one down to open the gate, and came toward her, smiling, then dipping his head in a self-conscious gesture revealing his pleasure at seeing her. She noticed that his skin had lost its summer tan yet remained rich enough in color, and his eyes, when he took off his sunglasses, seemed deeper and blacker than she remembered, and he swept them over hers thoroughly, as if to assure himself of her fidelity and devotion, something he wouldn't have to ask her about later since he had ascertained it in that instant.

By the look of it, he planned to stay with her the full four days. There were two large suitcases. He had insisted, when he had spoken to her from school, on having his place in her house: At the end of the previous summer, when Jimmy had come home from his grandparents', and she had not only devoted a great deal of attention to him (taking him to an all-day rodeo in Bellville, a picnic at the beach, and finally a trip to the new drive-in movie) but had not let Hugh stay with her the night, they had quarreled. Jimmy's presence had infuriated Hugh, and he had made no attempt to keep it from the child. Elaine's playing her role as mother shocked him; it drew her away from him; he resented it. Each of the three nights of Jimmy's visit, injured, stubbornly furious, and silent, he had driven her to a distant town and rented a room for them in which she would only stay a few hours, demanding to be driven home before dawn.

Elaine looked behind her into her own living room as if she were appraising it. The house—she had bought it one afternoon in early April of 1945, when she still disbelieved her widowhood, was still outraged and betrayed and, in the full flame of her grief, incredulous that she was buying anything alone, that her husband was not somewhere ahead of her, examining the roof, the porch, the garage—had never meant anything to her before she had met Hugh. To make it a home for her, the presence of a beloved man had been required.

He kissed her quickly, a token gesture, then put his arm around her waist and drew her past the door and into the house. She held her hand up to touch his face; he began to pull the sweater she was wearing over her head. She ducked and helped him, pretending to be at ease, but her face was hot, and she knew she had to be blushing. "Don't you like my sweater?" she asked. "It's new."

"It's wonderful, Elaine." He kissed her again and caressed her under her clothes. If Elaine had been made shy by the separation, Hugh had responded to her even more aggressively than usual. Since he had left Dansville in early September, he had stayed away from women, and now he was in a hurry to make up for the deprivation that his faithfulness had cost him. His forcefulness was almost vindictive. She sensed this, and it made her draw away, but he pulled her back immediately and seemed not to notice.

"How are you?" He grinned, waited for her to reply and, when she didn't, glanced quickly around the room, his eyes prepared to react with anger if he saw anything that displeased him. "Is Jimmy here?" he asked.

"No." The question annoyed her, but she hid her irritation from him. Nothing was going to spoil their time together, not even her uneasiness and guilt over letting her son remain with his grandparents for the holiday, giving in to Jimmy's request almost at once since it suited her to be alone with Hugh.

She moved out of his reach ingeniously, shy as a gull before an outstretched hand. Watching him and teasing him by relating an anecdote in which he was certain to have no interest, she kept him away from her a moment longer. The heat remaining in her cheeks shamed her for its betrayal of her desire. She wanted to go to bed with him—she had thought about little else these several months—yet she was timid with him now and slightly disturbed that he was not more reticent, that he was not giving her more time. "I guess you're here because it's more comfortable than the hunting camp," she said.

He shrugged off her remark as if she were teasing him for not being able to console her fast enough, and answered only with a "Hush, Elaine." In response to the lace-edged camisole she wore and his knowledge of the flesh beneath it, he was all business. His eyes were wide and fixed, and he held on to her as if he were engaged in a physical contest rather than an act of love, as if he thought he would have to secure her quickly to prevent her from struggling. And it was true: She would struggle, would insist on his repeating the proof of his domination. He had known on that afternoon when he had first made love to her that she would play a rich game; and that it was because of his understanding of its rules and complexities, that she had chosen him for her partner in it. Yet her struggling now would be merely ritual combat; they would not destroy themselves as they might have, had they continued in the manner of their first encounters.

She slid against him sideways to close the front door, but he kicked it shut with the heel of his boot, jarring the three panes of glass, which rattled in protest.

His face and his presence were beginning to reveal themselves to her. She stood embracing the man, the memory of whom had robbed her of sleep, had made her rush home each noon to check her mail, had kept her waiting for the telephone to ring, and had left her in despair and sometimes fury when she failed to hear from him. Often, she had gone out of her way to ride by the Littleton ranch, driving as slowly as she dared before it to look for his summer ghost, or any evidence of him at all: one of his horses, or even a glimpse of Matt or Luther, with whom she had seen him ride. "You look wonderful," she said, looking up at him, her eyes tracing his features as if to learn them again.

His rumpled hair curled around the threatening angularity of his youthful face and softened it, reminding her of his beauty so compellingly that she said, "I love you"; but she was embarrassed by her forthrightness, by her inability to present a protected, flirtatious front to him.

"You should. I brought you a present."

She stretched her arm across him toward the suitcases. "Let me see what."

"You owe me yet," he answered and, pulling her back, continued to remove her clothes.

She complained about the coldness of his hands and felt herself being lowered with him to the sofa. He was careful and slow, waiting for her to speak to him as she would have during the summer, a bawdy remark delivered like thunder after the flash, but she was just watching him quietly. He smiled defensively and stopped caressing her. "Elaine?"

His departure in September, when he had put the last of his things in the car and left her, now linked itself with his appearance of ten minutes earlier. Her hand had begun to pass over his skin in tentative motions, recognizing and accepting the man. The scent of him in the close heat blurred with her own, and her mind admitted the familiar elision. She explored his mouth slowly with the tips of her fingers while she watched him with an enigmatic complacency. She slid her hand around to the back of his neck and tried to pull him down to her, but he held himself above her and began to laugh, not at her for wanting him (for which he knew he would never have been forgiven), but at what he interpreted incorrectly as feminine guile and manipulation. So he was unprepared when, misunderstanding his reaction, she countered softly, seriously, disinterestedly: "Go on, Hugh. . . . I'm anxious to open my present."

Cursing her, he raised himself, upsetting everything—ash tray, cushions, newspaper, the watery remains of the Coke she had been drinking when he arrived—and pulled her up with him till they were standing. "Christ, Elaine!" he howled. She cried out once, since her wrists, trapped together, burned in his hand, but then buried her face on his shoulder, whispering an incautious obscenity relating to his condition, and began laughing. "You're crazy," he said, guiding her before him into the bedroom, kicking that door shut as well, for no reason other than to hear it slam in sympathy with his mood. He jerked the spread off the bed by one corner, scattering a colorful variety of throw-pillows all over the great moss-green leaves and rose flowers of the rug. After a pause in which he held her in his arms, neither of them moving, he pleaded with her in a somewhat muffled, much softer voice never again to tease him. She was reminded by his vulnerability of something that she had forgotten in these months of separation: that he needed not only a woman who would respond favorably to his prodigal sensuality but one who would also be solicitous and kind to him.

"You tease *me*!" she said softly, feigning in her expression and in her tone of voice a capitulation as serious and unfortunate as his own. She tried to reach the crumpled spread to fold it, but he refused to allow it, and stopped her when she reached down to rearrange the pillows.

"Okay," she said with a slow smile that began in her eyes. "I'm a liar. . . . Aren't you going to pull down the shades?"

He shook his head and caught her as she escaped to do so herself. They both laughed at his success, but she continued to grapple with him. "You're hurting me! What do they teach you in that school? Tell me about your professors, Hugh Clarence! Do you ever tell them about me? Do they know where you are? I wish they could see you now, losing to a woman."

"What do you mean?" he asked her, throwing his wadded shirt onto a chair. "I always win."

She pointed backward to the shirt. "I'm not going to iron that for you."

He shook her to get her attention. "I always win."

"You have a poor memory, Hugh."

He continued to insist on his superiority, but while the substance of his words retained the bravado of a few minutes before, he spoke with less conviction.

"All right, I give up," she said, biting down on her lip to diminish, if only slightly, the intensity of her smile. "That's all it is. I give up everything to you."

He understood her concession very well, and answered in a tone similar to her own, but sweeter, less solemn. She nodded in response to his softly spoken questions and raised herself slightly to kiss his mouth. With uncommon subtlety and gentleness, he drew away the last piece of her clothing that was in his way.

* * *

The four days of Hugh's Thanksgiving vacation they spent almost entirely in the house, going out only for long car rides in the country. He left her so late on Sunday afternoon that he risked missing his plane, and Elaine prepared herself for another separation.

In December, just before Christmas, he walked into her office unexpectedly, a day earlier than he had planned. Grave and serious, he asked her to go with him to the cottage, and she did so at once. On the way to the car, he had held her hand tightly; his expression was so set and still that he seemed on the verge of telling her bad news, maybe a change of plans; perhaps something had come up and he'd be unable to stay with her. When they were sitting together in his car, he volunteered no information and asked her nothing about herself, just drew her close to him, and when she asked him how he happened to be in a day early, he said, without elaborating, "I finished my exam, I had time to get to the airport." At the traffic light, he kissed her with so much longing that she feared he might pull the car into one of the side streets and insist on making love to her right there in front of a store or a café or before the house of someone she knew. Then, away from the town's center, when she began caressing him and kissing his neck, he turned to her frowning, her desire for him troubling him; and when she began to smile and he asked her why, she shook her head and looked out across the glaring meadow on which the harsh needles of the morning frost were melting into placid pools, wondering if there would come a time when making love to each other would be only one among many activities instead of the only essential activity that existed for them. At the house, he parked the car carelessly, didn't respond when she advised him to pull it farther onto the shoulder, then, clasping her hand again firmly in his, led her into the house with a familiar impatience.

He left her early Christmas morning before she was fully awake, whispering in her ear while her face was still buried in the warmth of the pillow that he would return by six o'clock. She and Jimmy had lunch with Felix and Lily, then Jimmy begged to remain for the night, since the Fullers' eldest son, David, had received the gift of an electric train, and at the time that Elaine was ready to go home, the boys were in the process of assembling it.

Hugh was as good as his word. In fact, he was even back in

Dansville a few minutes earlier than he had promised, and he returned triumphant with a carload of booty, carrying an enormous pot of his mother's poinsettias in one hand and a bottle of his father's finest brandy in the other, both of which he had taken while they napped after the big family lunch. "I missed you, Elaine," he said and kissed her in haste before he put down the gifts.

"How was the party?" she asked. She had been cooking dinner; the house smelled of roast turkey, baked sweet potatoes, and an apple pie.

"It was no party—just my cousins." He had finished discussing the matter; he never brought that part of his life to Elaine. She looked at him closely to see if his evasiveness was intentional, but nothing in his face indicated the slightest desire on his part to restrict her knowledge of him. Obviously glad to return to Dansville, the cold of the outdoors still on his jacket, the smell of the fire and the cigar smoke from his father's library still on his clothes, he smiled.

She took the poinsettias from his arms and lifted them to her face. "They're nice," she said, smiling back at him. She knew that he thought she was beautiful then; from his expression, she realized that he appreciated what he had in her, was perhaps even awed by it. Moving away from him, she put the flowers in the front window, where they could be seen, feeling in perfect harmony with him then, knowing that not only she herself, but her manner of life pleased him. About eight, they had their dinner, which Hugh completed with several glasses of brandy. Afterward he insisted on taking Elaine to Victoria to show her the Christmas lights on the big broad streets. Afraid to drive home with him— he had drunk a good bit more on the sixty-mile trip—and knowing that he would never relinquish the wheel to her, she wooed him into stopping at a motor court just outside of El Campo, and they did not return to Dansville until late the next morning.

During the rest of his vacation, Hugh seemed more relaxed than he had been at Thanksgiving. When she had business to do, he let her be away from him without complaining; he stayed at home reading his books, studying for his courses, or driving out to the ranch to visit with Matt or to discuss a particular concern with the foreman. Matt had been encouraging Hugh to assume more responsibility, and consulted with him on matters about which he would have formerly gone to Clarence. He sometimes telephoned Hugh with ranch business; the conversations were brief—perhaps he disliked calling at Elaine's—but he had clearly come to respect Hugh's opinions.

Elaine saw that Hugh was pleased with these signs of Matt's regard, just as he was pleased with his domestic life with her. He seemed content with what she had provided him, and to need nothing more—or whatever he did require was well within her province to supply. When she was with him, she gave him her full attention; when she was away from him she sought to return as quickly as she could—she sensed that he knew these things and appreciated them. She also believed that the more worrisome aspects of his character, his temper and his restlessness, were slowly being negated by her efforts. If not completely solved, their earlier problems now caused her less alarm.

When Hugh neglected to let Elaine know that he would be coming to Dansville, as he did in the spring, she accommodated him, made time for him, talked Felix into taking her place at the office, quickly arranged her house and her life to provide the diversion that he sought in her presence, pleasing herself as she pleased him.

"I always come to the ranch at Easter," he protested, surprised that she had not known he would be with her. "Elaine?" He pushed her hair away from her face and kissed her mouth until she staggered from it and forgot her complaint.

Although they rarely argued during his visits—to do so would have meant a temporary estrangement, and that she would never permit—their fights were fierce. An outsider might have judged that he treated her badly, hurting her by his selfishness, but she seldom thought so herself; and when she did, she said nothing about it. She would tangle with him only on matters that restricted her independence. He wanted to give her money; she would accept presents, but never cash. When he had attempted to send her an allowance, she had stopped it not by opposing him but by writing to his banker. When he had tried to give her stock certificates for her birthday, she had refused them, which caused Hugh to become so angry that he had not written her for two weeks.

Much of their time during Hugh's breaks was taken up with talking, with his either discussing ideas with her or convincing her of the validity of his opinions—never arguing with her, but persuading her, and being particularly pleased when she came around to his point of view. She loved to listen to him. She had known men with more wisdom than Hugh, she had known men

who, because of their maturity, were more discerning, but she
had never known anyone who possessed so much information.
Sometimes, he would lean his head against the back of her best
chair, his feet on the coffee table, his black eyes half-closed, his
shiny dark lashes curling toward the heavy bones above his eyes,
and tell her how things were, what they were coming to, and how
he meant to change them. When he finished his education, things
would be different, his generation would set them right. She had
heard such ideals expressed before, not as articulately, but with
the same optimism. She had seen Foley try to realize them, had
even helped him, but in his late twenties, he had settled back,
still idealistic, though more patient, and a little slower to step
forward with remedies—until the war, which he had all too
quietly not believed in waging, had killed him.

Hugh's exams ended early that spring, and by the end of May,
he was back in Dansville. There had already been a few hot days.
The trees, heavy with dark leaves, bent their branches toward the
flowered meadows. Blackbirds with red escutcheons, dragonflies
in iridescent armor, and butterflies with ragged wings floated,
almost asleep, over the fields of yellow flax and black-eyed
Susans, rich and golden with the scent of spicy heat. The winter
had been exceptionally severe, and although a number of trees
that had been standing for years were lost, most bushes and
plants, cut back to the roots by the cold, returned in May with
fierce new growth. The fruit crop was expected to be the best in a
decade; the blackberries were never finer, and Elaine suggested
that, as a celebration of their reunion, they go to the Littleton
hunting camp, where long, full hedges of blackberry bushes bordered the woods.

Hugh did not want to go—he reminded her of the heat of late
spring, the insects, the lack of anything to shoot at but squirrels
—and only at the last minute did he join her in the truck, spoiling
a little of her pleasure by doing it grudgingly. He seemed impatient during the drive to the camp, and when they arrived, he
picked faster than she did, sticking his fingers often because he
refused to wear gloves, though she had gone back to the cabin to
get them for him, and eating more berries than he put in his
bucket. "You're going to be sick," she said, laughing.

After a while, he wandered away from the bushes and began
throwing the berries he picked at targets. "Go on back," she told
him, "I'll come pretty soon. They're so beautiful. I'd like to stay
a bit longer and get more." She emptied what she had into his

bucket, and he left, telling her that he would wait for her on the porch of the cabin, reading in the rocking chair.

Soon the berries bushes thinned in the place where she was picking, giving way to holly and vines, or overpowered by sedges. As she bent down to retrieve her bucket, she glimpsed a nest of armadillo babies. Their mother was not with them, but they were obviously being provided for, because they were fat and active. They stared at her, an intruder, without the least fear, since in so protected a location, they had no predators. She stepped away and walked far beyond the old grove of pecans that no longer bore very much and across the clearing. As she passed over the crest of a small hill, she suddenly came upon a clump of bushes covered with berries even larger and of a better quality than those she had already gathered. Although the fruit grew so thickly that she could easily have filled the gallon can, she took her time and chose only the best of them, berries plump with juice, very black, without any red seeds at all. It was a cool and beautiful afternoon, the last weekend of the spring before the fields would become unpleasantly hot. At the edges of a wide, grassy alleyway, high, rustling trees flashed in the sun.

When she returned, the gallon bucket filled to its rim, Hugh was still on the porch reading, and he glanced up only briefly when she came into the clearing. She knew at once by the set of his mouth that she had left him too long, and that he was sullen and angry.

"Look," she said. She was certain that she could break his mood with her enthusiasm, her pleasure and pride in her harvest, her delight in the beauty of the afternoon and in his presence. She showed him the full bucket, touching the top with the palm of her hand, feeling the contours of the berries. Her gloves were stained purple. She drew them off and put them beside the bucket.

Without looking up, he muttered something, but she knew he had stopped reading because his eyes were still.

Her happiness made her careless. She pushed the bucket aside and squatted beside him, sitting on her haunches like a field hand, her arms over her knees.

He raised his eyes from his book. "You look like hell," he said. If he saw anything at all that pleased him, he gave no sign of it. His body and his demeanor expressed distrust.

Her hair was still tightly wrapped in a bandanna to protect it from the wind and sun. She had meant to comb it before she returned, but knowing it was late, she had hurried. She pulled the cotton bandanna off and ran her hands through her hair. She shook her head and then looked up at him and smiled.

"Where were you?" he asked. He tossed the book onto the floor of the porch and let it land on its side, without bothering to reach down and fix the crumpled pages. "I looked for you, Elaine."

"I didn't know," she said slowly. "I went along the hedges. I don't know why you didn't see me. I never entered the brush."

"I've been away for two months. Why in the hell would you spend the whole goddamned afternoon berrypicking when I'm here?" He squinted his eyes.

"The berries are ripe this weekend," she said, still modulating her voice, concerned that she had hurt him. "I had to work all this week. It's the only time I have because Felix. . . ."

He bent down near her and clutched her shoulder, shaking her slightly, throwing her off balance, so that she had to sit down awkwardly on the floor of the porch. "I'm what you have," he said, "just me, nothing in the goddamned world but me."

He stood up, rocking the chair back so hard that it almost fell. He went into the cabin and slammed the door, and she heard the bolt slide shut. She slipped for a second into the chair and rested herself, gaining time to think about how she should respond. The sun was low over the trees, slanting in long rays through the branches and toward the mound where the men that Hugh brought to the camp stood to shoot at targets or tin cans. She occasionally saved cans for him; once she had gone to collect some from the lunch counter at the depot. He never invited her here when he brought friends from home, but it happened so rarely that she didn't bother herself about the implications of this slight. She never really wanted to go, for what would she say to his friends? He would come to her on those nights when he had guests, late, long after supper, sometimes after she was in bed. He would spend the better part of the night with her, set the alarm clock, then leave for camp an hour or so before dawn. She had no idea how he explained her to his friends, but she guessed that he told them the truth. Hugh never lied, and had even hurt her with truth. It would not have been like him, either, to permit her place in his life to become the subject of ridicule; he would have defended her.

She got up and tried the door; he unlocked it, turning his back to her quickly. He was trying to prepare coffee, but doing it very badly, spilling the grounds on the rough surface of the table.

"Why are you so angry, Hugh?" she asked, standing with her

back to the door, leaning against it until it clicked shut. She needed the support of the door; she felt a knot in the pit of her stomach that she knew would remain until this was resolved. "Why are you sometimes so angry? Did you call for me? I didn't hear you. I thought you had something you needed to read, and that my being away for a while might be nice for you."

He paid no attention to her but went on ladling the coffee with a spoon, losing some of the grains before they reached the strainer.

She went to him and took the sack of coffee. "Let me do it," she said, smiling weakly. "Sometimes you're such a baby."

He stepped away from her, and she worked at cleaning the mess he had made until she heard him moving determinedly behind her. She turned and saw that he had begun packing what he had brought for the weekend. Her hands went cold and began to shake slightly on the side of the aluminum pot, yet she continued what she was doing, keeping her eyes away from him, searching her mind for the reply she should make, or for the thing she should do. She set out the two cups and reached into the cabinet above the table for the saucers.

"What are you doing?" she asked when he threw the bundle he had made out on the porch.

"I'm going home."

"To Houston?"

"Yes."

"What are you planning to do with me?" she said, but before she could reach him, he had left the cabin.

She watched him go and then emptied the strainer, put the dry coffee back into the sack, and folded it over carefully, taking her time. She was surprised at her ability to remain calm when she was so angry. She put away the kitchen utensils and began gathering her clothing off the floor, finding the things she had brought, cramming everything into her small canvas bag so that she would have a hand free for the berries.

When she left the cabin, she saw that he had gone down the trail to the car, thrown his things in the back seat, and was now waiting for her. He made no effort to help her with her bundle, though he usually treated her as if she were too weak to lift anything, an attitude that she had long since given up protesting. She went up to his window, which was rolled halfway down. "Give me the keys," she said. He took them out of the ignition— the car motor had been running—and handed them to her without lowering the window. She put the two cans of berries in a box in the trunk, then got into the car unassisted and returned the ring of keys to him.

He drove quickly, foolishly so, but she knew any criticism from her would be ignored. As the car sped over a pothole, she lurched forward, and he put out his hand to keep her from falling forward, but it was an automatic reaction, not a conciliatory gesture. Rounding the corners, she had to hold on to the door beside her to keep from being flung against him. When he finally stopped the car in front of her house under the branches of the water oak, he went on staring silently through the windshield.

"Are you coming in?" Her hand on the car door, she looked at his profile.

"No."

"Okay." She waited. "When will I see you?"

He lifted one shoulder and shrugged. "I don't know." He turned his head toward the neighbor's house across the street, as if the barking dog had caught his attention.

When the car pulled away, she felt an overwhelming sadness at having forfeited the pleasure of having him with her. She watched the car leave; her canvas bag with cosmetics, a sweater, and a change of clothes lay at her feet, sagging over the scuffed square toes of her boots. She stood perfectly still as the car disappeared among the heavy shadows that the trees made.

It must have been a half-mile away when she saw its red brake lights sharpen; it quickly reversed its direction, and swerved as it flew down the center of the narrow road toward her. It slowed as it approached the house; he must have seen the cloud coming off the shell road and remembered how she hated dust flung up into her trees, taking the brightness off the leaves, spoiling the color of the grass. He sat in the car a few moments, looking at her through the window. It was dusk. The purple boughs of the trees cast lavender reflections beneath them in complement to the graying shadows of the buildings. She had taken off her dark glasses and set them on top of her hair. She remained still, acknowledging that the next move would be his. He got out, went to the trunk of the car, and removed the two berry buckets. Reaching down with his elbow, he unfastened the latch on the gate, and when he lifted his head, she saw the flash of his teeth in a smile. "You left your goddamned blackberries," he said. Without setting down either of the buckets, he came forward until he was directly in front of her.

"Why did you bring them back?" He was so close that she was almost speaking against his mouth.

"I thought it was sad, your working so hard all afternoon, and the berries spoiling in the back of my car."

"You could have given them to Cana."

"I didn't think of that."

"You can go to hell."

"All right."

The tears glistened on her pale lashes, but it was too dark for him to see them, not even the ones that slid down her face and landed unchecked on her jacket; but when he kissed her, he felt the wetness on her cheeks and, putting down the buckets, took her face in his hands.

She turned away from him, retreating into the velvet sympathy of the shade.

"What do you want?" he asked.

"I want you sorry."

She struggled away from his hands when he tried to restrain her; she meant to go inside and lock the door against him, but she got only as far as the porch, where he followed her. They both sat down on the steps, and when she looked away from him into the weakening sky, he turned her face toward his and said quietly, "Well, why don't you put your berries in the house . . . and then we could go somewhere. You want to go back? You want to eat in town?" he asked, nudging her. "I'll wait for you, baby. You want me to do it, to take them in?"

She threw down the remnant of a leaf that she'd been tearing apart, the pleasing fresh smell of it remaining on her fingers. "I don't care what you do."

He tried again to make her look at him. "You want me away from you?"

She closed her eyes, shaking her head, but then turned quickly to see his expression. She could tell immediately that he was not sorry but merely greedy—he just didn't want to give anything up.

She went inside, taking the buckets of berries into the kitchen, dumping them out into glass bowls, and covering them with waxed paper. By doing this slowly, making him wait, she would call him to account, though something inside her urged her to hurry, even as he would have done had he stood beside her. She attempted to dally; she went to her bedroom, bent down before the mirror on the dressing table to comb her hair and check her lipstick, holding back, yet combing through her hair too quickly, and leaving the room in precisely the spirit of anticipation that she had meant to avoid.

When she returned, she saw that he had put her things back in the car and was leaning against the door, his arms folded across his chest, watching for her. She started to go around to the other side of the car, but he took her arm, opened the door for her, slipped her through under the wheel. When they got back to the hunting camp, he took a flashlight from the glove compartment and led them through the vines on the trail to the clearing where the cabin stood. While she waited in the doorway, he lit the kerosene lamps, hanging one on the porch and the other in the yard.

"Are you hungry?" she asked.

"I'm always hungry."

He was; but then, since noon, he had only eaten berries, and it was now past eight o'clock. He lit the charcoal fire he had prepared earlier in the small stone pit. "What are you going to cook?"

"Steaks."

She called from the yard where she was getting water from the pump. "I'll heat the beans inside. Do you want a salad?"

"No."

"When will the fire be ready?"

"Forty-five minutes, maybe a half-hour."

She came up behind him, put her arms around him, and pulled out his shirt. The fire was licking around the charcoal, sparking at grease from an earlier time. "That's long enough," she said.

"For what?" He took her by the shoulders and turned her toward the firelight so that he could see by her expression what she meant; and then, he went with her toward the cabin, fixing her arm under his. He was pushing her before him into the dark cabin. She felt the toes of his boots hit against her heels. He apologized but it happened again. Against one of the walls, the flashlight glared briefly. "You have the most ridiculous drawl, Elaine," he said, undressing her as adeptly as a nurse tends to a child at bedtime. "Why don't you do something about the way you talk?" he asked.

"I talk just fine . . ." She took one last swallow from the bottle of beer that he was attempting to take away from her and then put two of her fingers over his mouth, as if she meant to stop it from criticizing her. "And anyway, Hugh, I don't think you much come here to listen to me talk."

He pulled down blankets from the shelf above them and arranged them on the floor beneath her, thickly to make them soft, and made a small pillow with his shirt. He reached across her to turn off the flashlight, tugged at his boots, and threw them in the corner. "That's so," he said.

The following Saturday it rained, and Elaine spent the afternoon in the office writing letters to possible buyers of a quarter-section of farm land that she had just listed. She returned home near suppertime; Hugh, who had arrived before her, was in the kitchen pouring himself a whiskey, and when she kissed him, he returned her kiss with reluctance, hardly greeting her at all. She knew that he resented her working on Saturday, or for that matter on any other day. Yet he insisted on coming and going as he chose—to drive into Houston whenever it pleased him to do so, or to work long hours at the ranch with Matt, but when he returned to her house, she was to be there, whether or not he was late, or she had even expected him.

As he walked away from her into the living room she asked him if he still wanted to go out for dinner. They had planned to drive to Freeport to a seafood restaurant that a friend of hers had recommended.

"If you like," he said, without enthusiasm. He lay down on the sofa, picked up the newspaper, and buried his face behind it.

She went into the bedroom to get ready, but she was upset. She wasn't going to spend the rest of the summer crossing cautiously the glassy surface of his moods, needing to fear those times when he might isolate himself from her, punishing her or even threatening to leave her. But at the same time, she couldn't risk another quarrel as damaging as the one of the previous weekend. She sighed to remember it, reasoning that they had unwisely permitted their relationship to enter dangerous territory. It annoyed her that she had to be anxious about angering him, but she knew that she had to be wary of Hugh, he could injure her badly. Steeling herself against anger, determined to avoid spoiling their evening, she changed into a dress, got her raincoat, and ran with him through the downpour to the car, and was compliant when he suggested going to a steakhouse in Richmond rather than the place in Freeport, though this was to her a much less interesting choice, and she felt that he must be aware of her disappointment.

The rain lashed against the windshield, and the wipers thumped furiously to push it aside; houses and barns vanished behind the gray scrim, and in the cornfields, the long, slim leaves bent to their stalks, silvering under the assault. As they drove, Elaine's resolution to remain pleasant seemed to decrease in proportion to the apparent return of Hugh's good spirits. She was

angry at him, and increasingly impatient with herself for feeling
irritation and letting him see it.

"What's the matter, baby?" he asked, after she had remained
silent for a long interval.

She looked into the driving rain, wishing she could find some
intriguing landscape beyond it to distract her from the resentment
that had been festering since the incident at the hunting camp,
when he had treated her so unfairly, but there seemed nothing out
there to change how she felt, nothing else to think about at all.
"You're not like Foley," she said, startling even herself by making this allusion to her husband. "He was always considerate. He
thought of me before himself. You want everything without giving anything in return."

She had lost her temper then, taunting him with Foley's perfection, and she regretted it immediately. In that instant Foley
might have been her secret lover and Hugh the legitimate spouse
to whom she had just revealed her adultery. "I don't want to talk
about it," she said quickly in an attempt to erase her fault. She
dared not look at him, fully aware of what she had done, how he
would react, and what her action might cost her.

He had drawn back the hand with which earlier he had covered hers in an effort to console her, to please her, and to bring
her into his contented frame of mind. Predictably he was
wounded and defensive. "Good, Elaine," he said harshly. "You
can tell me about him. I guess you can do that now." His words
were almost lost in the clattering of rain on the windshield and on
the hood of the car. He searched for a place to stop, and when he
saw a drive-in in Rosenberg, he pulled the car under the awning.

He asked her again to tell him about Foley, but she answered,
"I can't," saying it so softly, and so obviously unnerved, that he
had to ask her to repeat herself. "Don't ask me. I never . . ."

For well over an hour, they spoke over the pelting roar of the
rain on the canvas above them. After the first few minutes, Hugh
stopped his hurried, systematic interrogation and let her speak
freely, her head on his chest or pressed against his arm, stopping
her monologue only when she thought he might react to what she
was telling him, and when she had finished her benign history of
a couple who had married for love, lived in a small town, gone
about the business of raising a family, and participated in rather
unexceptional events, it was only in her tears that he had discovered her. She had not denied that she had loved Foley, and im-

plicit in her affirmation was the fact that she would never have left him. There could have been no question of that.

A car that had been parked beside them pulled away and a battered black station wagon with a noisy radio took its place. The rain had let up. A mist rose from the chinks in the broken pavement; the blue satin of the waitress's sleeve emerged out of the rainy haze like a jay's feather from a tufted wing. The waitress, a young woman with shiny blond hair, approached each car, speaking in a friendly voice, taking orders and bringing food and beer, and smiling generously when, just before she unhooked the tray to return it to the kitchen, a quarter or a fifty-cent piece resounded on its metal surface.

They finished their beers and sandwiches in silence, and Elaine had thought the subject was closed when Hugh asked, "Do you still think about him?"

"Yes. . . . How could I not if . . . ?"

"Do you love him?"

"He was my husband, Hugh. What difference does it make? I love you. I've told you."

"Promise me something," he said with an edge to his voice. Whatever joy he had felt at the beginning of the evening was completely gone, and his request had a solemnity to it that disturbed Elaine. "From now on, just one man, just me. Okay, Elaine?"

She realized immediately how long he had waited to say this, and how much silent anger he had borne before admitting it. Yet if she stopped mourning for Foley, who would do it? If she forgot him, what would become of his memory? She thought of the time during which she had lived without him, how she had reminded herself: This year, he would have been thirty; this year, thirty-one; now thirty-two. She had taken particular care to notice men who were Foley's age, but they were never like Foley, and the more time that passed, the more the comparisons hurt her, since with each year his image faded. When occasionally she looked at his picture now, took it out of the drawer and held it under the small dresser lamp to see it clearly, she noticed that with his soft eyes shaded by the visor of his hat, he hardly looked older than Hugh. What had happened to the audacious man who had come to her, had loved her, and had given her so much undisturbed happiness? She could never renounce her youth, or her reverence for the man who had set her on a pedestal and kept her, and the family she gave him, in his powerful protection. Yet she understood that if she preserved Foley in her heart, it would have to be in a different way, and it would have to be kept from Hugh. If in any way Foley remained Hugh's rival, she would have to make it up to him, to lavish her love on him, a thing that now more than ever she strongly desired to do.

They kept to themselves that summer, rarely attending public functions, coming into Dansville only for business and shopping. In the evenings, a little after six, when the light had mellowed and the sun sent long shadows over the fields and roads, they would drive through the countryside: to Freeport, to West Columbia, to Cuero, to Richmond. If they went as far as Rockport or Port Aransas they would eat in a seaside restaurant, then walk along the beach, barefoot in the wet sand, watching the moonlight ducking the endless streamer of its likeness in the turning folds of the water. When there was no moon, they would pick out the best stars, identifying the ones they could. Sometimes they would spend the night in a hotel, sleeping late the next morning, ordering breakfast in their room. Once home again, they would spread their treasures of shells on the kitchen table and look up the names of the ones they had forgotten or had never known.

Most nights, though, they would remain at Elaine's house, reading on the porch by the yellow light, or sitting in the metal furniture at the center of the yard, enjoying the cool of the evening, talking softly over the sound of the breeze in the tops of the ripening cotton. In full moonlight, the shadows of the trees would be so sharply traced on the blue lawn that it was possible to walk the paths of their outlines. These nights were noisy with insects and sweet with the smell of honeysuckle and the rich musk of ivy.

The summer passed, and despite her realization that problems were being created that she would one day have to deal with, it would be forever perfect in Elaine's memory. She had Hugh, she adored to be with him; his love for her, his ability to express it, the energy with which he came to her, dazed her still. She needed Hugh as she had needed Foley. The peacefulness of her sleep, without dreams and without worry, the composure with which she now accepted her work and the disgrace of her position, were testimony to her contentment.

On September 8, Hugh's twenty-first birthday, they drove to Corpus Christi and stayed at the Breakers, a beautiful hotel on the beach. That night, in a covered pavillion in the harbor, they sat on a bench eating oysters, making a mountain of their mossy shells at the end of a redwood table. Hugh sent a boy to buy them a bottle of champagne, and later, in a little bar at the back of their hotel, they danced. Two days later, Hugh left her to begin his last year of college.

Chapter 6

EVEN THOUGH SHE had known Hugh for over a year, and their relationship had been tested by quarrels, long separations, and opposition from friends, Elaine often imagined that she would receive a note from him asking her to return his things to the ranch; or he might make a brief telephone call. Maybe Lettie or Opal would drive over to tell her that he was never returning to Dansville, would hand her a letter that he had scrawled out quickly, sitting at a table in the cookhouse, or standing nonchalantly by his car. It wasn't that Hugh gave her any reason to believe he would abandon her but simply that he never obligated himself to her, whether by plans, commitments, promises, or any acknowledgment of a future for them.

Yet all through his final year in the East, he continued to come back to her, though his visits now were always unannounced; he would show up at her house, come in, take off his shoes in the middle of her living room, and fling his jacket on the sofa or one of the chairs, as if he were a husband returned from a trip. He would fly home from college for the weekend just to see her, to surprise her, he said; on Saturday, he would study for eight to ten hours at a stretch, sitting at the table, sucking on his pencil, putting his stocking feet on a white kitchen chair, moving his lips soundlessly, leaning over his work, his head jammed between his fists. She would leave him and tend to the garden, or work in the living room at her desk. Late in the evening, he would come to her, insisting that she listen attentively to what interested him, demanding that she stop whatever it was she was doing to be with him. When it suited him, he would lead her into the bedroom, which now held evidence of his presence everywhere: his pipe in the ash tray on the dresser; his shirts hanging in the closet among her blouses; his jacket on the hook beside hers; books he didn't want to throw away but probably wouldn't read again in a tall stack by the windows; photographs of him or the two of them together wedged into the frame of the mirror.

She had learned how to please him, how to soothe his frustration, and even occasionally how to make him calm. Being with her, she knew, provided him with a relief from the ambition that drove him. She guessed that at school he never relaxed: He had to be first in his class. But the competitiveness hurt him and wore at his spirit. When he told Elaine that he would prefer to have been born Luther Kelly rather than himself, she understood him and half-believed that he was right. Like all driven people, he was his own prisoner, compulsive and sometimes cruel. His well-being became the barometer by which she measured her actions, and she surprised even herself by the extent of her understanding and compassion. There seemed to be no limits to her tolerance. He was never able to shock her or wear her down; she had infinite patience for his sometimes outrageous behavior: Not only would she tolerate his onslaughts, but she would often encourage them. Her submissiveness fit with the image of him that she had created for herself; she seemed to desire him for those very elements in his character that made him able to dominate her; and neither did he realize that his behavior was unique to his relationship with Elaine, that with her he was rarely defensive or unhappy, and that she was responsible for that contentment. Yet she understood that their relationship was not one that she would consciously have chosen and that her character had had to alter to accommodate it; that in her effort to keep Hugh, she was losing herself.

Elaine did not allow this to trouble her any more than her loneliness did. People in town had, for the most part, stopped telephoning her (Hugh had been right when, after the fight at the dance hall, he had told Matt that in the future no one in Dansville would bother his girl), but if she had had to sacrifice most of her friendships because of her affair with Hugh, she could manage the loss. Nothing, in fact, worried her or stood in the way of her complete commitment to him—except her son. Jimmy despised Hugh, not just because of what people in Dansville said about him and his mother, or the taunting he sometimes received from other children on those weekends and brief vacations when he left his grandparents to stay with Elaine, but because of the arrogant, rude, incorrigible man that Hugh himself was. Whenever Hugh arrived, the boy left for a neighbor's or kept to himself in his room, playing his radio and tinkering with his balsa wood models of airplanes and ships. Hugh never referred to Jimmy; it was as if he were never present. It was clear to Elaine that Hugh had no intention of sharing her with anyone, that she existed now solely for him, for his pleasure and his consolation. He obviously felt that she could make it up to Jimmy after the weekend or vacation was over; and the next time Hugh came, if she wanted it, he would bring the boy a present.

In any case, Jimmy was rarely in Dansville, and his stays were short; he had to return to go to school, or to go on a fishing trip with his uncle Albert, or to get back to the calf he was raising for a contest. He loved his mother—he would have acknowledged that to anyone—but his life and his interests were elsewhere. Elaine knew this and regretted it, and she had to remind herself constantly that she had sent him to her parents, not because of Hugh—she had not even known Hugh then—but because Jimmy had needed the guidance and discipline that she had believed could only be provided by a strong male, and since he'd lost his own father, she had permitted hers to assume that role. But she questioned her motives now and wondered if she continued to allow her parents to keep Jimmy with them more to forestall her lover's resentment than for the welfare of her son.

Yet if Elaine increasingly arranged her life to accommodate Hugh, and if some of those accommodations seemed extreme, he was no less absorbed by his involvement with her. That past year, each time he left her, drugged, heavy-headed, he tried to account to himself for the power of his feelings, yet the reasons he invented were never adequate, and, in fact, really explained nothing, so he stopped worrying about his passion or trying to justify his actions. When the impulse overwhelmed him, he went to her as inexorably as a stream courses toward a wider body of water. He went unmindful of consequence, eager to be surrounded and nurtured by her. The woman, the cottage, the landscape around it—all burned in his mind. He could hardly believe that he was flying home on so many weekends. He would plan out his studies, morning and afternoon, hour by hour, intending to stay at school. He convinced himself that he would be content to telephone her on the weekend, but on Friday morning, he would suddenly leave his bewildered roommate in a swirl of papers and books and clothes to catch a plane, reaching Elaine's nine or ten hours later. Sunday night, he would travel back to school, arriv-

ing at his first class exhausted and with an expression on his face
of content and gratification that would stay there long into the
afternoon.

He felt neither guilty about nor responsible for their relationship. If she believed that they were living in sin, it was she who
would have to worry about that stigma. As far as he was concerned, it was her burden. And, in fact, he was right about this.
The women in Dansville, who considered the affair shameful and
unpardonable, blamed Elaine more than Hugh. They held her in
contempt for letting a man use her without guaranteeing her future, letting him break the rule that he, in his natural superiority,
must bend for a dropped handkerchief, open doors whether they
are heavy or not, walk on the street side, and marry the woman
whom he habitually troubles with his demands. She was setting a
dangerous example.

The men responded differently. Each of them, from the
youngest to the oldest, had in his imagination Elaine's image, and
they dreamed about what Hugh experienced. Occasionally one of
them would make a sly aside to Hugh, who ignored him. On the
subject of Elaine, he kept his thoughts to himself.

Their second Christmas together—Hugh was to graduate from
college in May—the weather was cold, damp, and disagreeable.
The days were gray, and there was a perpetual canopy of clouds,
with all the depressing aspects and none of the benefits of rain.
But Elaine had made her house look beautiful for them with red
candles and bouquets of red and green pyracantha and pine that
she had gathered at the ranch. She had taken her truck in on the
dirt road that ran parallel to the fence and then beyond the old
pond, where a cascade of pyracantha bent to meet the ground
cover of leaves that had fallen the month before. Lettie had seen
her enter the front gate and had soon joined her, pulling her truck
up beside Elaine's, insisting on going into the depths of the
bushes with her clippers, then passing the cut branches back to
Elaine, warning her of the thorns, giving her more than she could
possibly use, urging her to take them all, delighted to play hostess to the woman Hugh loved.

Elaine had saved to buy him boots for Christmas, a pale,
dun-colored pair in fine leather, almost without decoration, made
by a retired shoemaker in Cuero who was known for doing the
finest work in the region. She had met him at a church encampment weekend several years earlier, when he had impressed her
not only with his beautiful leatherwork but with his love for the

craft. When she had first telephoned him with her request, he had refused, claiming that he had no time, but after she had visited him in his dusty back yard, practically stripped of its grass by the scratching of a flock of scrawny chickens; had sat an hour with him and his wife on a hard metal swing, listening to several long stories in which his role as hero or missionary was certainly embellished; and had drunk his homemade wine and praised it, he had agreed. On December 24, the boots were still unfinished, and she had stood behind him in his workroom while he put the final touches on them, details she did not think were necessary but which he, as the artist, insisted on. There had scarcely been time to wrap them, and it had been hard keeping the package out of Hugh's sight, but they were beautiful, and they had pleased him greatly. He had given her a string of perfectly matched pearls, worth approximately—though she would never have imagined it—half the value of her house.

On Christmas night, Elaine's living room was lit warmly by candles and by blinking colored lights on the little pine tree that she had set on the table by the front window. Hugh kept a fire blazing, getting up at regular intervals to adjust the logs. They were sitting at the dinner table when he began telling her of his plan to go to law school at the university in Austin after his graduation in the spring, and, when he obtained his degree, to look for a job in Houston.

Amazed at this news, having had no warning that such an idea was even in his mind, she leaned toward him and touched his arm. "I thought you'd come to live at the ranch after graduation," she said.

"And not continue with school?"

"Why should you continue it, Hugh?"

She picked up their empty salad plates and rose to get the rest of their dinner. When she returned with the platter, he stood up to carve the duck, taking his time and filling the two warm plates with the dark meat and the steaming dressing.

"I thought you wanted to live here," she said.

"There's nothing for me to do in Dansville, Elaine."

"You could run the ranch."

"Matt does that."

It hurt her that he hadn't discussed this with her or asked her how she felt about it, hadn't even hinted at it, and she wondered why he hadn't confided in her until he'd made up his mind. She tried to eat, to put aside her concern at least until the end of dinner, but her anxiety spoiled everything. For the first time, she mentioned her fear that he would leave her.

"Why would I do that, Elaine?" Nothing at that time could have been further from his mind. For weeks, he had looked forward to being with her, and as always, he was in no way disappointed at their reunion.

"Oh, you will," she said. She was sorry that she had mentioned it. "You'll meet someone your own age, and then it will be over. You'll want to have children."

He looked up at her and shook his head, to deny not that he wanted a family but that his time with her would ever end. While he'd never allowed himself to think of Elaine's place in his future, he'd assumed she would have one.

"Don't worry about it," he said, picking up a duck leg, leaning over his plate, and pulling the last of the dark meat away from the bone with his teeth. "I don't." He wiped his mouth with the stiff white napkin.

"I know damn well you don't," she said.

She cleared the table and brought him coffee and a hugh piece of fudge cake with chocolate ice cream.

He watched her as he ate, concerned about the sadness he had seen in her face. "Don't keep thinking about it, baby," he said. He expressed himself as a much older man might have, as if he had borrowed the proper conciliatory tone from his father. He got up from his chair, walked around the table, and crouched in front of her, taking her hands in his, and asking her if she would like to go to a movie.

She laughed. "Hugh, there's no movie around." The theater downtown had closed, and the two new drive-ins had shut down for winter.

His dark eyes searched the room, as if he hoped to find in it, among the decorations, the furniture, and the small pictures, the distraction that he needed to break her mood. "I'll drive you to Houston if you want me to," he said.

"It's too far."

"It's only an hour and a half."

She got up from the table, turned from him, and spoke softly, "I thought you wouldn't want to be seen with me at home."

"I don't give a damn."

"Yes, you do. I know that." She looked out the window into the bleak night sky. "And anyway," she said, drawing her finger roughly against the sill, "it's so bad outside. You can't even see the stars . . . and it would have been a full moon."

He came from behind her, put his arms around her waist, and pressed his face into her hair, and then, whispering, compared the beauty of the pearls he had given her to her own. His praise was excessive—she came out so far ahead that the necklace might have had very little value—but it was ingeniously phrased, and it pacified her, a well-timed endearment that made up for a period of neglect. She turned to him and put her arms around his neck, hiding her eyes against him, and trying to convince herself that in this embrace that brought her so much pleasure she could read no sign of betrayal, no sign that, one day, he might try to reach for those things that she was unable to give him in the simplicity of her commitment.

He was in love with her that night, and he made her especially aware of it. He looked after her, took time with her, showed her unusual care and attention, and afterward praised her lavishly for pleasing him. He was softened and soothed by his love, and for the remainder of the vacation, until he left after the New Year, he was gentle with her, solicitous of her wishes, and less selfish. She considered that she might have underestimated him; he was growing older, thinking about his future, and after all, the next step in his plan would bring him closer to her. She believed that he had considered this when making his decision.

In the fall of 1949, Hugh began law school at the state university. He was happy to be home again with people he'd known all his life or whom his parents had known, people whose friendship he could look forward to keeping for the rest of his life. He anticipated being hired by a major law firm: If he did well, and he was certain that he would, he would join one of the firms with which his father had contacts and to whom over the years Clarence had given business. Hugh had been in law offices many times, accompanying his father at his frequent meetings. The paneled walls, deep carpets of sober colors, wide desks of dark, varnished wood, high-backed chairs, and leather-covered books appealed to him—a comfortable ambience, genteel, quasi-intellectual, and vaguely aristocratic. He appreciated the respect, security, and, sometimes, fame that a successful man in the profession enjoyed, and he had never objected to hard work, long hours, or responsibility; on the contrary, he welcomed them, and he looked forward now to beginning his professional training, seeing no impediment to his chances of achieving success. As for Elaine, Hugh supposed that he would always spend a part of his life in her house on the road close to the end of the town, where, from the back windows, you could see a meadow flanked by stands of hickory, oak, and pecan. In the spring, there were blue-bonnets, buttercups, and Indian paintbrush; in the summer, Queen Anne's lace, sage, and daisies. How many times he had watched the sunrise from the bedroom, turned on his side to see it flare up apricot and golden between the bottom of the shade and the sill. He would get out of bed and pull the shade high so that the dawn glowed on the walls and reflected in the closet mirror, still and shining.

And he loved Dansville. Some of his friends from home might think the town was too restrictive, ugly, tawdry, with its shops of inferior merchandise and cafés with slices of cake under glass covers and metal stands on which cellophane sacks of potato chips were clipped, but to Hugh it was ingenuous and restorative, and the people were attractive in their straightforward ways and uncomplicated reactions, in their wholesomeness and their gener-osity. Away from Dansville, he felt a nostalgia that he had for no other place on earth he'd seen—he missed the shaded streets; the banging doors of trucks; the folk sentiments in country music; the easy summer days, when he might stop for a half hour to talk about cattle and sheep, politics and farming, with someone he met on the sidewalk, or when he might go into the drugstore to order a sandwich and learn from the waitress everything that had happened in town that morning, and not because he had asked her but because, as she wiped a spill of milkshake off the counter or dipped dirty Coke glasses in and out of soapy water, she had volunteered it. He might be critical of the people, disparaging of their crude manners and their sometimes painful candor, but away from them, he would speak in their defense, saying that they would stop in the middle of their most urgent tasks to help a neighbor, that they organized their church activities around ser-vice to their community, that their social events were designed not only to amuse their most prosperous members but just as often to reach out to and raise up those who were less fortunate. He imagined that when his business activities permitted, he would find time to be there, maybe not so much in the first years (he knew that young lawyers often worked far into the evenings and sometimes all day Saturday and even Sunday), but later in his career when he became established, then he might live in the big house at the ranch and commute to Houston, remaining on his land in November, taking his vacation to do that, inviting clients to shoot the ducks and deer that were always abundant on the huge acreage his family possessed. He might even buy more land, eventually competing with the Dearborns, the Basses, and the Kennedys. That would please Clarence, who had often spoken about it but didn't seem to have had the time or the inclination to send Hugh again on that particular errand.

When he couldn't get to Dansville even for the weekend, when studying for an exam kept him at school, he assumed that Elaine would understand. He spent whatever time he could with her, but it never occurred to him that he might owe her more than that, or that she might in fact want something more secure. If she complained of his behavior in a letter, he ignored it, planning to make it up to her on his next visit. Their relationship continued with one central theme taking precedence: Hugh's need to have Elaine continually available to him and uniquely his. He made plans without consulting her, then was angry if she objected; if she spoke of her son, he changed the subject; if she wanted to do things independently of him, he forbade them. He had only a hazy awareness of his neglect of her, and when he did perceive it as neglect, he blamed it on his necessary commitment to his work. Yet sometimes he regretted his dereliction, and made up for it by extravagant gestures—giving her presents, and on several occasions, treating her to short vacations.

In September they spent three days on the coast of British Honduras; and on a weekend in October, he invited her to Santa Fe, sending her an airplane ticket and asking her to meet him there. They left their hotel room only long enough for meals and brief shopping trips, on which he would insist on buying her Indian jewelry, turquoise and silver, which was unbecoming to her fair complexion, and which she really did not want, but for which she thanked him warmly. He would grab her arm and pull her into shop after shop, standing beside her and encouraging her to look at everything, then ultimately urging her to select a necklace, a bracelet, a pair of earrings, the prices of which embarrassed her. He chose a restaurant where the tables were covered with stiff white cloths; where long-stemmed tea roses stood tall in slim silver vases; where exquisite china soup dishes reposed on silver place plates, and crystal goblets rang out purely when their rims were hardly even touched. He ordered for her, then delighted in her enjoyment, spoiling her, he thought.

For the last four years, he had attended a school where there was almost no social life; now he attended one where parties were held continuously, where even the most conscientious student could be corrupted, and Hugh found that he had to be care-

ful. He avoided the rowdy fraternities, where often several cases
of whiskey were consumed in an evening; he took no part in the
heavy drinking that went on in bars and in the popular open-air
German restaurant, although he did enjoy having a drink or two
with classmates, discussing the future with them, or the best
ways to arrive at a brilliant start in a career.

Despite his resolution to resist all temptation that would divide
him from either Elaine or his studies, a weekend came when
Hugh was invited to the party of a friend—a man whom he had
met in law school—in San Antonio, and he decided to go. On
Friday he telephoned Elaine and told her he would not be coming. Late on Sunday night he called her again, and in the course
of their long conversation he spoke of his friend's sister, imper-
sonally yet with obvious admiration for her industry in having
taken her degree in medicine, and for being exceptionally bright.

Then one Saturday shortly after, Hugh did a thing he had
never done in all their time together. He brought friends with him
to Elaine's—the man from San Antonio, his sister, and one of
their cousins. She disliked all of them instantly. They followed
him into her house laughing and talking, letting the screen door
slam, and though they nodded politely when he introduced them
to her, their discomfort was obvious. The young woman was tall
and slim, with hair that was pushed into waves around her face
and then caught up with hairpins in a French twist. She was
dressed in a bulky cable sweater, slacks of lightweight worsted,
and English boots, tapered to fit the calves of her legs. She wore
no lipstick on the shapely lines of her mouth, nor were her cheeks
rouged, but to heighten a feature of an otherwise weak appearance, she had brushed her eyelashes thickly with mascara. She
had the kind of clear blue eyes that, when ringed with black,
suggest that behind them lies a keen judgment and understanding,
and Elaine noticed that the men listened to what she said with
attention. When she sat down on the sofa and took a cigarette out
of a flat gold case, her sophisticated gestures were only a fraction
away from being mannered—but she had clearly mastered them,
the final impression causing no more harm to her than a slight
isolation. She tried lamely to make conversation with Elaine,
complimenting her on her house, admiring a vase of silk flowers
on her desk, and confiding that she envied her the calmness of
life in a little town.

Elaine smiled and momentarily stopped tapping her fingers
against her thigh but did not bother to reply. She was about to
excuse herself to go to the kitchen when Hugh came back into the

room to serve them the beer that she kept in the refrigerator for him, and then asked her to make sandwiches while he sat with them. Not once while she was busy in the kitchen did he come to pass a moment with her alone.

"Elaine," he asked when she returned with a tray of food. "Don't you have any whiskey?"

"No," she answered, setting the plates down on the table and turning to him with surprise. "You know we don't keep whiskey, Hugh—It's only here when you bring it." The girl turned her head quickly toward the window; the implication of Elaine's remark had clearly discomfited her.

Furious, Elaine felt as if she were performing in a play in which all the actors were professional and seasoned except for herself, and in her inexperience she was ruining the piece. She began to speak in a slurred, velvety voice; she made deeply sensual movements that were designed to negate the influence of the others in the room. She saw that Hugh interpreted her gestures correctly, and his expression revealed that he was aware of something that he had known before but had not wanted to believe. A shudder of fear swept over her; and from then on, she avoided the eyes of all the visitors, including Hugh, who, changed by these people and the inappropriateness of their visit, seemed equally alien to her. She played with Emma, the Persian cat Hugh had given her, murmuring to her softly, and kept to herself.

Hugh continued talking to his guests, introducing esoteric subjects that he must have known would leave her out of the conversation. Apart from politics, real estate, or matters that required practical skills and common sense, Elaine was lost, and realizing Hugh's intentions quickly and with profound regret, she made no attempt to contribute. Out of the corner of her eye, she saw the young woman watching her, fascinated. She looked from her to Hugh and then back again, as if assembling the facts and summing up the debit inherent in their sin. As the afternoon passed, even Hugh seemed to grow nervous. He began to look at Elaine furtively, as if afraid to meet her glance. To whom was he comparing her? she wondered. To this anemic-looking girl? Was it possible that her bantering, the aridly clever remarks, the outpouring of useless information and idle conjecture had anything to do with what interested Hugh in his life away from her? But what was the good of all this talk? She realized then how removed Hugh and his friends were from the realities of making a living, that they were able to devote the better part of an afternoon to metaphysical speculation, letting their imaginations run loose, their minds roam the blind sides of the universe, just as children play with a pinball machine, losing quarter after quarter —and these people had so many. Hugh had made a mistake in bringing them here, in thinking that her house was anything other than a tiny oasis that was uniquely his, that it could remain fecund and green if it was made accessible to others.

At the end of the afternoon, when the sun had gone below the bare branches of the tallow and the breeze had lifted, but before the evening colors had begun, at the prettiest moment of the day, Hugh took his friends off to the hunting camp, leaving her house littered with smoked cigarettes, partially eaten sandwiches, plates, and beer bottles. He had neither invited her to go with them nor told her when, if at all, he would return, and though he had stooped before her for a second to caress the head of the cat she held, he had never touched her. When she could no longer hear the sound of their departing cars (Hugh's new silver-gray convertible followed by a noisy bright-red Porsche), and was certain they would not be back, she sank her face into the cat's fur and cried.

Later, her eyes still misty, she stood at the window watching the long streams of thin winter clouds invade the darkening sky; a butterfly's wings filled and refilled on the currents of air that rocked the hollow stalks of the dry flowers; a grackle cried out in the lonely, raucous monotone of his breed.

That night, Hugh stayed at the camp. She hated him; she hated herself, and it shamed her considerably to have waited for him so tense and alert that she had become exhausted. She asked so little in return for loving him.

The next morning, he telephoned early from the ranch, waking her. She had stayed up most of the night and was so tired and angry that she was unable to be kind to him. He was telling her about the success of the evening, about his good luck on the morning hunt, the huge number of birds he had sacked, as though nothing was wrong.

"If you've been a good girl, I'll bring you some," he said.

She took a slow, jagged breath, and her words came out on the wild current of her exhalation. "If I had been a good girl, I would have sold you a piece of land, taken my commission, and called it quits. If I'd been smart, I'd never have let you get near me, except to sell you something."

"How many do you want?" he persisted, now with an obvious note of indulgence.

Using an obscenity that she had heard him use many times,

and which she had never before uttered in all her life, she told him what he could do with his ducks. He answered her aptly, cleverly. He would not be provoked; he had had too good a time. Yet she could tell by his forced gaiety and the hoarseness of his voice that he had drunk a lot the night before, something that she disliked intensely.

"What the hell's the matter, Elaine?"

She was silent.

"Did I call you too early or something?" he asked, his voice now settled, almost normal.

"You know what's wrong; and it makes me mad as hell that you pretend not to. I hate that."

After he had begun to reply, she eased the receiver into its cradle, turned her back, and dropped her head. There was no pattern in the loose little rug by the phone chair, but she seemed to be studying one. The phone rang. She closed her eyes and ignored it.

Lighting a cigarette, she blew the smoke in small clouds that were slow to dissipate since the windows were closed against the cold, and while her coffee was brewing, she paced her living room, throwing hostile glances at the sofa and at the chair where he liked to read. She must break with him; she imagined that without Hugh in her life, she would have control over it again and could return to the times of peace and rest; but when she stood in the doorway of the bedroom and saw the bed, which was scarcely disturbed, only the edge of the quilt making a triangle where she had turned it back when rising, she felt first grief and then bitterness that he had deprived her of the night with him.

She lit another cigarette and, forgetting it in an ash tray, set herself to tidying the bedroom, putting away her slippers and gown; then she sat down on the ruffled stool before her dressing table and gazed into her mirror, leaning quickly forward to examine the circles under her eyes caused by her trouble and lack of sleep. She sighed deeply and covered her face with her hands, overwhelmed by the abjectness of her position in having become so much Hugh's mistress and so little his equal or friend. She feared that she would have to pay a heavy price for allowing her love for him to lead her to this debasement. The fact that she held him mainly by her sensuality humiliated her, and she knew that this condition was contrary to her welfare, yet she was unwilling to abandon it, since it drew him to her and united them in a way that nothing else could. Even so, she knew that if she let him stay with her now, it should be on a different basis, and she ought to exact from him a promise. And yet, what could he promise her when his experience away from her prodded him daily into renouncing not only her but the entire mode of his past life?

After enough time had passed for him to clean up and get to her, she heard the brakes of his car screech to a stop in front of her house, and then the car door slam on the cold electric air of the day. From the bed, where she was sitting, she could look across the room into the mirror. The light was at her back. Despite her distress, Elaine had prepared herself for him carefully. Her red hair was tied back with a green ribbon that matched her blouse, which was open at her throat, where she had arranged the strand of pearls that Hugh had given her. She smelled wonderful and expensive, and she looked lovely. On a scarlet-colored spread that Elaine's mother had crocheted for her during the war, Emma lay curled. She stretched, drawing her long claws over the locked-in octagons of coarse thread, and lifted her head toward the noise outside.

Hugh let himself in with his key and called to her. He had behaved typically on the porch, stamping his feet noisily and slamming the door as he entered, but once he stepped inside, she could detect a change in his manner. He crossed the living room warily, and after he repeated her name, she heard no other sound. She answered from the bedroom, where she had not moved from her place on the bed. A book was open on her lap, and her fingers were riffling its pages. She did not look at him when he approached the room silently. He leaned against the edge of the door, waiting without a word, as if he had first to obtain Elaine's permission to be admitted.

She glanced sideways and saw the discomfort both in his face and in the peculiarly sharp angles of his lean body. She wondered if there was any other creature in nature that could look as awkward as a finely made man who has wronged a woman, and who needs, for his own well-being, to make it up. Instantly it hurt her to see him so subdued, and she smiled weakly, knowing that she was defeating herself, going against her own interests, and that even if she were unable to send him away, she should at least prolong his suffering.

"Well?" she asked him.

"Well, what?" He took a step into the room.

"Did you bring me the ducks?" She knew he had not.

"I didn't bring them. I thought you didn't . . ." He looked puzzled, and he waved his hand backward toward the front door. "Do you want me to go back and get them?"

"No."

"It wouldn't take me very long." He waited. "Do you . . . you want to go with me, baby?"

"No," she said softly. "You don't have to take me out there, Hugh. I know you're sorry you brought them here yesterday. Why the hell did you do it?"

They were both silent, and Hugh was the first to lower his eyes. Elaine glanced at her stretched-out hands as if she were checking on the length and smoothness of her nails. He had given her an amethyst, which in the brilliant light of the morning was glittering on her finger.

A flicker of discontent crossed his face, as if he knew that his fate was being decided, and that her choice, though it was his preference and he would have fought hard for it had it been denied him, was singularly disturbing. "Elaine, what do you want me to do?"

She pulled slowly on the end of the green ribbon that held back her hair and kicked off her shoes. Forgetful of her future and pushing her fears to the back of her mind, she looked toward the window and smiled—at the man, the day, the appearance of the birds in the field, and the way she felt at that moment. "I want you to come to me," she said.

Although he valued her more than any other woman who had come into his life, Hugh did not know what to do about Elaine. Among his friends at school, his situation was an anomaly: The men he knew were either recently married or dated the sorority girls who lived in the white colonial houses on the west side of the campus. Hugh's affair with Elaine had never before embarrassed him, but perhaps, he realized, that was only because he had kept his life with her separate from the world at the university—a world that was becoming ever more important to him. When he had taken friends to Dansville, he had been experimenting, standing back as an observer to see if the two disparate elements would blend. He would rather not think about the results; in the meanwhile he kept coming back to her, and when he was away, when he was not occupied with his studies, he yearned for her company. He felt as if he were walking on two parallel lines: one, his ambition; the other, the pleasure of his life with her. As the lines gradually began to separate, he was still managing the small leaps from one to the other. It was his belief that he would always be able to do so.

Their separations, arguments, and misunderstandings were

unsettling to them both, no less to Hugh than to Elaine. Early in their relationship, they had often tried to effect their reconciliations in rational ways, but now, more volatile and less patient, they abandoned these attempts: After fights that were, at best, a flood of abusive words from one interrupted by a heated denial or protest from the other, only love-making could restore their calm. Finally they knew this so well that, to settle their conflicts, they almost abandoned language altogether. Only when one of them was able to attract the other to bed did the powerful, bittersweet reunion begin—although both Hugh and Elaine sensed that, one day, their method might escape the bounds of what was acceptable even to them.

Hugh believed that he would never be content without Elaine, and he was certainly unwilling to test that belief. He needed someone who would continually strive to remain independent of his will, as she did. He feared a relationship in which a woman might not be able to put him in his place, demand that he toe the line, and remain somewhat separate. Yet the violent physicality that he sometimes experienced with her during the worst of their quarrels worried him. He thought that since he was older now, he should be different—not that he meant to deny his sensuality, only to keep it in check. And so it was, that in reaction to several unsettling periods of trouble between them, he began to arrange distractions for their times together, to avoid spending those long, quiet weekends alone with her in her house, where most of their disagreements seemed to occur. In November, he asked her to go deer hunting with him; if she didn't want to hunt, she could simply accompany him.

Elaine rarely went hunting; she hated to get up while it was dark and cold, when it was still night. It was sinister and unhealthy. Her heart would beat quickly, and she would feel sick to her stomach. But, as in everything, she went with Hugh now for the pleasure of his company. She had hoped that he might have changed his mind about going, but he shouted to her from the front steps, cheerful and eager. In her depression at arising in the blue starlight she hardly recognized his voice or knew who he was, and she put her jacket on gloomily. On the way to the truck, Hugh spoke to her through the damp chill of the air, but her attention was roused only when a star of drizzle fell on the sleeve of her jacket.

The moon was soon swept away by the rainy dawn. The light rain slowly put a sheen on the hood of the moving truck, and as they drove, the wheels marked precisely the newly glazed pavement. Hugh was talkative in the truck, but as they walked into the woods and approached the stand, he became quiet and serious. Ten steps, short planks, were nailed to the side of a sinuous tree; a box four feet square, one side opened partially to effect an entryway, rested between the main part of its trunk and the forking out of its branches. They climbed up, reaching to grasp the steps above them, then crawled into this structure, the floor of it already damp and the walls marked with splotches of moisture. Hugh arranged his equipment; Elaine made herself as comfortable as she could, kneeling in the corner adjacent to the opening; and they began to listen for the movements of the deer, feeling the drizzle, waiting for the wet pearliness of the sunrise. After a while, the sky began to lighten, and then the edges of the clearing took on pale hues, lavender at the horizon blending to a silver winter blue. The rain increased until it was difficult to see even the base of the tree. Elaine pulled the hood of her jacket low over her face, shivering in silence.

A doe crossed the clearing and grazed briefly, tugging at the yaupon branches, and then lifted her head in the direction of the lake and darted forward, losing herself in the thicket.

The buck appeared almost at once, but from a different direction. Hugh hadn't heard it; he had anticipated that it would enter the thicket where the doe had come in, rather than from behind the tree on which the blind was set. Unprepared, acting almost on reflex, he swung around, pushing Elaine backward, notching an arrow, aiming, and releasing it in one fluid movement. He could not have afforded to spend more time preparing the shot, but he immediately regretted it because it was badly made. The arrow hit the upper curve of the animal's right shoulder, penetrating it, yet the wound was not deep enough to bring him down. Hugh reached for the rifle behind him, but again he was not quick enough: The buck, snorting and clamping down his tail, had already spun around on the points of his hoofs and plunged into the thicket in the direction of the lake. Hugh sucked in his breath. "Jesus Christ! Oh, Christ!" He cursed not only his ineptitude but the unpleasant task that was now before him: He would have to track the wounded animal in the rain; the search might be long and difficult, and he might never find him. He took the rifle, climbed down to the ground, and then turned back to Elaine, who was watching him from the blind.

"Throw down the knife!"

"Let me go with you."

"No," he answered. "You'll slow me down."

The knife stuck in the ground at his feet, straight up. "Don't use the knife, Hugh. . . . Shoot him!" He disappeared into the thicket exactly where the buck had whirled around and broken through. Flashes of blood—a few on the branches, most on the ground—marked the path of the animal's escape. Farther on, splashes of red dissolved in the rain at a spot where the buck must have tried to free himself of the arrow. Hugh winced to think of the agony of his effort. He found a part of the arrow that had broken off, then a series of sharp hoofprints on a clay embankment. Although the spoor was widely spaced, he was able to follow it as it digressed to the left and toward the water. From time to time he stopped to listen but heard nothing except the leaves rustling in a rain which was now beginning to penetrate the thick canopy of the forest. The glistening blood he saw on the damp carpet of leaves was darker now, a deep scarlet. The buck's trail, after rising slightly, switched directions and began to run parallel to a brake. As Hugh came nearer to the lake, he could smell the mud and the rank richness of moss, water lilies, and swamped reeds.

Half an hour later, after crossing a ravine and climbing onto higher ground, he heard the thrusts of the animal's breath and the pawing of his hoof. The buck was half in the water, lying on the shore, protected by the undergrowth, three of his legs folded under him, the fourth striving for a footing. In the drizzle, the lake was flattened out, without reflection, and seemed to extend everywhere; it was hard to tell where the water ended and the beach began. The buck's tongue was dangling thick from his muzzle; he was exhausted, nearly dead from the loss of blood; the hole in his shoulder was torn wide and deep; his breath was irregular and forced, yet when he saw Hugh approach, he threw his neck sideways in an effort to rise, one great surge of muscle rippling through his side. His eyes were frenzied and sparkling, as if all his energy and power had gone into them, as if from these whirling centers might come the strength he needed to renew himself and set himself against the man. He snorted and again swung his head around; blood flowed from his mouth, mixing with the rain that coursed down his neck. He tossed his head again, trying to lift himself.

Ashamed of witnessing the scene, greatly moved by the animal's courageous struggle to survive with no chance of doing so, and furious at himself for having caused the buck such pain, Hugh dropped the rifle and went for him with the knife. The blade gleamed in the sunless, rain-streaked morning, as if it had taken on all the light of which the sullen landscape had been deprived. Carefully making his way around the antlers, knowing that a swift, unexpected movement of that head could kill him, Hugh grabbed the buck's neck, jerked it upward and back, and drove his knife in up to the hilt, slashing it sideways across the throat, blood splashing hot and fuming over both of them. The buck sagged backward and fell sideways onto a crest of black earth that was patched with lichens. He trembled violently, and his hoof cut into his assailant's boot, laying back the leather in the same kind of ragged, arc-shaped slash that Hugh had made to open his neck.

Thrown off balance, Hugh fell back toward the lake, then regained his footing and waded in. He scooped up water with his cupped hands and washed the fresh blood off his face and arms. The water was freezing cold; his boots were heavy and his feet were numb. Panting, he stepped from the water, his arms shaking from the exertion, and knelt beside the buck, gently touching the horns, running his hand along the great curve of his neck over the crest of the shoulders, and down the wet flank. It was a beautiful animal, and he decided he would take it to Matt.

Still mindful of the rack, he turned the buck on his back, and with his knife, opened the belly from the top of the ribs to the groin, one shallow incision that cut the hair and skin, exposing the red and gray entrails. He reached into the cavity and pulled out the steaming innards, throwing them in a pile on the wet leaves. Before dark, they would be removed by birds or a wild-cat; by nightfall, the soiled floor of the forest would be clean again as if neither he nor the buck had ever been there. Getting under the animal with the rifle strapped beneath his belt was the hardest task. After three tries, three times staggering and then losing his grip, he succeeded in hoisting the weight to his shoulders. For more than a mile, he followed the blood tracks back to the clearing, losing and finding them again a half-dozen times. At least two hours had passed since he had left Elaine; it was now after ten o'clock.

Elaine heard his footsteps on the leaves; she had been sleeping fitfully off and on since he'd left; she rose on her knees to look over the edge of the blind. She saw him make his way through the brush, streaming with blood and water, so absolutely in keep-ing with the sinister aspects of the gray, rain-soaked, drizzling landscape, the absence of sun, and her own acute physical dis-comfort that he seemed to be the personification of ruin. He stood below the blind and looked up at her. His dark hair under the hood of his jacket curled toward his face, and though he tossed his head once in the silver light, he was unable to keep it from falling into his eyes. He smiled at her; she smiled back, stunned. The buck was flung over his shoulders, his head and neck slightly stiffened, his feet dangling against Hugh's waist, his eyes wide, not yet completely glazed. The two beings, one murdered, the other so flagrantly alive, fused in Elaine's mind, and she wondered how it was that she had replaced Foley with this man.

It was a single instant, but the most poignant that had occurred between them, making her fear that she would never forget it, that it would come to her always, piercing through her most engaging thoughts and activities, and that she would have no control over its appearance. He stood planted on the earth as if he had sprung from it; he seemed to describe in his stance all that he was in her image of him, all the obduracy and heat of his life, as if his interior had risen to the surface, and been exposed to her. Any man after him would be an insipid counterfeit of this one, who had filled more than two years of her life with his presence and, if he left her, would fill the rest of it with regret that she had lost him. Yet it occurred to her that she must be crudely masochistic to see him as he was now and to love him so much, to love him at all. She suddenly saw herself as she was: dependent on his good will, as any victim is dependent on the compassion of a stronger force. She was a willing victim, one who had sacrificed herself, and though one part of her wanted to escape, the other, the more insistent, demanded that she play the situation out. This homicidal image of him in blood was the symbol of her subjugation. She knew now that she must lose him and suffer, and that he would avoid that suffering, being less vulnerable, and never having entrusted himself to her as she had to him. He had never loved her, or rather, he had only wanted her, and when that passion played itself out, what would be left to her?

When had she lost herself to him? When had it happened? When had it become irreversible? Was it right then, or had it been that morning more than two years earlier, when she had been late for him, and he had been waiting in her chair in her office, browsing through maps and aerial photographs of the land he wanted? She had run into that room; her face had been hot and her breathing fast and short. She had leaned back on the door she had just closed. She remembered that he had been angry, and that he had insulted her, but that she had been able to deflect that insult. Maybe it had been then, when she was confronting the look in his eyes which held hers for an instant or two longer than was right. He had been dressed like a country man in a faded blue work shirt, faded denims, and boots, but his speech was from the city, perfect, learned early; and he had begun to track her at once, and so deftly that she had given herself to him in three days.

She had made misery for herself by letting him come close to her. Her relationship with Foley had been simple, straightforward, inevitable; it was based on his superb strength and her compliance with it, their mutual attraction, their love. It had been healthy. With Hugh it was a voluptuous meeting of apostates. Why? What kind of woman was she? It was no good, it never would be. *I'm going to end it,* she thought.

Hugh let the deer slip off his back, propped the rifle against the tree, and stepped forward, placing his foot on the first scrap of wood that was nailed to the trunk, and grasping a branch above, as if he would scale the tree like a cat. She turned, feeling with her foot for the first step down, but he had already climbed halfway up, his hands gripping the steps before him. "No," she said. "No. I'm coming down." She knew that he meant to prevent her from doing so, that she was challenging him. She was certain, too, what his response would be, and she acknowledged her guilt for leading him into it.

He climbed up behind her, wiping his face on the rough canvas sleeve of his bloodstained jacket, and held her, not yet pushing her back up into the blind.

"No," she said. She strained forward, away from him. "No . . . no more. I want to go down."

He spoke without inflection. "The hell you do. You're lying." He smiled cautiously. "I always know what you mean," he said. His voice, muffled and weightless, sifted through the soft rain between them. She wrenched her body from his embrace. Abruptly, in reflex, he closed his arm around her waist. "What the hell are you doing?" he asked. There was a thread of nervousness in what he said, but he jerked her against him, tightening his grip, and lifted her backward toward the corner of the blind, accomplishing his purpose as if she had never objected.

"No," she said. "I told you . . ."

She was going to stop him. Just this once, just to let herself know that she could do so. She reached behind her on the floor of the stand, closed her fingers around the flashlight, and struck him with it on the hard bone of his cheek. For all her willfulness, for all that she occasionally baited him, indulged herself in a kind of hostility that brought him to her as ineluctably as a fish to a feathered and scintillant lure, she had never hurt him. He was

stunned; below his eye, a cut had opened where the edge of the
flashlight had hit him; and then, while he was looking at her in
disbelief, not yet understanding his situation, she struck him
again. He grabbed her hands, and the flashlight dropped to the
floor of the stand, bounced along the slope of the tree, and fell
onto the ground.

He did not look angry when he hit her, but confused. The back
of his free hand struck her face with a sound like that of the hard
rain on the soaked carpet of leaves. She bit her lip to keep from
crying out, and before she could free herself from his grip, he hit
her again with the same peculiar detachment. She closed her eyes
to stop seeing him, or the moving shadow of his hand as he
struck her, yet again, without rage, only a measured righteousness. Finally, he spoke to her with a hatefulness she had seen him
use against other people but which he had never turned on her.
He pulled her up to him in the small space on the floor of the
blind; she held on to him to keep from falling, no longer knowing
how close they might be to the opening of the stand. She felt him
thrashing against her, her conscious resistance alternating with
unconscious complicity. She caught brief glimpses of him, his
collar, his cheek, and of the gray branches and limbs that blew
over them in the changing wind of an increasingly irregular rain.
She smelled the burnt blackness of his hair; the musky odor of his
drenched skin; the faintly sour scent of his wet jacket. She heard
his boot hit the wall of the blind like a report. She tensed her
body, resolved to give him nothing soft and female, to deny him
everything that he demanded, but the protest was futile because
her flesh refused to obey her, any more than his had obeyed him
after she had smiled at him from the blind, and he had interpreted
it as an enticement, a result of her approbation and pride. She
groaned aloud in a rebellious, final complaint, not at him, but at
the thing she was—helpless, all nerve and skin and unlucky
predilection.

He stayed with her, obstinately patient, watching and shadowing her bewildered face, until her quivering and whimpering had
begun, until her fingers had driven themselves into his back, and
until, finally, he had felt her hands in his hair. She rocked her
head from side to side while the soft rain fell into her eyes and
between her partly opened lips. Above her was the blackness of
his face, etched against the streaming background and the milky,
water-stained walls of the stand. She saw the inquiring light in
his eyes, but then they moved so close to her that they bled into
his eyebrows like a mask. As she twisted to free herself, a spot of

red from his injured face splashed onto her jacket. She looked away from him, cursing him, cursing herself, cursing their alliance. She called him a name which she had once heard her father call a hired man who had stolen from him; she had been quite young then and hidden from the sight of the two men, or her father would not have said it. Never had she heard the image used at any other time of her life, yet it was now apt, and Hugh could not have denied it. She hid her face in the crook of her arm, so not to see him at all.

He arranged his clothes and replied with an obscenity, an accurate description of what had just occurred, and then took off his jacket and threw it over her. She heard him climb down the tree, and she heard him when he lifted the buck, then the sound of his boots, sloshing through the leaves, the underbrush catching on his clothes. She rolled into the corner of the blind, drew up her knees, and covered her face with the sleeve of the jacket. Immediately she passed into a condition in which she was heavy and static like a stone that has been thrown into a river and is still, except when sudden rushes of change upstream cause it to jerk or to sway, though each disorder is short.

Exhausted, coatless, his clothes wet and clinging to his skin, Hugh climbed onto the slick and glistening porch and let himself in the antique door which was always unlocked. It had been two years since he had spent the night in his parents' house at the ranch; even before he had got it in his head to move in with Elaine, he had usually stayed in the bunkhouse with Matt or Stephen, or until his marriage, with Luther.

"What a goddamned waste this place is," he said wearily. He blinked and looked up, as if he were speaking to a tall butler who had met him at the door with the intention of taking his wet things. He put his hand on the mahogany bannister of the staircase, smooth as glass, bleakly glinting. His father spent no more than a total of two weeks here each year, and his mother no time at all. *Though it was a present to her,* he thought.

In the hallway, he stripped off his clothes; in the living room, he dried himself on a sheet and then pulled a blanket off a chair and wrapped himself in it. He wondered if anything could keep him warm. He did not plan to go back for Elaine. "She can take care of herself," he said, speaking this time to a window over which the curtains were drawn and whose valances were covered with strips of cloth, these too, remnants of sheets. "She damn well can."

He switched on a lamp, which glittered amber under an Italian parchment shade, but turned it off quickly with an intolerant gesture that canceled the sympathetic circle that it had made on the tea table. He stood up and, banging the heels of his hands against each side of the sash to loosen it, opened a window and watched the rain wet and darken the floor; then he slammed it down, and not because he gave a damn about what happened to the floor of his mama's house, but because . . . yet that was untrue. He loved this house; he loved everything about it; and suddenly he loved his mother. The only person in the world he hated, he realized, had really ever hated, was Elaine. She baited him, she lured him, and then when she had got what she wanted out of him, when she had succeeded in turning him into a savage, she became quietly judgmental. Instantly this idea, this understanding of his situation, turned his nightmare of a morning into an epiphany. He would begin a life without her, ordered and safe.

He was not a paragon. He would never be perfect. He had been brought up irresponsibly. When he was a child, the only person kin to him that he had been close to was his grandmother, and she had treated him as if he were God Almighty. He was an egomaniac; but Elaine should forgive him—he could not be a reincarnation of her husband, and that was what she wanted. He had not been born on the wrong side of the tracks; he had not pulled himself up by his bootstraps; he had never been a football hero, or any other kind of hero.

He squinted as though he were studying an object at the horizon rather than staring at a blank wall, a doorframe, a painting of a palomino horse, and a gun rack made from the feet of deer. *Foley was not a savage, but I am. Foley was devoted, kind, loyal, loving . . . and what else?*

Angrily he lit a cigarette and drew the smoke deep into his lungs. *Foley must have been a hell of a lover, though; he must have known just how rough she could get. I know that, damn it! I know it because she would never in God's world put up with a man who wasn't. She'd have thrown him out on his ass, and all the virtue and hard work and moral strength couldn't have saved him. Foley came from nothing and wound up a gentleman. I come from everything and am still a savage.*

He sat in the shadow of the ceiling before the hearth. The fire had been laid, but he did not bother to start it, though he was shivering and the house was cold. He wished that Matt would come; he knew that it would be impossible to seek him out. If he did, Matt would guess his predicament; but if Matt came to him, he might succeed in fooling him . . . and it was possible that Matt disapproved of his relationship with Elaine enough to join him in a diatribe that would serve to end his infatuation.

He looked down at himself, at the contours of his exhausted body under the blanket, acutely aware that nothing was available to him now that might allay his feelings of enervation and dread. He stood up, his eyes earnestly searching the room for something to distract his mind. Not finding it, he went upstairs to the bathroom, rummaged through the cabinet for a clean towel, and bathed, using a piece of soap and razor his father had left there months, maybe a year ago. His cheek was bruised and discolored. He thought of the way she had hit him. His lips moved but he made no sound. Why did he love her? Why couldn't he stop loving Elaine, stop leading a goddamned double life, hiding, even lying sometimes? He tried to imagine her in his mother's living room with all that Louis Seize furniture, the Boucher painting, the pair of Fragonard sketches, and the Fabergé eggs. She'd be the most substantial and beautiful thing in it, but she would never be suitable because his mother would not let her be. God, how Clara would hate Elaine; his mother, who had never done anything in her life when she wasn't hiding behind Clarence, and Elaine, who had never done anything in her life hiding behind anyone! And yet the outcome might have been different if Elaine had given over more to him. Suddenly he wished she were more like his mother; that's it, like Clara. . . . He shut his eyes, half yawned, and sighed heavily. "Clara . . . ? Christ . . . !"

He touched the wound on his face. The cut had closed neatly. On the high shelf in the closet, under a pile of his father's soiled and neglected hunting clothes, he found a silver flask of brandy, engraved HCL; his initials, too. What would his father think about this morning? He threw the soiled clothes on the floor so that one of the women would collect and wash them, and then filled the cap of the flask twice, drinking each capful in a single swallow, scalding his throat. He lay down on the bed and noticed that the room had the smell of cloth and wood and wallpaper, the flat, arid smell of a room that is never occupied. *I've been with her long enough,* he thought. *I'm going to tell her. She will have gotten a ride on the highway, and she'll be home. I'll sleep, then tonight I'll go and tell her.* He raised himself on an elbow and drank straight from the flask, finishing what was in it, and for the first time since he had left that morning, he was warm. "I don't need her," he said with the affable and chilly detachment of his youth. "Not anymore." He felt relieved of a burden. He looked at the ceiling; rain on the window was reflected in pastel, a tinted parallelogram. He would work and study. He would never again be involved in a passion like this, never. One day he would marry, but his wife would be an adjunct, not a partner. He drew his hands onto his chest. He hoped to sleep. He was vaguely aware that the day was going to go down without ever having risen.

Clean and shaven and wearing fresh clothes, he went to her house and found it unoccupied and shadowy with a chill on it. She was not in her office in town, and Felix had not seen her. Hugh left quickly, running down the steps to the street and backing the truck around so fast that he narrowly missed grazing the fender of a parked car. It was nearly dark when he returned to the blind. Twenty yards from the foot of the tree, he had begun to call to her over the final peckings of the rain on the packed and drowned carpet of leaves.

He climbed up the tree slower than he needed to, as if he were putting off the time when he would have to see her, to see what he had done. He knew that she would be there, that she would have outwaited him, that her patience would have been greater than his. She raised herself on one elbow, brushing the side of her lip and then the bruise on her cheek with the back of her hand. He reached out, groping for her, as if he were unsure whether she would let him near her. When he climbed onto the floor of the stand and crouched beside her, her eyes held him to her, static, until he reached under her and pulled her to him, rocking her, saying to her words that were impossible to understand; nor did he understand the reply that she whispered into his jacket. He eased her down, pulling her over the wood-scrap steps of the arched tree trunk in such a way that she never quite touched them, though his own body scraped against the bark and the stiff little resurrection ferns that grew all along the trunk and swung back like springs as soon as they were released. He took her to the truck, sometimes bracing her against his side, sometimes carrying her, depending on the terrain. "I went to your house first," he said. "I thought you would be there."

In the truck, she sat apart from him; and he, having accomplished the rescue, did not reach for her again, nor did either of them say anything to the other. The brittle fronds of palmettos and the twigs of yaupon snapped against the truck. The muddy water in the ruts and holes dashed at the fenders; and in the depressions in the road, the wheels jerked out of rhythm to right themselves. They were still so wrapped in their thoughts that they were unable to give each other comfort. They had struggled too deeply, fought so bitterly, and the union had been harmed.

The headlights fanned out over the lake and then swept across wide clearings bordered by trees that were shaggy with moss. The truck clattered over the last cattle guard, then moved smoothly over the shimmering black top. Rather than be slowed down by the lights in the center of town, Hugh took the road around Dansville, crossed the bridge, and pulled the truck into Elaine's drive.

The damp little house seemed foreign to him; he disliked it; he no longer belonged there. Working as quietly and efficiently as a spy in an enemy camp Hugh lit the gas heater in the bathroom, wrapped Elaine in a blanket, and fixed her a cup of hot bourbon and sugar. He wanted to leave her then; he wanted to get out and never come back. He would send her money; he would do something. He drew her a bath, and while she soaked, he went out for food and cigarettes. When he returned, she was sitting on the sofa with a magazine in her hands, the cover doubled back to isolate the single column of a story. Her heavy hair was damp and pinned in loose curls on top of her head; she was dressed in a green kimono with frog closings and a fringed sash. Without speaking to her, he handed her a cardboard container with a lid. She glanced up at him quickly without seeing anything other than light and shadow. She slipped aside the tab to open the carton. In it was steak and fried potatoes, aromatic and still hot. The meat was rare and soft, just as she liked it, yet the plastic fork and knife in the carton were inadequate for cutting. He saw her difficulty and went to the kitchen, getting the two pieces of silver she needed.

She pushed the carton toward him. "Don't you want some of this?"

"No."

She ate a little, then offered it again. "Don't you . . ."

He shook his head. His face was pinched and closed, and he sat with peculiar rigidity.

She ate slowly but persistently, hungrily, neither looking at him, nor stopping the rhythm of her movements until the container was empty and she had placed the greasy knife and fork across it as correctly as if it had been made of china. She put the carton on the coffee table, leaned back on the sofa pillows in the same attitude she had been in when he had entered the room with the supper, and took up the magazine again.

Both of their faces were bruised; Hugh's was cut as well. His eye was partly closed, and there was a swelling over his lid. Their bodies were stiff and sore; their spirits, tired to death. They were ill with fatigue and dejection, and they had done it to each other, only one more event in the solving of the unconscious dilemma of their flesh.

He touched the shoulder of her dressing gown. "Do you want me to leave you for a while?" he asked.

"No." She looked up at him briefly, trying to smile, and when she was unable, she turned her attention back to the words on the slick pages.

"I could come back early in the morning before I have to leave," he said. He hesitated, waited for her to respond, and when she was silent, he picked up the empty cardboard container and went to the kitchen. She heard him rinsing the utensils, heard the foot pedal of the garbage can, the squeak of its closing lid. He must have opened the back door. The screen door shut gently, as if he closed it fearful of disturbing an invalid. He came back in the house with an armful of wood, put it down on the black tile hearth, and laid the fire, leaving extra wood in the brass basket. He lit it, and it blazed up at once, generous and unexpectedly nurturing, quickly warming and coloring the small room. He pointed to the extra wood. "You can put that on later, Elaine. . . . Is it going to be enough? Do you want me to get more before I leave?"

She looked up from her story, but not to answer him, since she knew he did not expect it, but to give herself the luxury of watching him since he was facing away from her. He sat on his heels, staring into the fireplace, his hands hooked over his knees; occasionally he would turn himself a little, as if he were going to speak, but he would soon settle back on his heels again, as if the need had passed. Elaine could see the tension in the attitude of his body, but still he said nothing.

She turned off the light behind her to see the flames better. The highest of them disappeared at the mouth of the chimney. Slipping off the sofa, she went to the fire, untied the sash, and opened her kimono, hoping that the warmth might heal her. The light and heat of it glanced along her thighs onto her belly and upward to her neck and face, stopping at her earrings and flashing into her hair. She raised her chin toward the ceiling to make herself straight, and when it became too warm for her, she stepped back onto the edge of the rug. Under the logs, the fire hissed, and jets of blue flame curved around them in attenuated wisps. Hugh stood up, his body grazing her back, and raised the kimono, his hands on her as if he would shield her from the heat, yet borrow it from her at the same time; and then, all at once, he spoke to her quickly, trying to tell her what he'd been thinking, what he had tried to tell her since he'd returned with her from the blind. She turned her head as if to get her bearings, and then twisted full around to face him. She looked up and touched his face below the place where, that morning, she had hit him. He continued talking, persisting in one idea that encompassed grief and guilt and misunderstanding, yet implicit in all he said was an admission that, were it all to begin again, he could not do it differently, that it was the result of circumstance, of the confluence of events, not of the man's choice.

"It's nobody's fault." She had interrupted him to make him still. "It's not."

He started to speak again. "No," she said, and she spoke in a tone that matched his own. "I'm not sorry." She was a little angry, not at him, but at something ineffable. "I'll never be sorry for anything we do. I accept it. It's going to stay this way until it runs out, until it's over. Forget it. The trouble is in me, too."

As the fire murmured, he bent his head down to hers, he answered her, slow and gentle, his words as revitalizing to her as the warmth from the hearth; then for a time, between the firelight and the plumelike shadows that the fire made on the wall, they stood together, silent, their faces almost touching.

The rain started again, first the big drops on the steps of the porch, then a shower on the roof. They walked over to the sofa watching the fire die out, listening to music on the radio, talking very little, sometimes falling asleep in each other's arms. Near five o'clock, he eased away from her and prepared to return to school.

As he moved toward the door, he looked at himself in the mirror over the mail table, hardly recognizing his image, and not because the dawn light was yet so tenuous, or because he was bruised and cut, but because of the uneasiness of his expression. He glanced back at the sleeping woman on the sofa, her hair swept across her cheek, her arm fallen limply to the carpet, her beautiful hand half-opened. Emma rubbed against his leg. He frowned at his own thoughts and reached down to stroke the cat's fur; then, picking up his small suitcase, he left, closing the door as quietly as he could.

Chapter 7

THAT WINTER, ONE crisp, cold day followed another, most of them filled with sunshine. In January, usually a slack month for the sale of country property, Elaine sold two farms, one of which brought her a commission large enough to take a vacation for the next six months if she chose to do so. In late February, Hugh pleased her with a trip to the Mardi Gras in New Orleans, where they stayed in a hotel in the French Quarter. For four days, they enjoyed the festivities, and at last, from the elaborate wrought-iron balcony that gave off their room, they watched the parade. In early March, Elaine's garden blossomed with hyacinths, tulips, and daffodils; the snapdragons, red salvia, and poppies would follow, and she could look forward to Easter on the first weekend in April, when she would have a full week with Hugh.

Elaine had begun to feel their situation was growing more and more secure, almost unassailable. Hugh had begun to write to her more frequently; he would telephone her from Austin and talk to her for an hour or more at a time. He was growing up, becoming considerate, developing the embryo of a conscience; she believed that when he had fully matured, he would have unusual integrity and a strong sense of honor. She saw now the promise of what she had sensed in the difficult, irascible youth—the thread of a fine humanity which had been obscured by the scars of his up-bringing.

In April she turned the office over to Felix and waited for Hugh to come to Dansville, and when she did not hear from him for three days after she knew his Easter vacation had begun, she telephoned his home in Houston, something she rarely did because it frightened her, and because she worried that she might make trouble for him. When he came to the telephone, he was as courteous as a stranger but hardly seemed able to concentrate on what she was saying. He told her that he had been busy, that other things had demanded his attention, that he was deeply sorry. He was in a tennis tournament, and he had been working with his father. There had been some . . .

She knew at once. There had never before been any question of another woman, but still she began to shake with grief, as if her body would suffer more acutely than her mind over this, as if the pain originated there, the shock crossing over via the senses to her brain. "What's her name?" she asked.

"Shirlee." He had spoken so softly that she could hardly hear him, spinning the name out without anchoring it anywhere. She knew by the tone of his voice that he was smiling, but that he did not mean to communicate his happiness to her.

"Is it someone there at home?" She tried to keep her voice still.

"Yes."

"Where did you meet her, Hugh?"

"At a party."

"Are you coming here at all?"

He did not answer.

"If you're coming down to the ranch," she said, "I'd like to talk to you."

His voice was heavy and strange. She was, she realized, pushing him for the first time where he did not want to go. She imagined him winding the spiral twists of the telephone cord through his fingers trying to talk to her, trying to care about what he said since he had loved her, but being so preoccupied with his infatuation with the girl that he was numb, unable to control his emotion or to think clearly enough to be kind. "Maybe I can get down on Friday," he said.

"Will you stay the night?"

"Sure."

She neither wept nor despaired, but with a swift, instinctive reliance on her seductiveness, she planned. He would come to her; he always did what he promised; she would have this chance. And if she could get him beside her, she could make him forget. He had made a mistake, and he would see it. She reasoned that he needed to know what it would be like with a woman of his own background. It might be good; he would try it for a while, and then she would have him back. You had to see things as they were. It was foolish to jump to conclusions. It wasn't strange that Hugh would want to see someone else; what was strange was that he had never tried it before. It would be a kind of experiment, and if she gave him a free rein, he'd be back. Perhaps he'd never really leave. She expected that he wouldn't, and she prepared carefully for his visit.

Late Friday afternoon, she sat near the front window waiting for him, her hair rolled away from her face beautifully, its color complementing perfectly the jade earrings that he had given her, which were just a shade darker than her eyes. She was wearing the silk dress that was his favorite, and she had on new shoes which she had shopped for that afternoon. For a while, she read, and then, as dusk set in, she made the final arrangements for dinner. As always, when she served him meals, she was using her wedding china and her grandmother's silver. The napkins were starched, the glass compote was filled with lilies. She would light the candles when she heard his car at the turn.

She was patient; she picked up another magazine and did things that had already been done; and when she took a walk, she stayed close enough to the house so that she could see the approach of his car. For a time, she sat on the porch, and then, though it had become quite dark—a tame, comfortable night without a moon—she went into the garden. She would have liked to telephone a friend; she could have waited for him at the window and been distracted by the conversation—but she put that thought away: since he was late, he might try to call her. She would have to keep off the phone.

She turned the radio on to a news program, yet her mind wandered quickly from what was being said to her thoughts about what it was going to be like—their new relationship, when she might have less of his attention than she'd had in the past. It would be difficult at first; she would have to adjust perhaps, but she had done that before. She had learned his ways, and she knew what he needed. No one else would know that; no one else could do for him what she could. She flipped through the pages of a Russian novel Hugh had brought her, but it was so thick and heavy that she felt too weak to hold it, and the hero's reflections were so interminable that reading it was work instead of pleasure. She would come back to it again sometime when Hugh was there and could explain the reason for these long passages. A pair of headlights swept across the house. It was not his car. She paced the floor in front of the fireplace; she stood at the window in the bedroom. Finally she went to the kitchen and began to put away the food. She was calm and efficient; she went about her work as if she were advising a client on the value of a piece of land, knowing the facts, taking account of the variables. Maybe it had been necessary for him to see the girl and explain things; maybe this girl named Shirlee had been slow to understand the change in Hugh, and so the explanation had taken longer than he expected. Elaine was still certain that he would come. He had told her he would. If she knew anything, she knew Hugh's character. He might hurt her, hurt her badly, but never this way.

From the highway came the sound of a fading horn. There was a continual whispering in the bushes and trees. The wind picked up, and the painted glass chimes on the terrace began to tinkle and sing. Jimmy had given her those chimes a whole week before Christmas, but he had insisted that she open his gift. They were from China, he had said. Embarrassed by the beauty of his present and his mother's reaction to it, he had acted silly, imitating Chinese words and pulling at his eyes to make them slant. She had taken him in her arms and kissed him over and over, and then the two of them had gone outside and hung the chimes on the long, low branch of a live oak tree. The day had been cold, but without wind, so Jimmy had had to blow on them to show her how they worked. Bundled in her coat, Elaine had sat on the grass, listening . . .

She looked at her watch—it was half past two.

She finally fell asleep on the sofa without having either undressed or turned off the porch light. Near dawn, she was awakened by a car that was certainly his; its flaring headlights were approaching the cottage quickly. Dizzy from standing up so quickly, she reached to a chair for balance and walked unsteadily to the window, where she raised the blind fully and stood in the light so that he could see her. She hoped that the nap had refreshed her. She might have waved; she certainly smiled. Across the black bed of the horizon to the north, broken only once by the slack and shadowy bulk of an ancient barn, a strip of opal began to stretch itself; the sails of a windmill coaxed the stirring light into the flowered pasture behind it.

There was no woman better suited to him, no place where he would ever be so well loved, no nature more complementary to his, and he had found her at the start of his manhood, wise enough to recognize it, but too restive to stay.

He did not come.

* * *

That night, Hugh had been with Shirlee Faris in a club in Galveston, a gambling house on the end of a long pier that featured a floor show; rich, salty seafood; dancing; and expensive games. He gave Shirlee twenty dollar bills to spend as she needed them. Whenever she lost, she would turn back to him, laughing and crying playfully, until two hundred dollars was gone. It was nothing to him: He would have given her much more, but she put her hand to her chest, pretending to be out of breath from the exertion, and begged him to let her stop. She was charming, she was intelligent, she was well educated, and she was lovely; and though they had never seen one another before the tennis matches at the club, they had so many friends in common that they had joked about how funny it was that they had often crossed each other's paths without meeting.

Six afternoons before, she had lost three sets out of four to a better player, but she had given her a fight that Hugh had thought was particularly valiant. A hush had fallen in the stands among those others who respected such determination. She had an innate sense of the game; she had talent and courage.

That night he had gone to a friend's party with no purpose other than to meet her. She had been there with a date; Hugh had kept them in sight, and at a moment when she was alone, he had approached her, complimenting her on her tennis game, and asking her to join him on the country club courts the next morning.

The day had been cool and calm, with fresh spring sunshine stirring softly in the new lime-colored leaves of the trees. After they had played two sets, they had gone into the club grill and had lunch. It pleased him to talk to her; and when they disagreed, she could hold her own. She was quick and intuitive, and he thought she spoke beautifully, without either the puling accent or the dearth of vocabulary of most of the local girls who had taken their education at home. She had gone to preparatory school in the East; she seemed startlingly competent, yet she was not afraid to show that there was still plenty of the little girl in her that needed to be instructed.

She had refused several of his invitations to dinner, so when she had finally accepted one, he had decided to take her to Galveston in order to prolong the evening. After the gambling, they turned away from the noisy roulette table and, agreeing that they needed some fresh air, walked out on the long pier high over the water. The gulf was agitated; waves lashed at the base of the pier; even without the lights from the hotels and restaurants on the sea wall, the large churning whitecaps would have been visible. Because of the roughness of the salty wind, Shirlee stood close to Hugh, teasing him by saying that he acted as a hedge against it for her, then made mock complaints that he had invited her to dinner and was now starving her.

The tables in the dining room were arranged around the dance floor; behind the orchestra, a huge picture window framed a violet sky that was filling gradually with stars. He ordered a champagne cocktail for her; she held it up between them so both could watch the dissolving sugar cube, stained orange with bitters and rising in the sparkling wine. Briefly he remembered Elaine; he looked for a telephone but, when he found it being used, he returned to the table. The food had arrived; he had seen Shirlee turn her head toward the door to look for him. "You shouldn't be gone so long," she said. The shrimp in the cocktails were oversized and fleshy, and their sharp coral tails hung over the sides of the stemmed glasses. A freshly opened bottle of champagne smoked in a bucket of tear-streaked silver.

"I missed you," she said, smiling.

"I love you," he returned.

She took a swallow of her drink and leaned toward him. "You hardly know me."

He put his hand under her chin, raised her face to his, and kissed her. Yet he realized that his affection was not spontaneous; caution and fear made him, for the first time in many years, self-conscious. She was seeing another man; when he had inquired about her, his friends had told him as much. His mother had also known about this, as did one of his girl cousins. But he was unable to do anything about his rival. Not yet. Not until she loved him.

She pushed away from him, though without much resolve. "You like me," she said softly. "Maybe you'll love me later."

He was afraid of the way he felt about her; the emotion seemed new. He kissed her again. She squirmed in her chair; her eyes brushed over his face, and she spoke to him more affectionately. "People are looking at us," she said.

Turning only his head, he gave the couple watching them a look—an acquired skill of his increasing urbanity—that caused them to leave their table for the dance floor. He grinned and took Shirlee in his arms.

* * *

Two days later, on Easter evening, he took Shirlee to dinner and a movie; afterward, he should have driven back to Austin, where he had classes the next morning at the university, but he stayed behind to see if she had lied to him. He parked his car in an alleyway near her house. At half past midnight, in the dark of the side porch, she received a visitor. If the man stayed where he was, if they stayed under the awning talking, it would be all right, just a visit. Shirlee would be doing what she had promised repeatedly that she would do: telling the man that it was over between them. But minutes later, they left the house, and he put his arm around her. He said something to her, and Hugh saw her nod. They got into a car and kissed—Hugh was sure of it—and then the car pulled away quietly. Enraged, yet determined to keep her from seeing that side of him, anxious that she should never witness for herself what her friends might have told her, and certain that he must resist the impulse to drive after them, to intimidate the man, to fight him if necessary, and then to drag Shirlee into his car, he sat silent and still. For now, he would live with it; he would drive back to school, let time pass. He would not lose Shirlee through an act of reckless stupidity.

He pulled the car out onto the open road, safe. The headlights, two thick silver wedges, sliced into the space before him; the wind from the car stroked the bluebonnets and Indian paintbrush beside the road; the highway was his, and he was making good time. In seventy miles, he encountered only a few hauling trucks and two or three cars. He crossed over the featureless, night-thickened Colorado River into Colorado County and was well into the town of Columbus—past the filling station with its brick-bordered flower bed of ageratum and narcissus, past the boarded-up icehouse, and the mansion with the giant cedar hedge, past the lilac clouds of wisteria in the mayor's side yard and the magnolia-and-pecan-shielded courthouse—when suddenly the scalding humiliation of his defeat overwhelmed him, when all at once there was nothing good in the world ahead of him, and nothing but what had hurt him behind. Wounded, tired, and cheated, left alone to founder in the hostile climate of his failure, he made a wild turn south on a dusty farm road that would take him directly the seventeen miles to Eagle Lake and then the other thirty-three through Matthews and Egypt and Glen Flora to Dansville.

It was dark morning when he arrived. He braked the car too

urgently, and it skidded on the dusty shoulder of the road. In her sleep, Elaine seemed to hear him: the slam of the car door, the footsteps on the walk, the scraping sound on the porch. She tried to pull herself into alertness; she knew that she must be ready for him, and that if she were not, she never would be again.

Then the key.

He passed the light switch without touching it; he knew his way. Warm with the heavy scent of sleep still on her, she felt him pull her up, unbelievably harshly, too rough, too distraught, a child again; his behavior terrified her, and she tried to twist away. "Elaine," he said, and at first she thought he was drunk, but then she heard the resolute, clear, unarguable: "I can't come here anymore!" He held her against him and talked to her; his voice was rushed; he cursed violently, damning neither her, nor the woman he claimed he loved, nor himself, but rather the situation that bound him, the trap he had fallen into through nothing more than good will and affection. He had meant merely to have her listen; yet he moved against her, borrowing from her, asking for a different kind of sympathy, confounding them both. He expected understanding, and when, in a little while, he made love to her, his feelings for her spun backward to the scenes of their times together, the prodigality of autumn colors, the swish of leaves under her feet, the twists and turns of the tallow tree, the copper sun falling between the limbs' shadows, and onto her hair; and these memories provided more evidence of the finality of his statement than his words—though they were less urgent than his determination to lose his pain by loving her, as if it were the flesh that granted mercy while the mind circled above it, remote in its reminiscences until the body sated itself, and the legs and the numbed torso rested, wet and trembling from their work.

She lay beneath him, trying desperately to invent something that would hold him. Since the act of love had failed to bind him to her, since he had used it merely to ease his own suffering, she probed her astonished mind for the words that would succeed in keeping him with her, but she found none. She sensed a tragedy so deep that she felt as if she were a helpless child again, hearing of her grandmother's death and then hiding behind a pile of leaves raked into the corner of the yard, where she could grieve unseen by the others, not because she objected to her grief being observed but because there was something fundamentally wrong and unnatural in sharing it.

Without speaking to her again, Hugh got up, dressed quickly, and was gone as unexpectedly as he had come. She listened to

him retreat, slam the door, and walk through the yard between
the beds of tall roses, disappearing from the scene of her devasta-
tion so fast that he did not hear her call after him, not with the
redundancy of a curse, but merely his name.

She listened until the car roared away, until the small sounds
of daylight—the birds, a truck changing gears far out on the
highway, the wavelike roars of a train stopping at the stockyards
—filled the void it had left. She turned her head to the side; the
dawn was coming low over her garden. The iris were not yet
open; the snowdrops and hyacinths had already quit; the buds on
the roses were still tight and green, rigid and uncompromising as
they went about their task of reproducing their kind against the
lilac beginnings of the day.

At some point she got up, went to her closet, and threw a
canvas jacket of Hugh's around her naked body. The hem of it
fell midway down her thighs. She tried to button it a little and
then went outside and lay on the dewy ground under the tallow
tree, staring straight into the low-slung sun until her eyes
throbbed with its brightness. She didn't know how long she lay
there, but before she made her way back to the kitchen door, the
day had become quite warm and a cloud of insects was buzzing
over the tall, heated grass of the field. She neither ate nor dressed
nor answered the telephone; and it had been dark for hours when,
without turning on the bedside light, she felt with her hand into
the drawer for the cold metal of Hugh's pistol, lifted it out, released the cylinder, and searched with her fingers to make sure
that each of the six chambers was filled. She laid it beside her on
the sheet, prepared to use it if she could not control her suffering;
and then she settled in with the sickening grief that started in her
stomach and rose boiling and smoking into all the recesses of her
brain, making her head split with pain and throb at the back of
her neck. Both times that she reached for the pistol, it was raining, not in torrents, with lightning and thunder, but slow, gray,
silky rain that fell on the new leaves and the hard buds, not
clattering and harsh, like a healthy summer rain, but soft, like
caresses sweetly given, like mothers comforting their distressed
children. And both times, Elaine laid the pistol aside and went
out to walk. The wetness increased the intensity of the smell of
Hugh's jacket; she turned her head inside the collar, touching
with the tips of her fingers the stains accumulated from animals
and plants.

She began to think that as long as she stayed in her bed, where

Hugh had last been with her, she would retain some possibility of recovering him. He had left her there; he would think about her; he would come back. But later, after she had slept, and after her dreams had cleared her head of illusions, she knew that he was lost to her. Hugh was gone.

The first days, her stomach cramped from hunger, but by the fourth day, she felt nothing, and she no longer cried. She was perfectly quiet and still and did not allow anything to occupy her mind for a long period of time. Once she sat up in bed and looked at herself in the dresser mirror across the room, but the image was too harsh; she turned back and covered her head with the jacket. She could see the sun through the rough weave of the cloth, an orange light that showed a spot of moisture just above the pocket. The patch of morning sun moved across the bed over her feet, then onto the rug, elongating until it was straight, narrow, and incisive. When she looked down at her body, it looked strange and sunken; she pulled in her breath with all her force to see it become even smaller, to make it disappear in the rumpled sheets. She pulled the blind down, and the oblong of light disappeared, leaving an amber brightness behind the slats. She felt dizzy, she could hardly stand up, but she found that she could cross the room to the bathroom without falling if she moved very slowly, made no sudden changes in position. If she was careful and held on to the back of the armchair and then gripped the edge of the buffet, she could even get to the kitchen to put milk in Emma's bowl, though when the cat looked up at her, its eyes were no longer twin circles shot through with vertical black spears, but one continuous band of gold.

Back in the bedroom, Elaine braced herself against the dresser and looked again in the mirror; her skin was pearly white; her eyes, huge and green; actually she had never seen herself so beautiful. She had used to deny her beauty, to blush and refute it. She would not deny it now.

She spoke in German. Rapidly. The verbs were right, the vocabulary was rich. She seemed to be reaching into a subconscious repository, and soon she was reciting bits of poems that her grandmother had taught her. Maybe her mother thought that she had forgotten these poems. She laughed at that thought. She had always been smart. She had been supposed to go to college, but Foley had stopped all that.

On the sixth day, words and definitions of words rolled through her mind; when she stared at the blank spaces on her bedroom walls, maps of the counties she knew appeared to her.

She had them by memory. Never again would she have to refer to
a map, since the roads and paths were projected in her awareness,
like the veins in a familiar body. She took pleasure in thinking
that she had mastered geography. As long as she knew it, she was
safe from harm. What could hurt her? There was even a map for
getting out of this world, and if she found the right turn, maybe
she wouldn't suffer. Foley had not learned that trick. That Foley
had died, had ruined her life; that he had suffered, that he had
regained consciousness after he was struck, and then known that
nature, whom he had served so well during every moment of his
short life, had betrayed him and given him up to suffering, had
broken her heart.

The cat cried. Elaine would have to feed her. "Emma!" Was
that the cat's full name? "Emma Bovary!" Hugh had made her
read that sad book. "Emma!" Because cats are so self-centered,
Hugh had said. So damned selfish.

Her dreams lengthened, but they were sweet, and she was no
longer concerned about the cat's face close to hers, sniffing her
breath, then lying on her chest like an ornament on a tombstone.
Maybe she wasn't a warrior angel with a sword, or a cherub with
a wreath of flowers and a lyre, but Emma would have to do.

She reached for the pistol and laid the barrel of it across her
forehead to cool her skin. A window blind danced, then slapped
at the sill. The noise hurt her head terribly; she should close the
window. That afternoon, when she had poured the dry cat food, it
had clattered on the linoleum like hail. "Hail in April!" She
laughed slowly and soundlessly, as Emma sometimes laughed.
She went into a chill. She made a great effort to roll over on her
side and then pulled the quilt over her, drawing her knees up to
her chest. She was unable to keep her teeth still, nor could she
leave the bed.

The next morning, she heard movement in the bushes beyond
the blinds. The sun, trying to get in, had gone around to the back
of the house and was shouting. Elaine strained to understand; the
voice was loud, insistent, but it seemed to be talking in a foreign
language. Not even the old farmers spoke this unintelligibly.

A pane of glass broke in the kitchen; she heard bits of it
shatter on the floor, some of them falling into the cat's water
dish. Elaine opened her mouth to speak, then quickly covered it
with the barrel of the gun. It passed over her lips, and she tasted
metal. A figure in an indigo dress appeared in the doorway; it
flung down a purse and cautiously approached the bed . . .
speaking, coaxing now, lovingly and yet with fear: "Elaine,

Elaine, Elaine . . . good Lord, honey." She had a round face and particularly scarlet cheeks.

Someone let out a yell, the protest and lament of a cornered animal. Elaine was never certain which one of them did that—maybe it had been she herself, maybe it had been Felix's wife, Lily.

They telephoned her father.

He was difficult to talk to, not because he didn't understand all that they were saying but because he believed, as a fundamental principle, that what they were telling him was impossible. Practical and lucky all his life, he was unable to comprehend how the fruit of his loins could have so much go wrong. He listened carefully, though, and by nightfall, he was in Dansville. He was thorough; he left nothing undone that needed attention.

Elaine went to the hospital, frail and sick. For more than a week, she was unwilling to speak, but after two or three days, she had the strength to manage for herself: to eat, to remove her gown and paper slippers, and to take a shower without help. She leafed through the magazines and mail: a letter from Jimmy (for the last year he had been living with Albert and Arlet on their farm near Brenham, happy to be with their two sons), letters from her aunt in Michigan with photographs of her young cousins included. Friends came to see her, stood at the foot of the bed, looking at her with serious faces, telling stories, relating to her and to one another their own illnesses, talking softly among themselves, trying not to bother Elaine, who didn't seem to appreciate these visits anyway.

Bent straws stood in half-empty glasses of orange juice and milk; trays went back to the hospital kitchen half-eaten; Elaine's flesh pulled away dangerously from the hospital gown. The doctor cautioned her.

She cried when her minister came—she knew him to be kind, charitable, and steadfast, qualities that evoked in her profound empathy—but she refused to share with him the source of her grief. She let him sit beside her and hold her hand; but while he talked, she kept her gaze on the sheet's coarse weave or on the framed print of two little girls at a piano. When he asked her if he might do anything for her, her eyes blurred, and she shook her head. A woman from the church brought her cookies and fruit, but after she had left, Elaine gave them to the pregnant black girl whose duty it was to clean the hospital rooms.

Her father sat with her for hours. Mostly he read; she appre-

ciated his silence. When occasionally she glanced at his profile, it
occurred to her that a woman should never marry a man who is
less than her father: If the father is courteous, the husband must
be gallant; if the father is strong, the husband must be a rock . . .
and so on.

In early summer, she heard from Hugh when he sent her a
check. There was only one thing in the world that would have
made her cash it, and she did so. In July, after arranging for Felix
and Lily to take over the business until she returned, she packed
her belongings and went to her parents in Seguin.

Chapter 8

THE DECORATIONS WERE on the theme of a French garden: Fresh
flowers, brought in by the armloads, had been tied to the columns
in the ballroom and placed elsewhere in huge urns throughout the
other rooms of the club. The scent of florist roses blended with
those of French perfumes, liquor, and exotic foods. Chains of
ivy, pegged with white daisies, hung in scallops from each of the
lintels of the double doors, then formed swift cascades of sweet-
smelling ropes that trailed on the beige carpets like feathered boas
on well-kept arms.

Hugh had driven home from Austin for this party, one of several in celebration of his engagement, after the last of his law
classes before the Easter break. It was being given at the old
country club, a rambling frame building with verandas; thick,
stubby columns; and gloomy, reassuring interiors. Black servants
in white coats bowed to the members and their guests, welcoming
everyone with their quiet ways, showing their good will in spontaneous gestures and smiles. Their service was perfect, and their
voices were warm music.

In a pale-pink taffeta dress, Shirlee stood beside Hugh in the
receiving line: too diminutive to be beautiful, and looking even
smaller in relation to the big man next to her, who was dressed in
a black cutaway and a white wing collar that set off his dark and
very striking face, crowned by an abundance of hair grown
slightly too long over his ears. On the table behind him, which
was polished like a mirror, stood a glass of whiskey and soda;
and though the glass was emptied with mechanical regularity, the
waiter, who had known the younger Littleton from childhood

swimming matches and tennis tournaments (Paul had been in charge of the thick towels and the yellow tennis balls), kept it filled. Shirlee had the gift of remembering the names of everyone and often had to remind Hugh of them, looking up at him with her cool blue eyes, certain that he would now remember them forever, since they had been sealed in his mind by her voice. It was her habit to look up at her fiancé without raising her head in the slightest. It made her look innocent, and wary of him, as if she expected him at any moment to lash out at her. This feminine mannerism suited her, but it was by no means a defense: He was hers now, and she knew it.

Hugh's mother and father were in the reception room among friends. Clarence was loud, sociable, and, like his son, already a little drunk. Clara watched the room out of the corners of her eyes, delighting in the perfection of the decorations and the impressive numbers of mauve candles. The glamour of the rustling dresses and heavy jewelry; the magnificent effect of the men's black and white evening dress; the drama of the flowers in urns on pedestals so high that the very tallest of the gladiolas and forsythia grazed the winking teardrops of the crystal chandeliers gave her such pleasure that, on first seeing them, she had almost cried. It was a scene for an artist, and Clara wished that, instead of standing there in her silk dress with her matching shoes and her beaded purse, she could have been painting it herself, that she could have been in a studio, dressed in a smock, keeping this party alive on a very large canvas. In the brief intervals when she was alone or could hide herself in Clarence's shadow, her gaze went around the room, missing no detail. She was satisfied. Her child would never look back, and she trusted that he would be completely happy.

Clarence was less complacent. He had never been a vigilant parent, but he was a far more observant one than his wife. He was concerned about the mix rather than the alliance, and there were things about the girl that worried him. She lacked warmth; she was too reserved, and that reserve was not like a sturdy wall which she might have erected to discourage the attentions of men she didn't want and which she would remove for the one she did, but was rather like a gauze curtain that a man's ardor might cause to ripple and flutter, but never to vanish. Hugh seemed to be fleeing the flesh, making a precarious truce with convention, denying himself the kind of passion that frees and delights the body while properly imprisoning the heart. His past put him at odds with this marriage. *You can't dress him up*, Clarence was thinking, *stand him in a line, stick him in an office somewhere, demand that he go against his nature into the world of rules, and not sacrifice the fire.* He shook his drink to hear the ice tinkle. *Well, maybe fire is something he just can't afford.*

His thoughts were interrupted by friends who engaged him in conversation; he listened, reacted, nodded when he needed to, offered advice when it was asked for, took another pale, gold whiskey from the silver tray—yet this did not keep him from looking for his son every once in a while. Hugh was dancing with Shirlee. Even in exquisite silver sandals with heels like needles, she scarcely reached his shoulder. Clarence could not help comparing her with the splendid woman in Dansville, and he could not help but shake his head and wonder. Shirlee was almost a refutation of Hugh's first choice. *He was so long with the other one,* he thought. *I should have tried to stop that, I guess.* Yet what could he have done? If he had belittled her, Hugh might have reacted by drawing closer to her; if he'd forbidden him to see her, Hugh would have defied him. Once a romance like that gets started, nothing from the outside can ever stop it if neither of the parties is willing to have that happen.

He glanced behind him. His wife was talking to a cousin; the dress she had on, the flower she wore, and the smile on her pretty mouth reminded him of their first meeting. It humbled him still to remember how much he had wanted her and how much he had suffered on her account. But nothing in the world could have separated him from Clara. His feeble attempts to rid himself of his passion for her had been more to assuage his scourged pride than to release him from subjection.

Two bands provided the evening's music: A dixieland group, all the members black, fiery, fast; and an orchestra patterned after Guy Lombardo's. Its leader, dressed in tight gray pants, a gray silk shirt, and an orchid-colored bolero, swung the baton in an endless pattern of arcs; the men before him, unless they had a solo, for which they would stand, sat on velvet covered stools, reading their music from small brass stands. The dancers, in flashing clothes, rocked back and forth, holding on to one another. Hugh was no longer dancing but, with his hands in his pockets and a look of increasing discontent on his face, watched the crowd. Shirlee had gone over to greet several of her college friends and was now leaning on a young man with large hands, scant hair, and a pale complexion. She reached down and adjusted the ankle strap on one of her silver shoes and came up smiling.

Hugh went to get another drink and was soon joined by two
men, childhood friends. They stood on either side of him, leaning
into him like buttresses lean into the walls of a cathedral. Their
elbows rested on the wooden bar, their hands bracing their
cheeks, their lips curved in smiles that were sometimes genial
and at other times as grotesquely lewd as those of gargoyles.
They spoke confidentially, trading quips, often striking the waxed
and polished surface of the wood with a fist or the flat of a hand,
and between jokes, they reminisced. Hugh would smile, but he
never laughed and scarcely spoke. When one of them slapped
him on the back, he held firm; occasionally he made a faint
motion with his hand or shifted the position of his leg to secure a
new foothold on a rung of the bar stool. His aloofness, the slow,
vaguely suspicious movement of his eyes, in which the light of
exaltation never flared, increased his air of control and self-pos-
session, exaggerated the insolence of his maleness, and made
him more beautiful. The only thing that might possibly have been
interpreted as a sign of discontent was the rippling of the muscles
of his jaw, as if he had closed his teeth hard to ward off a flicker
of pain.

Briefly he glanced at the woman with whom he would soon be
living. She was fine. She complemented him. He thought of her
serenity as a foil for his intemperance. She brought to his impe-
tuosity and restlessness, grace, charm, and restraint; she was
quietly eager and guardedly happy; and she was to him like a
fresh stream is to an exhausted hunter on a withering summer
day. Maybe her people were the kind in whom he had never been
much interested, but they were comfortable to be with. Her two
brothers had gone to Princeton with him; although they were
older and had not been in his class, he knew them and liked them
both. One had finished graduate studies in archeology and had
been living in Ephesus for almost a year; the other was in an
executive training program at a bank.

Shirlee was not intellectual, but then, neither was he. He was
well educated; but he was no longer willing to contemplate ab-
stractions for much more than thirty seconds unless they had utility, which was why he thought himself well suited to the law.
Shirlee was practical, smart, able—as he was. She was slightly
rebellious in the small matters that made no difference; but, when
it came to the serious issues, she seemed to lack confidence in her
judgment, and she deferred to his. She would do as he said; she
would make a beautiful home for him; and when, after they married, his affection, so demonstrative and constant, had dissolved

her reticence, she would become a good wife. She did not need him particularly; she was not independent, and scarcely daring, but she was self-contained and, by temperament, self-sufficient. He appreciated that. She would never demand much of him.

If what had at first seemed to him to be independence was in fact an opaque reaction to those whom she would not have influence her; if what he had initially seen as bravery was actually skill in feigning it, together with an obsessive competitiveness which he understood and believed in since he had it himself— this was not to say that he found fault with Shirlee. If she lacked some of the qualities he found admirable in a woman, qualities that had so much seduced him at another time, she made up for it by her suitability to the partnership he wanted, and also by her love for him. She was now entirely his: She saw no one else but him, no one else demanded her attention. There was little emotional depth to their relationship—his feelings for her had long since stopped being accompanied by symphonic strains—but neither was there much conflict. And if he did not love her, he adored her. She was too fine and perishable an ornament not to adore. He was in awe of her; she held him spellbound in between reality and an illusion, one that had stamped itself on his consciousness in the figure of his mother. He could remember sitting on the soft carpet at Clara's feet, playing with his blocks and toys while she powdered her face and applied her lipstick and rouge, and Cana, standing behind her, combed and arranged her golden hair. He would look up at her in wonder at her elegance: her fine hands removing the fragile stopper from a bottle of perfume, incapable of damaging anything; the delicate way she straightened the lace at the neck of her gown; the gentleness of her expression when she told Cana about a reading or a musicale that she had particularly enjoyed. As his mother had been then, Shirlee was hard to approach—when her body was hugged, she hesitated to go soft and supple, as if she would rather retain the appearance of imperturbability than experience pleasure—but doll-like and precious, even intoxicating.

If he seldom worried about Shirlee's somewhat chilly sweetness, it was because he was certain that once she had lived with him—specifically, once he had taken her to bed—her cool veneer would crack. She had yet to give in to him, but he attributed that more to her upbringing than to her inclination. That she might not desire him would never have occurred to a man like Hugh, who had known so much carnal affection, who had been so gratified early on that there could be no question of his suc-

cess. If he was confident of his appeal, it was because he had had
confirmation of it in countless demonstrations, so powerful and
so perfect that it would have been unreasonable for him to have
imagined that the fault in a flawed physical relationship could be
his. That Shirlee could become a passionate woman, he did not
believe; that she could satisfy him, he was certain, and this not
because he credited her potential but because he trusted his own.
And he believed he could be the agent of Shirlee's transformation; it was a challenge to him. He did not realize that a ride on
the fiery chariot that he offered might devastate her, that his energy might destroy her, and so cause her to look elsewhere for
relief, as some distressed personalities satisfy themselves with
mediocrity to find calm.

She had left her group and walked radiantly across the room to
where he was sitting. One of the men with him surrendered his
place on the stool to allow her to sit beside her fiancé. She in-
spired politeness. In this small society, everyone was good to her.
Other women liked her and invited her places; for any number of
the men, she would have been a fine match, all they might have
hoped for, and this irrespective of her family's money. She put
her head on Hugh's shoulder and rubbed her forehead on the satin
of his lapel. She often showed her fondness for him with little
gestures like this, either alone with him or in front of people they
both knew. The wedding, she complained, whispering in his ear,
was so far away, but she was obviously enjoying the excitement
of her engagement, this betrothal to a slightly tarnished but nevertheless superior man.

From a number of girl friends, who considered it a duty to
inform her, each independently of the others, she had heard about
Elaine; and then Hugh himself had admitted it when she had
confronted him. One sunny afternoon in January, a few days after
he had taken her to the jewelry shop with him to choose, to be
encouraged to select the biggest diamond solitaire in the case;
after the ring was glittering on her finger, and tears were glistening in her clear-lit eyes, she had accused him, and he had told
her. It had lasted for three years? Almost. Was she really six
years older than he? Something like that. Had he loved her very
much? Yes. Was she as beautiful as they said? Yes. Had he actually lived at her house? He had. Well, did he love her now? Only
as one loves one's past. No, he had stopped loving her; it was
over.

"Dance with me, Hugh," she said. He kissed the top of her
head and finished his drink, holding the glass up until the ice fell

against his mouth. He dabbed it with a napkin—at another time, he would have used the back of his hand, and not because there had not been a napkin available—and looked down at Shirlee. She and her kind had almost made a gentleman out of him. He liked the discipline that these costumes and rituals fostered. Once he had been too wild; people had been hurt, and he was sorry. The pride and satisfaction he felt at his conversion made him particularly sorry. Shirlee had given him a fresh start. Like a novice in a monastery, he had been given a second chance, with no penalties for his flirtation with hedonism, for the slipshod morality of his youth.

When they danced, she held herself close to him, raised her head so that his cheek could touch hers, and let him pull her hand in with his until his arm was against her small, tight breast. The other hand she let fall gently across his shoulder, where the diamond he had given her gleamed. As much as she was his ideal of perfection, marrying him was, at that time in her life, her idea of the highest attainment. He had a future that was conventionally desirable; he was intelligent, handsome, and rich, so rich that it was inconceivable that he might be marrying her for her money. There would never be any question of that, something she knew that her father had feared before her engagement, when he had questioned the advisability of her dating certain men, and she had answered in a playful tone, reserved just for these discussions: "I'm just playing the field, Daddy. Don't worry, I'm not thinking of settling down."

Shirlee's cousin had come across the dance floor and now moved to cut in. "This may be the last time I'll have to dance with Shirlee while she's single," he said pleasantly, with his hand on Hugh's shoulder. "I hope you don't mind." Just home from Oxford, where he had been a Rhodes scholar, he spoke in British idioms and with a pronounced British accent.

Hugh smiled, gave way, and left them. He went back to the bar, where he and his friends talked about school and women and work and money, interspersed with politics and the war, all of them worried about being drafted, but not too seriously, since they were in school, or had children, or were the sole surviving son, or had another good reason for deferral. It was an unpopular war; people in their class, at least, were not enlisting, not as they had been a decade before.

By the time Shirlee returned to him, the party was thinning out, and many people had already come to him to tell him good-by, and thank him for inviting them. He had drunk a great deal but was neither belligerent nor clumsy; he replied to everyone courteously; if he could be criticized, it might have been for being distant and a bit preoccupied. His drinking was the thing that Shirlee liked least about him. She drank little herself. She took him by the arm and pulled him into the alcove under the staircase.

"I'm not going to drive with you, Hugh." Without lifting her head, she looked up at him. "I'm going home with one of my brothers," she said. "I'll see you tomorrow afternoon." She started to walk away. As she turned, the flounce of her dress, swishing at the toe of his gleaming shoe, was more threatening to him than her words.

He leaned into her, grasped her arm, and began to lead her outside. He held her firmly while they waited for his car to be brought around. Without listening to her protests, he helped her into the front seat and went around to the other side. She raised her chin and showed him her profile, making herself more than usually unapproachable, out of reach. Yet he had to overcome her resistance; he had to have her whole-hearted commitment if this was going to work, and there was only one way that he could think of to get it.

On the way home, in the brashness of his intoxication, he decided that that night, in the parking lot by the lake across the street from the zoo, he was going to make love to her. He was not going to wait until June; he was tired of going to bars after he had taken her home to pick up prostitutes because she had teased him, led him on in front of friends, and then, when they were alone, refused him. Actually, that had happened only once, his needs otherwise having been taken care of by a good-looking if sullen waitress whom, one night, after five or six beers, he had had the good sense to pinch. But he felt sorry for himself. He slightly enjoyed the melodrama he was creating, and he enjoyed his place in it; he relished parading his courage in front of her and his certainty of success. "Shirlee, do you know where we're going?" he asked with the impertinence of a badly used slave whose master thinks he is still chained to a bench. She would have guessed from the route he had taken. They should have turned right at the drugstore with the great marquee and the massive red word *Coca-Cola* in script and lights; but they had gone straight. They ought to have been near the old lumberyard with its vacant buildings and its signs with vanished letters; but, instead, they continued past the art museum, then the bronze equestrian figure of the victor of San Jacinto, and then the entrance of the school of science and engineering where Hugh's maternal grandfather had taught.

One moment, Hugh felt malicious and evil, the next, he was weak with desire; one moment he knew exactly how to proceed, the next, he would think of something better. But he felt good. The wholesome wantonness that he had finally recaptured, thrilled him. With a certain lack of precision, he reached to the dashboard for the glass of whiskey he had taken from the club. In a desperate move, Shirlee tried to grab it from him; but he held her back with his arm while he swallowed what remained and then let the empty glass drop onto the rubber mat of the floorboard beside his left foot. He was drunk, and he felt ashamed, but not ashamed enough, not this time. *This is going to be the night,* he thought. His bravado increased in proportion to Shirlee's earnest contempt.

"I have to go home," she said. He just wanted to frighten her, she supposed. She would never believe that any man who knew her would go against her wishes. When he had failed to take the proper turn back at the drugstore, she had told him that she had to go home at once: There was a wedding shower for her the next afternoon, and she was very tired. He had not listened. And when he pulled up in the parking lot among the other cars—for there were always several in this lover's lane, which was so evocative of garden and jungle, of freedom and captivity—she had moved away from him, sliding to the corner against the door and folding her slight arms across the flower-pink bodice of her dress. After carefully arranging her features to express a mixture of petulance and disgust, she looked out the window. On the lawn sat a group of sleeping geese, fat and frozen in the solidity of their rest. She had taken it for granted that the attitude she had assumed would make her feelings clear, so she cried out in surprise when Hugh pulled her across the seat to him. His hand was hard, and it seemed to squeeze her arm to the bone. He was serious. She stiffened all over.

This was not the way he had responded when she had refused him in the past—though she had been acutely aware of his disappointment and had tried to make it up to him in other ways. She bragged about him; she loved his beauty, and she told her friends that she had never seen such patrician features. In public, she showed him immense affection. She embraced him and called him darling often; she listened to every word he said and then repeated his opinions to others in front of him. She admired him because he was clever and adroit, and because everyone

whom she knew thought so, too. The dark side of his character,
his sensuality, she distrusted; nor was she yet ready to free her
mind in order to understand it, to let loose the restraints in a
moment of abandon, to order the guardian of her chastity to retreat a little so that she might at least consider its attractions.

He tried to approach her gently, subtly, and when that failed,
he used harsher methods. But she was adamant, she refused him,
and finally there were tears. At last, since it was intolerable to
him to hear her cry, he restored and arranged her clothes and his
own and pushed away from her. He leaned on the steering wheel,
hiding his face in the crook of his arm; when he lifted his head a
few minutes later, his eyes were wide, clear, and sober. He
blinked a few times and then looked at the woman who would be
his bride. Her face had swollen very little from the crying, and
she stared at him with the concern of a trained nurse who has
been sent to sit at a sick child's bed until he wakens, and then to
take note of his every gesture and activity. He drew in his mouth,
shaking his head slowly, and when she tried to smile, he touched
her folded hands until she opened one of them inside of his. He
turned the key in the ignition and backed the car around to take
her home. From the parking lot, he drove down Main Street
under the black shade of oaks that had been planted along the
sidewalks thirty years before. She was quiet for a while and then
she asked, "What's wrong?"

"Nothing."

"You're not angry?"

He ignored the question, and she repeated it. "No," he said,
throwing her a glance, yet keeping hidden behind the twin curtains of his thick lashes a look of secrecy that, had she seen and
interpreted it correctly, she might have protested so vehemently
that it would have forced him to reconsider his plan. But she had
not seen it, and he drew her close and left his arm around her. His
fingers caressed her and played absently with the dress material
on her shoulder. Nothing mattered now; he had made a decision.
An hour and a half had passed since they had left the club, and he
was much soberer now. On that night, after months of anxious
and frustrating pursuit, he had decided to do something that he
had longed to do for nearly a year. He was going to take himself
out of captivity, do himself a favor. And he was unwilling to wait
until he was more clearheaded or rested. He was going now.

He took Shirlee home, and just inside her door, he answered
her troubled questions: Yes, he did love her; no, he was not hurt;

yes, he understood; yes, he would pick her up at seven for the cocktail party tomorrow evening.

"Mother and I are going to the church tomorrow to see about the decorations and talk to Mr. Smith," she said. "We're going to . . ."

He listened to her; he liked to hear these plans; he was as interested as she. He had seen the wedding gifts as they had begun to appear on the tables in the Farises' den. It was reassuring; it told him that he would be married, that his future was certain and would be orderly, expected, traditional. He smiled at his fiancée; she was all that he wanted; and when he kissed her just inside the door, she responded to him with unusual warmth. Her arms were tight around his neck; she seemed to want to keep him there. He suspected that he had upset her earlier, and that he could look forward to realizing the benefits of her discomfort.

"Hugh!" She had called to him as he was halfway down the walk, past the giant camellias that were planted on the summits of the leaf mold mounds and near the beginning of the chain of azaleas that twisted in and out among the trees, and whose branches made such shady caves. He had gone back and kissed her again.

He had not been in a hurry then; he had proceeded with the caution of his new maturity. But as soon as he was alone, as soon as he was out of sight of Shirlee's house, something in his spirit broke loose and drove him toward his objective rapidly and without any other thought. As he turned into the drive before his house, the tires of the car swept up the fallen petals of the dogwood. He let himself in, ran up the back stairs quickly, and searched for the pair of dun-colored boots in the back of his closet. Although they were scuffed and the heels were worn down, they were shaped to his feet, and they were the only boots he had worn since she had given them to him. He changed into faded jeans and a flannel shirt, grabbed a bottle of Dom Perignon out of the liquor closet, snatched a bouquet of roses out of a vase, shaking their water on the rug, and brushed past his father, who was standing in the kitchen behind the door of the refrigerator, pouring himself a glass of milk.

As Hugh went by, Clarence's free hand brushed his arm. "Where are you going this time of night?"

Clarence followed him to the door and yelled through the screen. He could see the white-shirted figure veering through the darkness like a moth.

The car engine roared as Hugh turned the key in the ignition.

In a voice made full and jubilant by a conclusive action long
considered, he shouted back an answer over the noise of the
machine, and Clarence brought a fast whistle through his teeth.
"Good God!"

The taillights of the car were like red votive candles followed
by two pale streamers. Soon there was the squealing of tires at a
corner, and Clarence saw a fuzz of light over the trees, moving
south.

He heard his wife call out a question to him from the staircase.
Her voice was high and stressed.

He answered her immediately: "Dansville!"

"Is he going to . . . to Mrs. Menutis?"

He was; and he was going to make her a radical proposition
that he had been contemplating for a long time, ever since the
first bloom of his infatuation for Shirlee had faded, and he had
fallen into the tedium of a long engagement. It was not that he
would have denied Shirlee; she was simply a different kind of a
companion, a helpmate necessary to his future. Yet he felt that
his health was sinking; he craved joy. He was a vigorous man,
and he needed not only the body of a certain kind of woman but
her spirit as well. He needed someone who could come back at
him, one for one, an equal. He needed to be loved completely,
and he knew where he could get that, where he could get excitement and pleasure and peace.

Just beyond the pink stucco gates that marked the entrance to
his neighborhood, just before he reached the highway to Victoria,
he lit a cigarette and rested his arm on the edge of the open
window. As he drove, passing through towns where street lights
shone only along the main avenues, commercial establishments
shut their doors at dinnertime, and the last showing of the movie
had finished two hours before he had left the party at the club,
images of the woman flashed before him in recollection, causing
expressions of content and anticipation to alternate on his face
until he was in Dansville, slowing down on Main Street, slowing
down particularly as he passed the dark service station where he
could be sure that, in the shade of the porch roof, in his black
ensigned car, Lonnie Teague waited like a lynx in his cavern.
Lonnie had never had a good word for him since the night in the
dance hall when he and Gerdine had fought over Elaine; yet now
he saw him raise a thick, dark hand in a gesture that seemed a
return of his greeting rather than a warning. He even thought he
saw the flash of a smile.

Her house had never seemed so far from the courthouse

square. When he did pull up in the car before it, he stopped for a moment to look at the garden and the moonlit fields behind, at this landscape that had seen so much of his history. All his sentimental attachments to people and events seemed to spring from this place.

He had expected to see Elaine's truck in the drive; he imagined that it must be behind the closed doors of the garage. It seemed odd that there were no baskets of fern hanging from the eaves of the porch, and that the lawn chairs were gone; but everything else was as he remembered it: the stone walk, the neat flower beds, the swing on the porch. The house, hit full by the moon, appeared small and vulnerable. He had spent so much of his time during the past year in large places—his own home, the huge houses of his friends, the immense law library, the great lecture halls—that the contrast hurt him. *I'll have to do better for her,* he thought. He had lived with her for too long on credit; he would have to make that debt good. He wanted to do wonderful things for her; she would have missed him; she would let him help her now.

A light went on in the bedroom, then was so quickly extinguished that he assumed the unexpected visit had frightened her. He regretted that he hadn't telephoned from Houston, but there hadn't seemed to be time. She must have heard his car pull up, then heard the car door close, though he had tried to close it softly. His heart pounded against his ribs; his breath was short. He should wait here a moment; he shouldn't let her see him like this. No—maybe she would be pleased to see that the anticipation of making love to her could still affect him this way, that in this respect, nothing was different, nothing had changed. He wondered what she was feeling. Whenever he had wakened her in the past, she had tried to prepare herself for him in some way. He had never been as fastidious: When he wanted her, he took her as fast as she would let him, with nothing else on his mind. With Elaine, delays annoyed him; they would surely annoy him tonight. But he would, he realized, have to be careful with her. If she wanted to dawdle around in the bathroom; if she wanted to talk to him awhile from that straight-backed chair she liked to sit in when she was playing mother instead of mistress; if it would please her to sit awhile on the porch, drinking the champagne and telling him of her activities of this past year, he would be obliging. He would court her again; he would do whatever she wished. Absolutely. He had been right to bring presents; he was happy that he'd taken the time to get them.

He went to the gate and opened the clasp carefully. He would
not rush at her; he would go slowly. Would she approve of his
acquired gentleness, a by-product of his relationship with Shirlee? She would probably tease him, but she would like it. And if
she didn't, he would forget what he had learned, or put it away
for her. He could be two people, two men. He would have to be.
He looked down at his clothes; he was a little mussed up, but she
had always liked the way he dressed—she sure as hell would
have rejected that man who had stood in a receiving line four or
five hours ago wearing a black suit with a satin stripe down the
side of the pants and a white shirt with a collar so stiff it burned
his neck.

Stepping out of the shadows of the trees holding the flowers
over his arm and the champagne in his hand, he was bathed in the
same flood of moonlight that washed the house and the garden.
The stones on the front walk felt familiar under his feet. *In minutes,* he thought. Even if she were hurt, still a little mad, he knew
he could coax her to him; even if she upbraided him a little and
tried to start a quarrel, he would be patient. She might be intractable, difficult, even vicious, but he planned to let her air her
grievances against him without uttering a word to defend himself.
Then after a time she would forgive him. He was certain of it. He
knew her emotions like a thief knows safes; he had studied and
learned the combination to every one of them. He could always
get her to give in to him, to become suddenly warm and soft and
ready. He could do that with Elaine. He imagined that it was her
flesh that gave up to his, never her will to his will, nor at that
moment did he remember that he had ever wanted any other kind
of submission from her. The worn soles of his boots brushed the
steps. He touched the swing and smiled; he could never pass it
and leave it still. Holding the screen door open with his shoulder,
he put his key in the lock.

With the quiet alertness of someone for whom the predictable
sequence of events has changed radically, Hugh sat up straight
behind the wheel. It seemed to him that he had been in the car on
a highway for days, watching the center stripe of a road. He had
forgotten the party at the club; had anyone asked him about any
detail of it, he could have given no information. Only one fact
existed for him, one question, one problem, one acute sadness.
There was room for nothing else in his mind.

His gaze was steady, transfixed, and his mouth was strained.
He did not think he had ever had a headache in his life, but now

his eyes were heavy; a dull pain began to throb behind his lids, and he could feel it getting worse. The monotony of the road, the failure of the trip to end quickly, annoyed him and set him on edge.

When he arrived at the ranch, it was nearly three A.M., and the poker game in the bunkhouse living room was just finishing up. There were no visitors; five players were present instead of the regular seven.

With a sleeping baby lying across her lap, Lettie Kelly was sitting quietly behind her husband. She was the first to see Hugh, and she gave him a feeble wave of her hand. If he saw her greeting, or noticed her at all, he gave no sign of it. That a man of the stature of Luther Kelly had married a woman like Lettie was understood by Hugh as one of those anomalies that crowd into perception and are changed or integrated there; only this one hadn't changed and hadn't been softened by time, circumstance, or his own maturity. He never paid any attention to her except to tease her, and because of Luther, he was careful about how he did that.

He stood in the door a minute, unsure of what he wanted to say, and realizing that he had forgotten how to talk to these people. It had been months since he had seen Matt—he had made no telephone calls, sent no letters—and Matt had been unhappy with him the last time they had been together. A stable had had to be built for the English Thoroughbreds that Mrs. Littleton wanted imported, a stable and fences painted white like the ones she had seen on her trip to her cousin's in Virginia. In the past, Hugh would have objected to this kind of waste, which demoralized the cowboys and embarrassed Matt in front of the foremen of the ranches that were run for profit, but at that time, he had just been implementing a decision already made, something Clarence had given in to; his heart and mind had been elsewhere. Hugh was losing sight of what was important; Matt realized it, and it hurt him. Hugh had even left before lunch, though the women, knowing he was coming, had cooked what he liked.

"You're getting white and lazy," Matt had said as he was leaving. Until then he had avoided personal questions, or any comments at all that did not have to do with the business that Hugh had come for. He had crushed out his cigarette in an empty coffee cup, making it stagger in its saucer. "You better come out here and herd some beef for me, Hugh. City life don't agree with you."

"I've got all I can do," he had answered.

Yet Matt never allowed the ranch community any criticism of Hugh: "You hogtie a calf like he does, you ride a bronco as well as he does, and then you can talk to me about him. He ain't no sissy sitting around here while the others work. I never was out with him that he didn't work double to what I did." All of this was said without passion, but he was inflexible in his defense. "Whatever you think, he's boss, or he will be one day. So you keep your mouths shut. Clarence don't think like you do. That's his boy; we don't need to pass no judgment on that part of our boss's fortune."

So now, after Matt had glanced up and seen him, he shifted his attention back to the poker table. "What brings you down here? The game's closing. You come here a little earlier, and we'd have dealt you in."

Luther leaned back in his chair and smiled. He twisted his fingers together and stretched them back to crack his knuckles, but Lettie touched his shoulder, so instead he folded his big hands across his chest. "Where's your lady, Hugh?" he asked teasingly. "She don't stay up so late? Or was one visit here enough for her? We too rough and dirty?"

"She'll be back," said Hugh. He stumbled over the words because they were far from his mind. "She liked it all right," he added after a bit, as if his first statement needed explanation.

Mark slid his chair back and stood up, as did Alton Higgins and moments later Stephen, but none of them moved to leave. They asked Hugh about school, his grades, how he liked the life in Austin, and after answering them quickly, he suddenly said, a bit too peremptorily to settle well with any of the men: "I'd like to talk to you, Matt."

Matt moved a stack of white chips toward the container. "Okay, I ain't going nowhere . . . got no appointments." He glanced around. "You're not honoring us with your company for the night?"

"No."

While the men cashed in their chips, Hugh was silent, and they were careful to look away from him. He used to be their friend, but now he was their boss, a carbon copy of the man who came down occasionally to pay his respects, do a little hunting, take a look at his prize animals, ask Luther a few questions, and give orders to Matt. Hugh was no longer the young man with whom they used to ride, or play cards, or cut up with in town. Ill at ease, they counted and pocketed their winnings with exaggerated care and left, walking slowly and throwing glances at each other that didn't quite make contact. Only Luther and Lettie stayed behind—Luther because he did not believe that Hugh's implicit request for privacy had been meant to exclude him, and Lettie because she was unwilling to leave. Luther took a cup off a hook and lifted the coffeepot from the warmer. He spooned sugar into the pungent circle of heat, and then held the cup all around with his thick fingers, as if something other than the weather made him need to warm his hands.

Hugh watched him. Luther looked like he was waiting for the opportunity to deliver one of his short, quiet sermons, the ones he put his heart into, that he had thought about for maybe a long time, knowing that the moment would come when he could say what he had to say, and being sure that it would be what he meant to say because he'd culled out all the nonsense during his long periods of silence. But when he spoke again, it was still about Shirlee. "I guess we didn't have a horse gentle enough for her," he said, trying to figure out the arrangement that Hugh had with this girl that he seemed to like so much, but who didn't match up with him—for no careful livestock breeder would put animals of as disparate temperaments as Hugh and Shirlee together in a million years.

Hugh knew that Luther would never say anything derisive about Shirlee, so that could not be the subject he was leading up to. He looked at Luther as if he'd offered something significant, but Luther only pulled the chair that Alton had been sitting in away from the table, as if inviting Hugh to sit down. Hugh remained standing and looked back to Matt, who was now leaning over the table, stacking the chips in the cups of the container.

Matt avoided asking Hugh why he was there, what problem he might have that he couldn't figure out for himself. Hugh was so book smart, so dollars and cents smart, so careful with that part of his head. It was the other part that he was unable to handle. And he was a big man, as big as Clarence now, strong as hell, and filthy rich. But he was so goddamned selfish; he was an arrogant aristocrat in a land where, to Matt's thinking, there shouldn't be any.

Clarence was different; Clarence was like a lizard changing colors to suit everybody—to fool them, too. And down here? Oh, God, he played the egalitarian game. But never Hugh. He looked hard and steady into the young man's black eyes. Never Hugh. Look at the way he had walked in here tonight among these men who would willingly break their necks for him and his daddy, yet hardly given anybody the time of day. He'd had that woman and trampled over her, too. With half a lick of imagination, any man just seeing those two together would know what they did when they shut the door of that little house in town, and squirm in his chair or in his saddle just thinking about it, yet Hugh had left all that, and as far as Matt knew, had never looked back.

Interrupting his task, Matt took a cigarette, and even though there was no wind, he cupped a trembling hand to light it. He sat back in his chair and stretched out his legs, habitually crossing his ankles so his legs would not bow or look so old and gnarled. He was playing host, keeping the distance between him and Hugh as long as he could. "You want a beer?"

"No."

"No?" He could tell when Hugh had come in that, although he now showed no signs of drunkenness, he must have been drinking earlier.

"I'm going to stay sober awhile," Hugh said. "Maybe I'll be able to figure out what's happened to me."

He sat down in the chair Luther had offered, but he addressed Matt. He leaned forward, his hands hanging over his knees, and squinted a little, as if he were expecting a blow or bad news. "Where's Elaine?" he asked Matt. "The lady I just woke up says she's renting the house, that she's been renting it since last summer. She says she takes her rent check to Felix Fuller; she's hardly even seen Elaine." His speech had already slipped into an easy drawl, but he still intended to lead the conversation and keep Matt from either changing the subject or lecturing him, because right now he didn't have the patience for either. "Where's my girl, Matt?"

Hugh saw Matt wince at his last question, but he went right on looking at him, expecting an answer. Matt picked up the cards and shuffled the deck in his short, scarred hands. He turned the first card up, then placed six more side by side, face down. The cards clicked one by one as he made the seven ordered piles. He turned them up until no more of them worked, and then he went through the deck, making more noise than he needed to. He would never get away with what he had rehearsed, but he would try it, and at least his face wouldn't give him away too soon. He put a red queen on a black king, then turned up the jack of spades.

"Do you know where she is?" Hugh was making an obvious effort to be patient with Matt, knowing that somehow he had wronged these people, and that because he had wronged them, everything was going to be difficult for him now. Stephen, Mark, and Alton had scarcely been cordial, Luther was acting funny, and Matt was mad.

The rudeness of Matt's silence crushed Luther; Hugh might have made a few mistakes, but punishing him in this way was wrong. "She went home," he said quietly. "I think she's with her folks."

Hugh's head jerked around. "Since when?"

"Since sometime last summer."

"Is she coming back?"

"Maybe. No one hears from her."

"You know why she left? She marry someone up there?"

"Might have. We ain't heard."

Luther was finished talking and went back to looking at his coffee. Stirring nervously in his chair, Matt took off his hat and threw it on the table, scattering the remaining chips. Lettie leaned down to pick up the half dozen that had sprinkled at her feet and then reached over to put them in the cups of the container. The baby fretted, and she whispered something to calm him. Her eyes went back and forth among the three men, but so that Luther would let her stay, she kept as still as possible, hardly breathing; and she made an effort to keep the baby hushed, too. Her mouth began to tremble as it did when she was planning to do something that Luther disliked. Luther saw it.

Matt turned all the cards up and shuffled them.

"Why do you think she went home?" asked Hugh. "She had everything here. The business, I mean. She would need the money."

He felt awkward talking while the others were silent. He had sent her money. She could have lived off that awhile, and he would have sent her much more if she had ever asked him for it, but she never wrote him, not even after she had cashed the check. But then, he had included no letter with the money; he had let his banker take care of the matter, handle everything. He had thought it better to leave her alone, to make a clean break because of Shirlee, and perhaps Elaine had resented that.

He hesitated before asking what he hated to ask these men because he knew that Matt, at least, was angry about him and Elaine, and that he stayed that way most of the time. "You think it had to do with our breaking up . . . that she left town?"

"That's unusually sensitive of you, Hugh," said Matt, swinging around to him. "That could have been one of the reasons, I guess. Might have been a few well-meaning people thought she'd got what she had coming—little country girl thinking she could keep your attention. But then, you left out of here. If there were any stones thrown, they missed you. You didn't even have to bother yourself to defend her, neither . . . that's not so bad."

Hugh was silent, and Luther had bent his head down a little. Lettie started to speak, but then she sat back in the chair with her troubled eyes on Luther's broad head and kept still. When the baby began to cry, she picked him up and put him over her shoulder, singing under her breath one of the nursery tunes she had learned from Opal.

"He's got fever and a sore throat," she said softly. "That's why I'm sitting up with him." Turning her head, she strained her neck to look at the baby's face. His eyes were closed, but he was frowning and moving his mouth. "He's taking penicillin," she added proudly. She wanted it known that when their children were sick, they were taken to a doctor, and expensive medicine was prescribed, and that, without it hurting them at all, Luther paid for it and paid the doctor, too. Some people were fast about calling the doctor, and slow in paying him, but not Luther. He said you can never ask a man for his services and then fail to pay him in the same spirit in which you asked for his help. You either have the money or you don't, he said. He wouldn't buy a truck on time, as the other families did, and he'd even paid cash for all the furniture for the babies, the new record player, the section of land west of El Campo, the Chevrolet sedan for her and the kids, everything.

Lettie continued murmuring to the baby, whose head lay on her shoulder and whose full, rounded arm fell limply across her back. He was a big baby, almost six months. They had been married more than five years, and this was her third child. Luther had said three, but she planned on four. With the beef herd on the new land, there was plenty of money for kids—there was plenty anyway. And she wasn't ugly when she was pregnant; Luther liked her just as well, and came to her just as regular. Pregnancy never made her feel lazy or lose her color, either, like some women—Valerie Higgins, Alton's wife, for instance. She got her work done no matter how tired she was; she never complained of the heat the baby made for her; and she made a point of walking quick and light; as if she weren't off balance or carrying a burden.

"Take him to bed," Luther finally said as the baby woke again and began to cry. "He'll sleep better, be better off."

Lettie stiffened a little but said with a quiet, false submissiveness, "He's all right."

"Go on, Lettie." Luther shot her a warning glance, and she knew she was trying his patience.

"I ain't at all tired," she said carefully. She shifted the baby on her shoulder. "Now, don't talk so loud and bother him, honey."

She picked up a cigarette, which looked unusually large in her little mouth; Luther removed it. She frowned, but when his hard look remained unchanged, she eased into a smile.

She stood up then and walked to the corner of the room, an area where the light from the lamp over the table could not reach, her pale hair and slender body moving into the dark pinched angle of the room. She would hardly trouble anyone, and if she could just keep the baby still, she could stay.

Hugh sat at the table, his arms crossed tightly over his chest, his expression as steady as he could manage, patient in the way he knew he would have to be if he wanted to get any more information out of them at all. They were balking; he didn't know why, but unless he was watchful now, unless he avoided a misstep, he would have to stay here the entire weekend to find out what he needed to know. "It's not likely that Elaine let herself be run out of town," he said. "I won't buy that."

Matt sat upright and pulled himself nearer to the cards, scraping the floor with his chair as he did so. "You may have to."

"Maybe so, Matt."

"You ain't seen her, then?"

"No."

"How long?"

"Maybe a year."

Matt had been sorting out the suits to see if a card was missing from an old deck he had found in the table drawer. "You write to her?" he asked.

"No."

"You send her money?" He picked up a pack of cigarettes from the table, shook one partway out, offered it to Hugh, and took one for himself. In a half-closed hand, he struck a match and held it for Hugh; then off the same match, burned down so low now that it must have hurt him, he lighted his own. In the close air, the smoke clouded around both their heads.

"Yes."

"She take it?" Matt asked, without lifting his eyes. "She take money from you?"

"Once . . . she did once."

Matt left the cigarette in his mouth, and when he talked, the end of it bobbed like a struck cork. He squinted an eye when the smoke rose along one side of his face. An ash dropped on the felt-covered table and disintegrated in the deep sigh he let out of his open mouth in a breathy whistle. "Only once?" His tone was that of a priest behind a screen.

Hugh nodded.

"Huh?"

"Yes . . . once."

"How much?"

"Two thousand."

Matt whistled. "Knowing you, you got off cheap. How many visits you figure that paid for?" He lifted his hand as if to ward off an answer.

Luther had leaned back in his chair, still holding his cup, letting his coffee get cold. He followed the conversation diffidently and made no attempt to join in it.

"The one you're getting married to . . . does she know about you and Mrs. Menutis?" asked Matt. He started to smile and then thought better of it. He began making the seven piles again. Hugh leaned over him and placed a two of hearts on a free ace.

Matt turned his head sideways. "If you're getting married in June, Hugh, what were you doing in Dansville after hours? That little blond fiancée know about that? Or is this business conducted on the side?" His expression was ironic and showed not a spark of good will. He shuffled his feet on the hard wood floor, dragging the heels of his boots against the much eroded grain. "God, you ain't even married yet, and you're looking backward."

Hugh held his temper down and started to say something that he thought would amuse Matt, but Matt lifted his hands up toward him, almost touching his face, and shook his head. "It's none of my business," he said, a muscle in his cheek twitching. "I'm out of it. Don't explain nothing to me."

He stood up, and Hugh followed suit, so that they faced each other. "I don't see how it's helping anybody, your coming down here right now . . . unless, that is, you've changed your mind about something."

"And I don't see why this has you so upset, Matt. Why are you riding me so close about Elaine? Why don't you give up trying to keep me out of that house where I'm invited, buddy?"

Matt refused to raise his eyes. "You ain't invited now."

"That pleases you, doesn't it, Matt?"

"In a way."

"It's none of your goddamned business."

Matt screwed up his mouth and nodded. "You're making it my business by coming down here, stud. I didn't send you no engraved invitation to pay me a visit and badger me about her." He turned around, glanced quickly at Luther and then back at Hugh's chin. "You're getting ready to marry and settle down. I just want you to get on with it, that's all."

"I don't believe you."

Matt looked up then. His eyes were focused sharply on the young man. He was extremely myopic, and at that time of night, the pupils of his eyes were huge. "I don't care what you believe, Hugh. That's one thing don't trouble me a damn no more."

"Then why the hell are you so mad?"

Lettie had stopped walking the baby, and he rested quietly on her shoulder. She faced the men, the light rippling the willowy length of her form, and stared at them all accusingly, a separate offense incriminating each of them. Lettie's judgment was always harsh; she took it for granted that other people had not suffered as much as she had; in order to even the ledger, she reacted severely, always on the flashing crest of any action. Matt and Hugh ignored her since, as yet, she had said nothing. But Luther kept his eye on her, in the same way he kept his attention on any maverick in the herd. From the first, he had always had to be vigilant, and by now it was second nature; if he failed to watch after her, he would pay for it in some way.

Yet, especially under these circumstances, Luther was strangely curious to see what Lettie would do; her outspokenness was the one serious fault he found in her, but paradoxically it was an aspect of her character that he also loved and respected. Perhaps it was because he saw how she strained to enter the mainstream of civilized humanity, yet retained her feral orneriness, which neither time nor domestication nor his guidance could completely eradicate.

She stood there watching awhile in a position that, because of the weight of the baby, might have been uncomfortable, but if it was, she never showed it. Her body seemed elongated and strong.

Hugh looked down at Matt and tried again. "Why are you so mad, Matt?"

"Hell, Hugh, I thought you had all the answers." Matt laughed insultingly and, to make it worse, said incautiously: "Ain't you the one used to be the expert on Elaine? Everyone in town sure thought so."

Hugh drew himself up, blinking his eyes once, and his face became rigid. The vulgarity, the crudeness, the officious, stubborn righteousness of Matt, which had so often in the past amused him, even when directed at him, ground into him this time and cracked his composure like a stone pestle on a piece of newly fired bisque. He hated Matt, and as in the old days, he wanted to fight him. His jaw trembled and sweat broke out on his forehead. "Get off me, Matt!" he shouted.

Hugh could be dangerous when he was mad, and though Matt was not afraid of him (like an old wolf, a veteran of disasters, he was too seasoned to scare), he knew the game was over. He half-closed his eyes and spoke quickly: "She said she don't want you coming around her no more. I went to see her a couple of days before she left. I'm just delivering that message. That's what she told me to say, and only if you was to ask about her. She said I wasn't supposed to get in touch with you or volunteer nothing. There was no reason for me to go against her." He waited. "I'm sorry if it hurts you."

But Matt didn't sound sorry—Hugh had seen him use this blend of sarcasm and good will on cowboys whom he intended, by the end of the interview, to have set straight or fired—and Hugh was not hurt, he was startled. Why would she say anything like that to Matt? What the hell was Matt doing at her house? He grabbed his father's foreman by the arm. "What is it, Matt?" he asked. "Did she talk to you about me? What did she say?"

"She didn't say nothing else, but what I told you . . . but I'm saying this: You ran her for all she was worth, you got tired of her, and left her. Okay? That's okay, Hugh. She knew what she had when she took up with you, and as far as I'm concerned, she deserved what she got for doing that. She stood by with a contented smile on her pretty face and let you ram it down the throats of everybody in town that you were going to live with her in plain sight and beat the tar out of any decent man who chose to court her. If the folks with families disapproved, that was tough! She knew what I thought. Hell, I told her." He crushed out his cigarette and picked up his hat to leave. "Well, she had her party. I wouldn't give nothing for either one of you, and I ain't defending Mrs. Menutis!"

But he *was* defending her; Hugh knew the style of Matt's rhetoric; and he knew that Matt was taking her part. Hugh gave Luther a look of supplication. "What the hell's going on?" he asked him.

Luther threw a quick glance at Matt. There was a trace of

alarm in it, but Matt's face stayed expressionless. Yielding to the foreman's wish, Luther, his eyes shifting from embarrassment, replied slowly, "Matt told you what she said. She said she don't need nothing from you, and not to tell you where she was."

It didn't fit. Elaine would never do that to him. She had never denied him her company, never once. There wasn't one chance in a thousand that she would refuse to see him now. He lost his temper in the same way that he would have lost it a dozen years before if Matt had refused him a ride on a wild horse, or not let him accompany him into the sleet to find a stray animal. "Matt's a liar!" he cried. "Matt's a goddamned liar!"

Matt let out a yell, and though Hugh ducked the first punch, which he had seen coming (he knew that nobody could call Matt what he had called him with impunity), the next one got him in the center of his chin.

Five years earlier that blow, placed where it was, would have knocked him out, and right now someone would have had to be pouring cold water over his face and slapping his cheeks; but Matt was not as strong as he used to be, and Hugh was solider and bigger. Still, it caused him to stagger, to cry out in pain, and to catch himself on a chair to keep from falling. His stomach churned, and his legs almost deserted him.

Matt beckoned to him; he was hunched, waiting.

"I'm not going to touch you, you crazy bastard," Hugh whispered. He was breathing heavily, and blood was dripping from his lip onto the boot-shined, sand-colored floor. "Everyone around me is nuts!"

"You got your share."

Feeling as if he had a knife in the back of his neck causing a pain that was going to cut off his head, Hugh looked at the old rancher, who, tense and breathing hard, was watching him, still expecting the fistfight that he had started to be continued, unable to believe that he could hit Hugh that hard and not lose a lot of skin for doing it.

Hugh raised his hand to calm Matt and said, "Tell me why in the hell you're so goddamned mad at me, Matt. Why does my wanting to see Elaine get to you so much? You beating me up for you or for her? Huh? What's going on? You want to tell me what I did?" His voice broke because of the pain.

"I'm sick and tired of you running over everything comes in your way. I'm not going to try to fix that up no more."

"Elaine?" he yelled. "Running over Elaine? You told me for years, Matt, to end it with her! What are you talking about? You wanted it over, Matt, and so did Dad. Why do you think it's over? Because you liked it the way it was? I thought you'd have a celebration when I got engaged! You ran the hell over *me*!"

Matt waved his hand toward the door. "You gone crazy, Hugh? Get out of here! Why don't you go the hell back where you belong?"

Hugh tensed, but he kept still. "Where do I belong, Matt?" he said. "You tell me. Say what you think for once without protecting Dad's interests."

From the corner, there had been a cry of indignation when the blow was struck, followed by a moan. Now the baby began to whimper, feverish and sick, and Luther, knowing the limits of his wife's understanding and guessing what was about to happen, was immediately beside Lettie. But she avoided him successfully (she was agile even under the burden of the infant), wiped the tears off her own face, and shouted at Matt. Matt stood stark still, the lower part of him in the circle of light, the upper, unreadable in the shadow. By then, Hugh was standing beside Lettie, too, because he finally understood what everyone else already knew: that it was Lettie who was going to tell him what he needed to hear.

"Ain't you ever going to tell him the truth, Matt?" she cried, looking at Hugh, her wet eyes blazing. "Ain't you going to give him a chance to do nothing about it?"

"Lettie!" She was going to defy Luther; he foresaw everything that was going to happen. "No, honey." He was trying to herd her, nipping at her with words, gestures, and looks, as a good shepherd dog nips at a lamb. She broke away from him. She had that expression that he knew so well and feared so much.

Hugh wiped the blood off his face with his handkerchief, smoothed his shirt, and ran his fingers through his rumpled hair. Unconsciously he moved closer to her, and he nudged her hand when she did not speak at once.

Her glittering eyes stayed fixed on Hugh, and every word she said was directed at him. There was, in fact, little to say, and since, by her revolt, she had risked unleashing her husband's rare but unpleasant rage, she did not wait to see the color leave Hugh's face, or for a flash of comprehension, awe, shock, and terror to seize him, or for the imprecations, not so much against Matt and Luther for keeping him ignorant as against his own lack of prescience and the pettish incorrigibility of fate. She banged the screen door behind her; the disturbed baby shrieked and only seemed quieted by the increasing distance Lettie was putting so quickly between herself and the bunkhouse.

Hugh's eyes looked anxiously for something to focus on, but found nothing. In an instant, his life had been totally altered. It was richer—a trouble, certainly, but richer, and he was unable to be sorry about it; it would be the worst error of his life if he were sorry about this. His face broke into a smile that would stay with him for the rest of the time he was in the room.

"Okay," he said aloud, but largely to himself. "So that's how it is." With her it would be hard, but on the other hand, with her, he could always set things right. All he had to do was to visit her, let her see him. A year ago she would have done anything for him, anything, and she had loved him. Chances were good that she still did. She would let him fix this; she'd have to, because no one else would care about it as he did. God, she must have a world of backs turned on her.

He walked over and stood behind Matt, who was facing the window away from him. He put his hand on Matt's shoulder and closed his eyes. "Oh, Matt," he said, trying to stop smiling, since it hurt his bleeding mouth.

Matt kept perfectly still, unsure what emotion he wanted to show; though he promised himself when this was all over, he was sure as hell going to kill Lettie Kelly and fire Luther. "I first figure she was still crazy from what she did," Matt said, "from being in the hospital and all, and then I started thinking that she was right. She said she'd handle it . . . that it would mess you up."

"Oh, it does," said Hugh slowly. "It does, my God."

"You going out there?"

"Yeah."

"Now?"

"Right now."

"Don't you think you ought to rest awhile, go in the morning, after you've had some sleep and can figure out what to do?"

"I know what to do." Hugh bent around so he could see Matt's face. "You're going to see, Matt." He laughed in his throat, but that hurt him, too. "I think I'll just let you wait and see . . ." He pulled at the old man's shirt. "You going to apologize for busting me up?"

Matt was silent.

"I didn't think so."

He slid his hand down to Matt's arm for a moment, and then he let it slip down to the table. He picked up a blue chip that Matt had overlooked when he was sorting the colors, turned it over a couple of times, and flung it onto the table, where it twirled. He stepped away from Matt, away from Luther, away from the place where he had last seen Lettie Kelly, and was out of the room and on his way to central Texas before it fell.

Luther stood in the center of the room, his hat in his hands, waiting for Matt to say the first word, but when Matt ignored him, opening the cupboard and replacing the poker chips, then returning the Mason jar of cornflowers to the center of the table, he said, "She don't know any better, Matt."

Matt's gaze shot to Luther. "Can't you ever do anything about Lettie?" he asked. "You haven't got one ounce of control over her. There's little kids here less out of control than your wife." He took a beer out of the cooler and opened it harshly on an opener fixed to the wall, then leaned over to keep the foam from soiling his shirt.

Luther knew that Matt wanted him to be tough on Lettie and to let him see that he was, but punishing her or making her feel uneasy for too long was something he would never do. "There's things she just can't learn," he said.

Matt felt uncomfortable to see Luther standing for so long in one place, waiting to be forgiven and dismissed. "Well, it's over," he said quietly. "Don't think about it anymore. I don't plan to."

Luther smoothed the front of his hair with his hand and slipped on his hat. "Just the same, I'm sorry for what she done. She causes trouble, and I know it, and if you want us gone, Matt . . ."

Matt interrupted him. "If ever I want you gone, I'll let you know." His irritation at Luther was finished. "We ain't nowhere close to that."

Luther started to leave, then turned back to say something more, but Matt spoke first, "You riding with me to Llano on Tuesday?" Matt was going to a cattle sale.

"Sure."

Matt pointed to the cooler. "You want a drink before you go to bed?"

Luther nodded, reached into the cooler and took out two grape sodas, one for him and one for the woman who would be looking out the window for him to come up the path and who was surely planning to speak to him softly and to put her arms around him before he could even say anything; and if she was scared enough, she'd be crying. He started once again to defend her, but realizing in the tense way that Matt was staring at him, that for the present Matt had heard all he was going to about Lettie, he moved into the shadows, opened the door, and was gone.

Matt turned off the bunkhouse light and went out on the porch to sit in the dark. Because the weather was turning, the animals were milling around in the pens, and the night birds were silent. Something was walking slowly in the flowers, an armadillo or one of the stray cats, wild things that hunted rats and field mice and snuck onto the porch for the leftover food the women scraped from tin plates. They never became tame; they would run away if you approached them, slinking tight to the ground, to disappear behind the golden lantana and the privet hedges that were thick and snowy with winged mites. And you never saw them in the daytime.

He put his feet on the porch rail and shut his eyes, and as often happened when he was alone, there rose before him the cornfield in front of his own farm, and himself a young man, big, vigorous, and not needing naps or dozing off in front of people but able to stay up all night drinking and never feel it; when he would sit on his own porch, which, though of a building of poorer construction and a tenth the space of this one behind him now, was nevertheless all his own (he had built it), as were the acres that stretched in front of him to the road and to the near hill. The stock had been his, and behind him in the house was the excessively difficult woman, who, according to his understanding of the law and the Bible was his, too, but who had given him so much pain by leaving him, drawn back to her folks whenever the least little thing went wrong: the drought he could do nothing about; the early frost; the tweed divan that she wanted but that he was unable to buy her until the following year; the garden he had no time to work on until he had brought in the crops. And her father had defended her right to leave him so emphatically that, after a while, Matt had had to give up going to collect her, since the sheriff had put him in jail both for shooting his father-in-law in the thigh (a shot the old man had returned grazed his own cheek), and to keep him safe from his wife's brothers. After a week or two, though, she would come back to him on her own, arriving silently with her eyes cast down, sulky or bitter, or both, but wanting something that she knew he would get for her, without her ever having to ask him twice, or even be especially cordial about it. She would move around their house, straightening things, preparing his meals, as if she had never left, and him hardly daring even to welcome her back. He would watch her cautiously, not wanting to say anything to her that might bring on another one of those arguments that might make her withdraw coldly into herself, to sleep on the old divan or to leave him again—though never in the heat of an argument, as normal people do, but fleeing when his back was turned, when he thought the problem was solved, when he had to be away working, out of sight of the house. When he returned home at the end of the day, he would sense that it was too quiet and begin looking for her, shouting and finally screaming to keep from exploding from the anguish she caused him. He would try to overtake her, but she would have calculated perfectly her lead time. He was left imagining that she had taken the company of the world with her, and that he was now finally and completely alone.

He had met her at church, and though she was plain and never said much—a quality that he had mistaken for serenity rather than sullenness—he had, at eighteen, loved her for her dignified, mysterious, and silent reserve, and for the fact that she had seemed to like him. After a few months of accepting his presents (a box of candy, a pair of red wool gloves, and finally a watch), she had accepted his promise that they would have a farm of their own, and then, his proposal.

He had loved her for twenty-five years without the briefest remittance and with only the slightest encouragement on her part. Until her death, she had seemed only to tolerate him, observing his passion for her as a spectator at a sideshow observes with horror and pity, but without the least involvement, one of nature's unfortunate creatures. She had been able to give him but one child, a frail baby that had died six weeks after his birth; afterward, she had never been able to carry another for more than a few months and was left so ill as a result that he feared to touch her. He saw her often in these quiet, late-night visions, in the shady wake of time, and a longing for her came over him. There remained in him an empty place that he had neither filled nor cared to fill with another woman; partly because he could not have borne being wounded again, but mostly because he despaired of ever finding one.

He thought about Hugh and the woman he had so nearly destroyed that she wanted to die of it. He wondered how it would be when they met and what would happen to them—if they would wreck it or pull it back together.

"It won't ever be the same," he whispered to the agitated night, whose winds blew hard in gusts and exposed the stars between the lashed limbs of the oak. "No, God. And this past year of getting citified and reading the law ain't going to help him with Mrs. Menutis, either. She'll hate it, and she'll let him know. Like I did."

The distant wailing of a baby reminded him of what a nuisance Lettie was. Witnessing her outburst had been like watching storm clouds that have already torn up everything in their path swing back around to cause even more damage:

"Elaine's got her a baby girl, Hugh. It's younger than mine, but it ain't quite brand new." She had patted her child to confirm that it was a baby she was talking about. "Lily Fuller seen it. I asked her who it looked like, and she said, 'Ain't Hugh Littleton her daddy?' I said I guessed so because she never stayed with no one else . . . not since I knew her." Lettie's eyes had darted to Luther, and then she had begun to sob. It was hard to understand her. "She told Lily she has to give it up, because she can't stay in town and make no living. Hugh, you listen . . ." Then her voice went completely. Little bitch cur.

Chapter 9

IT WAS AS if Foley were there with her, outside somewhere in the shop or in the barn, helping her father mend a saddle or repair a harness. She could almost look out the window and see him striding back to the porch with something to tell her or something he had made for her and wanted her to see. As the time for her confinement approached, her imagination became more and more often filled with her husband—not with memories of him, but with scenes of what might have been if he had returned home, as grieved and confused by the war as his letters had suggested, but basically the same, and after a while, completely restored to her.

The pregnancy had retrieved her from sadness, enabling her spirit to skim by it prudently, like a car holding to the edge of a mountain road. After she had gone to waken her mother early one morning as the yellow dawn melted the helplessness of her sleepless night, she did not have the crippling pain she had experienced when her other children had been born. She didn't know why—maybe her maturity accounted for it—but this baby was easier: The clawing at her lower back failed to hurt her, and the constricting steel band that stretched around her failed to make her fearful. This birth was different; she was somehow able to go out to the pain and confront it, and then to turn it away. It was only near the finish that she lost control and vented her terrific suffering in moans and stifled cries in which she had said her husband's name, calling to him in her delirium.

But almost at once, she heard her mother and the hired hand's wife crying with relief, and then the baby, too. She saw the child lying across her, splotched with blood. "Sophie," she whispered.

Her mother thought that she was calling to her, and she came close to listen.

Elaine shook her head and touched her child. "No," she said, "it's her name." She felt the full curve of the baby's back and its strong little chest expand.

When physical peace came to her again, when she lay washed and cool and drowsy with the child asleep in the curve of her arm, she dreamed of Foley crossing the room, as he had done the other times her babies were born; and as she drifted into sleep, it seemed that the big blond man had pulled a chair close to the bed and eased himself down beside her. The breeze came in from behind him, folding back the hems of the white curtains, lifting the edge of the lace doily on the dresser, and then sweeping into his thick hair. He was there to help her as he had always been before; he would take her and the baby home. When her mother had given the word that the convalescence was finished, he would carry her downstairs in his arms, put her in the car, and they would resume their lives again with a slightly fuller family. In her dream, she thought, *Foley won't care that she's not his baby; he will love her because she's mine*.

But this baby was not Foley's. Not blond and fair like Jimmy and Laura . . . Laura, her little girl who had died before she could quite walk, when she was still holding on to the edges of tables and chairs, making her way to a shell, an ash tray, or a pillow with birds, and then suddenly sitting down and looking up at her mother in surprise, her huge blue eyes wet with instant tears. No, this one was stamped with the Littletons' darkness. Her eyes were eager and brown; her color and her quick interest in all that was around her belonged to Hugh, as did her sudden, inexplicable changes to gloomy satisfaction just after she had been fed or amused.

Sometimes the man in Elaine's imagination became Hugh, without her knowing why—just as, after Foley had died, the dreadful recurrence of memories of him would take her in fear and by surprise. Hugh was too near yet. One evening, when she burst into tears at the dinner table, her mother covered her hand with her own and said, "You must keep the baby, Elaine. Write to him. Ask him to help you."

Elaine left the table.

Most days were cold, with no wind at all; the meadows sparkled in the wheat and straw shades of late winter. The sky was the sapphire blue color she remembered from childhood. Every afternoon, she would take the baby out for a walk, holding her up to see the animals—the big, fleshy, milk-scented cows, the lean horses, the rooting pigs—all of which Sophie would disregard, to stretch back against her mother, her body smelling sweet of milk, too, and baby powder and recently washed clothes. Elaine would carry the child bundled up in wool blankets and clothes that she and her mother had made during the months she had stayed on the farm. Only the baby's face peeped out, her tiny mouth and lovely dark eyes watching no one but her mother. Yet she was so like her father that often, when her eyes rushed to meet Elaine's, she thought she saw Hugh, and her heart jumped with admiration, not only for the child, but for the man.

Sometimes she would sit with Sophie in the sun in front of the well and uncover the baby's arms and legs. "You'll have a little sunbath," she would say, kissing her and laying her across her lap. She would sigh and adjust the tiny blankets. "Poor baby." The dog would come to her and lie at her feet, rolling over to expose its belly to the warmth. Sophie would sleep, and the windmill would squeal on its journey, tipping slightly at each revolution of its blades.

Once she took the baby over the hill behind the barn, along the steep skirts of the ravine, across the meadow behind the abandoned stone house. On the weekends before their marriage, she and Foley had made love in the cobwebs and the dust of that house. They would find themselves sneaking away, both of them knowing where they were going, and neither of them saying anything to the other. He had only to touch her—with a hand that was a little too warm, a touch that meant to waken rather than to remind—or to give her a fevered look, or more rarely, an imperative glance of possession, for her to feel that distinct pain start in her breasts, wind along her thighs to her knees, weakening them so that, even if she had wanted to, she could neither have fled nor argued. It still hurt her to see those stone walls that had hidden their delirium so sympathetically. She turned from the ruined house abruptly, veering off solidly in another direction through sharp weeds that cut at her legs and caught at the hem of her skirt as if to hold her back for a moment to remind her of these things.

Although most of her attention was now taken up with her baby, Elaine often thought of Jimmy. The summer before, when she had had to tell him of her pregnancy, they had sat alone on the awning-shaded porch of the farmhouse kitchen. She had considered leaving the responsibility to her mother, but then decided that no one should be punished but herself, no one else condemned to witness the disappearance, once and for all, of the last trace of respect that might have remained as a result of Albert's having repeatedly told Jimmy that it was his mother who worked hard for him, put aside money for his education, and let him leave her only for his own good and not at all for her convenience. That morning in late August, she had had to watch a son who was just beginning his adolescence try to cope with the news that his mother, who for three years had lived with a man whom he disliked, would now, after having been deserted by him, bear his child, and that this baby would be his sister. Elaine supposed that the news she had given him strengthened his already firm conviction that, since his father had been killed, nothing had gone right between him and his mother: first her mourning, then such obsessiveness with her work, that she seemed never to be with him—and after Hugh came, no place for him at all. He had probably learned to take comfort wherever he could get it, and mostly—though she had never actually denied him, had sent him his spending money, bought all his clothes, and written to him constantly—that had been apart from Elaine.

After Sophie's birth she had wanted him to visit her, and suggested the weekend of his birthday, but a party had been arranged by some of his friends, and his letter responding to her request had contained a firm refusal. He came weeks later on a date of his own choice, well into February. On the day of his arrival, Elaine drove herself to the bus station, where she stood nervously in her jeans, thick sweater, and tweed jacket, watching the passengers alight from the bus, until finally Jimmy came quickly down the steps carrying a green duffel bag.

At fourteen he was tall, and his body told of the heavy build of his father. He already carried himself well, seemed especially sensitive to the unmanliness of either too much talk or too much enthusiasm, and knew how to keep his eyes from revealing his mood. His bearing spoke of an early maturity or perhaps of an inurement to painful personal entanglements. The problems that had caused Elaine so much trouble in rearing him, that had precipitated her father's urging her to put him under his care, had all but disappeared. His teachers no longer complained that he was difficult; on the contrary, he was often praised. He had become a fine athlete and fair-minded; he had steady companions now.

In inviting him to visit, Elaine planned for him to return to her; there was nothing now to keep them apart, neither Jimmy's own obstreperousness nor the presence of Hugh. She knew that he preferred living on a farm—during the previous year, when she had made similar overtures, he had been clear on that point

—but she was confident of her ability to coax him back. She wanted her time with him before adulthood made his absence permanent.

On the drive back to the farm, he spoke of his activities, his teachers, his continuing success with sports. When she attempted to turn the conversation from these subjects, he replied only briefly, giving a minimum of information, guarding answers that might lead to intimacy. He greeted his grandparents, who had come out on the back porch to meet him, crouching to pat and to speak affectionately to his grandfather's hunting dog. He made no mention of Sophie until he and Elaine had stepped into the front hallway and removed their coats. "Where is she?" he asked uneasily. "I guess you want me to see her first." He looked upstairs and then glanced toward the parlor, just as Foley would have done if something was wrong; a particularly sad or upsetting situation that he was reluctant to face.

Elaine reached for his hand. "She's upstairs in my room."

"Who does she look like?" he asked, permitting himself to be led toward his sister. "Does she look like you?"

"No," she answered. "Not at all like me."

"Like Hugh, then?"

That Jimmy mentioned Hugh's name with such ease startled her. "Yes, she's like him." She felt his hesitation only when they reached the top of the stairs. Looking over her shoulder, with an encouraging smile, she preceded him into the room.

Jimmy, silent, stopped far from the crib, leaning against the foot of Elaine's bed, his arms folded across his chest. "She's pretty," he said when Elaine lifted her and brought her close. "I guess she's like Laura, too."

"No, Laura was small and blonde like Mimi." Mimi was Jimmy's name for Foley's mother.

"Arlet says you may send her to live with us."

"I don't know."

He touched the baby's arm, and then made one quick stroke across her dress. "Albert's taking me to Colorado this summer when he can get away," he said, his eyes shifting toward the window.

"On a fishing trip?"

"Yes, we've planned it for a long time."

She touched his hand and his warm cheek. "Then afterward you can come to me. Live with me, I mean."

"Why?" he asked abruptly.

As Sophie stirred, Elaine raised her to her shoulder and

stroked her back. "Well, why? You could be a help to me." Her voice shook a little. "I miss you."

"Would you still have to work?"

"Yes."

"Aunt Arlet thinks you'll get money from Hugh."

"No, I won't," she replied quickly. Somehow she had imagined that her situation was never discussed by her family, and certainly never with her son.

He turned away from her. His decision distressed him, or perhaps he thought if he saw her face, he might say something he would regret. She realized, with a little stab of pain, that in his time away from her he had made his own life. He had his friends; he had a room, trimmed with plaid curtains and matching spread, the walls covered with things he liked: a red and yellow high school banner, photographs he had taken, magazine cut-outs of racing cars and planes. And Arlet had become a successful substitute mother to him. When he had hurt his shoulder in football she had come to the practice field at once; when he had the flu she woke him for his medicines at intervals throughout the night. Albert had taught him woodworking, and now allowed him the full run of the workshop; he often picked him up after school, and as a birthday present, was teaching him how to drive. "No, Mama. I should stay with Albert and Aunt Arlet. I'm fine there."

He looked at her questioningly, with no little alarm. "Unless it's Albert and Arlet not wanting me," he said.

"No," she said. "This has nothing to do with them. It's just me wanting you. That's all."

Jimmy stepped away from her to the dresser and picked up a photograph of his father in a football uniform. Elaine supposed that when he was living here with his grandparents, he had sometimes entered this room of his mother's childhood, and studied the picture, glancing up in the mirror to determine whether his own soft, childish features would ever resemble the strong, solid ones of Foley. Yet he must have been profoundly moved by his father's image, and perhaps afterward, when he had slipped back downstairs or into his own room, he had felt like one who has brushed too close to the abrasive reality of his own life's loss.

He had told her of a recurring dream: that he was confined to a school room without openings, the walls covered with blackboards. He knew that if he could write a message, the hero of the dream would free him, yet nothing remained to write with, only a pyramid of crushed chalk on the smallest of the desks. The sleep in which these dreams appeared never restored his force in the normal way, he said, but instead seemed to rob him of it, and he wakened worried and weak.

Elaine imagined that he remembered his father very well—how Foley had come at any hour of the day and shouted for him, hugged him, sometimes carried him struggling and laughing under one arm, to take him out to play, or for long happy rides in the countryside, and while the trees and bushes and flowers streamed by the open windows, had talked to him over the wind and made plans. Maybe in reverence Jimmy would feel that he had to do something for his daddy, since years ago on a winter night, Foley had come to him after he was in bed, embraced him with his habitual warmth, and promised to come home soon, yet never had, and so all their projects had gone unrealized.

Jimmy replaced the picture gently, taking care to steady it on its stand. Then his strong glance returned in the mirror that of his mother, in the independent manner of her own character. "I'll spend June with you," he said. "Before Albert and I go on the trip."

Elaine nodded and adjusted the baby in her arms. "But think about what I asked you," she said quietly. "Please don't just say no all at once."

He attempted a smile, but his nervousness and the certainty of disappointing her caused the smile to dissolve. He touched the baby again, and then let his eyes meet Elaine's only briefly, not able to rest on them for fear of revealing the kind of disapproval that a son must never let his mother see. "Well, she's nice," he said, a courtesy to Elaine, praising her for an accomplishment that had nothing to do with him, and which he must regret. She listened to the quick fall of his footsteps on the stairs, an almost running gait to the kitchen, and then the bang of the kitchen door.

She moved to the window and watched him cross the yard to his grandfather, who must have been waiting since he heard Jimmy call to him from the porch. The two of them stood talking in the sharply incised shadows of a blackjack oak, which threw its veinlike patterns over their bodies and over the ambered winter lawn. Undoubtedly the subject they discussed was the sorrel colt that her father intended to give to Jimmy when it was a yearling. Jimmy with his hands thrust deep in his pockets seemed relieved to be away from her and this baby whom she suddenly felt rather more alone in cherishing.

That night, she served him a belated birthday dinner—baked fish, roast beef, and an elaborately decorated cake with candles—at the end of which she gave him the sheepskin jacket that he

had asked for in a letter. He thanked her, and later she saw him
stop at the mirror to admire himself, to see how the jacket looked
buttoned and with its collar turned up. He pushed back his hair
and cocked his head, appreciating the strength and solidity of his
masculine beauty.

On Sunday afternoon, still as reserved and unapproachable as
when he had come, he asked her to drive him back into town, and
he was gone. Nor did he, as he might have done in times past,
watch her from the window until the bus had turned off the main
street and disappeared behind the theater and the bank.

In the time that followed, Elaine worked hard, not just looking
after Sophie, but also in caring for her old home and her parents.
Mrs. Mueller reminded her that she should conserve her strength,
that she was nursing a baby and recovering from the lying-in, but
Elaine had to keep busy. It was a way of distracting her mind.
Together she and her mother and the wife of the hired hand
cooked, arranged, and cleaned. They mended things in the house
and sewed dresses and skirts for themselves and particularly
clothes for the baby: a quilt, a coat, and a wardrobe that would
last for the next three years. They embroidered pillow slips and
sheets, as if royalty had been born instead of simply a pretty,
healthy child to a woman who offered it no future, could never
give it a father, and whose soul was tortured every day by the
thought that she was going to have to give it up, that realistically
she must plan on that, that she should talk to her brother and
sister-in-law about the adoption, and that the longer she waited,
the more difficult it was going to be. Sophie was nine weeks old.

The thought of going back to Dansville alone, of returning to
the house without her daughter, brought interludes of painful regret. It had occurred to her that she might find a husband, make a
marriage of convenience. She was beautiful still, and she knew it
from a more truthful source than the mirror. She never went to
town, to church, or anywhere else without feeling the warmth of
a man's eyes upon her—not just the gentle, floaty looks of desire, but also the hard and anxious ones of proprietorship. But
wedding herself to a man whom she could never love just to keep
her child was an option she preferred not to consider.

A bachelor farmer, not much over thirty, began to call, ostensibly to talk to her father, but really to see her. He was formal and
grave, gentlemanly in the old style, and he attended church and
Sunday school as regularly as did the members of her family. She
liked him for his character and accomplishments, and for the
forgiveness that was implicit in his attention. So far, there had

been only visits, but she had agreed to have dinner with him in town the following weekend.

She wished for the days to pass slowly; she savored the time with her child. Yet she knew she must soon leave her family and live apart from them as she had always done. Desirous of her independence, she was gradually becoming anxious to retrieve it.

One morning, after two piercingly cold days of a drizzle that caused the blacktop road to glisten and the white gravel road from the farmhouse to almost disappear, she felt that she had to get out and move, that her health required it. She took a coat off a hook in the hallway and shouted to her mother that she was going to the mailbox.

"It's all right, Ely," her mother called from the kitchen. "Daddy will get the mail when he drives down to the pasture. Don't risk getting wet, honey."

It was nice to have her mother treat her like a child again. She enjoyed that; it was a welcome anachronism.

"Listen for Sophie," she shouted. "I'll be back soon. I need the walk." She put on a loose raincoat of her mother's and tied a plaid wool scarf under her chin, tucking her unruly red hair under it as she stepped out onto the porch.

The rain dripped steadily on the road and on the meadows. The clouds were low and watery; in the early morning, there had been a dense fog. The great oaks of her childhood, their limbs heavy with the damp, looked as if the coming of spring had overlooked them, and they would remain in an eternal grisaille. She walked down the road, relieved to be free of the confines of a warm house, of the feeling of closeness to other human beings; of the smell of pies cooling, baby clothes being washed, and smoke. She wondered what she was going to do to earn a living. She would have to go back to Dansville. She would have to talk to Arlet about Sophie. Yet she knew with each passing day that she would be unable to give up the baby, though there was no question of returning with her to Dansville. It was impossible to live off her parents indefinitely, either, and the money she had received from Hugh she had invested for the child.

The mailbox was gleaming silvery with water. The entire valley seemed to be at the bottom of a transparent pond, cold and artificial. It was disconcertingly beautiful, yet she felt herself to be only a visitor in the landscape. Even when the spring came, even with the green and the new colors, she was still a stranger, and nothing but her baby kept her alive. She felt incapable of action; the sorrow she had so long expected, had known was inevitable, had robbed her life of momentum and direction, and she had taken no steps to find an alternate place in nature, other than to fulfill her duties toward her parents, who had helped her so much, and toward her infant, who needed her. She was rootless, a failed adult come back home; and though she was fighting to return to normalcy and to take up her own life again, she was—and she acknowledged this—losing ground.

She had stopped at the mailbox and was reaching into it when she saw a black Mercedes leave the road, glide onto the shoulder, and approach her, suddenly halting, then continuing hesitantly to where she was. She stared at it weakly, dull and transfixed, like a person about to be lifted by a wave and helpless to resist it. The car was unfamiliar to her, and because of the rain, she was unable to see through the window, but she knew before the man got out of the car that it was no stranger asking directions or assistance. Somehow he had found out, though she had done all she could to keep that from happening. She heard the articulation of a perfectly fitted door on a very fine car: It shut with a precise click. He stood still for a moment and then came toward her, not in the spirit of his character, she thought, but in the spirit of his mood and the day. Behind him, opaque clouds labored across the anonymity of the slate sky. The form of his gray Stetson had lost its definition, and the highlights of his dark eyes were conspicuously absent.

His manner was so different from her memory of it that their being together on the road seemed to her a chance meeting of acquaintances. He looked haggard and exhausted, but he still put to shame the men she had become accustomed to seeing. She felt that she had never known him, never been with him, never slept beside him, never held him in her arms, never comforted him at all; though in the house, less than a hundred yards away, she had his daughter sequestered—sequestered, she realized suddenly, not so much from the shame and illegality of her existence as from him. He was a stranger now, and as a stranger, he had probably come not simply to see the baby but to take her away; he would be powerful enough to do that, and she would be unable to stop him. The fear of it rose in her, but she was prepared. She had decided long before to keep her baby away from the Littletons, not just from Hugh, but from all of them.

She stood beside the mailbox, sensing that she contributed to the gloominess of the setting. She felt heavy and awkward, with weighted feet, as she had sometimes felt in troubled dreams. She was ashamed that she looked so shabby—the raincoat, the scarf, her hair disordered in the rain. His presence had always prompted in her a desire to be beautiful, and this moment was no exception. She now desperately needed every advantage; before this man, she felt inadequate, cheated to be female, the harshness of nature's unfairness now that the love that had made her whole in allowing her to bond herself to him no longer existed.

"How are you, Elaine?" he asked. He approached her just as he had always done, assuming command, as if not a day had passed since they had separated, as if this were the very morning that he had deserted her, and that, instead of leaving conclusively, he had simply driven as far as the highway, or even as far as Needville or Rosenberg, then looked out his car window into the blinding sun of the full spring, the ice-blue sky shattered with lilac and lavender, and had turned the wheel sharply, returning to her house, committed to letting her hold him in her arms for the rest of his life.

"I'm fine," she responded. She ran the toe of her boot along the back of her ankle, holding the mail to her breast like a shield. "What did you expect?"

Her words tumbled out without guidance, arranging themselves in odd expressions, but serving well enough for what was unrehearsed, what she could never have planned to say. "Where did you get that car?" she asked. Her mind sought frantically an escape from this confrontation, and her heart, uncomfortably tight and hard, raced in terror in anticipation of the conclusion of their meeting. Her face must have been flaming; her skin felt as if it were being scalded despite the cool rain that fell on it.

"It's not mine," he said.

"You steal it?"

He smiled. He looked different. Her blood beat against her temples.

"It must be your mama's," she said. "She's the only Littleton insensitive enough to buy a German car."

"At least you haven't lost your sense of humor."

"It's my one remaining asset." She did nothing to temper her sarcasm, because in her amazement at his arrival, she had nothing with which to replace it.

"What about your daughter? Isn't she an asset?"

She felt herself jump; he must have seen it. "You get right to the point." She turned to leave him, to return to the house, to lock herself up and her baby with her. She had been careless.

Reaching out for her, he seized her arm.

"What do you want, Hugh?" she asked, facing him, ugly in

her anger. "What in the hell are you looking me up for after a year? Take your goddamned hands off me!"

Her resistance seemed to shock him, and he released her. "It is true?" he asked suddenly.

"You wouldn't be here if it weren't!" She looked back toward his car. "Is there anyone with you? Did you bring your girl friend to see if she wants to play mama to my baby, or is your daddy here to back you up?" She knew he was alone, but taunting him was a way of making him uncomfortable and keeping him at bay.

"No," he said, refusing to let her draw him into a quarrel. He wanted to see the child, and if he had to defer to Elaine's extravagant manifestation of her pain, it was all right, what he deserved. He searched for the right words to calm her and make her trust him.

She stepped away from him quickly, the mail tight in her hand, and began to make her way back to the house until he moved ahead to stop her. "Where is she, Elaine? Do you have her here?"

She looked at the house, wondering how she could succeed in getting back inside it and have this meeting in her past, finished and done with, just one more among her nightmare memories of her experiences with him.

"Do you have her here?" he asked again, more insistently.

"She's here, but she's not on view."

"You mean . . . not to me?"

"That's right." She stood there spellbound, no clear thought in her head. After that night almost a year earlier, she had reconciled herself to never seeing him again, and after Sophie's birth, she had stopped wanting to see him. She had all she needed from him forever in the gaze of her daughter. He was too rich for her blood; he had hurt her too badly. She realized now that the years she had spent with him had been brutal and terrible, and they had been blackened with the ever present fear that he would leave her, as indeed he had. It was over. She resented the cruelty of his coming; she knew her mistake in ever having loved him at all. She had wanted her girlhood back, and he had brought it; she had wanted a fair duplicate of the man whom she had married, and, with his sensuality and masculine pride, he had provided it. Now she had come to believe that her desire had been sinful and a sacrilege; doing penance for it had almost killed her.

He was wearing jeans and a long-sleeved shirt. His sleeves were rolled up to his elbows, as if he had prepared himself to do some dirty labor. His shoulders and chest had filled out; he seemed taller and more heavily muscled than she remembered, but his features had that same alertness and intensity. Yet the restlessness of his body was diminished, replaced by a composure that Elaine sensed was ingenuine; it was as if he had been calmed by something that would eventually prove toxic. "You must be freezing," she said stupidly, like an anxious parent. "Don't you have a jacket?"

"I'm okay." He had felt her unintended maternal caress and was soothed by it.

"You been drinking?"

He looked at his watch. "No." He smiled slightly. "I've been sober for almost three hours." In spite of the smile, the hint of charm and ease, he could not hide his fatigue or troubled spirit.

"You stay up all last night?"

"That's right." He was shivering. His chin and his cheeks had the bluish tone of a dark man who hasn't shaved for some time.

"Why?"

"Because I was on my way here, wondering what you were going to say to me, what kind of welcome I would get."

"Now you know," she said, not without hoping to wound him further, to see his perplexity and disappointment intensify.

"Oh, I knew, Elaine," he said, narrowing his eyes and squinting. She had rarely seen that expression because she had rarely hurt him: While she had been his mistress, she had been so sensitive to him that she had handled his somewhat fragile feelings as a maid handles fine crystal whose damage she will be held responsible for out of her meager earnings.

"Did you?" she asked, her mouth trembling and tears streaming into her eyes. "I always thought you were oblivious to my reactions. I don't remember you listening much to me—certainly not the last time you came to me." She had never seen him look so hounded and tired, but she reminded herself that he could be a cruel, a self-absorbed child that thought only of itself; even if he had been brought up that way, his behavior was vicious, and though she had once imagined that she was the only one who cared enough to coax him toward humanity, she was glad to be out of it.

The lines at the corners of his mouth were more sharply incised than his father's, and the contrasts in his face were more pronounced, as if they sought to emphasize his virility. As she watched him and he became more familiar; as she began to recognize a look, a nod, a stance, and she remembered him, he was restored to her as a portrait arrives inevitably on a piece of photographic paper. She marveled at his image. He wore a big silver watch on his wrist, the black hair on his arm curling around it, and she knew that if he removed it, she would see the white band of flesh of a man who was active and always in the sun, outdoors whenever he could be. He was tanned, and it occurred to her that, this winter vacation, while she was having his child, while she had stayed alone to bear the baby, he had probably been vacationing in a rented beach house on Bermuda or Jamaica with Shirlee, who would have been well chaperoned, and a troop of his friends, like the ones he had brought to her house one day, and with whom she had contrasted so drastically that it had shaken his love for her, and this had finally led to his ceasing to love her altogether. There was no place for her in his adult life. She had been good enough for the spirited, barbarous child, whom she had understood, but not for the mature man, whom she would never know.

"You didn't dress up to come to see me," she said. "After a year, you . . ."

His visit was unexpected; she realized now that she would never have believed that fate could be so perverse as to let her see him again when she had taken such care not to let it happen, when that had been the focus of her prayers in the red brick, steep-roofed Baptist church, during the singing of the hymns or the interminable sermons, or at odd hours when she was riding in the car on the country roads, during the long empty times when there had fallen a silence between her and one of her parents.

"And what could I have worn that would have pleased you, Elaine?"

She might have been able to be civil to him, to give him a hearing, had he been careful. Had he approached her somewhat differently, she might have let him see their child, or at least do something for her. But she did not. And if Hugh was incautious, it was because he had come close to making a decision as radical as cutting off the mast of a sailing ship in the heart of a storm.

When a truck passed on the road, Elaine nodded her head in a vague greeting, but Hugh, fixing his attention on the woman before him and on the problem that his desertion of her continued to cause him, took no notice of it. The information he had received only hours before from Lettie had sent him straight to Elaine. When the car had turned onto the road that led to her family's property, and he had seen her, as if she had been waiting for him, his heart had caught in his throat; and the scenes of their past life had filled his mind, canceling out even his most pleasant recollections of the period of his engagement. He had wanted to get out and relinquish his freedom to her at once. Not only was she the woman he wanted, but she had his family! He knew what he wanted to do; he had made his decision at the ranch, then decided how to implement it on the journey here. He needed only the moment when he could tell her, yet that moment was slow in coming. She was so much changed that he didn't know how to approach her, much less to propose a plan.

Slightly aggravated by her failure to be relieved to see him, to be accommodating and welcoming, he caught her by the shoulder and turned her around, as a person turns a young child to see if it is lying; but it was a futile maneuver, no more than an unconscious assertion of dominance, and she, from experience, recognized it at once and jerked back from his grasp.

He stood apart from her then, his irritation increasing. "I just want to see my child, Elaine." There was such a crude, defensive insistence in his tone that Elaine pursed her lips, and looked at him in disbelief. He had driven two hundred miles to see a child whom he claimed as his solely on the basis of hearsay, whose mother he had neglected even to telephone for a year.

"You should have asked your father for advice before you came here, Hugh," she said. "He would have told you not to worry yourself about a German farm girl's bastard. I can take care of her. I know what to do about my baby." It had always been Elaine's prejudice that Clarence had dozens of women. He looked that way, and in the presence of women, he acted the part—quiet and furtive. He should have had a harem.

"I know that. You're not exactly helpless."

She pulled harshly at the ends of the scarf under her neck, tying it more securely, as if that gesture might arm her and make her defense more effective. "You mean, I wasn't an innocent girl whom you took advantage of? Well, it's all right with me whatever you think. Just leave me and my baby alone."

A new thought seemed to have come to him, and he frowned under its weight. "Who was with you? I wasn't there. Christ, that kills me."

"And what would you have done?"

He looked toward the house. "Your mother deliver her in one of those upstairs rooms?"

"That's right. And we did just fine." Her eyes were green behind the rain and so much anger.

"Why are you fighting with me, Elaine? I've come all this way to see you. We need to talk."

"Two hundred miles after a whole goddamned year?" Her voice, through the thin rain, sounded strained and distressed. "And why do we need to talk? So you can arrange to take my baby away from me amicably? Tell some judge your daddy pays off that I'm a fallen woman because I let you live with me? And now you want to reach in and grab the results. Why, Hugh? I can't see why. Your daddy tell you to say that? I give you credit for not thinking it up yourself. Clarence fill you in on what to do about your illegitimate children? Or has he already hired you a lawyer?"

Then, as her voice started to tremble, she squinted her eyes, and her honeyed lashes touched together in a fluttering motion like filigree birds beating their wings over a brace of emeralds. Although to a stranger, her gesture would have appeared virginal and absurd, Hugh knew that it was caused by grief, and he let his grip tighten on her and his hand slide down her arm.

"For Christ's sake, Hugh . . ." Two great tears burned at the corners of her eyes until, disturbed by the agitation of her lashes, they splashed onto her face and joined with the rain. "Did you go to Dansville to see me before you knew? Or did you and Matt get drunk, and he tell you by mistake—one more story among a dozen others?"

"I went to see you."

"Did you think I'd let you in?"

Almost breaking into a smile, he caught his lower lip with his teeth. "I still had my key," he said. He took it out of his pocket and held it up before her, where it shone like a piece of gold on the floor of a stream.

"Strange souvenir," she said impatiently. "What were you going to do with it? Frame it? Give it to your girl for a wedding present with a signed and dated inscription, promising to stay away from licentious women in backwater towns?"

She saw in his eyes the pain her words caused him, and she had a moment of pity for him—perhaps all he wanted was to see Sophie, just once and never again—but the weakness in her passed quickly. Still she was amazed at the powers of spoken language, what a phrase could evoke, the damage an exchange of phrases could do, the danger in a chance word, or an inappropriate answer, or an ill-chosen tone.

Elaine tasted the water on her mouth. Her face was wet from looking upward, the collar of her blouse was cold and soaked. Rain dripped off her lashes and into her eyes; rain that had collected in the rim of Hugh's hat fell at intervals in a stream. She had denied herself the pleasure of touching him. She considered that a triumph, the domination of mind over flesh.

"Where is she?" he asked quietly. He looked beyond her. "Is she in the house? Let me see her, Elaine."

"No." She spoke clearly over the muddle of water and rage and misunderstanding; she would keep him from seeing Sophie; she would prevent that absolutely.

She could see that he was going to lose his temper, and she was relieved. His jaw was set, she saw the heavy movements of his shoulders, heard his quickened breathing, and she knew that it would be easier from now on. "Why the hell not?" he yelled. He was caught completely, engulfed at last, by the pain of what she was doing to him.

Maybe he would hit her, and she could hate him that much more. It would give her pleasure to nurse a bruise or a swollen lip and despise him for it. It was essential that she continue to hate Hugh. She could never continue her life, she was certain, if she were ever to stop hating him. "Because she's mine, and only mine, and you can't prove otherwise."

"I sure can, Elaine!"

"Try it, Hugh."

She was a mother, and however formidable the adversary standing before her, bullying her, she was as invincible as any maternal figure at the approach of a cave that houses her young. A hundred yards from where they stood, she had a baby waiting for her. Her breasts were heavy and ached with the milk for that child; she would remember all her life the shame and stupidity of an illegitimate pregnancy. Hugh had had no part in this. "Try it," she repeated. "You bother me once more, and I'll leave here, and you'll never know where I've gone."

"What's wrong with you, Elaine? Let me see her! Christ!"

"What for, Hugh?" She had said all she was going to say.

She turned to leave, but he was beside her. He spoke flatly. The landscape behind him was like tin, a huge, uninterrupted piece of metal. "I'll get an injunction," he said. "I swear to God I will. I'll drive back to town right now. You want a deputy sheriff to walk into your house, pick her up, and carry her out?"

"How?" she shouted, turning around. The rain was coming down harder; the needles of it stung her face. "Prove me an unfit mother? I had her, I gave birth to her! Without you! One hundred percent alone! One year. All the work is done. It's over! You weren't here when I needed you."

"You didn't get her alone."

"Conceive her alone? The hell I didn't! The night I got her, I was alone! You attacked me in the middle of the morning, when you were in love with another woman, and telling me so every second of that time—telling me how bad *she* was hurting *you!* That's making love alone, you son of a bitch." She pushed back her wet hair. "I wasn't your psychiatrist, you bastard!" she howled. "I was in love with you! What are you doing here, Hugh? I absolutely cannot figure that out."

"I'll see her," he said.

"Over my dead body. I promise you!"

In all the time she had known him, she had never dared to talk to him like this. It shocked him, and he showed it; he didn't know what to do with her.

Then, unexpectedly, she stepped close to him and risked touching him. Her flesh had become neutral. She took his arm in her hands. "Listen to me, Hugh. You have the whole world before you, a career, a girl who loves you . . . everything. I have Sophie. Period. Living with you lost me my son. You forced me to choose between you and him. You remember? You know that's true."

He tried to speak, but she interrupted him. "Jimmy is ashamed of me," she said. "He always will be. He wouldn't even come to see me now unless my brother made him. I'll never get him back, Hugh. Never. Now, don't mess me up with my baby." She shook him a little. "I'm doing you a favor. I have not and I will not ask you for anything. Do you hear me? But leave us alone. Forget this. That will be the best thing you've ever done in your life."

There was so much water falling between them that he could see only the exquisite colors of her: the ivory and copper, the brilliant flashes of green. "I'm going up to the house with you," he said.

He had failed to listen to her; he had disregarded her appeal; he had not changed. Even the fact of this disaster had nothing to mellow Hugh. "You do," she said softly, "and I'll tell my father to kill you." She still held his arm. Her nails drove into his wet shirt like the points of a rowel; she held him as if she were in pain, and putting pressure on his flesh assuaged it. "I've told him about you. You may not believe it, but to my father, I'm still a little girl, and he's not exactly delighted that, after my being your mistress for years, you simultaneously get me pregnant and leave me. That's all right with me, but it's not with him!"

She was alarmed that Hugh's insistence had forced her into such desperation that she lied. She had never discussed Hugh, or any aspect of their relationship, with her father, nor would it have been like him to inquire. It would have been inconceivable that he would harm the father of his grandchild; if he were to take any action at all, it would be conciliatory. He was the kind of man who held his children responsible for their folly, rather than the people on whom they might blame it, even when the accusation was as justified as it was in this case. He had taught them to stay away from bad people and bad behavior, and if they chose to ignore that lesson, they were liable for the consequences. He had never thought to chastise Elaine when she had come home pregnant; that was her affair and not his. He could only be sorry to the extent that this affected his grandchildren. He pitied Jimmy for his mother's shame; he pitied the baby for her hard future; but the idea that he would have taken vengeance on Hugh for causing Elaine's pregnancy, after she had allowed him to live with her openly, not only in front of the community but in front of her young son, was preposterous.

Hugh cleared his throat; the anger had left his voice, though the distress had not. "Lettie thinks that you tried to kill yourself last Easter," he said. He tried to take her hand. "That's not true, is it?" He looked as if he were in love with her then, as if he, too, had been wounded, but that had to be an illusion brought on by the thickening screen of rain between them. She lowered her eyes. "I don't know," she said softly.

"You know you were pregnant?"

"No," she said, raising her eyes quickly to his. "But I should have. I should have known you wouldn't leave me before you'd wrecked even the part of my life you didn't want!"

Perhaps now, after having seen her in the ugliness of her anger, he would leave. He would want no part of her child, nor would he care to retain the least memory of their encounter. But he seemed strangely complacent, as if he had not heard what she had said, or at least had not been injured by it. Maybe his thoughts had returned to the more agreeable subject of his future. Finally she asked the obvious question, the one she should have asked at first. As if to avoid a blow, she ducked her head slightly. "Are you married yet, Hugh?"

"No."

"You engaged?"

"Yes."

"When will you marry?"

"In June, when school is out."

Yet as he answered he looked at her with a softness in his eyes

that belied a marriage, or even a romance; she had seen the expression before, and she understood perfectly its meaning. Her
face went white, and she said quickly, "Then what are you pro-
posing, Hugh? What do you want? Why are you here?"

He had known what he would offer her from the beginning,
when Lettie had told him about the child, for he had only to alter
slightly what he had planned to suggest had he found her in her
house in Dansville as he had expected. It was a solution that
pleased him in its simplicity; and he was certain that he was rich
enough to carry it through, without too much inconvenience to
anyone. He loved the ranch; he meant to continue to spend a
good part of his time managing it. Shirlee, like his mother, would
have no interest in it, would never accompany him there. He had
taken her once, she had disliked it. She had found the people
coarse, the manner of living too primitive, and the recreation
boring. Her entertainments were in the city; all the things she
wanted to do were there.

"I'll take you back to Dansville," he said clearly, without any
strain in his voice. "Right now, Elaine. You can live where you
were, or I'll build you a house, or you can buy what you want. It
doesn't matter. Do as you like." The bulk of the clouds had
increased, and the sky had become motionless behind him. As he
continued talking, she felt her hands going up either to attack him
or to cover her face. "It's better for the baby that you don't work
anymore, Elaine. In the past, you wouldn't take money from me,
but this is different. I'll give you a thousand dollars a month, I'll
pay for the baby's education, and I'll get you anything you need
for her, and for yourself. And I'll come to see you. I'll be with
you as much as I can."

For a time, neither of them spoke, and their eyes held each
other steadily until Elaine dropped her gaze. She shook her head
and walked away from him; he followed her closely, sometimes
touching her in aimless gestures. When he made a confused attempt to hold her, she struggled with him briefly, using her full
strength against him, and pushing away from him, turned and
ran. As she slammed the gate behind her, she tripped, but caught
herself quickly and ran on. She avoided the curving road lined
with trees and took the straight path across the meadow, where
her legs soon became soaked to the thighs, and the wet grass
pulled against her feet, but she was determined to escape. The
house grew larger and larger; she reached the fence, the walk,
and then the roses. She slipped on the slick, glassy treads of the
porch steps, but then rushed through the front door and locked it,

panting and crying, still holding the mail, wet and clinging to her hand.

She had worn her boots in the house and left a trail of mud and water on the rich, dark floors. She went the length of the hall to her father's gun case, opened the door of the glass front, and lifted down the deer rifle. Out of the drawer below, she gathered up five cartridges. Her hand shook violently as she pressed each one quickly against the spring and clicked it down, then pushed the bolt forward until the first round was thrust into the chamber.

Carrying the gun in both her hands to steady it, she went back down the hall to the front alcove. The baby was silent. Elaine did not know where she was: perhaps in the cradle in the living room; perhaps still upstairs, put to bed after her bath. She heard voices in the kitchen, her parents quietly arguing, an old disagreement about how many chicks her mother intended to start. No one must see her; absolutely no one must see. She unlocked and opened the front door, put the gun to her shoulder, and trained her sights on the man who was still standing on the road beside the black car. His hands were in his back pockets, and he was looking toward the house. If he saw her in the shadow of the doorway, if he was aware of the gun pointed at his chest from a distance of a hundred yards, he gave no sign of it; he was slightly stooped now, humbled, yielding, and devastated by his position. She could kill him easily; Foley had taught her to shoot; she confounded her husband with God when she prayed to one of them to steady her hand.

She fired once, shot the bolt quickly, and fired again. How many times she had fired that gun; what satisfaction she had taken in shooting it so well—and how that had pleased Foley.

The first shot was considerably above his head; the kick of the old rifle had burned into her shoulder. The second lobbed off a branch of the pecan tree. The other three she fired smoothly and steadily into the chalk-white vapor of the receding rain.

She would not remember either leaving the doorway or closing the door. One of her hands had been burned on the hot barrel of the rifle, and she had cursed the pain for recalling to her that she had indeed fired at Hugh, and not just once but many times. She threw the gun down the hallway, against the coat rack, hoping to make it fall into the darkness beneath the hems of the wraps.

She heard a renewed clatter of rain on the roof. Somewhere in the house the baby cried in terror, but Elaine was unable to go to her, unable to provide any comfort. Guided by a slant of light that fell through its partially opened door, she moved into the sitting room, her legs trembling so alarmingly that she knew she could go no further. Only one idea remained clear to her: She might have been wrong in attempting to be the instrument of Hugh's destruction, but she was right to hate him, and right to wish him dead.

She lay face down on the sofa and screamed, and when her mother shook her hard, questioned her, and turned her over on her back, her eyes, horribly swollen, were wild, and her lip bled. She tore at her mother's sleeve and told her what Hugh had said, and then she asked her mother to go to her father with her request. "If he comes back here, Mama, have Daddy kill him!" she cried, her head lolling back and forth on the disarranged embroidered pillows. "I couldn't do it, but he could.... Promise me, Mama." She rose up on her knees and threw her arms around her mother's shoulders. "I thought it would have been better.... I wish I had died. I wish Lily had let me die ..."

"And not have had your baby?"

"Yes!" she cried. She was a child in the grip of a tantrum. "And not have had her!"

Mrs. Mueller held her at arm's length to look at her face. "It's a sin to wish yourself and a baby under your protection—"

"I love him, Mama," she kept on. "I'm going to have to love him all my life!"

"You loved Foley—"

"Foley is dead!"

"If you loved God—"

"No! No, Mama ... if God loved *me* ..." She repeated these words over and over imploringly, smothering them against her mother's breast until she was exhausted. "If God loved *me* ..."

For a while, Mrs. Mueller was silent, but then, as a woman who had had five decades in which to arrive at an understanding of the penalty that must be paid for the indulgence of almost every delight, she said: "Stop trying to take on the whole world, Elaine. You're strong, but you can't do it all. You told me yourself that it would be easy for him to support his child. Let him. He will. He wants to. And let him take care of you, too. You can't afford the luxury of punishing him. Make it easy on yourself"—she stroked Elaine's back and tried to arrange her hair—"and on all of us, Ely. Ask him for Sophie's care and yours, too. Make him give you what you need."

Elaine flipped over and looked at her mother hatefully, with abhorrence for her mother's failed morality and for God and for all mankind, with loathing for everything for having betrayed her—for killing Foley, for seeming to make it up to her by giving her Hugh, for taking him away, and then, cruelest of all, for letting her see him once more. She shouted a series of inarticulate phrases, then buried her body and her face in the bare recesses of the sofa and wept bitterly, hopelessly.

Outside, a few rays of sun flashed a smile of encouragement on the desolation of the rain-battered garden, but Elaine refused to open her eyes to it. Her breathing was shallow, and her eyes were half-open, like those of a person in a coma. Even when the child was brought to her and had begun to nurse, she lay still, and her body felt none of its usual pleasure.

The next morning—it couldn't have been six o'clock—when it was still dark in the upstairs hallway, so dark that she could hardly see to find the receiver, trying to think over the roaring in her head, her baby struggling in her arms, she telephoned Arlet.

Chapter 10

CLARA LITTLETON HAD known that her position in society had
changed when she had been forced to leave a luncheon, not only
before the medley of salads and sherbets could be served but
before the chairman of the board had been able to ask her to
underwrite the expenses of the symphony ball. She had overheard
three women discussing the long, serious, and apparently permanent liaison between her son, Hugh, and the woman in Dansville.
Had Clara been able to imagine that the women pitied her and
understood her position, she might have been able to overlook the
incident, but they had converged on one another smiling and sly,
like a trio of nymphs decorating a rococo fountain. Not only had
Clara refused the request for money that was made later in the
living room of her home (after several attempts on the part of the
chairman to make an appointment), but she had withdrawn her
maintenance pledge. In a way, she had considered the young,
eager chairman responsible for the affront.

Her son's affair had humiliated her. Her misery over the matter had begun in the late summer of 1947 after she had first
learned of the affair; when, in the spring of 1950, Hugh spent his
first school vacation at home in three years, she cried, hiding in
the dark little alcove between the butler's pantry and the breakfast
room. The spell seemed to have been broken: Hugh was spending
the nights in Houston; Clara's prayers had been answered. She
would walk past his disordered room, not complaining about the
chaos, only happy that he was there; gratified even to hear him
yell down the service stairs to Cana:When was she bringing his

breakfast? Where were his tennis socks? Had she seen the tie with the thin blue stripes?

Then she saw him fall in love with Shirlee; her friends saw it, too, and they pointed it out with what seemed to Clara to be pleasure and approval. Impressed by the suitability of Hugh's new choice, they believed that the son had seen the light, and they were willing to show him forgiveness by giving parties for him and his intended. It was an interesting match, anyway, made more interesting still by Hugh's past.

From the start, Clara had known that Shirlee's dates with with other men had troubled her son. Shirlee's indifference to him when he drove the one hundred and sixty miles from the university in Austin just to take her to a party, to have a few hours with her, and then be dismissed (his rival had the advantage of attending a school in the same city) bewildered him and sent him into fits of irritation that surprised Clara. She had not supposed that a young woman's treatment of him could affect him so, plunging him into a state that neither she nor even Clarence could do anything about, since he was unwilling to discuss it. He stayed in his room, he ate poorly (sometimes he even refused to come down to dinner), and at the mention of Shirlee's mistreatment of him, at even a hint of sympathy from Clara, he would get in his car and roar away. She was certain that he was in love, and rather than pitying her own child and despising Shirlee for tormenting him, she was glad. She had to be. Shirlee, cruel as she was in her double game, apparently insensitive to the pain she caused, had taken him from Mrs. Menutis, had captured him, and held him in the sphere in which Clara believed he should move, would have to move if he were to take his place, that place that she imagined she had participated with Clarence in preparing. Mrs. Menutis, on the other hand, would have ruined him.

When finally the engagement was announced, after that cold, drizzly night in December when Hugh had met his father at the airport and told him, and then Clarence had told her, and awkwardly she had congratulated him, she relaxed, once and for all, and buried an unpleasant memory. The conflict between the two young people had worked itself out, and the diamond gleamed and hung heavy like a rich fruit on Shirlee's hand. Clara observed that the girl, having sweetened since her engagement, looked up at Hugh with love in her soft, quick eyes, listened to everything he said, clung to his arm whenever they were together, and never seemed to regret abandoning her other suitor. Shirlee praised

Hugh, and she teased him cautiously; she was knitting him a sweater, and she was making him happy.

More and more rarely did Clara discuss the scandal with her friends, and she began giving them the very coldest looks if they dared allude to it. She felt that she was absolved from sin, that the entire family had received a benediction and was free. Hugh loved Shirlee; he would finish law school in the year after his marriage. Clara contacted an agent in Austin, and a house was found and rented in the best neighborhood, on a hill close to school. The garden had a view of the city and the state capitol building and the university tower. She arranged to have the house painted and refurbished by a contractor whom Clarence knew; she planned to have the furniture moved in when Hugh and Shirlee were on their honeymoon in England.

She wanted Hugh's wedding to take place quickly.

"This engagement is too long," she told Clarence at the beginning of Lent, after she had noticed, for the first time, a hint of annoyance in Hugh's behavior with Shirlee, a restlessness coming back into him, a discontent that she had thought he had lost. "We should let them marry at Easter," she said. But Mrs. Faris, Shirlee's mother, overruled her, and Clara learned through the grapevine that she was still concerned about Hugh's past with Mrs. Menutis. She wanted to be assured that there would be no turning back, and if there was, she wanted it to take place before her daughter was married and not after. One afternoon, sitting in the back of Clara's chauffeured car, her white-gloved hands folded and resting on her shiny lizard purse, she informed Clara that there had never been a divorce in the Faris family, and Clara was quick to counter that there had never been one in their family, either.

Since the beginning of Hugh's relationship with Shirlee Faris, the thing that Clara herself had feared most was that he would indeed go back to Mrs. Menutis. But even though Clara had noted in her anxious mind the indications of trouble with the engaged couple, she was unprepared the night when Hugh left for Dansville. When Clarence came into the bedroom, her thin body, which was wrapped in a robe the color and texture of a slick green plum and half-lost in the satin of her bedcovers, shook with the grief of disappointment. This last escapade of Hugh's was just another in a long list of outrages he had committed against her, beginning with his birth, which had hurt and confused her.

She had never understood Hugh, and certainly she had never understood his involvement with a country woman, a redheaded real estate agent of German extraction in a little country town where you could buy neither a good meal nor a good book. At that moment, she hated Hugh; and she thought the worst thing she could think about him, which was that he was like her husband. No one in her family had ever been the slightest bit of a renegade. And if Hugh was bad because he took after Clarence, he was also bad because Clarence had not brought him up properly, had not corrected him as only an older man can correct a younger man, by drawing upon his experience to advise and discipline him. Just as Clara blamed Clarence for Hugh's errors, she blamed him for her own unhappiness. If she had never understood Hugh, Clarence had never understood her. He had been too liberal; he had never punished Hugh sufficiently (as she would have done had it not been for his father's interference); he had given him too much, indulged him in everything. When Clarence had pointed out that Hugh took care of himself, was hardly ever home to bother her, and made good grades in school, she had answered that his independence and absence from home were due to his dislike of her; and if he was smart in school, it was because he had inherited that facility, not because he had earned it. "And if he is wild, he gets it from you," she said, raising her lovely eyes slowly to Clarence's patient face and seeking in it what she would never find: a desire to restrain his son. "My people were never reckless," she had said.

Hadn't she done everything she could to encourage his engagement to a young woman from a good family: the little candlelight dinner parties on the lawn, and then the catered party on Hugh's birthday, when Shirlee came to him like an exotic lily in a saffron gown, flowing with veils of silk chiffon, her pale blond hair crowned with green orchids that Clara had ordered specially to match the table decorations? Hadn't she entertained Hugh's future in-laws a dozen times, and even persuaded Clarence to include them in their vacation in Spain, where they had rented a huge, sprawling villa on the Costa del Sol, with a team of servants to keep everything delightful for everyone? She disliked Shirlee's mother: Both the Farises bored her. Jerome Faris had wanted to go out in the boat all the time, or to drive into the fishing town for the loud entertainments; and his wife, Betty Jean, had insulted him constantly: at restaurants because he ate too much bread and always finished off the meal with a rich pastry, but especially over the bridge table, since Betty Jean used the Goren system of counting and Jerome, with an intuition for cards, used no system at all.

The night Hugh went to Dansville, Clara turned to Clarence, her face red and swollen from her tears, and they talked as only a husband and wife can talk: Outwardly the conversation lacked logic, but its progress was clear to each of them. Little information was exchanged, and nothing constructive occurred; nor did they reach a conclusion of any sort. But the ritual had to be played out because it was essential to their partnership, and the conversation consoled them in their grief for their son and themselves, though they grieved for different reasons.

While Clarence tried to calm her, Clara pulled a tissue out of the ruffled box on the bedside table and patted her face. She suppressed a frown and lowered her eyes. "It's all sex with them," she whispered.

"Probably."

"They have nothing in common."

"They have that."

The room was blazing with light from every lamp. The Chinese lamp bases, the opalescent silk shades in hexagonal shapes with shimmering tasseled hems, the polished surfaces of the tables, all vibrated with a radiance that was enhanced by the metallic peach blossoms in the design of the wallpaper. Every object, every detail of the decoration, either shone or sparkled. "I introduced him to the children of our friends," she said weakly. "I arranged all those parties. He never would have gone to that woman, except for Matt."

Clarence took his wife in his arms. He had always loved Clara, and he had always hoped that he could make her love him unreservedly; but, from time to time, he lost her somewhere: Part of his obsession with her was in trying to find out why. He wanted to make love to her then; he wanted to be distracted and soothed.

"Maybe he just went to explain to her how things are," she said.

Clarence laughed as he removed his tie and studs.

"He won't stay!" said Clara. "He left her before. Why should he stay with her now? She'll never hold him."

Clarence shrugged. "She had something nice. He must think she still has it." He thought carefully about what he could say that would not upset his wife. "I expect she was hard to give up. It should never have started in the first place. I never understood it." But he had understood it, and he had envied his son for being able to go down to Dansville tonight, to just run down there months after having abandoned her, knowing that he damned well could, and that she would receive him in the most expressive implication of that word.

Clara sat up straight, and the chignon at the back of her head fell to the sheets. She retrieved it and went to her dressing table, where she dabbed the heat from her face and neck with cotton balls soaked in a green astringent that smelled of basil. "She's trash."

"I don't think so."

Clara turned to him. Even on a vanity chair, she looked small; her buttocks failed to cover even half of it. Her inadequacy made her beautiful. From where Clarence was sitting, her frailness was that of a child. He stood up and moved toward her, but she turned away. "Clara."

She was being absurd now, and even she knew it, but her disappointment and her desire to overcome it made her continue, and she lashed out again at Elaine. "He was a minor when she enticed him!"

Clarence lifted his hands in a gesture of fatigue, but his voice was kind. "Clara, there's not a judge in the world who would rule against a woman for seducing Hugh."

She tilted the mirror and began to comb her hair, but she watched Clarence to see if he would try to conceal his thoughts from her. His shaggy dark head was bent to the side, his fist rested on his hip, and he rubbed his cheek against his shoulder. His expression disheartened Clara. She had seen it before at those rare times when he had lost a large amount of money or missed out on a deal. She began to speak about a luncheon on Monday at which she was to review a new book by a great and misunderstood writer from Mississippi, whom she championed. "I won't be able to do it now," she said. "I'm too upset. I'll have to telephone the chairman. Cana will have to."

Clarence sighed heavily and shook his head. His eyes hurt, and he realized that in his haste to get upstairs to his wife, he had forgotten to pour himself the drink he so much needed after Hugh had answered his question and the car had disappeared under the moon. He went to the table in front of the chaise longue, where he poured some sherry into a tiny bell-shaped glass, tossed it down like medicine, and poured another.

"Clarence. . . . Please . . ." she whispered. She hated his drinking, especially now that she went once a month to a special club and had stopped herself. She chewed on her lip and stared into the carpet, as if something in it were going to reveal to her the cure to her husband's vice. She threw him a despairing glance.

"Telephone him," she said. She turned her wrist and looked at the face of her little watch.

"At Elaine's? Phone him at her house? Good God, Clara!" Their talks about Hugh always made Clarence tense and regretful. He hated to hear his son criticized, especially by Clara, whose disloyalty startled him. "If I telephoned, what would I say?"

"I thought it was over," said Clara. She closed her eyes and rubbed her forehead. "He's been so long with Shirlee."

"I know," he said, his voice low and softly caressing. "But the question is, why does he still need to go running down there to Mrs. Menutis? If he's still in love with her. . . . You do believe in love, don't you, Clara Fay?"

Although Clarence was seriously contemplating Hugh's latest dereliction, he could not help but think about Clara, also. Her face, which only a few hours before had been radiant and girlish with happiness over the success of the engagement party at the club, was now drawn and anxious. Like a defeated general leaving the field of battle and having to clear a path through his own dead, she pulled her gown tightly around her, lowered her head, and made her way hesitantly from her dresser toward the bathroom, as if she were no longer certain where it was. But some of her histrionics were for Clarence's benefit, and he knew it, so when he heard the bath water running and smelled the scent of bath oil, and before she could look out the door to see if she still had him worried, not just about Hugh but about herself, he went downstairs for a whiskey.

When he returned, all the lights would be out except for one tiny bedside lamp by which he could see his way to bed. She would be waiting for him, whiny and sad and soft, knowing that what she would offer him then would be a satisfactory escape for them both. It was what he had known he could expect of her since that night over thirty years ago when he had seen her in an anteroom, a pretty, yellow-haired girl, with her corsage lost, trembling like a caught bird, astonished, completely his, always his in spite of the few infidelities that he had thwarted. Why? Because without dominating her—his weakness for her made that impossible—he could protect her from those who would.

When he had seen Elaine run back to her parents' house, Hugh had not moved but stood in the rain, hesitant to stay because it would accomplish nothing but unwilling to go because she might think he wasn't coming back. He was exhausted and stunned; he had thought she would be overjoyed to see him and grateful for his offer of financial security and a sure, if limited, place in his heart, that she would forgive him everything, as she had done in the past. She had seen him filthy, bad tempered, drunk, sick, yet had never seemed to love him the less for it. And that morning on the road, when he had gotten out of his car, he had seen that she was shaking. *I've got her,* he had said to himself, *and I make her do that. All I have to do is stand around a few minutes and she'll invite me to bed, and we'll work out our differences there.* Why hadn't that happened?

Through the translucent veil of soft, slanted rain, he had watched her retreat; but after the door had slammed, it opened again, and the next thing he remembered, he was lying face down on the muddy shoulder of the road, his head in his arms. Five shots. He looked up. The door was closed, the meadow was empty; there was no sign of her. He rolled over, half-expecting to find blood on his clothes. When he was certain that he wouldn't suddenly feel severe pain, numbed only temporarily by his shock, he crawled to the car and worked the key into the ignition. Shivering with cold, he felt the enervation that comes after abrupt fear. He drove to a bend in the road and dried himself on one of his mother's scarves, which he had found in the glove compartment, then turned on the heater and tipped the rear-view mirror to see himself. His face was haggard; he looked miserable; his chin was bruised and slightly cut; he was filthy with mud and wet all over. He frowned, cursed the woman's insanity, cursed himself, and turned the mirror back. As the car moved on the wet shoulder of the road, he looked again at the house.

She had fired five shots and missed. It was unlike Elaine not to hit her target. The only thing he could figure out was that she had at first meant to kill him, then changed her mind, like an animal that heads toward a trap it has baited, then veers off the path because it has sighted better prey. What had she seen better, he wondered? What was she planning against him?

She's insane, he thought conveniently, absolving himself of blame. But he knew she was not insane; she had just learned to live without him, to manage her life alone. Everything he had said had been a mistake. He blanched at his miscalculations, what the lapse of eleven months of not being with her had done to his memory of her character. He wondered if she might have given in and behaved differently if he'd been agreeable, more tactful with her. She might have acquiesced to his proposal if he had waited until they had been to bed and he had gentled her a little and made her happy. He had looked forward to that—to seeing her stretch out her limbs in satisfaction, smile at him, and say something teasing or complimentary as she often did at those times. Was it possible that nothing beyond the care and defense of the baby had any interest now for Elaine, and that he himself moved about her mind a figure in a distant perspective of whom she no longer wished to have a clearer view? Perhaps the birth of an illegitimate child had changed her, increased her wisdom and dulled her senses. But whatever the situation Elaine would not now settle for what he had given her in the past—or what he had offered her that morning, and if in the past he might have been able to cajole her into accepting a life whose terms were profoundly humiliating and hurtful to her, he could do so no longer. He had not understood this during the long night drive from the ranch to Seguin—but he understood it now.

As he began to reflect on her reaction, it occurred to him that the love she had lavished on him had seemed an immutable fact of his life, a gift he could depend on whenever he went back to her. He had taken it for granted. In the secret part of his soul that longed for affection and warmth and sensuality, he had kept Elaine, and on a certain level he had almost imagined that he had been faithful to her. He had continued to believe in her love for him even after he had left her to solidify his position elsewhere, to prepare to marry and to lay the groundwork for a family in the way he had always intended, never considering that he was betraying her. He had never meant to hurt Shirlee and he had thought that he could depend on Elaine to act out of love for him, if not as an accomplice, at least as a silent and accepting partner —but that expectation had been secure only in the certainty of the night before.

He tried, as he had been trying for hours now, to imagine how the child would look, and resorted to attempting to picture any baby at all. He regretted that he had never really paid attention to one. He thought of Luther's newest child: He was a big infant, and when Lettie held him, he covered her breast. He had held his solid red arms around her neck, his head on her shoulder and turned into her neck, his white curly hair wet and clinging to his skin from the fever. Lettie had had to keep brushing it away from his face with her fingers and wiping his mouth with a cloth. But his own baby would be dark, not fair; and she would be younger and smaller.

Then a disturbing thought struck him, followed by a realization that he needed desperately to ask Elaine something that he should have remembered when he was with her. If she wouldn't let him provide for her, and she wished to remain independent, she'd have to go back to Dansville—and necessarily without the baby. What would she do about Sophie? He slowed the car and began looking for a farmhouse or a store.

At the junction of the farm road and the highway he stopped at a gas station in front of a sag-roofed cottage. It had no telephone, but since Hugh had decided that she would probably have refused to talk to him anyway, he opened the glove compartment, took out a tablet, and wrote a note while a stoop-shouldered, white-haired man, obviously the owner of the cottage and the two round-headed pumps, put gas in the tank. He asked for an envelope, which the man went inside to get from his wife. As he sealed the flap, Hugh, following the rules of country etiquette he knew so well, stood with him beside the car and talked to him about the war and the weather before he asked him to deliver the note to the Mueller farm, to Mrs. Menutis.

"It isn't too far up there," said the man, running his hand respectfully along the wet fender of the beautiful car. "Don't you want to take it yourself? They're real nice people." He kept his attention fixed on the Mercedes while the rain tapped outside the tin roof over the pumps on the pavement of broken oyster shells.

"I can't," Hugh answered. It seemed a stupid reply. He remembered how he must look: wet, dirty, unshaven, and bruised. "I don't think she'll see me."

The man looked grave and respectful, but when he nodded, he winked. "Yeah," he said, "they can be like that."

Hugh wondered if he knew about Elaine's child. People in the country usually heard about their neighbors' troubles—especially a misfortune as grave as this. He wanted to ask him if he had seen the baby, if he could tell him how she looked, what she was like, but he didn't dare. The man might already be suspicious of him. He had probably heard the rifle shots, and given Hugh's appearance and his request, it would be easy for him to conclude that he was the baby's father—that he was trying to see his little girl, and Mrs. Menutis wouldn't let him. Or worse still that he was running out on her and the kid, that that was what the note said and why he didn't want to deliver it himself.

The man pulled at his mustache and looked back at the Mercedes. "First one of these I've seen out here." The German car must have reminded him of something, because then he asked, "You know Mrs. Menutis's husband was killed in the war?"

Hugh's sleepy black eyes opened as full as a child's. "I've heard that," he said.

The man seemed to be depressed by this memory, and his glance fled from Hugh's, as if he were thinking of something other than what he was saying. "It's been a long time, though."

"You knew him?"

The man took hold of the brim of his cap and pulled it low over his forehead. He put his hands on his hips and looked out at the slackening rain. A watery light began to show through the branches of a hickory. "Everybody knew him," he said.

Even today, even when Elaine had his baby, the symbol of his primacy, Foley was there before him, perfect and indestructible because there was no way on God's earth he could make a mistake. *She probably tells herself that my baby is his,* he thought. Would she ever have denied Foley anything that he might ask of her? He didn't think so. He could tear at her, and tear and tear, but he could never eradicate Foley. It made him wonder why she hadn't accepted his proposal. She could have been rich and lazy, and had to put up with his lustful importunities so rarely that she could have indulged herself in fantasies of her husband and hardly noticed his presence at all. And not in the house Foley had provided for her—not Foley's house, but his! That would have been vengeance.

His anger sprang from his suffering at the loss of the most significant experience of love he had ever known in his life; his torment was clearly brought on by the gracelessness of their meeting and the frustration he had experienced during the last hour, and not just because of Elaine's rejection of him or because of the infidelity that he imagined in Elaine's memory, but also of his own treason. And Foley was always going to be present; he might as well resign himself. Eight years. She had told him.

He remembered how, several years earlier, during a rainstorm, she had explained Foley to him. "He was just like me," she had said, speaking with great agitation. "He knew what I was going to say before I said it because it was what he would have said. It was as if our souls were connected." To illustrate her statement, she had clasped her fingers, twisting them tightly together. "I know that sounds trite, but . . . " When she spoke that night of her love for Foley, it had been with the suppressed emotion of someone who has been wounded and is wounded still, and if she had told him more than she had meant to, she had seemed unable to stop: "While he was alive, I always imagined that our marriage was predestined—I even told my minister so. And after his death, because of the way that I suffered, I was certain of it. Foley knew me perfectly. For eight years, he loved me, and he never caused me any pain. I never made him unhappy—I couldn't have. And I never had to explain anything."

The man was talking to him about his car, then about foreign cars, and cars in general. He wanted to look inside the hood. While the rain warmed to a damp mist, they discussed how the engine worked, how it was put together like a watch, both of them knowing that Hugh's indulgence was the price of the errand. Finally he paid for the gas he had bought and tried to give the man some extra money. He knew it would be refused, but he understood, too, that it had to be offered. The man shook his head, looked down at the ground next to the pumps, and smiled. Realizing he wasn't going to catch his eye again, Hugh thanked him and stood with him a minute more, both of them staring down, their hands in their pockets, the man swinging one of his feet, grazing the dirt, until the correct time had passed, and Hugh could leave.

The glimmering day spread out ahead of him over the smooth, straight road and the gleaming pastures, over the rough, haphazard scattering of unpainted settlements, sometimes with a store, a tiny church, or a filling station, over the two-room tenant houses covered with composition fake-brick sidings, their porches scarcely wide enough for a rocking chair or a blanket-covered horsehair sofa, with rusted farm equipment strewn among the obstinate weeds. The sky began to clear, and as he passed through a small town, a soft, rinsed blue rose above the flowered yards. Clouds had grouped on one side of the sky, driven by shafts of sunlight that lit the mosaic of the pastures in metallic flashes. "I cannot live without her," he said aloud. "I just can't do that anymore."

He wondered what she would do when she received the note; he hoped it would not make her want to do just the opposite of what he had asked. He tried to think of what the next step might be, but it evaded him. *Because of Elaine,* he thought finally, *because she is so much changed, and because of me, because I haven't understood my position, and Elaine won't stand for it anymore, everyone is going to get hurt. Everyone, but that baby especially. Somehow I've got to keep that from happening. I've got to keep from quarreling with Elaine again, and injuring Sophie so badly that nothing I can do will ever fix it.*

* * *

Hugh walked quickly through the shining rotunda of the marble entrance hall in the hope that he would be able to get through the house and to his room before he was seen, so that he could avoid having to give any explanation of his activities between midnight and now. He would need to telephone Shirlee; she was probably already waiting for his call. If he took the central stairway, he might run into his mother, so he turned left and passed through the dining room, the breakfast room, and the pantry. He was halfway through the den, making his way to the service stairs, when his father called to him. He started through the door, but Clarence called again, and he turned down the long hall to his father's study. The door was open, and Clarence was sitting in the soft leather swivel chair behind a desk that was almost as wide as the room, great and gleaming in flame satinwood, with scalloped borders and inlaid panels on its handsome drawers. The light from the west was low and so bright behind him that as Hugh stood in the doorway to the study, he was unable to see his face. Responding to the motion of Clarence's hand, he entered the room, closing the hugh oak door behind him, and took a seat in the deep red chair directly across from his father.

Clarence moved forward uncomfortably and offered Hugh a cigarette, which he refused; he then put his hand on the neck of the whiskey decanter just above the silver disk that named its contents, and asked him if he wanted a drink.

Hugh shook his head and lifted his chin to look at his father through a hedge of black lashes that nearly hid his eyes. His face was unreadable, and his breathing was shallow. If he was nervous or felt any guilt or discomfort, he concealed it. In fact, he simulated boredom so successfully that, for a moment, Clarence was confused enough to wonder if he had misunderstood the rapid departure, the flowers, and the wine.

"So how is Mrs. Menutis?" he asked, smiling, but keeping his eyes steady. "I take it you weren't delivering those flowers to Matt." He waited for a response, but Hugh continued to avoid the engagement, so he went on: "She the one put that bruise on your chin?" Wounded or not, his son was as fine-looking a man as he had ever seen, and he liked everything about him. He was proud of him, and felt, at that moment, that there was no limit to that pride.

Hugh touched his face. It was sore and swollen. He had forgotten about Matt. That had been so long ago. "No," he answered. He crossed his ankle over his knee. His eyes remained impassive. "Matt hit me."

"How's Matt, then? You hit him first?"

"I didn't hit Matt," he said with exasperation. Out of context, it seemed strange that he hadn't piled into Matt for not telling him about Elaine, for letting Elaine persuade him to keep the knowledge of her flight to himself, and then for being so righteous about every damned thing.

In his soul, Clarence sighed with relief. "So you went to the ranch and not into town. You didn't see her, then?"

"Oh, I saw her." He drew down into the protective shadow of the chair's broad, padded wings. His head ached horribly, and to close out the bright light behind his father, he finally had to shut his eyes completely. "Jesus Christ," he whispered sorrowfully, complaining neither to the Savior nor to Clarence, but to the whole world for its insensitive and selfish willfulness in pitilessly pursuing its own ends and running over anything that got in its way—which, right now, was him and the three females for whom he felt responsible, since he was committed to all of them. He opened his eyes and leaned toward Clarence, whose face had lost all trace of amiability and equanimity. "I saw her, Dad."

Clarence picked up a pencil and tapped the eraser on the padded frame of the blotter, and to further distract himself, to keep his eyes from being too hard, from destroying all possibility of being taken into his son's confidence, he looked above Hugh's head at a photograph of them together on a hunting trip in Wyoming. He had invited Hugh to go with him when the boy was only ten or eleven. Hugh had always been big for his age; he had had stamina, and he had withstood the rigorous trip well, even carrying a heavy pack and the .22 that Clarence had given him for his birthday. Hugh had hunted seriously; he had never complained about the rugged hikes, and the only time he had cried was when he had missed a shot. He had insisted on building the campfires; he had got up early to prepare breakfast; he had helped everyone. He had talked a lot and laughed constantly, and on the way home, when they had left the stateroom that they had shared on the train, he had held Clarence's hand as they left the railway station, looking up at him and talking continuously about what they had done. For over a year, he had talked to Clarence about that trip. It was all he had seemed to think about. Clarence had wanted to go again, but there had never been time.

He looked at Hugh, at the creased brow, the eyes cast downward, and the hand patting the arm of the chair. What had Elaine

done to him? From what Matt had said, she had never hurt him:
She was a sweet woman, who had been pretty much at his beck
and call, and happy to stay that way. Clarence had never seen
them together; to do so would have been to acknowledge her
importance in Hugh's life, and he had felt that this was to be
avoided—though he had never disapproved of her in the least.
Now he wished that he had, wished that she had been the kind of
woman whom he could have raised hell about.

The silence had lasted too long. "When you met Shirlee, your
mother and I thought that you had come to some kind of understanding with Elaine—that you wouldn't be seeing her anymore.
It isn't going to help you much with the Farises if they find out
you've been down there." Clarence reached toward the tray for a
glass, and an ash dropped from his cigarette. "But I guess you
haven't seen her in a while," he said. Swiftly, with the side of his
hand, he brushed the blotter clean.

Hugh was surprised to hear his father talk about Elaine as if
their relationship were a subject familiar to him. "That's right,
Dad. Not since last April."

A tree rustled in the casement window behind his father. Because of the rain that morning, everything seemed washed and
fresh. Hugh's gaze traveled to the line of the lawn as it sloped
down to the swimming pool and then to the tangle of scrubs along
the bayou. He could see the roof of the gazebo, a place where,
last summer, he had sat with Shirlee, easing into the mystery of
being in love with a woman so unlike himself.

Clarence was speaking again. "You sure didn't give us any
warning of what was going on in your mind, Hugh. How come
you went out of here in such a hurry last night?" His voice was
uncharacteristically soft, without any of the masculine bravado
that he usually displayed when he was with his son and all other
men. "You care to tell me what happened?"

Hugh moved restlessly in his chair, as if he would rise and
leave the room. "I can't tell you anything yet, Dad; and I don't
want to talk about it until after I've had some sleep. I can't
think."

Clarence removed the stopper from the shimmering decanter
and filled his glass. "You sure you don't want one?" He held up
the glass, his hand steady and sure.

"No, thank you, Dad."

Clarence drank half of it, pulled in his lips, then shook his
head and put the glass down solidly. "She didn't want to see
you?" he asked.

"That's right. It didn't work out, and it's not going to. She doesn't want it anymore."

"There's someone else?"

Hugh laughed and reached wearily for a cigarette. Clarence pushed the package close to him and then handed him the striated silver lighter shaped like an ancient oil lamp. "There's someone else all right," said Hugh.

Clarence drained the rest of the whiskey. "She get married?"

Hugh waved the hand holding the cigarette in a back and forth gesture. "No, no . . ."

"I suppose you were upset by her reception."

"It was in no way a reception. I wasn't in the least welcome."

"Maybe it was just that you surprised her, and she wasn't ready for it."

"Dad . . ." He got up from the chair, crushed out the cigarette, and started toward the door. It was an amicable interrogation, but it was an interrogation all the same. He was not up to it; he had to decide on a course of action, and he knew that if he was going to protect his baby girl, Clarence must not have any part in the decision. "I'll talk to you about it later," he said. "After I've rested some. Do you know if Shirlee called me?"

"No, I don't."

"I'd better call her."

"What are you going to do about that chin?"

The question annoyed him. "I don't know. Maybe you have a suggestion."

"Your mother's going to want to know what went on last night, Hugh."

He looked back at his father in an agony of aversion to the suggestion that he talk to Clara at all, and answered him hard and quickly: "I'll tell her that Matt punched me because he thought I needed it, because he felt bad about not telling me what he'd decided not to, because he loves you more than he loves me, because he thinks he can pass judgment on things that don't concern him, and because I called him a liar."

Hugh stared at his father, but Clarence, preoccupied with questions Hugh's outburst had raised, had no reply. As the implications spun out before him, and his imagination, spurred to daring by the whiskey (which he was drinking in the middle of the afternoon on an empty stomach), spoke out in earnest, he felt his blood slow down and the color drain from his face. A tremble came to the hand that was clutching the neck of the crystal decanter, causing it to fall on its side. He retrieved it quickly, but at least a jigger had been lost, and it was a very fine blend. He cursed softly, not at the waste, but at the revelation. He examined his son's predicament. It couldn't be. Hugh had been away from her . . . since when?

"Dad, if she had let me know months ago," Hugh was saying, "I could have kept her from going out there. But I didn't know anything. Elaine. . . . Elaine's so goddamned . . ."

He started as he heard Clara's voice call his name from the sunroom. She had seen him come in, and she had been watching for him; she could only wait so long for the interview in the study to come to a close. She needed answers, and she was entitled to them. Hugh looked at his father beseechingly, asking in one quick, desperate glance for defense, but Clarence, helpless, shook his head and held up the palms of his hands. Hugh turned away from him, lowered his head and pressed it against the dark, rich library wall panel. Again Clara called his name.

Clarence followed behind him into the sunroom. Clara was standing in front of a rubber tree twice her height and ten times her width. Around her neck was a string of white pearls; her silk shirtdress was sky-blue, the color of her eyes. She looked like a character in a fantasy, and Hugh realized that he had always thought so. He disliked his mother's diminutiveness almost as much as he resented her serenity. He had always felt awkward with Clara, uncouth. He had never been able to look good enough, to behave well enough, to learn enough, to do anything well enough to please her; and now whenever she was present in a room, even in the house, he wanted to be somewhere else. He certainly didn't want to be with her now, and he would try to escape before ceding to her anything of what he knew.

When she saw his chin and the condition of his clothes, she covered the lower part of her face with her hands and gasped; and instantly her eyes filled with tears. "I suppose that woman . . ."

She had never before spoken to him of Elaine, much less forbid him to see her, and why she had either the interest or the audacity to do so now, why she didn't leave him to his father, as she had done for all the years of his life, Hugh could not conceive. He stood still, looking down at her, not moving a muscle, while she told him in no uncertain terms that he was never again to see the woman in Dansville, and that if he did, she and his father would withdraw from him both their sympathy and their support. She was speaking so fast, struggling with an argument based on such scant information and so little reflection, that for a time neither of the men knew what to do, other than to watch her.

She seemed to have no understanding of the need to be cautious, unable to break free of her indignation, and when, in a voice gone suddenly quiet and honeyed, she referred to Elaine as a whore, and Hugh picked up a potted plant, a cluster of remarkably beautiful Dutch iris, and threw it over her head, where it flew through the panes of a French door and landed on a glass table on the terrace outside, shattering it, her expression showed not only astonishment at his rage but ignorance of what might have warranted such a violent act.

The noise of the quarrel had been heard all over the house and yard, and the servants, led by Cana, quickly made their way to the door of the sunroom. With his hands lifted menacingly—not to hit his mother, but to shake her apart—Hugh stepped toward Clara, and Clarence blocked him.

"Don't you touch your mother!"

Hugh broke loose, uttered a cry of physical pain, and shouted at the only man in the world whom he wouldn't have struck for trying to restrain him: "Then tell her to get the hell off me about Elaine!"

Never in all the years he had been with her had he felt so close, so inextricably bound to Elaine as he did at that moment. Clarence realized this and knew that there was no question of what Hugh was going to do. But needing to hear a confirmation from Hugh of what he already suspected, and having decided that Clara would have to be told, one way or another, he asked: "What's wrong with you, Hugh? What happened in Dansville? You tell me now, or I'm getting on the telephone to Matt!"

Hugh groaned, and his eyes, like those of a wounded beast, glittered and passed over the room, as if they would find him an exit, not from the space but from the problem.

Then, while Clara cowered in the flowered taffeta corner of a sofa, terrified of her son and horrified by his life, he told them. He stood close to his father and spoke hotly, his muscles still quivering from his rage and exertion. Feeling that his mother would defeat him still, that somehow she would try to keep him from the family that he had unwittingly procured for himself, he refused to address her and spoke only to Clarence. He told him that on her parents' farm near Seguin, on the east side of the Guadalupe River, in the direction of Kingbury and Luling, Elaine had been living for months; that she had given birth to a daughter, that the baby's name was Sophie, and that this child was certainly his; that Elaine refused to let him see her; that he had lost his temper and unwisely told her that he would get a court order that

would enable him to see the baby; that he had threatened to take
the baby from her; and that she had picked up a shotgun to kill
him but had somehow changed her mind about doing that, and
that he was still in shock from the incident—and not just because
he had been shot at but because he had had to return home without having reached an understanding with Elaine, or having had
the opportunity to see his child.

"Do what you want!" he shouted to end it, in one of those
strangely inappropriate reactions to a suspected threat. "I don't
care! But don't ask me to give them up. . . . You hear me?" He
was looking at his father, but the warning was clearly aimed at
Clara.

The room was silent, but for Clara's crying. The servants had
discreetly withdrawn except for Cana, who was shaking her head
and looking down at the gleaming blue tile of the floor.

After watching Hugh for a moment, Clarence squeezed his
eyes tight and cleared his throat. When he opened his eyes again,
his expression was one of wonder at and admiration for the blind
obstinacy of the race, with all its mysteries and inconsistencies
and incomprehensible aberrations. He took Hugh's hand in both
of his and then embraced him. "Well, well . . ." he said so hoarse-
ly that he had to clear his throat again; and when he looked at his
son and smiled, Hugh, with a face still flushed and strained with
fury, returned the smile instantly.

Cana was holding Clara, both consoling and needing to be
consoled herself, so that while she stroked Clara's face and neck,
Clara patted the white uniform that was stretched so tightly across
the solid back. At last Clara reached out her hand to the two men,
and when neither of them took it, she let it go limply to her side,
her bracelets clanking together. Her head was lowered, and she
shivered as if from cold. "What can we do?" she whispered.
"What can we do?"

"Do?" asked Hugh. He was bewildered by what she might be
implying; his thoughts were still in the misty aftermath of the
instability that follows rage.

"Not to lose the grandbaby," said Cana, speaking for Clara,
"and not to have you killed by her mama."

But that was Cana and not his mother. He watched Clara.

Clara tried to smile, but her situation was too desperate; her
mouth returned to a thin, worried line, and she blinked her eyes
rapidly. "It can be settled in court," she said. "Your father can
find someone to keep her from. . . . Well, she's to blame." But
when her eyes met her son's, she sighed deeply, pressed her

hands together, and said with effort, "Please, darling, try not to . . . " She stopped and pulled at the corners of her handkerchief. "When you go back . . . well, before you do, you'll have to be sure that she won't . . . that she no longer feels so . . . "

Hugh went to her, offered her both his hands, drew her up to him, and held her, as he struggled to hold back the strong emotion that both his nature and his upbringing proscribed. He listened, nodded at her requests, and then, gently delivering her to his father, he left the room. Behind him, mixed with the murmurs of the servants, the mewings of his mother, and the low, solid voice of Cana, he heard the alerted yardman beginning to sweep up the spears of glass.

At six-thirty, Hugh was dressed and ready. He had sat quietly for a while alone in his room; his head was clear; he knew what he had to do, and what he wanted to do. The outburst with his mother had helped. The drive to the Farises' was not far, a few blocks through the dense shade; before him lay cool lavender and apricot clouds, underlined by a strip of red. He pulled into the great circular driveway, was admitted into the house, and stood in the columned hallway, waiting for Shirlee to come down the winding staircase, a circular complement to the driveway and the round window of the stairwell. Dressed in pink, with all the delicacy and charm of a freshly picked camellia, Shirlee floated down the steps and across the shiny floor, put her hands on Hugh's shoulders, and without calling attention to his badly bruised chin, waited to receive her customary greeting. While the butler made some redundant arrangement in the cloak closet, Hugh kissed her, and when the front door was opened for them, they left.

The party was in the neighborhood, in a huge white house with wide lawns, a long blue swimming pool, and an Italian garden—not unlike Shirlee's house or his own. The hosts were named Carter. They had made their money in banking; the family was learned and cultured and remarkably well traveled. They talked of Paris, Rome, and New York with ease; they were as much at home on the Côte d'Azur as in San Francisco. They knew the names of the parks in the major capitals of the world, the most fashionable streets, the places to shop, the internal politics. No one awed them; and as part of their understanding of the Christian message, they tried not to awe others. Their house bordered on a country club, so that, from the front, the lawn looked like an English park, and only an occasional golfer ever destroyed that illusion. When she had been in college in Tennessee, Eleanor Carter had belonged to the same sorority as Betty Jean Faris; they were still great friends, and it was for this reason that the Carters were giving a party for Shirlee and Hugh.

Shirlee let her silk coat be removed by the black maid who answered the door, and thanked her by name. A butler approached, and Hugh ordered a Scotch for himself and champagne for Shirlee. Shirlee's girl friends came to compliment her dress, a long, full-skirted silk which became her, both in color and in style. She was the center of attention that night, and her sweet eyes flashed, and she showed her teeth in a series of smiles while she and her friends discussed the details of the shower that afternoon. They were old friends, had been close all their lives. Those who were married were the leaders of the group, since, though they could neither drink alcohol nor vote, that ceremony had conferred adulthood upon them.

In the living room, as far as possible from the hired pianist, who was playing popular ballads and songs from Broadway hits, the men had arranged themselves in a cluster, the center of which was Wendell Carter and his thirty-five-year-old son, Dave, who had just been made a partner in a large and prestigious firm. They discussed the fighting in Korea, which at that time was uppermost in everyone's mind, questioning the wisdom of having entered the war at all, the position of Japan, the rearming of Japan, and the draft. Hugh turned his attention to a friend in law school, and they talked of their studies.

About half an hour later, Shirlee came to him, bored and complaining, half-teasing, saying that he had deserted her, and that she had missed him. She put her slender hand on the sleeve of his dinner jacket and guided him away from his friend into the room where the food was being served on silver platters and crystal plates, a room that smelled of roast beef cooked outdoors, shrimp sautéed in butter and herbs, lobster in a sherry sauce, and cheese melted with cumin over Mexican peppers. The only light was provided by candles in the center of the table and the crystal sconces on the watered silk coverings of the walls.

Shirlee began talking to Hugh about the wedding invitations. They were being printed; she had chosen to have them done in script, and she and her mother were pleased with the proofs of the engraving that they had seen that afternoon. She told him about the flowers. They had decided on orchids and stephanotis for the bridesmaids' bouquets; there would be white and yellow roses on the altar. She had just placed a piece of roast beef between the two halves of a soft, fragrant roll and was offering it to Hugh when he took the sandwich from her hand and told her. His face was very close to hers, and from across the table, an observer would have thought he was witnessing a warm colloquy between lovers instead of a violent rupture in which one of them was breaking their bond as irrevocably and with the same dire consequences as if a chain that held a ship to its anchor in a gale were sundered.

For a moment, Shirlee kept her eyes on the table of food, as if she were searching the silver platters, the candelabra, and the crystal plates for the lie or the mistake in what she had heard. The napkin that Shirlee had been holding fell to the brass-clawed foot of the table without her being aware of having lost it. She set her plate down slowly, as if the weight of it in her now powerless hand had caused it to happen, rather than her having willed it.

Hugh realized that it was cruel not to have told her earlier, and that the delay was a failure of courage on his part, since it was not simply her pain that he had wanted to postpone, but his own. If he had told her directly what he was thinking, he might have said: "I do not know what has happened to me. I don't understand it, but I have no choice other than to act as I am doing. I have no alternative and I don't wish an alternative. I don't know what I wish, really, but I know what I'm going to do, and perhaps that best expresses my wish. In any case, this is my choice, and it is not negotiable." He told her instead only of his predicament and his decision, and because he thought it would be less painful if there was no confusion or wavering on his part, he was firm. He spoke swiftly and carefully and clearly in order to prevent a misunderstanding that might give her any hope whatever.

He had never seen her eyes as beautiful and expressive as they were then, dissolved in their great pools of tears in which the candles were reflected like torches in a pair of troubled lakes. She was silent. She turned from him in the most resolute and dignified movement he had ever observed her to make. Without asking him whether he preferred to leave the party or stay, and without thanking the host or hostess, she glided out of the house, leaving her coat behind. Silently she waited with him for the car under the handsome porte-cochére, the waving candlelight playing on the slightly wind-blown folds of her gorgeous skirt, and she was quiet and isolated from him as he drove her home. She seemed to hate him; he hoped she did.

As they sat in the car, the only light coming from the porch, where the high lamp hung on its curved metal chains, she asked him in a delicate, childish voice he hardly recognized and which broke, even on the first word: "Is there any possibility that you may change your mind, or that Elaine . . .?"

He did not draw close to her. Any comfort that he gave her might be misinterpreted. "I can't change my mind, Shirlee." How could he tell her that he must now use all his cleverness and cunning and intelligence, not to plan for his future with her, the woman whom two days ago he had meant to live with for the rest of his life and to give his name, but to court, instead, the stubborn and willful and very much changed mother of his child?

He knew she was crying, yet still he dared not touch her, fearing that something might break inside him to challenge his resolution and to lure him back to the comfort of an existence without problems. If he were to hold her, to sympathize with her in any way, to see in her a hurt child and confuse the image with the woman in Seguin, he might irrevocably ruin his life and that of the two others.

Abruptly she tipped her head and put her hands under her hair to unscrew the diamond earrings he had given her two weeks before her birthday, the present that had been the pride of her twentieth year. She hesitated a moment, looking to him for guidance, but as he did not have the heart to offer her his open hand to receive them, she placed the jewels carefully on the dashboard.

Without looking at him again, she opened the car door, ran up the walk, put her slight weight against the massive whiteness of her front door, and disappeared. He did not wait at the foot of the drive, as he had habitually done, to see the light go on in her room, to see her push back the curtain and wave to him or open the window and call down to him one last affectionate farewell; nor, when he got home, would he expect her to telephone to wish him good night one last time, a practice that irritated his mother but pleased him.

The next morning at half past nine, Jerome Faris arrived at the Littletons'. Behind the closed door of his father's study, Hugh listened to a quietly and quickly delivered list of his faults, real and imagined. Whatever merits Mr. Faris might have thought he possessed had been washed away in the flood of his wife's and daughter's grief, and he intended, if he could not change Hugh's mind, at least to insult him. Hugh did not attempt to defend himself even when the remarks were unjust. This was part of the price. Like a treed animal, he would have to hear out the fury of the hound until he was spent and would go away.

While the coffee steamed untasted in the richly decorated silver pot that Cana had brought just before Mr. Faris had risen to shut the door himself, he accused Hugh of shirking his obligations, and Hugh reminded him of his obligation elsewhere. Whenever the man spoke, Hugh either nodded his head, agreeing with the accusation, or met his gaze with eyes faintly squinted, not out of hostility, but out of sadness and regret. He was not a man to easily accept being insulted, but, more important, he was not a man to easily forgive himself for a mistake.

"You must understand," he said, looking under his eyebrows at the furious father, "that I would never have asked Shirlee to marry me if I had known at that time what I discovered yesterday, nor would I have involved her in a courtship that could lead to nothing."

"When you asked me for Shirlee's hand, you chose to keep me ignorant of your relationship with this woman."

"I told Shirlee," Hugh said, "and I'm fairly certain that the information passed to her mother, and therefore to you."

Mr. Faris struggled to reply, and then was silent. He jerked at his tie and stretched his neck, and with a shaking hand, poured himself a cup of coffee, spilling a portion of it into the saucer. He picked up one of the starched white napkins and, without unfolding it, wiped at a stain on his jacket. This accident embarrassed him and caused him to change his tactics; like a ballet dancer who has fallen or a singer who has missed a note and so performs better, he became more circumspect, and the arguments he presented were more carefully considered. He crossed his legs and, though no less angry, relaxed a little. This was the second, more serious phase; Hugh recognized it and prepared himself.

"There is another possibility," Mr. Faris said, staring at Hugh with such resolution that Hugh knew that what he was about to hear was what he and Shirlee's mother had decided on, and that he had been sent there to propose it as an alternative to breaking their child's heart. "That you provide for the woman. Give her what she wants. Under the circumstances, it's in her interest to be reasonable and to take what you offer."

Hugh was still, but his expression changed a little, since this plan, coming from someone else, shocked him. He decided to tell Mr. Faris only half of what he had proposed to Elaine: "I tried that," he said. His mouth turned up at the corners as he thought of Elaine and how hardheaded she was, how she was ruining him without even trying, just by acting in character, and that he had let it happen, by pursuing her, loving her richly, and getting caught. It fascinated him still that she might have killed him, that the inspiration had come to her, yet she had been unable to quite carry it through. "I tried that, but she wouldn't have it," he said. He leaned forward, folding his arms on the desk. "I can't abandon them, Mr. Faris . . . not the way things are now. I'd be unable to live with that."

"Yet you're quite able to live with having made my child ill with grief; you find no problem in humiliating her and her family?"

"What would you like me to do?"

"What I told you: Support the baby. Work out an agreement that is satisfactory to the mother. Give her what she wants and be done with it."

"Renounce the paternity, except for support? Ignore the mother? Let her make out the best she can?"

"That's right."

"For the rest of her life?"

"Yes."

"The first part of her life hasn't been all that good," he said reflectively.

"I would say the same," said Mr. Faris, deliberately misinterpreting Hugh's words.

Hugh watched as Mr. Faris poured the coffee from the saucer into his cup. When he looked up at Hugh again, he had another idea. "I've heard that she is a beautiful woman and still young," he said. "She'll surely marry now that there is the necessity to find a father for her child."

"That baby is mine, Mr. Faris," Hugh said so precisely that it was unlikely to be disregarded. He listened to himself talk; he felt alien in that room; he wanted to be somewhere else. He was simply putting in his time, repaying a fraction of what he owed this man's family—a debt he could never make good. "She already has a father," he said.

Mr. Faris stroked his chin with the earpiece of his glasses. "Good God," he said slowly. "I can't be hearing you. There must be something that I'm failing to understand."

"I regret what has happened, and you are making me tell you more than I intended, but my actions disturb me only insofar as they hurt Shirlee; I can't be sorry for what I'm going to do, except in that respect."

Mr. Faris frowned at the man who had come so close to being his son-in-law, who had pleased him, and who, strangely enough, in the matter of honor, pleased him now. Still he said: "You've played your hand poorly."

"I haven't played it at all. I picked it up with no chance of improving it, and I'm arranging it as best I can."

Mr. Faris spoke quietly but with a note of hope in his voice, for he still felt he had a chance of changing the younger man's mind. "You're stubborn, Hugh; in fact, you are being so unreasonable that I suspect that you never cared that much about my daughter, but that you do love your baby's mother. My position would be stronger if it were otherwise. I've never heard of a man abandoning a beautiful and suitable fiancée for a woman who has been married, who is older than he, and whose life is blemished." He opened an initialed gold cigarette case, took out a cigarette and began to tap it on the table. "And I've never heard of a man as rich as you are going back to a mistress he'd left, for reasons of paternity alone. Never! Why should you do that?" Refusing to admit himself beaten, and wishing to God that he could avoid going home with such a dismal report for the two women he loved, Mr. Faris persisted: "I'm sure that it would be easy for you to give the mother a substantial enough amount of money to satisfy her. There is surely some figure to which she would agree. If I thought it necessary, I would even be willing to contribute to this. I see nothing objectionable in that." He lit the cigarette that he had been holding.

Hugh started to speak but rose and walked to the window instead. A light rain had begun, though at the foot of the garden, the sun shone brightly, like a gold medallion on a gray coat. The room had darkened suddenly, and when he returned to the desk and bent over the table to flick on the lamp, the light briefly caught his unhappy face. "I can't abandon my child, Mr. Faris," he reiterated. "And I can't regret her existence. I have to be proud of it. . . . I only wish I didn't have to embarrass Shirlee."

Mr. Faris sighed deeply and leaned back in the chair. The long ash of his cigarette collapsed and sprayed delicately onto an enormous bouquet of impossible flowers in the pattern of the rug. "Then you are in love with your baby's mother," he said softly.

"That's correct." He kept the same even tone that he had used since he had answered Clarence's knock on his bedroom door to tell him that Shirlee's father was waiting for him in the downstairs hallway. "If I have any understanding at all of what has happened to me in the past forty-eight hours, I would do Shirlee no favor either in prolonging our engagement or in marrying her. At some point, I would have to go back to Elaine." It was best to close the conversation, not to extend a discussion to which there could be only one outcome. "Mr. Faris, I was not going to Elaine because I had found out about the baby. It was only later that I learned about the child. I was planning to see her, to court her in the way that I used to, and to make love to her if she would let me."

Mr. Faris glanced away briefly in an effort to master his astonishment, and then his eyes flashed back to Hugh's. "Were you drunk?"

"I think that's immaterial."

Smashing out his cigarette, Mr. Faris replaced his coffee cup on the etched silver tray and stood up. He looked around the room carefully, as if reviewing its contents, and spoke out of a rigid face and through a mouth that was almost closed. "I'm glad you told me," he said. "It makes my task easier, gives me the ammunition I need. I appreciate the confidence, and I give you my solemn promise that I shall do everything in my power to convince my little girl that her loss is of no consequence."

Clarence, who was in the sunroom overseeing the repair of the windowpanes, did not come out to show him to the door. It was impossible for Clarence to address him in any way tactfully, and he thanked God silently that he was not that deceived father. Clara, who had taken a sedative the night before, was still sleeping and had not yet learned of the visit. Jerome Faris stepped into the glistening rain alone and took the car from Jesse, who understood, as all the Littleton servants understood that day, that comments to him about the weather or anything else would be out of place.

Hugh walked upstairs slowly. He wanted to go to Shirlee and comfort her, to do anything at all to ease her suffering and his, to make it up to her in some way, but all the avenues were closed to him. Elaine had left him no alternatives, and in his heart, he had accepted that. It was not giving up Shirlee that agonized him but his regret for having made her unhappy.

He made a telephone call to Seguin, one more in a series which Elaine had refused to accept; then he lay on his bed, his hands behind his head, and tried to imagine, to summon up some image of his daughter. He tried to picture the inside of the house and what the farm looked like: Since it had been raining when he was there, he didn't even know the orientation of the property. He had seen nothing but Elaine, and their drama had passed through his mind like a fierce wind, sweeping away all other impressions. He retained no memories of that afternoon but of the quarrel itself; he knew every word of it by heart.

That night he went out to dinner with Dan Carey, a friend from school who had come to Houston with him for the engagement parties, but who would be returning without him, starting back the next morning at sunrise. Dan was to have been a groomsman; it was at his house that Hugh had met Shirlee. They talked until ten o'clock, then played pool in a pool hall on the north side of town; and after refusing the solicitations of two prostitutes (both of them so young, childlike, and pathetic that they should not have been away from home, much less on the streets), they sat down on the torn seat of a dingy booth, discussed plans, and drank beer.

As the cool dawn crept over the empty city, Dan pulled his car away and Hugh drove home in quiet anticipation. The downtown buildings were brown and velvet gray against the yellow skin of morning; the bridges shimmered in alabaster. A flock of black ducks, leaving the dark shelter of pines in the park to the west of the city, cut across the bayou and searched for a place to feed. They seemed to dip a single wing and move in their wavelike patterns at the command of a single mind.

Once again, Hugh tried unsuccessfully to reach Elaine by telephone and then fell into a long and uninterrupted sleep, unsure of his future (for the moment, at least, having lost everything), and sorry about every misstep of his past but one.

Chapter 11

THERE HAD BEEN a warning in Hugh's note. No, a request: Until she heard from him again, would she stay at the farm and do nothing about the baby? For God's sake, would she please not sign anything? She tore the message up. Then a night letter came, containing an apology for the crude offer of two days before. He asked her again not to sign anything, not to give away their child. She put the note in her jewelry box, under the pearls that he had given her, and from time to time took it out and read it. She slipped it inside her blouse and carried it with her until, angry again with the one who had written it, remembering something he had said, she pushed it back in the box and clicked down the lid.

In the early morning and at sundown she took long walks, thinking about her problems, imagining what Hugh intended, and what her reactions might be. She sat on the porch and rocked the baby; she fed her in a place where she could watch the road from the window while her mother and the wife of the hired hand talked to her about friends and church and the change in government farm subsidies and criticized the state, and then the local politicians. Sometimes, when the discussions became heated, and objectivity was lost, the conversation deteriorated into aphorisms spoken in German. Elaine did not participate; she took care of her baby and thought of other things.

After the quarrel with Hugh, she had refused to eat, over which she and her mother had had a serious fight. The reason was the nursing of Sophie. Feeding a baby was, to Mrs. Mueller, sacrosanct; that Elaine jeopardized her health and therefore the baby's was a sin. The hunger strike had lasted the better part of a day and had been over, when, at six P.M., with both women in tears, Elaine had eaten to the last spoonful a bowl of vegetable soup, thick with beef and tomatoes, and drunk a glass of dark beer—and then pushed the empty soup bowl away from her, put her head on the table, and resumed crying.

The phone had rung many times that day and the next, and each time Mrs. Mueller had answered and come to Elaine to tell her that it was Hugh—and each time she had refused to speak to him. But on the third day, when the ringing of the phone echoed through the house, Elaine pushed her chair roughly back from the table where she was sitting, went to the phone herself and angrily lifted the receiver.

"I want to talk to you," he answered in reply to her harsh question. "I won't stay long. You don't have to let me in the house." He continued talking, softly, carefully. He coaxed her a little, then waited through the pauses.

"Where are you calling from?"

"Seguin. I spent the last two nights in a motor court."

His patience, and the fact that he was so nearby, confused her. "I didn't know you were here, Hugh. Is anyone with you?" If Hugh had brought his lawyer, she had no intention of agreeing to see him now; if that was what the errand was about, she would insist on a formal meeting in the law office of Lenn Ackerman, a friend of her father's. Since she had last seen Hugh she had spoken to Lenn; she knew her rights, exactly what they were, and that they were strongly in her favor. "Are you alone?" she asked.

"Yes," he answered.

"All right," she said softly. "When?"

Distraught with her capitulation, Elaine told herself that she had agreed to see Hugh because she needed to let him know that nothing he could do would make any difference to her, that he had died for her the night he had betrayed her—the night he had given her Sophie. And he was coming now, not because he cared for her, but to try to take Sophie from her. Yet, when she went to dress, she chose her best wool skirt and sweater and placed a cardigan about her shoulders not for its warmth but because its shade of green complemented the color of her hair. The shoes she wore were not for walking, but sling pumps made of a smooth taupe leather. She studied the effect carefully in the mirror—and then, angry at her concern, removed the outfit and replaced it with faded jeans, a thick cotton pullover, and boots. And when her reflection in the mirror remained alluring, when nothing she selected to wear was successful in making little of her superb complexion and features, she took her wedding ring from its hiding place and pushed it determinedly onto her finger. Then minutes later, again in her green wool, her hair tied back with a matching ribbon, she picked up the book on her bedside table and went downstairs to wait in the porch swing.

The day was clear, windy, mild. Wide streamers of clouds dipped to the horizon in flat swaths, swift and violent in their painterly descent. She held her book in her hands, reading a paragraph or two, losing the story line, then looking toward the road. A moment after she had despaired of trying to concentrate on her reading and had put the book on the seat of the swing, she saw the car turn into the drive and come slowly toward the house, stopping when it reached the picket fence. Hugh got out, stood beside the car door, not approaching but waiting in the spirit of his promise, while Elaine slowly descended the steps toward where he waited. They stood facing each other, motionless. As she glanced up at his features, it seemed to Elaine that the sky coming between the branches above him had shaped a kind of flower, but no, it was the blueness beside a particularly bright cloud. The branches behind him were covered in a new growth of leaves, almost transparent in their newness, and in the air, there was motion.

"You look beautiful," he said, looking at her with the kind of nervous tenderness that she remembered from their courtship.

Formerly she would have responded to his compliment and his mood. At another time, she would have taken him in her arms, then asked him about himself, listening to each word, almost committing to memory his responses. But now she imagined a method in his desire to please her, and since the tone of his greeting had simply intensified her distrust, she replied without regard, "You're dressed up. I hardly know you."

He looked down at his clothes. "I dressed up for you. You didn't like the way I looked the last time I came."

"I didn't tell you that."

"You did."

She had never seen him so carefully groomed. His suit was in a gray flannel material, soft and of a light weight, and his shirt looked particularly white in contrast with a dark-blue patterned tie. His laced shoes gleamed from a recent polishing.

He lifted his hand tentatively, then dropped it to his side. "You're wearing the pearls I gave you."

"They're mine."

"It's okay."

"I know damn well."

He reached for her hand, but she drew it back.

"I promised not to upset you—so I won't ask to see her," he said, "but I've been afraid you might make some arrangement to give her away. You haven't done anything—signed anything, have you?" For all their dark depth, his eyes were very clear.

Elaine was silent. She had never seen Hugh so careful, not since long ago, when an estrangement between them disturbed him, and he would scheme to bring about an accord. But she would never let him have Sophie—if only because she would never let the woman he preferred to her become Sophie's mother. Besides, she had made up her mind to keep the baby. Hugh might have other children, but Sophie was the legacy from her time with this man whom she had so much loved. She had already told Arlet of her decision. It would mean that she could not go back to Dansville, but she had been offered a job in San Antonio: One of Foley's cousins had a small dress shop in Alamo Heights and needed someone to run it.

"Did you?" Hugh prompted her.

She shook her head. "Nothing's signed."

The garden at this time of year was exceptionally pretty: The grass had come back up, the callas were colorful with great spotted leaves. Dozens of pruned rose bushes were clustered in beds enclosed by bricks set in at angles; several of the flower beds had seedlings, and displayed a fuzz of green. Clouds of pink hydrangeas bordered the house, and along a wire trellis a flowering jasmine tumbled in generous starbursts of yellow blooms. It was a handsome place, and Elaine was proud of it; since her childhood it had changed very little.

Foley had teased her mother about keeping things unchanged, being orderly, methodical; it was European, old country, not American, he said. She had loved her times here with Foley— Foley who had always been doing things, tearing down, restoring, planting new flowers, building with that terrible energy. Foley had tried to make improvements for her mother, not just repairs, but changes, and Mrs. Mueller had always refused, preferring the peacefulness of uninterrupted durations. They had always come here for vacations: Christmas, Easter, the Fourth of July. Jimmy, still in diapers that sagged around his thighs, showing the crease in his buttocks, a bowlegged baby with hair the color of corn silk, had followed Foley around, carrying the hammer in his chubby baby arms, dropping the nails out of the box, losing them in the grass, squatting to search; and Foley would turn back, speaking sweetly to him, coaxing him on. Jimmy had been Foley's shadow then, and in many ways, so had she. Elaine's eyes went to the road, where, a dozen years ago, she might have looked for Foley to come home.

But the man at her arm now was not Foley. This was a very different man—not blond and imposing but dark and terrible, and separated from her by age and class and opportunity; a rough man without the sympathy that her husband had had, not a person who would nurture her but one who had to be nurtured, a cruel child with a mind of his own that fascinated her, and a body that hers responded to in ways that made her blush to remember; a man she had begun to love because, in a certain way, he had reminded her of her husband. It was a vitality that they shared, which she had once tried to tell Matt about, but which he had misunderstood.

The man who had just tried to hold her and whose arms she had evaded was not one who would think and act and do everything for her as Foley had done, settle her in a charming house in a shady town and cherish her (and do it well, so perfectly that, for the duration of their marriage, she had abdicated her independence and been grateful to him for it), but one with whom, thus far, because of her terror of alienation, she had always been slightly at odds.

"You call her Sophie?" he asked.

"After my mother."

"That's nice."

"I thought so." She raised her eyes to his and narrowed them. "Sophie Menutis," she said. "It's on the certificate."

His face clouded for a moment, and she knew it cost him an effort when he smiled wistfully. "You don't think of me here, do you, Elaine?"

She shook her head, but it was not a negative reply: His question troubled her, and she did not want to answer.

"You think of your husband here."

"Yes," she said. "I met him here. We were married in the garden."

This time he could not hide his pain from her; a dark, wounded look passed over his face, as if he had just learned something he should have known, something that had been kept from him, and not by Elaine or anyone else, but by his own misapprehension. She felt a stab of pity for him, and when he uttered her name on a pleading note and reached for her hand, she did not resist. Murmuring softly that they must go somewhere to talk, he led her from the yard, and she followed.

They climbed a steep embankment. She let him hold on to her arm, but it was she who chose the way, and at the top, she took him to a moss-covered log, where they could sit. When Hugh was silent, Elaine began to pick up twigs from the woods floor and snap them between her fingers, trying to find a suitable, impersonal remark.

"If the baby had been a boy, I planned to call him after one of my brothers," she said. "Not after my father, since a nephew already has that name. But then Arlet would have wanted to choose the name herself—if that was the way it had worked out." She spoke to him with a slight lift to her chin, directly, and sometimes severely. It was her intention to keep him from approaching their child, even in his mind. She flaunted her own intimacy with Sophie and she made it clear that she would prohibit his involvement. Sophie was not really his. Not really.

For an instant, she looked up into the trees, as if someone had called to her from there, then she returned her attention to the remains of twigs she had broken. Hugh reached over to stop the activity of her hands and told her what he had done. "Three days ago," he replied, in answer to her question. "It's finished."

The vividness of his gaze disturbed her and made her turn away toward the more neutral landscape. For a fraction of a second, she felt as if she had just completed a tremendous race, like the difficult competitions she had taken part in years earlier at school, which she had prayed to win, fleeing down the dirt road behind the barns, far away from her brothers and her parents, kneeling and holding her breath, squeezing her eyes shut until they hurt, her lashes becoming wet and heavy. She touched Hugh's arm, and her fingers dug into the material that covered it. "You'll want to go back," she said. "Shirlee will ask you and you'll have to go." Her eyes were wide, then suddenly blinking. She wanted to shake him to force him to be truthful.

"I'm not lying," he answered a moment later in response to her accusation. His voice was quiet now, level and serious.

She could not take it in; it made no sense. She knew nothing of this version of Hugh. The man who had just told her that he had given up the woman he loved for the sake of an illegitimate child he had never seen was not the arrogant man who had stalked about her house, parading before her in his dark, brutal nakedness, like a young god; not the man who had appeared before her in the deerblind, his bloody trophy slung over his arm, tired and proud and demanding of approbation and a tribute that she had so determinedly refused to provide. He could not mean what he said; she was unable to accept it. She had taken it for granted that he would know how to get Sophie, just as he knew everything, was wise to the world of power in a way that she could never be because it had never been in her to want so much. But perhaps she had been wrong—perhaps he had discovered that there was no legal way he could take Sophie from her, and so had invented this story about Shirlee to trick her into giving her child up. She got to her feet and moved away quickly down the slope.

He was behind her immediately, and when she stumbled, he grasped her elbow to keep her from falling. A vine tore at her jeans. She heard his jacket catch in it, then pull loose. The wind was picking up, and she hugged her arms around herself, tugging at her cardigan. His hand on her arm stopped her, and he lifted the sweater from her shoulders to help her into it. She took it away from him and put it on herself, ashamed that she was letting him see her, not only petulant, but suddenly awkward.

"She's not your baby," she said coldly. "I don't think of her that way." Her words were like a refrain so much repeated that it has become more evocative of the interim suffering of the one who recites it than what it means to convey.

"That's a peculiar prejudice," he said.

At a bend in the path, he stooped to pick a blossom of a prairie verbena and presented it to her. She kept her eyes on the purple cluster of star-shaped flowers, working the rough stem through a buttonhole of her sweater, and refused to look at Hugh. Any return of affection she had ever shown him had cost her— yet what did he want? And if he had broken his engagement to Shirlee Faris, what was implied? It was too soon to accept an answer; she was unable to accommodate what he was explaining to her.

After a time they came to a pond where clouds of gnats flew thick and silent among the water reeds, the yellow-green spikes of reeds made a barrier between the shore and the water, and swollen buds of flowers among the lily pads showed early for the season. Cattle stood in the shade of trees, flicking their tails across their glossy flanks, disturbing the interested insects. Behind a wide, close-cropped hedge, a dog barked, and Elaine called to him. He appeared for an instant, then responding to a sound in the underbrush, disappeared behind clumps of hawthorn and yew.

The cows came over to them, curious as house pets, their white faces scattered throughout the cyprus trees, red and white in a blue and silver landscape. "They think we have food," Elaine said.

Hugh watched her closely. "I know."

They went on, and the silky red dog descended the rocky path toward them, wagging its tail, panting softly, the wind parting its hair raggedly along the center of its back. It walked purposefully now, as if it were delivering a message. Elaine put forward her hand to touch the dog; she spoke to it, and then followed in its anxious path.

She kept ahead of Hugh, reluctant to let him see an expression on her face that might reveal to him her increasing awareness of his intention. Yet she would never again place her hopes in him. What difference could his actions make to her when she could never trust him? When in a moment he came nearer, she stared up into the clouds, into the pasture, anywhere to avoid looking at him, reacting to his presence. His glances had in them the insistence of supplication, the precise meaning of which confused her. She must avoid seeing him and falling into his eyes like a downed bird falls helplessly into a lake. She was shivering.

"Are you cold? Do you want my jacket, baby?" he asked, beginning to take it off.

"No," she said. "No, thank you." If she put his coat around her body, it would be the beginning of acquiescence. She drew her sweater tightly around her.

Birds flew out of a hedge in a scattered group. Calling to one another, they formed into a wedge and dissolved into a single trail in the distance. "Does this place bother you?"

"Bother me?" he asked.

"I mean, the way we live. The farm?"

"No."

"Well?"

"Nothing about it bothers me—except your not wanting me here."

She realized that she had been taunting him and that it gave her no satisfaction. "I want you here," she said softly.

She turned away from him and began to walk in the direction of the house. Without slowing down, she lowered her head and looked back. Then she stopped and glanced at him through a fresh agitation of leaves. "You ever make love with her, Hugh?"

"No."

"You sleep with anyone?"

A wave of color went over his face and rested at the height of his cheeks.

She shook her head and waited. Her eyes caught an instant in his, and then she went on.

The chimney of the stone barbecue pit came into sight, then the fence around the house and the flowers. A woman on the porch called to Elaine and, in the course of relaying her message, said his daughter's name. From behind the woman came a baby's shriek, then a frantic, demanding wail. Hugh stood still, awed by this first communication with his child; and his eyes seemed to be focusing on what he could not see beyond the walls of the house. The woman gave him one swift, comprehensive glance, then slipped back inside discreetly, without showing any further curiosity.

When they reached the porch, Elaine turned to him, and when she spoke, her words were slurred and her breath was uneven. "I have to feed her," she said. "What will you do?"

He hesitated and stared ahead at the house. "Wait for you here."

"All right." She put her hand on the door, then paused. He had started to sit down on the swing, then changed his mind and moved to the corner of the porch to sit on the railing, his eyes averted, not, she thought, to gain her sympathy, but rather to keep from exposing his feelings and perhaps in some way further hindering his progress toward the child. He glanced at her sideways, suppressing his request—yet it showed in his eyes.

She had meant to prevent him from seeing Sophie, and to continue punishing him, but the conviction that what she was doing was right had gradually faltered, and she was beginning to accept his explanation for why he had come, and to dare to believe in it.

"Come with me, then," she whispered.

He rose quickly, reached down to steady a small table that he had disturbed, and in an instant his hand touched her arm as if he would have her lead him. As she crossed the rug, a shadow followed in a familiar rhythm. She glimpsed a flash of black in the hall mirror; not blond and fair, not her husband, not herself either, but near to herself, because she had seen that image and been thrilled by it so many times in the past.

Hugh opened the door to the living room for her, and in the bright sunlight she hesitated. For a moment, the sun went out, then came back, sparkling over the shiny varnish of the woodwork and on the huge knobs of the brass andirons. In her cradle by the fireplace, the dark baby, so much like the man standing by Elaine's side, waved her fists and mittened feet and howled in rage. She turned over and raised herself on her hands, looked once at her mother with huge brown eyes, and then shrieked again, refusing to be pacified even after she had been gathered up. She was not silent, nor did her struggle cease, until Elaine raised her sweater and brought the baby's mouth to her breast. Softly repeating her daughter's name, Elaine relaxed in a chair, then both mother and child shuddered and were still. Elaine's lips brushed across the top of Sophie's head, as the baby sucked noisily, catching her breath in short little sobs, one clenched fist opening and closing against the pale, full breast.

Slowly the redness left Sophie's face, and her eyes opened and darted to the man who still stood in the doorway waiting. Elaine, too, lifted her eyes and followed the gaze of the baby. In the tall slender window behind Hugh was the fresh yellow-green of the trees just then bending in the wind to reveal the blue above them. He had run his hand through his hair, his face dipped a little; he seemed unsure as to how to present himself as a father before a baby whose birth he had neither anticipated nor attended, and toward whom his body now strained yet dared not approach more closely. Elaine raised her beautiful arm in an encouraging gesture, yet Hugh, still unsure, hesitated a moment longer. It wasn't until the surroundings had become a bit more familiar to him, and Elaine's glances toward him had increased in sympathy that his confidence returned, and he was able to pick up a footstool, place it near her, and sit down.

From outdoors came the cry of a hawk; and, from time to time, animal sounds and the slow, unintelligible drifting of human voices. The hired hand came onto the back porch with the milk cans and in a hushed voice talked to Elaine's father. Hugh moved his hand across the baby's back. She stopped sucking, her eyes darting wildly to the stranger.

"You're distracting her," Elaine said.

He withdrew his hand and leaned away from the baby. "I'm not too good with her, huh?"

"It's all right." Elaine rocked Sophie in her arms until she started nursing again. They were quiet, and after a time, she pulled down her sweater and held the baby up before her, kissing her face and telling her things of which Hugh was not yet a part. Then she pulled her close, resting the baby's head on her shoulder, while one of Sophie's hands clutched and twisted into the sleeve of her sweater. The ceremony seemed to have come to an end. Hugh pulled the footstool closer and peered at the tiny face, so pale beneath the fringe of dark lashes. "Has she finished eating?"

Elaine nodded. It occurred to her then that he might want to hold his baby, but feared taking advantage of her concession. For a moment, she was unwilling to grant him that, but then she glanced at him and saw a look of such unguarded and unequivocal affection that it almost hurt her to witness it.

"Have you ever held a baby before?" she asked.

"I've never had one before."

"You have to be gentle."

"I can be gentle."

Slowly, guiding one of his hands beneath Sophie's sleeping body, and the other behind her head, Elaine gave her daughter to Hugh; she leaned close to show him how to hold her. As he took her, the baby opened her eyes and her small fists; her mouth drew up, and she shuddered as if she would begin to cry, but when he made a noise, a kind of sucked-in kiss, she started, and then smiled, her eyes almost shutting from the effort.

"She looks so little," Elaine said. "She's such a strong baby. You make her look like a doll."

Sophie's skin was white against the gray of Hugh's suit and the rich tan of his hands. Her eyes focused hard on him, and her fingers moved in slow motion, the index finger extended. When he put out his own finger, she wrapped her hand around it. He glanced up at Elaine, proud of his child's accomplishment. Elaine left her chair to sit on the rug close to him, and when she felt his fingers touch her hair, she stretched out her legs across a streak of sunlight on the floor, and rested her head on his knee. She was not sure how much time had passed when she glanced at the baby and saw that she slept.

"Put her to bed," she told Hugh. "Go on." She encouraged him when he hesitated, and she motioned toward the cradle. "You can do that."

Taking care to rise slowly and not to wake her, he got up and crossed the room to the cradle. Grave and intent, he lowered her to the sheet, tucked the flannel cover about her, and watched to see that she did not stir.

Elaine had gone to the window. Outside squirrels were shelling sunflower seeds on the walk, where her mother had scattered them. A sparrow splashed in the basin of the birdbath, hopped to the rim, shook himself dry, then folded his wings. Her gaze sharpened, as if she had seen something unusual, but it was the familiar landscape, the trees in a flood of sunshine, the flowers in the familiar beds. What was unusual was that Hugh was in this room; only an hour before she would have denied that possibility. That she had permitted him so close, suddenly frightened her.

He walked up behind her and buried his face in her hair. He cleared his throat, and she heard his fast breath. "I want you to marry me," he said. He kissed her neck, and in a nervous gesture, tightened his arms around her waist. "I love you and I want you with me."

She looked around at him quickly, dazed by the assurance of permanence and by the prospect of happiness implicit in his request, but then remembering past injuries, she shook her head. "No," she whispered. "I can't live with you again."

He took her face in his hands and kissed her mouth. "I love you, Elaine, and I'm going to take you home."

For a moment she remained close to him, trying to believe in his love for her and to imagine that even if she were not the mother of his child, he would have made this proposal. But the answer was surely negative, and necessarily hers must be, too. Certain that her decision was correct, that she was protecting herself from the greatest folly of her life, she broke away from him and started toward the garden, where she must wait to tell him good-by. If she remained in this room with him, she might not be able to answer for the consequences of the future, and, she suddenly realized, not just for hers, but for his as well. He would despise her if he sacrificed so much. She would not hurt him— she no longer desired that—but she would tell him what she had resolved. With her hand on the knob of the door, she spoke quickly without turning around. "I'm taking Sophie to San Antonio, Hugh. Jimmy's coming to live with me." She had wept when Jimmy's letter had come. Certainly Albert's urging had been part of her son's decision, but she would accept it because she had too long been deprived of him and she could no longer endure it. "You can visit Sophie whenever you wish," she continued. "I don't mind that. I'll send you an address as soon as I've rented a house."

But when she looked back at him in what she had meant to be a brief glance before leaving the room, her thoughts were broken off. He astonished her; she hid her face in her hands and moved her head back and forth as if to destroy the image, and she was unable to move or to further pursue her course. She knew now that until she had made peace with him once and for all she would be unable to leave the room or to proceed with her life and her plan. She had never seen him display so much grief.

"I love you," she said, her own tears rising. "I have suffered every moment of our separation. But I can't do anything to help you. I don't trust you. You can't expect it. You won't stay; I know it. When it pleases you to go, you'll leave us. You've never stayed anywhere or done anything that doesn't please you. I'm not going to set myself up for that possibility again." She glanced toward the sleeping child. "And I certainly won't do that to her."

"Do what to her?"

"Hurt her future."

"What about mine?"

She narrowed her eyes, and spoke quickly, her tone unrestrained. "You do pretty well by yourself, Hugh. Since when have you consulted me about your plans? You managed to live without me for nearly a year. Weren't you concerned with your future then?"

He was beside her in a second, taking her by the arm. She imagined his anger in that gesture, she thought that he was going to shake her or hurt her in some way.

"I'm not going with you," she said. "Nothing has changed, and I'm sure that it won't. I'm not going to put myself through that, not now, with the baby."

He held her wrist and kissed her hand, and then he spoke to her with such determined gentleness that his effort startled her. "Elaine, I've changed my life for you! I've gone back on promises and broken my word. It hurt me badly to do these things, but I did them, and I'd do them again without a moment's concern for the consequences to me or to anyone else—if that's what you want in return for Sophie and yourself." He looked at her beseechingly and spoke in utter frustration. "What more do you want of me? Tell me what more, and I'll do it. But don't tell me no! Not just no!"

She looked away from him; he took her chin and turned her head toward him. "Have you ever felt sorry for me?" he asked softly.

She shook her head. "Life doesn't touch you. You can buy what you like and buy out of what you don't like."

"I couldn't buy you. I tried that three days ago." And after a moment's pause, he added mournfully. "And I tried to love another woman. Jesus Christ, baby."

"You betrayed me for her. You loved her; you even told me!"

She raised her hand to brush away the beginnings of tears, but he intercepted it and wiped them away with his own.

"You betrayed yourself," he said, his voice breaking on every word. "Why didn't you tell me about Sophie, Elaine? Why didn't you let me know that you were carrying my child? Why? Why not even a note?" He looked back at his daughter and shook his head. "Nothing. All you had to do was pick up the phone."

"And have you tell me to go to hell? Have you gone crazy?"

He lifted up his hands, then let them sink to his sides. "What do you want from me, Elaine?" he asked, as he watched her still and silent face. "Do you need time to think? Should I wait in the garden? Is that going to be too close? Should I go back to the motel and wait for you to telephone? What do you want?" He paused, but Elaine said nothing. "Do you want Jimmy with us? Invite him. What can I do, Elaine?" he asked her. "You used to think you loved me."

"I love you now," she whispered.

"Then can't you forgive me at all?"

Weakening him this way was a sacrilege for which she felt both shame and guilt. She could not bear it. "Yes," she said. "But I'm not going with you."

She paused, looked away from him for a moment, then returned his glance with like intensity and feeling. "You almost killed me," she said. "I don't know how I carried Sophie through such grief. I nearly lost her. My mother thought I would." She bit down on her lip to keep from breaking into sobs. "You'll ruin your life, Hugh. You'll despise me, and you'll punish me for it. I know you will." She began to cry. "To hell with it!"

He might have tried to comfort her more emphatically then, but he was so amazed and bewildered by her accusation, and so unable to act predictably under his response to her disclosure, that he stood yet apart from her, stroking her arms and shoulders, and repeating his commitment and its binding promises.

It was impossible how much she loved this man, not only for what he had meant to her through so much of their past, but also for what he was doing now: for saying what was so hard for him; for loving her; for standing his ground to get her; for whispering promises of such absurdity that they would be impossible to keep and pledges of changes in his character that she would not even want; for the tears that fell as he ceased speaking—for everything. She knew what was going to happen then: that he was going to embrace her; that she was going to lift her arms to receive him; and that he was going to kiss her with so much passion that she would moan and cry from the pleasure of it. The knowledge that he loved her, that he intended to remain with her, to continue loving her with the commitment that he now expressed, washed over her, eroding the memory of the pain that he had caused her. Implicit in her forgiveness and consistent with her character was the fact that she would cease to admonish him for it. He repeated his request, then seeming to search her face for a reconsidered reply, and apparently not being satisfied, kissed her again.

"What are you thinking, baby?" he asked her. "Isn't it going to be all right?" He questioned her with such obvious concern for her present dilemma that her eyes met his quickly, seeking in them something that she seemed badly to need to know. For almost a year, he had longed to see that look on another woman's face, then gradually realized that, for him, it failed to exist anywhere else in the world. "I love you," he said, responding to her quest. "Tell me what you want." He kissed her hand and covered it with his own, and then he spoke gently. It was as if he had put together a puzzle, and he were waiting for her consent before laying down the last piece. "I need you to love me," he said. "I need you to go with me, Elaine."

He held her to him, as he continued to argue his case so adroitly that at last she began to nod in affirmation, and finally she lifted her head to ask him where he would take her, where they would live.

"Where do you want to live?" he asked her, coaxingly.

"I don't know," she whispered.

"In the big house? Wherever you like," he answered. "You can fix it up, make it your own. Do as you wish. I love you."

She smiled at a glance in her memory of the ranch, the herds of animals, the sweet greenness of the pastures, the dark river, the lush countryside near the beautiful town where she had spent so much of her life. But she wouldn't want to change anything. "I like the big house the way it is," she said quietly. "I don't think we should change it."

When she was in agreement with him, when he seemed to sense that he had made progress, that he was close to her acceptance of him, he dried both their eyes with his handkerchief, then continued caressing her, with the unmistakable intention of making love to her immediately if she would permit it. And when she heard the murmuring of voices approaching the living room, she was dangerously close to letting him satisfy a yearning that had tormented her for nearly a year.

"Are you going with me?" he asked her when she pushed him away from her, warning him that her parents were coming. He seemed unwilling to give her up, and he tried again to hold her. "Are you?"

She kissed him quickly on the mouth and neck; he had come back to her. He was insisting on taking her with him, and she was going to let him. "Yes," she said.

He sighed deeply, shut his eyes in gratitude, then tugged at his tie to secure the knot, smoothed his shirt, and tried all he knew to calm his heavy breathing. "I love you," he said, just before the door was pushed open. "And I'm going to make you very happy."

With considerable uneasiness, Hugh stepped forward to meet the Muellers; with considerable shyness, Elaine performed the introductions. When Hugh saw that they were not unfriendly, he spoke to them with the best training of his background, showing his intelligence and breeding with a degree of sensitivity that Elaine had rarely before witnessed in him. She was silent. Her eyes darted from her parents to Hugh and back again, anxious at first, then settling down. She was pleased by Hugh's regard for her parents, the respectful attention he accorded their rather circuitous remarks, and the care with which he responded to them— the rightness of everything he said, and not because the conversation was easy for him—Elaine felt certain that it was not—but because he knew it was important to her, and that mattered to him. He had his arm around her waist as he addressed her father and asked his permission to marry her.

Mr. Mueller glanced at Hugh and then at his daughter, studying their faces, observing that emotions had been liberally spent and knowing that the reunion had been tempestuous and necessarily upsetting. He set his gaze on his daughter. "And what do you say, Ely? Does this please you?"

Her eyes shifted from Hugh toward her father. "Yes, it does," she replied softly. The happiness that Elaine's expression conveyed was an emotion Mr. Mueller had not observed in her for many years. He was gratified and he returned her smile with uncommon warmth. "Then, that's fine," he said, reaching out to shake Hugh's hand. "That's all that concerns me."

Her father's eyes narrowed a little, and the emotion that he showed startled Elaine. "But we'll miss her," he said. "It's always difficult for me each time that my daughter leaves my house, and yet harder now because of the baby."

While the women went to pack, he offered Hugh a seat on the

sofa and brought in a pitcher of dark beer. The two men spoke
little; when the baby stirred, Hugh went to see about her, and
though she was still sleeping, he picked up a small silver rattle
and placed it close to her hand. Returning to the sofa, he prepared
to light a cigarette, then remembering Sophie, shook out the
match, and put the cigarette package aside, watching the door
nervously for Elaine to return. At the first sound of footsteps on
the stairs, he hurried to take the suitcases and to occupy himself
with packing the car. While Elaine said good-by to her parents,
he put himself very much in the background, though he shook
their hands warmly when her leave-taking was done.

Without stirring the dust, the car pulled away from the front
gate. Hugh glanced at the child on her mother's lap. Her grandmother had dressed her ceremoniously in a white dress with elaborate smocking, as if she were being taken to church or to a party.
Her hands rolled into fists, she sucked on her lower lip and stared
at Hugh with eyes that were veiled in lashes as black and heavy
as his own.

From the road Elaine had opened the car window and waved
to the couple on the porch. They had been so kind to her; she
would miss her father's stern but reliable presence and her
mother's fond attentions to both Sophie and herself—just as she
would miss this place, she realized as she caught sight of the
cattle coming in toward the barn, and the horses, up to their
hocks in water, drinking from the pond. Three cedars threw their
coarse shadows over the meadow, and as she watched, a soaring
goshawk was lost in their breadth.

They turned onto a sharp black road, sweetened by the waves
of primroses on its sandy shoulders, a familiar road. Elaine had
been over it many times in her life. Years ago, another man had
taken her away on it, pregnant with her first child. In what was
left of the twilight, she searched for the changes, for anything at
all that would tell her with certainty that fifteen years had passed.
She had been almost a child herself then, yet she had known she
was a woman, too; Foley's choosing her had made her one, and
the birth of her boy had affirmed that. The landscape, by refuting
the passing of those years, seemed to possess the permanence and
stability she had sought all her life, but which the experience of
her marriage had proved illusory. A flicker of grief passed
through her, yet she determinedly cast it aside and did not dwell
on it since it was no longer fair or wise to do so. If Hugh had
been able to give up the easy promise of success through paths of

power charted over generations, so too could she give up the habit of her mourning. Foley had already forgiven her long ago; forgiveness was implicit in so much love.

The wind swept harshly across a field of bluebonnets studded with pools of Indian paintbrush, lifting the color in waves toward clouds that changed from yellow, to salmon, to gold. A wild pine tree, completely foreign to the area, had struggled out a long life on a windy hill, its limbs nearly bare. Hugh remarked on the beauty of its isolation, and Elaine nodded. They came to a soft rolling hill dotted with small-leafed oaks; beyond it were a pond and a field with a stand of cedars. The curving road gradually straightened, cutting through treeless plains and gilded pastures, and across small, slow-moving rivers, the last of them bathed in apricot and orange. In the fading light, the white stones of an embankment shown topaz and garnet in the setting sun, astonishing her by their transformation; she had seen them before, but it was as though she were seeing them for the first time.

And this was how it was with Hugh: He'd have to begin again, and she would have to give him that chance by seeing him as he was, not as a replacement for Foley, but as a man she loved for some of the same qualities, though arranged in a different order.

Elaine had rarely tried to analyze love. It had caught up with her long ago, when she had been looking in the other direction, presuming that she would go to college, and then to some small town whose name she had never even heard and be a teacher. She had meant to rent a room, make her own way, carve out a place. She had been invincible then, and strong. But a man had claimed her, and she had gone with him, as if she had never planned to do otherwise. Something had happened, and it had never been directed by her. Yet this time she seemed to have control over the events, to have chosen freely, to have made demands and seen them granted. She wondered what she would give Hugh in return for the heart that he had been unable to recover from her. That he was taking her with him to Dansville, that he was no longer able to live apart from her, was surely her success, yet what price might a man as prideful as Hugh exact from her for this defeat, and how much should she rely on his conversion? If she had not trusted him, had not known fully the extent of his love for her and been prepared to return it as bountifully as she knew it would be given, she might have feared the life that awaited her. Yet she did not. She believed all that he had told her. He had made her aware of his pain, the necessity of gathering his family to him, and not only because of the strong love that he felt for her, but for the harmony of his life.

The lights on the dashboard gleamed, and country music came softly from the radio. Elaine reached for Hugh's hand and he glanced over at her, then slowed the car, pulled it over to the shoulder of the road, and stopped. With care not to wake the baby, he took her in his arms, kissed her forehead and cheeks, and her mouth. In a moment her arm tightened around his neck, and when he heard that childlike shudder of impatience that he remembered, he glanced around looking for a place for them—a bed, a rug, a sofa with flowers.

She laughed softly into the cloth of his shirt.

For the rest of the drive, she was settled against Hugh, looking from time to time at his profile, causing him to glance at her and smile, without caution. Her hand rested gently on the rise and fall of the baby's back. She had her family, and she had this beloved and difficult man. With him she would be like the backside of a coin, having almost nothing to do with its identification, yet everything to do with its value.

On the silver water tower, in neat black letters, was the name of the town. As the car went over the railroad track, the baby stirred; Elaine lifted her to her shoulder and spoke to her. A single yellow globe lighted the train platform, where a man, a stranger, sat on a bench reading a folded newspaper. He had a pipe in his mouth; sparks were torn out of it by the wind. The car went past the square, past the illuminated clock on the courthouse turret, the statues of heroes and founders, the public drinking fountain on a pedestal, the latticework bandstand, surrounded by a low, neatly trimmed hedge of viburnum. Elaine turned her head to a side street to see a gracious two-story house a block away, the place where she and Foley would have gone home. Lights were on in all the upstairs rooms. A big family lived there now, four children, little boys and loud.

They left the town and its homes and yards, some of them fenced, the prosperous mixed with the poor, some with swings and seesaws and flower beds, others with old furniture on the porches and battered cars in the yard, then the last little house, lit by the amber glow of lanterns, like a playhouse with paper windows. At each turn of the winding road to the ranch the headlights swarmed over the white flowers of the blackberry vines or plunged through the meadows, seeking out the fences, the pecan orchards, the sleep of animals grouped for warmth and safety.

The lights were on in the big house and in all the houses of the ranch. Hugh drove slowly up to the cookhouse, where Matt had just stepped out onto the porch. Without waking Sophie, Hugh opened his door and slipped her off Elaine's lap, experienced and familiar with his baby now, and handling her easily. As he walked toward Matt with Elaine following, Hugh had a smile that he was unable to do anything about; Matt ducked his head to suppress his own pleasure, yet failing, looked up smiling freely. Hugh lifted the blanket corner to let him see the sleeping child. "Her name is Sophie," he said. "For Elaine's mother."

Matt looked quickly from Hugh to the baby, and back again, amused at her startling resemblance to her father. "You sure left your mark on her," he said, raising an eyebrow. "Just the same, she's a beauty. I guess she'll be running things around here pretty soon. Well, that's all right with me." He patted the top of her head, not daring to touch either the rows of gathered lace on the fancy bonnet or its gleaming satin ribbon. He said the baby's full name, taking his time over it, seeming to enjoy its sound. Then he glanced at Elaine. "It's been a while since we've had your company out here," he said. "I'm glad to see that's changed."

Elaine shook the hand he was offering and thanked him, then went through the door that Stephen held open for her.

That night, she was very shy; she ate little; she seemed dreamy and calm; she would smile for no reason; she looked at the women only when they asked her questions about the baby. Because of her situation, she had felt obliged to avoid them on the few occasions that she had come to the ranch with Hugh; she had talked freely with the men but never assumed friendship with their wives. Their attention pleased her now.

While they drank their coffee, Matt lit a cigarette and spoke so quietly out of the corner of his mouth that Hugh asked him to repeat what he had said. "It's going to be a new life around here with the boss in residence," he mumbled, looking at Luther rather than Hugh.

"That scare you, Matt?"

"Everything scares me. Yeah. I guess we'll have to start off by getting you a case of Mexican beer, something to cool you down."

Hugh put his arm around the foreman's shoulders and spoke to him with a bewildered sweetness that had nothing to do with Matt, and everything to do with his future and his plans. "You will, Matt," he said. "You owe me a present." They moved away a little from the others and stood talking together, their faces close, each with his arms folded across his chest, each with the hint of a smile to indicate camaraderie and mutual respect rather than compliance. Yet everyone seeing them knew that the transfer of power had already begun.

As Elaine and Hugh walked toward the big house, the ranch hands fanned out toward their own homes, arm in arm with their wives, trailed by the children. The voices and the energies that had been so strong at five o'clock that morning had thinned and were wearing down. In the draw behind the fenced truck garden, an owl shrieked; bullbats and swallows twirled in arabesques over the hulky barn, circling, then swooping to the ground in swift arcs.

Early the following morning, the women who had risen to fix breakfast in the cookhouse heard a baby cry, the sound of it carried toward them by a breeze over the pasture. Lettie stood at the window and saw a light go on in an upstairs room in the big house, then heard the baby hush. In time the light went out, and she heard Elaine's voice calling Hugh's name, followed by a cry of indignation, then laughter softened quickly by a rise in the wind, finally drowned out entirely by a freight train, speeding along, crushing out the opalescent line of dawn, giving a sharp warning whistle before making the last road crossing into Dansville.

Gradually the night fell back into the mauve shadows of the trees as the light blued. When Elaine eased herself from under Hugh's arm and went to the window, meadow birds were already sweeping into the wet flowers, then lifting up again in groups to find a fence from which to share the freshness of the morning. She watched the roofs of the barns and houses regain their forms, the trees rest full and sturdy in the first soft light, not yet required to give up any part of their image for shade. Raising himself into this promise of renewal, a hawk soared, found an invisible current of air, and disappeared—a dot and then, nothing. The first colors melted; the sounds of men and animals, muted and intermittent, became sharp and continual; the first clouds dissolved into ragged fragments that would eventually blend and then dissolve again, going on and on and on, never aware of the inevitability of their patterns, having found in nature a suitable and genial form.

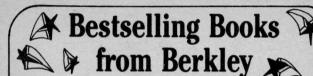

Bestselling Books from Berkley

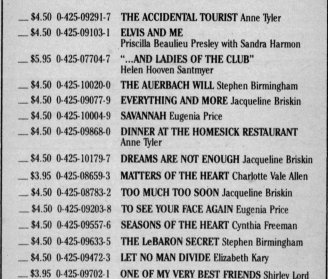

__ $4.50	0-425-09291-7	**THE ACCIDENTAL TOURIST** Anne Tyler
__ $4.50	0-425-09103-1	**ELVIS AND ME** Priscilla Beaulieu Presley with Sandra Harmon
__ $5.95	0-425-07704-7	**"...AND LADIES OF THE CLUB"** Helen Hooven Santmyer
__ $4.50	0-425-10020-0	**THE AUERBACH WILL** Stephen Birmingham
__ $4.50	0-425-09077-9	**EVERYTHING AND MORE** Jacqueline Briskin
__ $4.50	0-425-10004-9	**SAVANNAH** Eugenia Price
__ $4.50	0-425-09868-6	**DINNER AT THE HOMESICK RESTAURANT** Anne Tyler
__ $4.50	0-425-10179-7	**DREAMS ARE NOT ENOUGH** Jacqueline Briskin
__ $3.95	0-425-08659-3	**MATTERS OF THE HEART** Charlotte Vale Allen
__ $4.50	0-425-08783-2	**TOO MUCH TOO SOON** Jacqueline Briskin
__ $4.50	0-425-09203-8	**TO SEE YOUR FACE AGAIN** Eugenia Price
__ $4.50	0-425-09557-6	**SEASONS OF THE HEART** Cynthia Freeman
__ $4.50	0-425-09633-5	**THE LeBARON SECRET** Stephen Birmingham
__ $4.50	0-425-09472-3	**LET NO MAN DIVIDE** Elizabeth Kary
__ $3.95	0-425-09702-1	**ONE OF MY VERY BEST FRIENDS** Shirley Lord

---

Please send the titles I've checked above. Mail orders to:

BERKLEY PUBLISHING GROUP
390 Murray Hill Pkwy., Dept. B
East Rutherford, NJ 07073

NAME _____

ADDRESS _____

CITY _____

STATE _____ ZIP _____

Please allow 6 weeks for delivery.
Prices are subject to change without notice.

POSTAGE & HANDLING:
$1.00 for one book, $.25 for each
additional. Do not exceed $3.50.

BOOK TOTAL	$_____
SHIPPING & HANDLING	$_____
APPLICABLE SALES TAX (CA, NJ, NY, PA)	$_____
TOTAL AMOUNT DUE	$_____

PAYABLE IN US FUNDS.
(No cash orders accepted.)